W9-AHV-868

LITERARY PRIZES & PLAUDITS

The Debba won the **Arthur Ellis Award for Best First Mystery Novel** and longlisted for the **Scotiabank Giller Prize.**

Publishers Weekly: The Debba **Starred Review.** Sharp, biting prose… blends a murder mystery with a nuanced examination of the intransigent Israeli-Arab conflict.

Talking to the Enemy won the first **Sophie Brody Award for outstanding achievement in Jewish literature** from the **American Library Association**, was named **Best Book of 2005 by Kirkus Reviews**, and won the **J. I. Segal Award for Fiction.**

Stories anthologized in **the Best American Short Stories, the Pushcart Prize, Journey Prize**, and elsewhere.

"Mandelman … cast[s] the often grim news from the Middle East in a newly revealing and humanizing light." – **Jim Bartley,** *Globe and Mail (Toronto)*

"One can **qualify this masterful first novel as a post-political thriller.**"– Marianne magazine, France

"A **page turner.**" – Jewlicious

THE
UNDERTAKER'S
DAUGHTER
TEL AVIV *NOIR*

AVNER MANDELMAN

Copyright © 2023 by Avner Mandelman

All rights reserved. No part of this book may be reproduced, stored in a retrieval system or transmitted, in any form or by any means, without the prior written consent of the author. The author may be contacted at PO Box 26062, Toronto RPO Broadway, Ontario, M4P 0A8, Canada.

Caveat Lector

This book is fiction. Some historical figures may have inspired a few of its characters' traits, but just as a Picasso painting of Gertrude Stein is only daubs of paint on canvas, not the original, so the characters depicted here fictitiously are mere bits of ink on paper (or blips on screen), not real people. All are products of the author's imagination, used to attain two goals and two only: First, that once you started reading, you couldn't stop, and second, that once you finished, you couldn't forget what you've read. Please let me know in an Amazon review which of these two goals (if any) the book has managed to accomplish.

ISBN (paperback) 978-1-7388044-3-6
ISBN (e-book)   978-1-7388044-4-3
ISBN (hardcover) 978-1-7388044-5-0

Cover design Indie Publishing Group Inc
Interior design Indie Publishing Group Inc
Cover illustration by Shady Curi
Maps by mapsland.com, Creative Commons license CC BY-SA

For my sons, Ron and Dan, with love

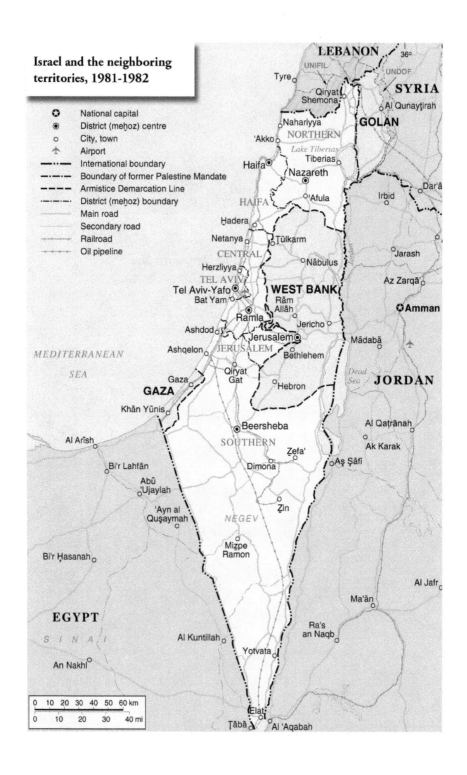

Israel and the neighboring territories, 1981–1982

✪	National capital
◉	District (meḥoz) centre
○	City, town
✈	Airport
—···—	International boundary
—··—··—	Boundary of former Palestine Mandate
————	Armistice Demarcation Line
—·—·—	District (meḥoz) boundary
	Main road
	Secondary road
	Railroad
	Oil pipeline

LEBANON   36°

UNIFIL   UNDOF

Tyre   SYRIA

Qiryat Shemona   Al Qunayṭirah

Nahariyya   GOLAN

'Akko   NORTHERN

Lake Tiberias

Haifa   Tiberias

Nazareth

HAIFA   'Afula   Irbid   Dar'ā

Ḥadera

Netanya   Ṭūlkarm

CENTRAL   Nābulus   Jarash

Herzliyya

TEL AVIV   Az Zarqā'

Tel Aviv-Yafo   WEST BANK

Bat Yam   Rām Allāh   ✪ Amman

Ramla   Jericho

Ashdod   Jerusalem

Ashqelon   JERUSALEM   Bethlehem   Mādabā

MEDITERRANEAN   Qiryat Gat

SEA   Gaza   Hebron   Dead Sea   JORDAN

GAZA

Khān Yūnis   Al Qaṭrānah

Al Arīsh   Beersheba   Ak Karak

SOUTHERN   Zefa'

Bi'r Lahfān   Dimona   Aṣ Ṣāfī

Abū Ujaylah

Ẓin

'Ayn al Quṣaymah   NEGEV

Al Jafr

Bi'r Ḥasanah   Mizpe Ramon

Ma'ān

EGYPT

S I N A I   Ra's an Naqb

An Nakhl   Al Kuntillah   Yotvata

| 0 | 10 | 20 | 30 | 40 | 50 | 60 km |
| 0 | 10 | | 20 | | 30 | 40 mi |

Elat

Ṭābā   Al 'Aqabah

Syria, 1981–1982

TURKEY

AL ḤASAKAH

Al Ḥasakah

AR RAQQAH

Aleppo
ḤALAB

Ar Raqqah

Idlib
IDLIB

AL LADHIQĪYAH
Latakia

Mediterranean Sea

TARTŪS

Ḥamāh ḤAMĀH

Dayr az Zawr

DAYR AZ ZAWR

Tartūs

Ḥimṣ

ḤIMṢ

IRAQ

Beirut **LEBANON**

DIMASHQ
Damascus RĪF
UNDOF Zone ALQUNAYṬIRAH DIMASHQ

GOLAN HEIGHTS
Al Qunayṭirah

1949 Armistice Line

ISRAEL DAR'Ā AS SUWAYDĀ'

Dar'ā As Suwaydā'

West Bank[b] 1994 Treaty Line

Dead Sea

★Amman JORDAN

ISRAEL

Boundary representation is not necessarily authoritative.

SAUDI ARABIA

[a]The Golan Heights is Israeli-occupied Syria.

[b]Israeli occupied with current status subject to the Israeli-Palestinian Interim Agreement; permanent status to be determined through further negotiation.

Syria
Administrative Divisions

——— International boundary
— - — Province (muḥāfaẓah) boundary
★ National capital
⊛ Province (muḥāfaẓah) capital
Syria has 14 provinces.

0   50   100 Kilometers
0   50   100 Miles

Lambert Conformal Conic Projection, SP 35°00'N/37°00'N

A HISTORICAL NOTE

The book's events take place in 1981–1982, in the year leading to Israel's First Lebanon War. At that time Lebanon was (and still is) a fragile tribal state, with political power shared among Christians, Muslims and Druze. Atop this ethnic cauldron sat Syria, acting as an overlord via several armored brigades led by the Syrian president's brother.

The arrival of hundreds of thousands of Palestinian refugees, expelled from neighboring Jordan, further destabilized the country, and as Palestinian terrorists began attacking Northern Israel from their Lebanese camps, Israel retaliated by bombing them. When the terror attacks escalated, pressure grew in Israel to invade Lebanon and cleanse the terror nests.

Yet that was not Israel's only aim. It is now commonly accepted that Israeli hawks also aimed to enthrone a Maronite Christian as Lebanese president, who, so Israel hoped, would also immediately sign a peace treaty with it.

The hawks' plan was resisted by members of the Israeli government who feared a long-term Vietnam-like entanglement, but this only made the hawks more determined. The book's events take place during the period when Israel's decision to invade Lebanon was hanging in the balance.

NOTE TO NORTH AMERICAN READERS

Most North American Jews are of Ashkenazi (European) origin, so what's considered "typically Jewish" in North America is really typically Ashkenazi. There are also "Eastern" Jews in the U.S. and Canada, born in Arab countries or North Africa, but their ingrained discrimination by an Ashkenazi establishment is unique to Israel, where the twin claims of Ashkenazi superiority and Eastern inferiority always lurk just underneath the surface.

WORDS OF THANKS

My deepest thanks to all the beta readers who have read early drafts of this book and commented on them (too many to mention), and to the skilled editors who gave me the benefit of their insights: Victoria Pryor, Richard Marek, Alice Rosengard, Howard Lovy, Marilyn Boake, and Marjorie Nicolaou. Thanks also to Shady Curi for his skill in creating the cover illustration, and to Chrissy Hobbs and her colleagues at Indie Publishing Group. I couldn't have done this book without them.

OTHER BOOKS BY THE AUTHOR

The Advanced Sleuth Investor,
Indie Publishing Group, Toronto, 2023

The Debba, 2010, Other Press / Random House, NYC, 2010

Le Testament de Jaffa, 2010, Editions Liana Levy, Paris, 2010

The Sleuth Investor, McGraw Hill, NYC, 2007

Talking to the Enemy, Seven Stories Press, NYC, 2006

Parlare al Nemico, Il Punto d'Incontro, Milan, 2006

Cuckoo, Oberon Press, Ottawa, 2003

Talking to the Enemy, Oberon Press, Ottawa, 1998

CONTENTS

PART ONE

NINEVEH

1981, Wednesday, October 7, to Saturday, October 10

-1-

**Wednesday, October 7, 1981, 6:40 p.m.,
the Carmel Market, Tel Aviv–Jaffa**

THE KILLER IN the darkened staircase put the note back in his windbreaker's pocket, inside the book that had changed his life.

Behind him the Carmel Market was quiet, except for the rain drumming on the galvanized roofs and the gurgle of the water rushing down the gutters to the sea. He turned and looked up and down the street, scanning it, the locked stalls, the shuttered shops. The street was deserted.

Yom Kippur, he thought. The Day of Atonement when we ask God, the "HolyName," to forgive our sins.

What about mine?

Like everyone else on the team, he had missed the Forgiveness prayer. But he knew God would understand. After all, everything he did was for Him. For a brief minute he debated with himself whether he had done the right thing in taking on the self-appointed extra duties. But then he fingered the book again and knew it had been the right choice.

He ran up the stairs as silent as a jackal, in his rubber-soled shoes, stopping on every landing, listening hard. But there was nothing.

There, the top floor. His safe room was a storage space right under the eaves, barred by a narrow door whose corner was clipped diagonally to accommodate the sloping roof.

He scrutinized the door: bits of string on the doorstep, wood sliver between door and frame—nothing had been disturbed.

He pulled a key out of his shoe instep, unlocked the iron lock, and pushed the door slowly, widening his nostrils as he had been taught, then his eyes. When no new smell came except wet mold, nor movement, he eased his body into the room, closed the door behind him, and latched it.

He stood still for a whole minute, and when he was absolutely sure the little space was undisturbed, he screwed the weak overhead bulb back in and sat down on the canvas bed, then breathed out slowly, releasing the Other—the protective persona he'd been taught to put on when he had to do the dirty jobs so that afterward he'd feel Clean and clear.

For the moment he was safe, but it had been close. His first act of private Cleansing had almost gone awry.

He removed his dark shirt and scrutinized his arms and upper torso. The scratches were already fading, but he still felt them as sharply as the sting of the near-failure. He tried to console himself—the first takedown at the end of the course did not go smoothly either. But later he improved. Perhaps it was the same here, in his self-imposed tasks...

The clicker in his pocket buzzed, and he froze.

For a brief second, he thought he had been discovered, then he pulled out the little gray oval, stared at the screen, breathed out with relief.

Just a routine query by Ehud. How did it go?

He pressed the little button, one long, three shorts. No problem.

Must be Shimmel, the Unit's commander getting jumpy in his old age.... Because what was there to check? They came in for a simple refresher course, a break from the killings up north, in Lebanon, two, three killings a day each, weeks at a stretch....

Not that he minded. It was a break, and besides, it also gave him an opportunity to embark on his private undertakings.

However, now that he'd done the first one here, how many more should he do? The task was so large as to be nearly discouraging. But then, so was everything else worthwhile, like building the Jewish state, even this city, previously so White and pure, now contaminated....

Through the narrow window came some yowling prayers from the Yemenite synagogue, and he felt his skin crawl with distaste.

Or was this the only sound? Was there something else?

Breathing shallowly, he pulled out of his toolbox the stick with a mirror at its end, crept to the narrow window and raised it, scanning the street through the small curved surface.

The houses on both sides of the Carmel Market lane, dating from the first days of Tel Aviv, were dark, their ancient plaster gray and peeling, the beautiful arched facades eaten by years of salty wind, the city now overrun by the dark breeds....

He scanned the street, end to end. But there was nothing. He withdrew the mirror stick and put it back in his toolbox alongside the rest of his tools: the pencil knife, the two-two single-shot, the garrotes, the serrated blades, the ear poison ampoules and sprays, the poisoned needles.

He locked the box and put it inside his side pack. He had all day before him to rest and fast. That evening he'd go out, look for one more *Ars* to cleanse before going back North to resume his regular duties with everyone else.

He rubbed again at the scratches on his arms, reliving them.

Once the little *Ars* understood he was about to die, the *Ars* struggled for all he was worth—he scratched and bit so tenaciously, it was hard to fathom where he'd found the strength, such a skinny, drug-eaten runt, offering himself for forty shekels, for the sake of another drug high, all of a sudden becoming a wiry little ferret....

Despite his training, it took a surprisingly long time before he managed to hold the runt down long enough to plug him just in the right spot, as he'd been taught. So now there was one less dark *Ars* to contaminate the purity of the land, and his own, the purity about which that unsung modern prophet had written....

Again he touched the book inside his tunic, pulled it out reverently, careful of the yellowing paper.

Although he knew it by heart, he reread the first few pages, lingering over the bold proofs of the *Schwartzes'* genetic inferiority, the list of dangers they presented to the Ashkenazi-Zionist state, the risk of their Arab-mixed blood....

From the first moment he'd seen the book in the stall on Lilienblum Street, he knew. And as he'd begun to skim the pages, before he even bought the book, the more he read the more he realized that this must be his new destiny.

Of course, he understood it would take a long while to cleanse the land. But one must start somewhere, and where to start if not with the most dangerous? Those who aroused in him the dark unclean passions that—he was sure—were due to their Arab blood.

Today he had performed the first cleansing act; more would surely follow. But will all others here understand his selfless act? Was he clear enough?

He reread his note's final draft in his notebook, the one he'd finally copied. It was clear enough—he could not wait to see it reprinted in the newspapers after Yom Kippur, explaining what he'd done for everyone's sake.

Or could he have explained it a bit better?

He considered the wording, then, clicking his pen, he began to compose the next note he'd leave behind, copying choice phrases from the book, modifying others, adding his own touches, his own stamp, to the Ashkenazi prophet's clear words that had by now been imprinted on his brain....

When he'd finished, he copied the note in Standard Square Script, used in the Service to disguise the writer's hand, tucked it inside the book, inserted both in his breast pocket, and went downstairs.

Behind the building was the Vespa he had stolen. He climbed on it, put on his helmet, and rode into the rainy streets of the darkened city—a city soon to be purified—to scout for his next target.

-2-

Wednesday, October 7, 1981, 6:45 p.m.,
Jaffa, then Tel Aviv

A FEW MILES TO the south, a dented cab stood in a Jaffa dark alley, hammered by rain. The driver's seat was vacant but two men sat in the back, a corpulent old man with a flat face and a younger one, curly-haired and muscular, both immobile and grim. They were watching St. Anthony's Church, its eaves cascading water as if a pipe had broken in its roof.

The younger man muttered, "You think they'll take your offer, Shimmel?"

The older man said, "My guy in French Intel thinks he might, but who knows?"

Outside, a bolt of lightning broke, momentarily turning the cab's interior into a ghostly tableau of black and white. A clap of thunder rolled, and another; the cab shook.

Neither of the men moved; a minute passed, then another.

The old man said, "He's been there an hour… damn… what's taking him so long?"

Just then a shadowy figure materialized in the downpour. The driver's door was wrenched open and a soaked man dashed in. His head was narrow and swarthy but his hair was fair and the eyes pale blue, an incongruity of mixed ethnicities.

He squeezed behind the wheel, wheezing and hissing as he wiped his glasses. "This fucking rain, Shimmel, I am telling you, we need an ark, not a car...."

The old man growled, "So? You met him?"

"Yeah, yeah, I saw the priest."

"And? What did he say that Rahman wants? Again, to ship more?"

The driver made a face. "Sure, also to complain that a shipment arriving at Marseille was short because someone here was stealing..."

The dashboard beeped.

"Wait!" The driver pushed his glasses up and peered at a panel by the glove compartment where a purple line on a small screen just shot to the right. "Yes, he's transmitting already."

"A condensed burst?" the muscular young man asked.

"I dunno, Ehud. Wait."

The driver fiddled with a toggle while the rain lashed the windshield. The purple line oscillated, stabilized.

"No message content—wait, here's another...."

The man called Ehud said, "Still no content?"

"No. Nothing."

The older man growled, "There won't be, it's pure timecode. Old French Intel method. Time interval is a Yes or a No, Message to Follow—"

"Here comes another one," said the driver. "I can measure the time interval—"

"Don't bother," the old man said. "Won't mean a damn thing without the cipher list. Shut it down."

The driver flipped a toggle and the cab's antenna slowly retracted.

A short silence descended. Presently the old man said, "So, Moshe? Tell me."

"I already told you," the driver said. "The priest said Rahman wants to ship more, like every time. And like always, I said no, only this time I also gave him your message to send back to Rahman, exactly like you said it..."

"Exactly?"

"Yes, yes, exactly, like I told you—"

"Fuck it, no!" the muscular man hissed. "Even what he ships now is too much..."

"Shut up, Ehud," the old man said. "You got any better ideas?" He turned to the driver. "Did he ask you anything after you gave him the message? An explanation maybe?"

The driver snorted. "No, he ain't dumb. But I think he paled a little."

Silence descended as the rain drummed on.

The old man said, "And you're sure no one saw you go in?"

The Security Service kept a twenty-four-hour watch on the church, whose priest served as an occasional conduit to Syrian bigwigs in Lebanon, via French Intel.

"Nah. These fools watch the front and I came through the back."

The old man grunted. "So when will we get a response? Did you ask him?"

"A day or two, he has to encrypt it first—"

Ehud broke in again. "And meantime we just keep up the killings up north? I'm telling you, Shimmel, the guys can't take this much longer... especially the new ones who aren't used to working alone... and in such volume...."

The older man snapped, "Goddamit, you just tell them to keep doing it or we'll have another Vietnam here if the whole army has to go in... it's a mitzvah you're doing there...." A religious good deed.

Ehud's voice rose. "But how much longer? We do two, three take-downs a day each. Last week I sent three guys to the psych ward in Haifa to get electroshocked. They'll be out two weeks, maybe a month—"

"So what? Better this than half the army coming back in body bags...."

The old man's breath came out as a rasp. He pulled an inhaler out of his shirt pocket, stuck it in his mouth and swigged a lungful of air.

The two others said nothing. Presently the driver said, "So you think Rahman will bite?"

"He'd better." The fat man put the inhaler back in his shirt pocket.

There was another short silence.

Ehud said, "But, Shimmel, even if he says yes, you have no authority to make this offer."

"Yeah? So? If he says yes, I'll go to the prime minister and tell him in secret, so the cabinet doesn't have conniptions…."

The driver snorted.

Ehud ignored him. "And what if the plan doesn't work? Then the army can go in? That's the deal?"

The old man said, "You have better ideas, any of you? Besides telling me what's wrong with mine?"

No one said anything.

"So shut up." The older man pulled out a pack of Kents. "Alright, enough, let's go."

Moshe said, "And you shouldn't smoke."

"You shut up too." The old man lit up and puffed, coughing.

As the cab moved up Jaffa's main boulevard toward the coastal road, all were silent. But as it turned into Tel Aviv, the old man asked how the refresher course had gone and whether there were any problems.

"No," Ehud said.

"Everyone passed?"

"Yeah, yeah. I could pass it in my sleep now."

Moshe snorted again but said nothing.

"You, Moshe? Problems?"

The driver shook his narrow head. "None."

"What about the other guys who came with you, also okay? No problems?"

Ehud said, "Come on, Shimmel, it's only standard knife work, it's not like we had to take anyone down for real—"

"Check with your guys, anyway."

Ehud rolled his eyes, pulled a gray Motorola clicker out of his pocket, lifted it ostentatiously, clicked a short staccato.

The driver's pocket buzzed. Just as ostentatiously, he pulled his clicker out, pressed three times, one long, three short. All okay here.

Ehud's clicker buzzed again, receiving.

"Happy?" Ehud said.

The old man grunted. "Wait."

They waited. Soon came five more responses, all alike.

Ehud said, "I told you, Shimmel, no problems."

There was again silence. Only the sound of the rain could be heard, then some wails outside, the all-night Yom Kippur prayers.

The old man snarled, "Alright, let's get away from this goddamn noise…. Can't stand it, these idiots sucking up to Him, after all He's done to them…. What? What?"

"Nothing," Ehud said.

The driver just shook his narrow head as the cab drove past a line of parked buses, a row of shabby cafés, stores of used furnishings, nooks selling cheap shoes, Judaica knickknacks.

The old man said, "When you all going back to Beirut?"

Ehud said, "This Friday."

"Alright, but Moshe, you stay."

The driver asked why since they were already shorthanded up North.

"To watch my back, that's why. If the plan works and Rahman bites, the Damn HolyName will send someone after me for sure, and I'm not as fast as before."

The driver said, "You're really crazy, Shimmel…."

"Oh yeah? The Damn HolyName just sent someone after Sadat, no? Because he signed a peace treaty with us. Didn't you see him gunned down on TV? Anyone in this place tries to stop the bloodshed, the Damn HolyName goes after him. You can't be too careful in this goddamn place…."

There was a short, uncomfortable silence.

"Don't worry, Shimmel," the driver muttered at last. "I'll watch your back." He tried to catch Ehud's eye, but Ehud avoided him.

Another silence descended as the cab drove through black puddles of water like an ark through a deluge. Presently the old man said, "Here, drop me here."

The cab stopped and the old man got out, carrying a side bag.

The driver watched the retreating man in the rain. "You think Shimmel's gone crazy?"

"Yes."

"I mean, thinking the HolyName will come after him—"

They were both silent. Then, just as the driver restarted the engine, the radiotelephone chirped. The driver picked up. "No. He just left." He listened. "No, I don't know where he's going." He listened some more. "Okay."

Ehud asked, "Who was that?"

"Chief Superintendent Levitan. Says he needs to talk to Shimmel, urgent. I told him I have no idea where he's going, but Levitan said he does, he'll call him there."

Ehud said, "Shimmel won't answer."

"So where's he going?"

"You don't want to know."

-3-

Wednesday, October 7, 1981, 6:50 p.m.,
Abu Kabir Morgue, Tel Aviv

TWO MILES FURTHER west, the Abu Kabir morgue was semi-dark. Only the mortuary hall was dimly lit by a flickering fluorescent, as two men bent over a cadaver.

"Can you hold the deceased's leg while I clip his nails, Your Honor?"

"Yes, but don't take too long. It's almost seven o'clock."

Judge Fishkin held the mottled leg steady while Sergeant Amnon Amzaleg snipped the long, crooked toenail with the morgue's clippers.

The judge said, "Why don't you clip the nails in order?"

"He was religious, Your Honor. The Talmud said you should clip the nails at random to ward off the evil eye."

"And from where do you know Talmud?"

"From Casablanca. I went to religious school there before my father brought us all to Palestine. Sabag went to one, too, here."

"Oh. You knew the deceased?" the judge said.

"Yeah, Nachum Sabag. He lived across from me in HaTikva quarter, with his parents. Went to school with my son Iddo. I arrested him in '78 for selling heroin. You gave him two years."

"I did? I see so many, all these *Schwartzes* look the same to me. Not you, of course. You are almost a White *vooz-vooz* now, ha ha. How did this Sabag get it? Overdose?"

"No, bullet, Your Honor."

The judge peered up close. "Bullet, where? I don't see anything."

"Here. Right under his ponytail. See? Two-two caliber…"

"Ah, probably the Ohayon brothers, when he tried to sell in the Yemenite Quarter."

"Yes, probably." Amzaleg's face was expressionless. "Now the other leg, please."

Judge Fishkin let down the first leg and held up the other. "How many good deeds did we do tonight? Three? Four?"

"Five, including Sabag."

"Five? I lost count. I hope God keeps tabs. The others were from HaTikva also?"

"No. Only this one." Amzaleg accumulated the nail clippings on the edge of the stone slab. "Can you pass me the hose please, Your Honor?"

"Here. But careful of the nozzle, it sprays sideways."

Amzaleg hosed the bony dead buttocks, which were covered with needle pricks, the back of the thighs too.

"You can't do this faster?" the judge said. "The prayers start at seven. These criminals found a good time to pop off, just before Yom Kippur."

"I'm almost finished." Amzaleg combed the dead man's hair down the back over the bullet hole. "Now can you roll the shroud over him, Your Honor? Then hand me the sticky tape, please."

"Don't use too much. It's the last roll. I told Munger we'd run out, so many at once, and we could get ten more next week. But go talk to the wall."

The judge certainly was talkative tonight. Usually volunteers at the morgue did their private act of charity and went home to enjoy a few hours of temporary atonement. Washing the dead was considered the truest good deed because the beneficiary could not repay it.

Amzaleg said, "We won't get ten more, Your Honor. Soon one drug gang will win and the others will stay quiet. Now please hold the shroud while I tape it. If we run out, I'll get some more from the office."

"From Munger?" The judge snorted. "He wouldn't give a paper yarmulke to a dying rabbi—well, well, talk of the devil."

The fat pathologist, Dr. Pesach Munger, strode in, munching on a dripping sandwich and holding onto his black skullcap. "Good evening, repenters. Pedicure finished?" He laughed at his own joke.

Amzaleg went on taping. "It's dark outside, Munger, Yom Kippur already. You shouldn't eat."

"Me? On Yom Kippur I eat double, since Auschwitz." He spit on the floor. "That's what I think of Him." Munger rubbed the spittle with his toe, twice.

Judge Fishkin rotated his finger near his temple, trying to catch Amzaleg's eye.

Amzaleg kept his eyes on the cadaver. "And we need more tape."

"What tape?—Hey, wait! No shroud yet. I need him."

"For what? Medical students again? Tonight?"

"No, no. Some Mossadniks are coming, for training."

"What training?" Amzaleg said. "They can't take a break for Yom Kippur—wait, they were here two weeks ago. The new course is not due until next month—"

"So maybe they have more courses now, for Lebanon. What do I know?" Munger muttered. "Here, I'll take the deceased. Oh, I see you washed him already. Doesn't matter. I'll tell them to wash the remains when they finish." He stuffed the sandwich into his mouth and threw the brown cadaver over his shoulder. "By then he'll be so white he'll look like a Polack." He laughed again at his own joke. Judge Fishkin laughed also.

Amzaleg put down the tape. "You have permission from the family?"

Dr. Munger grinned over his shoulder, above the dead buttocks. "Sure, signed with thumbprints…."

"Fuck it, Munger. You got permission, yes or no?"

Dr. Munger's grin faded. "What permission? From his father the thief and his mother the whore?"

"—So a warrant. Like in an autopsy."

Dr. Munger stood irresolutely, the brown cadaver over his shoulder. "What do you want from my life, Amnon? The Mossadniks will be here in a moment, and all the other stiffs are too skinny. Look. You guys finished your repentance? Go home, go to synagogue, go eat, leave me alone. Your Honor, tell him not to be a donkey."

Judge Fishkin said, "Amnon—"

Amzaleg said, "Here, Your Honor. You give Munger the warrant." He tore a swatch of shroud, tugged out his policeman's ballpoint and clicked it open. "You sign for him."

Judge Fishkin rolled his eyes. "Everyone is crazy tonight." He said to Dr. Munger, "Go on, take one of the others."

Dr. Munger's little eyes darted. "What is this? Why? They are all the same—"

Amzaleg said, "So take another one."

Dr. Munger flung the half-wrapped body down on the slab. "Suit yourselves."

When he was gone, Judge Fishkin blew out his lips. "Amnon, you're a donkey son of a donkey."

"Yeah." Amzaleg taped around the deceased's torso, then the tape ran out. "Wait here, Your Honor, I'll go get some more. Just hold the corner here so it won't unravel."

He marched down the basement corridor and pushed Dr. Munger's office door open. Inside, five young men in gray T-shirts and jeans were standing under a fluorescent light around a concrete slab on which was slumped a bloody lump. On the radio an Ashkenazi cantor was starting on the Kol Nidrei prayer.

Dr. Munger raised his head as Amzaleg entered. "What do you want now, Amnon?" He was holding a sprung jackknife, its blade dripping.

Amzaleg said, "I need some more tape."

The five Mossadniks raised their heads. They were young, trim, and fair-haired. He could see himself through their eyes: old, fat and swarthy, two chins, a wide belly, a Moroccan *Schwartze*.

"It's in the middle drawer," Dr. Munger said. "Then get out. And next time knock before you come in."

Amzaleg grabbed three rolls of tape and left. Over his shoulder he saw the men lean once more over the slab, then Dr. Munger slammed the door shut.

Back in the mortuary hall Amzaleg taped the last ends of the shroud carefully.

"Don't waste," said Judge Fishkin. "Keep some for next week. We're sure to get more. Where you sending him, to his wedding?"

Amzaleg taped on, doubling up.

"Alright already," Judge Fishkin said. "That's enough. Let's say the blessing and go, or we'll miss the Kol Nidrei prayer."

Outside it was raining. Behind Amzaleg's patrol car were parked three gray Subarus, their windows curtained. The license plates were carefully splattered with mud. Behind the middle car, one of the trainee Mossadniks was bent over, puking into the wet ground. Dr. Munger was clutching the man's forehead from behind. As Amzaleg passed, Dr. Munger muttered, "You ever want to rejoin, Amnon, let me know, I'll call Shimmel."

Amzaleg went on walking toward his patrol car.

Judge Fishkin waddled past. "Have a good fast, Amnon."

Amzaleg squeezed into his beat-up patrol car, saying nothing.

"And don't repent too many sins." The judge got into his own Fiat. "Leave some for next Yom Kippur."

"I can't remember them all," said Amzaleg.

He sat in the damp cruiser and watched the other cars leave one by one, all turning into Ben Zvi Road toward Tel Aviv; then the metal gate slid shut. When the cars were gone, he sat smoking, watching the tall eucalyptus trees bending in the wind, listening to the rain hammering on the cruiser's roof. He had trouble breathing. He saw before him the bullet hole in Sabag's scrawny neck, and his finger twitched involuntarily as if he himself had pulled the trigger—which in effect he had, just as surely as he had caused his own son's death....

A bolt of lightning broke above the clouds, somewhere over Jaffa: fast-fading, crooked and multi-pronged, then a dull thunder cracked and Amzaleg's heart followed.

What business was it of his anymore? He should stay quiet, wait for his retirement, get his rank back, and his pension...

He crushed his cigarette on the dashboard, grabbed the scuffed radio handset, and before he could change his mind, called the private line of Superintendent Klinger, personal flunky of Chief Superintendent Levitan.

He half-expected to be shunted to Dispatch, but to his surprise Klinger's nasal voice answered immediately. "Who's this? Amnon? You know what time it is? I'm on my way to synagogue!"

Amzaleg could almost see Klinger's small eyes, long teeth, thin lips, but tried to keep his voice calm. "Who's doing the Initial on Nachum Sabag?"

There was a long pause. Too long. "Sabag? Who's he?"

Feeling his temples throb, Amzaleg began to explain, but Klinger cut him off. "Fuck it. For a dead *Schwartze,* you call me just before Kol Nidrei?"

"No, Klinger, listen—"

"That's Superintendent Klinger for you now." Klinger's high voice rose half an octave. "And I think Chief Levitan warned you to stay away from anything—"

"Listen… listen…" Amzaleg stuttered, "this dead guy, my son used to know him—"

"No, you listen, Amnon—and let me give you some advice. Don't break any more rules for your *Schwartze* neighbors, okay? Just wait for your retirement and get your rank back, alright? Now go to synagogue, go pray…." Klinger's voice trailed into a Yiddish drawl. "Count it overtime. Half our Wanteds are there anyway. End."

It was probably meant as a joke.

Amzaleg slammed the handset into its receptacle and cursed at length in Moroccan Arabic, which he hadn't done in a while.

Where would Iddo be, where would Nachum, if he had not kept them from leaving?

He parked under his flat in HaTikva.

The flat, a dank cubicle with a tiny kitchen and two miniature rooms, was dark. Here—he still didn't know how—he and Ilana had raised two children, Iddo now dead, the wife gone, his daughter Zohara with a criminal record, hating him….

As he switched on the kitchen light, three framed faces above the bookshelf stared at him from under diagonal black mourning stripes: his two brothers, and Iddo. All dead in the wars.

He averted his eyes. Outside, through the downpour, he saw the light in Jacqueline's hair salon across the street. Zohara was most probably there, waiting for him to leave.

What was he waiting for? Prayers should start soon.

Pulling a bottle out of the fridge, he poured a glass of araq and saluted each of the three framed photos in turn, then one more time, for the dead Nachum.

He shivered. Contrary to what he had told Judge Fishkin, he was sure it was not the Yemenite gang, nor any other gang, who had killed Nachum. Tel Aviv drug gangs did not use two-two guns for hits, and they certainly did not shoot with such medical precision, the kind Dr. Munger taught to state assassins, like Amzaleg himself used to be, years ago.

But what business of his was it now?

He raised his eyes to the three photos and got no answer.

Nachum's photo, he knew, would soon be on the wall at his parents' flat. Dead not in war yet dead just the same.

But dead how? And why?

Amzaleg cursed, slammed down the empty glass, and dialed Dispatch directly. "Who's doin' the Initia' on Nachum Sabag?"

The line crackled. "Amnon, that's you?"

It was an old civilian hag, an Ashkenazi policeman's widow who worked nights.

"Yeah. Who's—"

"Sorry, Amnon, Superintendent Klinger just called. He said if you call, to tell you in his name to fuck off. End."

She hung up, cackling.

Amzaleg glared at the black phone. He felt the questions churning inside and tried hard to prevent them from congealing.

Finally he got up, grabbed his prayer-shawl bag and left for synagogue, staggering down the stairs into the rain.

- 4 -

Wednesday, October 7, 1981, 7:00 p.m., Jerusalem, the Prime Minister's Office

I N THE PMO'S canteen, two emaciated men in badly fitting suits were drinking boiling tea: Prime Minister Menachem Begin and his cabinet secretary. Their two prayer-shawl bags were thrown on the Formica table beside them.

It was half an hour before Yom Kippur would start, and both men, having had their pre-fast dinner with their wives, had stopped at the PMO en route to synagogue for the Forgiveness prayer: the PM needed an answer to a question first.

There was no one else in the canteen, only the swarthy Yemenite guard on a chair by the door, picking his nose diligently.

"Nu, Kiddush?" the PM said.

The CabSec's name was Tzvi Kadishevitz. The PM called him Kiddush ("benediction") in jest. It was the only joke he knew.

The CabSec blew on his tea. "What do you mean, 'nu'?"

The PM said, "Someone told me Shimmel had a bit of trouble with his Undertakers, up north."

Undertakers was the colloquial name for the Anonymous Recon's assassins.

The CabSec said with alarm, "Who? Who told you that?"

"I can't remember. Someone."

The CabSec leaned forward. "Don't listen! You shouldn't know any of this!"

"So who says I know? I'm just asking. What kind of trouble?"

"Shush!" The CabSec pointed a thumb at the guard.

"Nah," the PM said. "He doesn't speak the holy tongue."

The holy tongue was Hebrew, but old Ashkenazi men often said it about Yiddish, which is what the PM and his CabSec were speaking now.

The CabSec said, "Yes he does. He only picks his schnozz to show he's not listening. But he reports everything straight to Feldman."

Avigdor Feldman was the head of the Internal Security Service.

The PM half-turned in his chair. "Ovadya," he called out in Yiddish, "you can take a little vacation maybe?"

The guard blinked, eyes darting, then he rose and left, closing the door behind him.

"See?" said the CabSec.

The PM shrugged. "So he learned a few words, so what?" He waited. "Nu?"

The CabSec stayed obdurately silent.

The PM tapped a bitten nail on the CabSec's tea glass. "What trouble, and who told you?"

At last the CabSec muttered, "My nephew is there also, in Beirut... He says half the Unit guys went to the psych ward in Haifa after the first month, so many jobs they were doing.... Then the other guys said—" he stopped.

"So?" the PM said. "They said what?"

"They said enough is enough. They can't do it anymore."

The PM's eyes flashed. "What do you mean enough?! They don't know what it's for?"

"Yeah, sure they know. But still they said no."

The PM's small mouth pursed. "They can actually say this? Refuse orders? In the army?"

"It's not the army, Menachem! It's the Unit. They do *dreck* so the army doesn't have to."

There was a long silence. Snatches of wailing prayer came from across the street. The CabSec reached for his prayer-shawl bag but the PM put his own palm on it. "Nu? So Shimmel sent them to jail?"

The CabSec snapped, "Jail? What jail? So who'll do the *dreck* jobs? Anyway, Shimmel spoke to them and they're back on the job."

"Ah-ah." The PM let go of the CabSec's hand. "What did he promise them?"

"I don't know."

"Yes you do. *What?*"

"This, no. You don't want to know from this. Listen to me, Menachem!"

At last the PM gave a long sigh. "Alright, Kiddush. I won't. But keep an eye on it." He picked up his own prayer-shawl bag, a brown velvet thing that had belonged to his father in Poland. "Enough yacking. Let's go ask Him for forgiveness, and for this sin too."

"You won't have to ask for what you don't know."

"But He knows," the PM said.

The two men, groaning, got up and ambled to the canteen's door, shuffling their feet.

The buzzer, as usual, didn't work, so the CabSec knocked and the Yemenite sentinel opened the door, holding two umbrellas.

The two men made their way across the street to the small Warshauer synagogue, the sentinel ambling in their wake without an umbrella, two burly Samsons further behind.

The rain was coming down hard.

- 5 -

**Wednesday, October 7, 1981, 7:10 p.m.,
Tel Aviv, HaTikva Quarter**

FROM ACROSS THE street at the HaTikva Hair Salon, Zohara glared at the rain, then at the clock. It was after seven o'clock and the place was deserted. A pile of peroxide bottles on the floor, spilled skin bleach, sink overflowing with blonde dye, evidence of why the brown-skinned *Frehot* came to the salon, to look like the blonde Ashkenazi women in the magazines whose pages were tacked to the wall.

"Pirchiya!" she called out, "come help clean up! It's late!"

No answer.

As she swept the floor Zohara peered through the back window. The light in her father's apartment across the street blinked through in the heavy rain.

Damn. Still there!

She'd have to wait for him to go to synagogue before she could dash to her room, change out of her stained smock and go out to the club. If he saw her going, there'd be a scene because of damn Yom Kippur. But she simply had to go. The peroxide fumes got in her throat and she coughed. She hated the smell, hated HaTikva, detested Israel, couldn't wait for June next year when her criminal record would be expunged and she could finally leave, emigrate anywhere… anywhere but this insane place….

Seven months in the reformatory. Seven fucking months!

"Pirchiya!" she called again.

Still no answer, just muffled crying from the storage room.

Why Pirchiya came to work today no one knew. She cried so hard she could barely work. Jacqueline said she'd pay her anyway, just take the rest of the week off, sit *Shiva* for her brother properly. Yet she came—for what?

As Zohara swept faster, the crying rose in volume. Finally she could stand it no longer and hammered on the closed door. "Go home. I can finish by myself."

But all she got for her trouble was more crying. It was too much, really, especially two days before the anniversary of her brother Iddo's death, when she herself was barely holding it together.

She tried to show sympathy. "Listen, when my first uncle died in the '67 war, I cried for two weeks, then when Iddo died in '73, only one week, then when my second uncle died right after, just two days, see?"

But if anything, her words only made Pirchiya cry harder still. Finally Zohara had enough. She wrenched the storage room's door open. "Go, go home. There's not that much to clean, only three days. I'll do it."

To her relief Pirchiya complied and meekly rose. "I told Nachum to stop using, all the time I told him, one a day, okay, you can shoot, but he had to do two—"

"Three," Zohara snapped, her generosity exhausted; then it came back. "But it wasn't an overdose. It was the Yemenites did him because he was barging into their territory."

Pirchiya flared a little. "No he wasn't. He was only using himself, never sold anything…" She began crying again.

Zohara handed her a towel. "Enough. Go eat something, go to synagogue, your parents are there already probably—wait, you can't go like that."

Picking up a brush, she combed Pirchiya's long hair. It was light brown and all the girls envied her for it. It was rumored that Pirchiya's real father was an Ashkenazi client of her mother, when her mother had all her teeth and could still work. "When's the funeral?"

"F-Friday."

"You want me to come too?"

"If—if you want."

"Well, you came to Iddo's." This threatened fresh weeping, so Zohara quickly asked, "You have enough to pay for the burial?"

Pirchiya shook her head. "*Adon* Leon said he'll pay for it."

"Well he should. Nachum made him enough money selling shit."

"No, no, Nachum only worked in the restaurant kitchen some-times—" but Pirchiya did not look up as she said that.

After Pirchiya was gone the work went faster. When Zohara was done it was seven fifteen. She looked out the window—the light was still blinking.

Damn! How long must she wait in this stink?

As she lit a cigarette, a discordant singing came in through the window—the early Yom Kippur prayers from the Iraqi synagogue. She cursed out loud in Moroccan Arabic and dashed to the window to close it. She'd rather have the stink than this noise.

Fuck them all and their insanity. Her children won't be born here, that's for sure.

As she closed the window she looked across the road. The light was still on.

Damn, damn! When would he leave?

-6-

WHEN SHIMON "SHIMMEL" Gershonovitz retired from the Interior Ministry, he thought he was leaving for good.

But how could you say no to a prime minister?

He was seventy-seven years old, three months into his retirement, living with a much younger Habima actress. Mornings he played chess with old farts in the boulevard, taking pains to avoid talking politics. Let others carry the burden from now on.

Then one day the cabinet secretary called. "Shimmel, can you come in maybe?"

"For what?"

"Not over the phone."

He already suspected. But when he walked in and Prime Minister Begin spoke to him in Yiddish, he knew.

The current Unit's commander, like many of his charges, had succumbed to the Blackness, that peculiar soul malady of Israel's lone assassins. No one else wanted the job.

"Can you do this again, Shimmel? Temporary."

Years ago he'd helped found the Unit, to do the state dirt that must be done.

"Why? To do what?"

The PM shrugged one shoulder. Wasn't it obvious?

Gershonovitz said, "Arik still pushing to go in?"

Defense Minister Arik Sharon, nicknamed the Bulldozer, had been pushing to invade Lebanon, to liquidate the Palestinian terrorists and put the Christians in power. Before his retirement, Gershonovitz was adamantly against it. Such a war, he knew, like America's Vietnam, could tear the country apart.

"Yeah," said the PM. "You think you can do something to stop this invasion?"

"Do what?"

"Whatever dirt you used to do," the PM said. "We don't want to know details."

When Gershonovitz said he was retired, had lost his touch, the PM said, "Shimmel, please. I'm begging you."

If it was that bad, how could he say no?

He sighed. "Alright, if I must. But I'll have a year to do it, and no interference. That's the condition."

"Sure," the PM said. "You have my word."

But suspecting that Begin's word was not final, Gershonovitz knew he must also strike a deal with the Bulldozer himself.

His proposed deal was: Send all of Israel's assassins to a hideout in Beirut to "take down" as many PLO leaders as possible. The silent mass butchery should set the PLO back several years, postponing the need for an invasion.

Then, during the hiatus, try to convince the Syrian strongman in Beirut, Rahman al-Assad, to depose his brother, the Syrian president, with Israel's help. In return, Rahman, once installed in Damascus, would cleanse Lebanon of Palestinians, whom the Syrians hated too, then sign a peace treaty with Israel—just as the Bulldozer hoped to do with Lebanon's Christians.

It was a crazy, convoluted plan, but the only one that could prevent a full invasion.

In a face-to-face meeting, Gershonovitz presented it to the Bulldozer. "How about it?"

The defense minister was incredulous. "First you want to off Palestinian chiefs one by one, then help this Syrian thug depose his brother? It's an idiotic idea. It'll never work."

Gershonovitz snapped that it was no more so than invading Lebanon to liquidate the Palestinians and put the idiot Christians in power so that *they*'d make peace with Israel.

The Bulldozer became enraged. He snarled that it was not the same thing at all! The Christians were willing, while Rahman was busy selling drugs and ruling Southern Lebanon on his brother's behalf. "He'll never even talk to you."

"You leave this to me. He'll talk to us if we agree to let his drugs go through our ports to Europe so he could sell more there. We'll go slowly, to draw him in first—"

The Bulldozer eyed Gershonovitz with grudging admiration. "You are crazy, Shimmel."

"I know I am. But so what? It can work."

"It never will."

Still Gershonovitz kept pushing. "What do you have to lose? Just give me a year, and if it doesn't work, then you can go in with the army and clean up the place...."

Which meant "don't leak it meantime."

The Bulldozer scowled.

"A year," Gershonovitz insisted. "When I agreed to come, Begin promised me a year."

"So? I didn't promise."

But when Gershonovitz suggested they call the PM in, the Bulldozer gave in with bad grace. "Alright, nine months."

It took Gershonovitz two weeks to hammer out the deal, with his French Secret Service contacts serving as middlemen. Improbably, Rahman al-Assad, the Syrian president's brother, agreed to provide the assassins with local cover. Both because he also hated the Palestinians and because it would help his drug business.

"Sure, sure," the Bulldozer said when he learned of it. "Kill as many of them as you want. It'll save us work later when all this blows up in your face."

"You just keep it quiet," Gershonovitz said.

"Alright, alright. Nine months, not a day more."

What did leak, though, was not the deal's details but some of Rahman's drugs as they passed through Israel, and these were promptly stolen and sold locally… which knocked down drug prices, which in turn made the crime bosses mad at him….

How long he could keep them quiet, Gershonovitz didn't know. Luckily, Rahman had swallowed the initial hook, and so Gershonovitz could at last make the ultimate offer.

But would the Syrian thug bite?

Gershonovitz did not know. But he was sure that, if the idea worked out, it would be the culmination of all he had ever aimed at in his public life.

If only the Damn HolyName did not stop him from doing it…

Because, and this Gershonovitz firmly believed, the Jewish God was not on the side of peace. He was on the side of war, to keep His people apart from the Gentiles. It had started with the ovens when the Damn HolyName forced the Jews out of Europe by killing half of them—and it went on in Israel too. So it was now up to men like him and his soul-Blackened assassins to save the Jews from their crazed deity. Of this, Gershonovitz was certain.

But could he do it in time? Could his assassins keep the pace of killings till then? Or were they too late?

Wednesday, October 7, 1981, 7:30 p.m., Tel Aviv, HaTikva Quarter

AMZALEG WAS LATE for prayer. As he came in, all turned to stare, then their eyes slipped away. He felt the sliding eyes like a slap.

They had once been so proud of him—the first Moroccan police Sergeant, even as he arrested them and rose on the back of his arrests... then first Moroccan police inspector... first Moroccan superintendent... his rise proving that dark Jews could be as good as the European Jews, the Ashkenazim—now he was a walking proof of their inferiority.

His ears burned as he sat down besides Superintendent Meir Suissa, now head of the police Clandestine squad that Amzaleg had headed before his disgrace.

Amzaleg leaned over and whispered, "Who's doing the Initial on Nachum?"

A few men hissed, shushing him.

Suissa mouthed back, "Amnon, leave this one alone."

Loud weeping rose from the women at the back as the cantor raised his arms, two voices rising above all. Amzaleg turned, saw it was Pirchiya, Nachum's sister, part-time hairdresser, and her mother, the former hooker.

They, too, quickly looked away.

The prayer went on and on and Amzaleg mouthed the old words.

Yet absolution did not come. Amzaleg's throat felt so hot he could hardly breathe. He rose, squeezed through the congregants, scrambled out.

He thought about Iddo, gone eight years, about Nachum, gone two days, both as good as killed at that same moment thirteen years ago, when he saw their pale faces inside the ship's hold and ordered them to come out....

As good as if he had pressed the trigger on both.

As he lit a cigarette, there was a rustle behind. Suissa. Also gone out to smoke.

Amzaleg rasped, "Their *vooz-vooz* synagogue no good for you anymore?"

Suissa had married an Ashkenazi secretary, a shrew, moved to the suburbs. All during the year he went to her parents' synagogue. On Yom Kippur he came back.

Suissa said, "All year I can take it, but Yom Kippur I gotta come here. The cantor there, he weeps too much."

"So weep along."

"This I can do at home," Suissa said, "every time I talk to her."

Amzaleg watched lightning flash over Jaffa. "How are things for you at the Clandestine? Guys behaving?"

The Clandestine was the nickname given to the police's detective squad, half-hidden in a small hut behind Army HQ in Tel Aviv.

"It's okay now."

"You sure?"

"Yeah, I am sure. Come visit, you want to see. You need a map?"

Amzaleg shook his head.

Suissa said, "Everyone says hi. They asked me to tell you—"

"No. Tell them you are the boss now."

"You can still come visit. We won't tell Chief Levitan."

"Levitan give you a hard time?"

"Nah, he leaves us alone so long as we don't fuck up. Just catch some thieves or drug dealers, here and there, nothing too big."

Nothing too big meant "leave the crime bosses alone."

Amzaleg said, "It's your job to fuck up sometimes."

Suissa looked at him askance, raised his chin, as if to say "look who's talking."

"What? What?" Amzaleg said, "So I got demoted for stepping on *Adon* Leon's toes.... So what? Six months, I'll get my rank back...."

They smoked in silence. Some snatches of prayer came from within.

Suissa said, "Smoking on Yom Kippur... if we're not careful, He'll write us in the wrong Book, we won't finish the year."

"Let Him write," Amzaleg said. "I did so many bodies today, I'm good for a whole pack."

"For Munger? How many?"

"Five, six, I can't remember. Also Nachum Sabag...."

Suissa's cigarette glowed hard.

Amzaleg rasped, "He got it in the neck, two-two, in the third vertebra... Who's doing the—"

"I told you, Amnon, leave this shit alone! Will be better for you."

"Yeah? You and Klinger." Briefly he told Suissa about Klinger and the dispatcher. "So who?"

Suissa just kept smoking as if his life depended on it.

Amzaleg said, "Was a friend of Iddo, you know, before..."

Suissa smoked on, furious.

Amzaleg said, "Three years ago I arrested Nachum—"

"Yeah, yeah. The heroin thing."

Amzaleg's voice was thick. "Before, at age sixteen... they tried to stow away on a boat from Haifa... escape the army and stuff... I made them come back...."

"No shit.... I didn't know...."

Amzaleg persisted, "And why has no one talked to the family? It'll get cold."

No answer.

Suissa had already gone back in.

Back at his flat, Amzaleg had another araq and smoked two cigarettes, one after the other.

Nachum Sabag's killing had all the marks of a hit by a military assassin from the Unit: the gun's caliber, the bullet location…

But why would a lowly drug pusher be killed by a Unit Undertaker? It made no sense.

He stubbed out his cigarette and looked for Ehud Reznik's phone number in Jerusalem.

Ehud was in the Unit many years after Amzaleg. But Amzaleg had met him in Reserve Service and also later. Ehud ran a small theater in Jerusalem ever since he'd separated from his wife.

No Unit members could stay married for long, apparently.

Finally Amzaleg found the phone number in his old notebook and dialed. It rang for a long while, but there was no answer.

Maybe he, too, was in synagogue.

Then Amzaleg felt ridiculous: A Unit member in synagogue. He, Amzaleg, was probably the only one who went.

He drank another araq and called the morgue. Munger answered after the tenth ring.

"What? No, I don't know the names of everyone I train. You crazy? They don't tell me and I don't ask."

Amzaleg had one more araq. His head began to swim.

There must be another way of finding out the current list of assassins. But who to call?

Many owed him. He had done so many favors but never asked any back. The only ones he did no favors for were his son, and Zohara, and his former wife….

As he wrenched his mind away, he thought of his long-ago police partner, Feldman, now head of the Internal Security Service.

How long was it since they had talked? Five years? Six?

He looked up Feldman's old home number and called, but there was no answer. He made two more calls to old Unit members whose phone numbers were in his notebook.

No luck there either.

As he hung up, he realized he just might have to visit his old commander, now suffering from Blackness in his halfway loony bin. Maybe the old man would still remember...

No.

Amzaleg didn't want to see what he himself might one day become.

Maybe there was still another way?

Wednesday, October 7, 1981, 8:45 p.m.,
HaTikva Quarter

AMZALEG HAD ANOTHER araq then walked over to speak to Nachum's family.

There was no one in the flat except Eli and Bracha Sabag, Nachum's parents. Eli's arthritic hands were so thin there was hardly any flesh on them. He couldn't pick pockets anymore but his hands still gave him a good living, panhandling. Eli's wife Bracha, more a bag of skin and bones, no longer hooked, just did cleaning occasionally.

Pirchiya came in and stood to the side, her soft brown eyes puffy with crying, Nachum's photo behind her with its fresh diagonal mourning patch.

"No," she said after Amzaleg mumbled his condolences. "No one from the police came."

Amzaleg flushed. "I am... so sorry for your loss."

"Ha," Bracha said.

Eli said. "So they sent you to investigate this?"

"No, no...."

Pirchiya bent over, said to her father, "Amnon is almost retired, not working much."

Amzaleg felt a pang.

He said. "I—I'm still working, it's just—" He paused, not knowing what to say about the demotion and his being a "floater" now.

Eli said, "So you told them you'd do this, before you retire?"

"No, nobody sent me."

"So why you asking all this?"

Amzaleg stuttered, "—to see if maybe I can help—"

"Help?" Bracha snapped, "If you hadn't brought him back—"

"Quiet, woman," Eli said. "He brought Iddo back too."

"Yes," Pirchiya said, conceding. "Yes, he did."

Amzaleg threw her a covert look and felt a slight shock at how pretty she was. With her dark eyes, the flowing hair, the white shoulders, she could pass for a *vooz-vooz*. More than one pimp kept trying to recruit her but she always refused. She could've made more but instead preferred to dye hair and bleach skin. She only sometimes went with the other hairdressers to Tel Baruch beach on Fridays.

Amzaleg tried to keep his eyes off Pirchiya's breasts, forcing his mind away.

Eli said, "So you are going to try and find who did this?"

"He can't," Bracha said. "They won't let him."

Amzaleg opened his mouth, but Bracha went on. "He was a good boy, now the Yemenites killed him. May the HolyName avenge his blood."

"Sha, woman," Eli said. "We don't know who did this."

"Amnon will find out," Pirchiya said. "Whoever did it."

There was a short silence.

"Yes," Amzaleg said. "I will."

The fog in his head clearing a little, Amzaleg asked a few more questions but did not learn much. No, the police did not come, neither from Jaffa nor from Tel Aviv, and no, no one asked them anything.

"No, no one came," the old pickpocket confirmed. "Just neighbors."

Pirchiya said, "But no one from the police."

"No one," Bracha hissed.

Pirchiya said, "What do they care, one more *Ars* dead?"

Only now, Amzaleg thought, someone seemingly did.

-9-

Wednesday, October 7, 1981, 9:45 p.m., Tel Aviv

A S GERSHONOVITZ MADE his way up Allenby Street, flashes of lightning cast flickering shadows in his wake and the whipping wind carried the rotting smell of the sea.

He knew exactly where he was going but did not want to think about it. And as he passed by the shuttered kiosks, watchmaker nooks and old Judaica stores, he felt tense and angry but also oddly exhilarated.

He was seventy-seven years old, but his live-in actress told him he looked like the trunk of an old Galilean oak that the years had rendered as hard as the basalt from whose cracks it grew. His vaguely Mongolian face had once been as well-known as Ben-Gurion's shock of white hair, Dayan's black eye patch, or Golda's thick legs. But after his retirement, he made sure to keep away from the public eye, and in this he succeeded until three months ago, July 1981, when he reluctantly allowed himself to be pulled quietly back into service.

He had always enjoyed preternatural robust health, like many of the First Ones who had built the state. But ever since he'd come back, all of a sudden his hip turned arthritic, his digestion acted up, and his asthma, which he had first thought a passing cold, now silenced him just when he needed his lung power most.

The rain was coming down but he ignored it. Lightning flashed but he didn't see it either.

Perhaps, he thought, he should skip the Feast tonight, go instead to his office to bone up on the latest intel on Lebanon and Syria. But then he recalled he'd been going to the Yom Kippur Feast ever since its inception and walked on.

He had only missed the one Feast in 1973 because, at the time, as director general of the Defense Ministry, he had to help plan the blocking battles against the Arab onslaught expected the next day in what became known as the Yom Kippur War.

During those awful first days, when the Syrians already broke into Israel, Gershonovitz had come to believe that the Arabs' imminent victory was really payback for all Yom Kippur Feasts past. Yet if anything, this made him ever more determined not to miss any future Feasts. Because if there was one thing he hated more than the Nazis who had murdered his first wife and children, more than the Arabs who murdered his second wife and baby son, it was the Damn HolyName who, he was certain, had ordained all this for His own selfish ends.

Once Gershonovitz had thought he was mad for thinking this, but no longer. He now allowed himself to hate the Jewish God with all his old encrusted heart, as did those he was about to meet at the Feast intended to celebrate this hate and keep it alive.

The Apostates' Feast was started in the mid-fifties as a lark by a famed radio comedian who, together with five other bohemian Auschwitz graduates, decided to hold a drunken feast on Yom Kippur eve as a way of "sticking their fingers up the HolyName's ass" on behalf of those whom He had had burned in the ovens—"which wouldn't have happened if the original Patriarch had the sense to tell the Damn HolyName to go fuck Himself when he asked him to sacrifice his son."

"But," said the comedian, "better late than never."

The comedian himself died during the 1959 Feast (stroke) but the affair still went on, and by the sixties became a regular secret event. Attendance peaked temporarily in 1966, when during the rendition of the blasphemous Yom Kippur prayer no less than four participants suffered heart attacks and had to be rushed to Hadassah Hospital in Gershonovitz's jeep.

When the following year none of the stricken returned, the Feast was moved to a more modest safe flat near the police station in Jaffa. By that time, Munger had reintroduced the Bible-page burning ceremony and scandalously rewritten more prayers.

In 1981, the Feast's attendance was still twenty strong, and so it was held for the second year at the same safe flat as the year before.

When Gershonovitz finally arrived there, it was about nine forty-five. The safe flat was on the top floor of an old apartment building in the Bauhaus style of old Tel Aviv, and both the rain-drenched street and the buildings were dark.

The flat's door was unlocked. Inside, a few dripping umbrellas stood against the wall, and clumps of people, none younger than sixty, milled about.

Mutters arose. "Shalom, Shimmel." "Happy holiday, Shimmel," as if this were joyous Purim, not the Day of Atonement. "Brought any food, Shimmel?" Then they let him go around while Pesach Munger, the master of ceremonies, clattered in the kitchen and threw out high-voiced war cries. "Fuck the HolyName! And tell Him I said so!"

Gershonovitz passed from one group to the next, nodding. He saw a celebrated journalist in a wheelchair and the elder Reznik whose chocolate factory had gone bankrupt, also in a wheelchair after his stroke. A few oldsters he knew from the Service, also a handful of old actors. Nearly all had their right sleeves rolled up, showing concentration camps' blue tattoos.

He threw his wet clothes in the bathtub, pulled out fresh clothes from his side pack and put them on. A white-haired ancient put a glass of brandy into his hand and he drank it gratefully.

"How many came?" Gershonovitz took two framed photographs out of his backpack.

"Twenty. Two couldn't make it, may they rest in peace."

"Cowards," cackled the old journalist.

The elder Reznik smiled feebly. "All the more food for us."

But of food there was no lack.

In the room's midst sat a long aluminum table covered with a tablecloth laden with foodstuff, the kind cooked by men for men: herrings in a glass jar, misshapen gefilte fish, boiled carrot in a Pyrex plate, crudely sliced challahs, and in the middle, the piece de resistance, a cracked porcelain plate heaped with blackened pork chops.

"Eat and drink and curse His Damn HolyName!" yelled a white-haired spy recruiter, waving his tattooed wrist. "Munger! Hey, Munger! Where's the stew?"

"Soon, soon!" Munger appeared in the kitchen's door. "We thought you chickened out, Shimmel."

"I wouldn't do it to them." Gershonovitz put the photos on a bench, kissing them tenderly.

"Give them some schnapps!" Munger handed him a cup and went back to his cooking, and soon Gershonovitz could smell fried gizzards. Munger prepared them every year because his little sister in Poland left them on the stove when she was taken to Belzen. No one liked gizzards so every year he ended up eating it all himself.

"Oh, Shimmel," someone said, "there was a phone call for you, he said it was urgent."

"Who called?"

"Don't know. Reznik talked to him."

But old Reznik couldn't remember.

The journalist called out, "It's the Damn HolyName called for you, saying you made so much trouble for him, He's putting you in His Book."

Soon Munger came out of the kitchen, wearing a gray apron emblazoned with "Police Medical Services," and said, "To the table, Apostates, to the table!"

Chairs were pushed in, leaving two gaps for the wheelchairs. Munger made sure all had plates and utensils, then said it was their solemn duty to eat and drink on this day of fast and curse the name of the Villain who had killed half His people for His own private ends.

It was the same speech he made every year, and all listened dutifully.

Toward its end, the phone began ringing, but although all knew the speech by heart, none dared get up. After a while the ringing stopped.

After the first two courses had been guzzled, Munger delegated a youngster of sixty-two, a comedian who had been to Buchenwald, to pour sherry brandy all around, and one by one all laid scatological curses upon the Damn HolyName and drank up. Every now and then someone rose from the table, calling something like "Velvel, this fish is for you!" or "Rivkele, this goose liver is for your little children!" before kissing the photos they had brought. Gershonovitz rose when his turn came, knowing they had made an allowance for him because his second wife and child had been killed by Arabs, not by Nazis.

Presently a clamor went up for Munger to sing his famous mock prayers. At first Munger feigned reluctance, then at last raised his head. "But it's the last time now!"

Voices rose. "Here, come in! He's singing it!"

Someone who had been reclining on a bed straggled in. Another came from the enclosed terrace. Munger raised his eyes to the ceiling and began to sing the prayer whose words he had blasphemously changed.

"And so let Thy eternal shame sink Thee, for Thou art our Enemy, eternal…"

A few mumbled "Eternal" as if in synagogue.

"… And let us acknowledge the shame of this day, for we are full of anger and disgust, and on this day Thy eternal shame shall be proclaimed…"

All around weeping voices rose.

"… And Thy throne shall be swept away by the blood of all the innocents…"

Old Mr. Reznik sat straight in his wheelchair, repeating the words.

"… And You shall be thrown away from Thy throne because of Thy crimes. Truly You are Satan, not God…"

In the bedroom the phone began to ring again.

"… And You are the prosecutor and litigant and the false witness and the accused, and the executioner of our kin, and Thy crimes shall always be written in the Book of Records, until only they will be remembered, but Thy own accursed name shall be blotted out…"

"Yes, blotted out," said a pale oldster, staring at half a dozen photographs on a separate bench. "Tell Him, Munger."

Old Reznik was weeping openly now. "Enough, Munger, enough."

"No, not enough!' the pale oldster shouted. "Not enough!"

Yet Munger was in full swing. "And justice shall be rendered as we curse Thy name until the end of days, until a thin whisper of sound will be heard as all our butchered innocents will emerge from the ovens, and You shall be gripped by trembling and shame as they pass their terrible judgment upon Thee just as You had decided their fate—their fate—" Munger's voice broke but he resumed, "so shall they decide Yours, and on this Yom Kippur we declare, solemnly… solemnly…"

His voice broke again, "—solemnly and in their names… in their names we declare Thee dead and gone, by fire and by water, by smoke and by gas, by bullet and by knife…"

Gershonovitz saw old Reznik swaying back and forth in his wheelchair, his eyes open.

In the bedroom the phone kept ringing.

"… No matter if we are strangled, or are devoured by beasts, or are stoned…" Munger's voice rose to a scream, "We curse You forever and ever. You and Your accursed name, for what You have done and for having forced us to glorify Your name after all You have done to us, for this we curse You, and command the host of Seraphim and Cherubim and all Heaven Dwellers to curse Thy name and turn their backs to You, and… and… and so today all inhabitants Above and inhabitants Below… are thrice cursing Thee—may Thy accursed name be blotted out forever and ever—"

And all, as one, called out, "Accursed! Accursed! Accursed!"

There was utter silence. Munger whispered in Yiddish, "A glass of water please."

In the other room, the phone began to ring anew. Someone went to answer it finally. Someone else slunk away from the table to the bathroom.

Presently the journalist came and said to Gershonovitz, "It's for you."

"Who is it?"

Old Reznik said, "It's the Damn HolyName, calling Munger to give Him an account."

Munger raised his head. "He should give an account to us."

The old journalist said quietly, "It's Chief Levitan, he says it's urgent."

Gershonovitz rose unsteadily to his feet. Clutching the photographs, he took the call in the other room and to the background of drunken cries behind him, "Put Him on trial, like Eichmann!" or, "Make Him eat some pork too!" He heard Levitan's voice saying there was a problem. "And if this fucking Klinger had any brains he would've called me right away when he found it, not only after the Kol Nidrei."

"When he found what?"

"The note," said Levitan, and cursed in vulgar Arabic. "One of your guys got crazy, offed a drug dealer and left a note."

-10-

Z OHARA WOKE UP in the shampoo chair with a start.

She had dreamed of the women's jail—she was again spread-ea-gled on the bed in the isolation cell, her ankles and wrists chained to the corners, Red Betty poking between her legs, the wardens watching from afar, cackling.

She could still feel her shoulders bunched up, trying to tear the plastic restraints.

She got shakily to her feet. The rain still hammered on the window, but the damn prayers had thankfully ended. She looked out—the window across the road was dark. Her father had gone to synagogue.

She quickly scrubbed her hands, threw her cigarettes into her bag and locked up.

She must rush home to change before he returned, then leave.

They'd be waiting for her at the club.

When she left, the clock above the sink said ten fifty-five.

-11-

**Wednesday, October 7, 1981, 10:55 p.m.,
Tel Aviv Harbor Quarter**

IT HAD TAKEN Gershonovitz almost an hour to walk to Chief Levitan's apartment in the rain.

The police chief opened the door in gray underwear and undershirt.

"Sha," he whispered. "My wife is asleep already. She fasts."

Gershonovitz went in, dripping water, careful not to shake himself too hard. It was a nondescript low-ceilinged flat, with faded kibbutz style sofas and chairs and the usual row of photos of family gone with Hitler. But the wall opposite was a veritable shrine of photos to Levitan's son, from circumcision to recent photos in army uniform. The last Levitan.

"Your son home?" Gershonovitz asked in a low voice.

"No, he's in armor camp."

Gershonovitz looked for a place to deposit his hat and finally put it on the floor.

Levitan did not invite him to sit. "Anyone die at the Feast this year?"

Gershonovitz shook his head. "But two look half-gone."

From behind the frosted-glass bedroom door came a staccato snore, a sort of snuffle.

"She got asthma all of a sudden," Levitan said, "when Dudi was drafted. Now she gets it every time he goes back to camp."

Gershonovitz, who had pulled out his cigarettes, put them back in his pocket. "Show me the note."

A clap of thunder sounded but the curtained window stayed dark.

"Here." Levitan handed Gershonovitz a blue police file, the corner marked with a red triangle, indicating it should not be removed from the office.

Inside, in a cellophane protector, was a half-page torn from a school copybook. It was written in Standard Square Script, used in the Service to disguise the writer's identity. Gershonovitz read and reread it, his face turning darker, then put it back in its cover.

"You put it in the safe, don't show this to anyone. Who else saw this?"

"Only Klinger, he's the one doing the Initial, brought it straight to me."

"Good, he's an idiot, but not a dummy. Will he keep his mouth shut?"

"He'd better."

There was a short silence. Then Levitan said, "Um… Klinger said he got a call about it, from Amzaleg."

Gershonovitz cursed in Polish. "What'd he tell him?"

"To fuck off, what else?"

"Why did this damned Amnon call?"

"Klinger said the victim was a friend of his dead son, something."

Gershonovitz said, "It's a double problem."

Levitan said, "Don't worry about Amzaleg. I'll handle him."

"You'd better."

"Now what about your side?"

"What, my side?"

Levitan hesitated. "You think this madman is maybe—one of yours?"

Gershonovitz kept his gaze straight. "Can't be. They are all in Beirut."

"You sure?"

"Yeah, yeah, I am sure."

Levitan peered at him. "What about reservists, retirees, anyone with training—"

"Reservists and retirees all working now too. Everyone."

"All? Your guys, Asa's, Feldman's?"

Asa ben-Shlomo was head of the Mossad, Avigdor Feldman, head of the Internal Security Service. Each had its own assassinations unit.

Gershonovitz said, "Yeah, everyone. They are all in Beirut, or in the psych ward and can't get out, or getting electroshocked."

Levitan said, "Maybe someone came back from Beirut on the quiet—"

"Maybe."

"Or maybe it's someone not connected? Some upstart thug, or a foreign gun doctor, came to do a job—"

"On a small drug pusher? Who'd pay?" Gershonovitz raised his voice, "And then write a note like this? And in SSS?"

"Shhh," Levitan said. "Quiet."

Gershonovitz nodded, breathed in, out.

Levitan said, "Or maybe Munger got crazy, decided to do what he teaches—"

"No. Pesach is in the morgue all the time, working, sleeps in his office, even. You check the security cameras there. I bet it's not him."

"We will," Levitan said.

There was another clap of thunder, and the rain strummed on the window.

Levitan said, "You think maybe this madman will do it again?"

"You read the note, no? He wants to cleanse the land."

Levitan cursed in Arabic at some length.

"Yeah," Gershonovitz said.

Levitan said, "You want me to put someone else on it, maybe, not Klinger, someone not an idiot? Put together a bigger team—"

"God forbid! Bigger team, it will leak. Newspapers, radio… can you see this note in the paper? The prime minister sees this, he pulls everyone back from Beirut, gives the green light to the army to go in…" Gershonovitz breathed heavily, pulled out his inhaler, took a few gulps of Swiss cortisone. "Before we go after him we gotta know who he is, or—" He looked at the wall, where photos of Levitan's son were plastered: the last of the Levitans, now in a tank somewhere, whose life hung in the balance, like many more.

"Alright." Levitan said, "Can you check on your side?"

"You bet I will."

"And if you want anything else done here—"

"No, no, just keep this quiet and keep me informed."

They sat a while in silence, the rain a steady machine gun outside.

Finally Levitan said, "Alright, Shimmel, I'll drive you home."

"No, no, I can walk."

"Don't talk nonsense. Not in this rain, all the way to Rothschild Boulevard. You'll catch something, then what?"

"Alright," Gershonovitz said at last.

As Levitan's cruiser stopped before the flat where Gershonovitz's actress lived, Levitan said, "This note, did you read it? 'To cleanse the inferior dark breeds'... like it was written in German."

"You shut the fuck up, Leizer! It's not the same." He slammed the cruiser's door, went into the building, and climbed the stairs in the dark.

His actress was already sleeping. He went straight into the little laundry room, closed the door, picked up the mic, pressed the scrambler button, and dialed.

-12-

Wednesday, October 7, 1981, 10:55 p.m., Road to Jerusalem

EHUD'S VOLVO CLIMBED the snaking mountain road to the Unit's HQ near Jerusalem. Rain lashed the asphalt, pines and olives growing in vertical cracks of rock.

He had not seen his father for three weeks and wanted desperately to visit him at the old folks home in Ra'anana, but he had to pick up extra poison ampoules for the guys in Beirut.

All at once he felt a need to hear his father's voice, the one for whom he was doing all this. He grabbed the radiophone and dialed his father's bedside number at his nursing home.

The phone was picked up after one ring and he heard hoarse breathing, but no words.

"Dad?" he said. "Dad? Is't you?"

There was a stuttering croak, then angry weeping. The stroke effects came and went.

The home's nurse picked up. "No," she said. "He's not so good today, after the Feast. Maybe tomorrow."

Ehud waited until his voice came back. "Just tell him that I called."

"Of course I will."

Ehud wiped his eyes and hung up, cursing softly, but in mid-curse, the radiophone buzzed.

He grabbed it, hoping beyond hope it was his father, but it was Shimmel.

Gershonovitz had almost given up when his scrambler's green light went on.

He grabbed the mic.

"Put your scrambler on, Ehud. Did you off anyone here after the refresher?"

"What? Fuck no!"

"What about the others?"

"The others?" Ehud's scrambled voice was faint. "We only practiced some knife work indoors. What the—"

"Shut up and listen. D'you know if any of the others offed someone...."

Ehud's voice came suddenly crisp and clear. "Wait, Shimmel, wait! What the hell happened? Someone was offed? Who?"

"Some drug pusher from HaTikva."

"So why do you think it was one of us?" When Gershonovitz did not reply, Ehud said, "What was the MO?"

"Not over the phone."

Ehud said. "Listen, call the operations officer in Beirut, Ronen, ask him who else was—"

"No, you call. Tell him to call me on the scrambler." Gershonovitz paused. "How many of ours came with you on the boat from Beirut? Five?"

"Yes. With me, six. With Moshe, seven."

"Have them all call me. Not together, one by one. And not Moshe, I'll talk to him. End."

Gershonovitz leaned back, shut down the scrambler.

The killer could equally have been one of the Mossad's or the Security Services' guys—the quick retraining might have thrown one of them over the edge... but no. He felt the MO had Unit written all over it.

Yet who could it be? Who was mad enough to write such a crazy note?

And such archaic language too.... It reminded Gershonovitz of something he had read long ago... something equally crazy... a book perhaps...

What was it?

He searched his memory but couldn't put his finger on it.

-13-

Wednesday, October 7, 1981, 11:00 p.m., HaTikva Quarter

AMZALEG SAW THAT his flat's door was unlocked and there was a light in Zohara's room. As he entered, she came out.

Under her old raincoat she wore her tight red dress, nylon stockings, her mass of frizzy hair tied with a red sash. In her handbag were her high-heeled pumps.

He bellowed at her. She tried to make a beeline for the door, but he blocked her way, his heart racing with rage.

Zohara heard the door open as she came out, and there was her father. She tried to bypass him but he blocked her way.

"Where you going, like this?" he bellowed.

As she whirled to evade him he tried to grab her wrist, and, without thinking, she whipped the straight razor from her handbag and flapped it before his face.

"You touch me, I'll cut you, Amzaleg, do you hear?" She felt a wet trickle roll down her cheeks. "I swear I'll cut you!"

She saw him recoil. "—it's Yom Kippur—Day of Atonement, what're you doing?"

"Going dancing!" she hissed, pointing to the leftmost photo on the wall. "I'm going dancing, in Iddo's memory! You going to stop me?"

She flipped her blade in his face again, snick snack.

He hollered. How could she go dancing on Yom Kippur—he would not let her!

As she flipped her blade to keep him off, she saw him bring one leg forward, his hands circling, trying for her knife arm. His army training probably, whatever it was, years ago.

"Let me go, Amzaleg!" she hissed, edging away.

"Look at you, on Yom Kippur…. Iddo saw you he'd roll in his grave—"

She screamed, "Don't you dare mention his name! If Iddo saw me, he'd be happy! He never had the chance—"

Amzaleg made another grab at her but she had been watching his eyes and twirled away. "Yah! Go ahead, just try!" She spit straight at him, saw the spit trickle down his jaw.

He rubbed his face, then he let down his hands, stopped moving, staring right at her.

She couldn't stand his stare. "He could've been out of this goddamn place!" she screamed. "You made him stay. He died because of you… because you forced him…"

When Amzaleg hadn't moved, she circled around him, inching toward the door, him just turning to face her, his eyes so black-anguished she couldn't bear it.

Waving the razor in front of her, she shouted at him, "You think he'll forgive you, doing these fucking repentance washes?" Her voice was so thick she could hardly recognize it. "You kept him here, you won't keep me—"

She slashed at him but he stayed in place, not even trying to evade the blade, and she pulled back.

"Let me go!" she cried.

He said something in a low voice, but she just let out another scream, and as he stepped aside, she slashed twice in the air, hit at him with her handbag and ran out.

-14-

Wednesday, October 7, 1981, 11:05 p.m., Tel Aviv

ZOHARA ARRIVED AT the Velvet club after eleven p.m. and parked under a concrete awning.

Pushing her father's image away, she changed her shoes, locked the scooter and made for the entrance.

Before it, under a tattered canvas awning, snaked a short line of boys, some girls, beige- and brown-skinned and frizzy-haired Eastern Jews. They pressed against a rope guarded by the beefy selector in a black leather coat, his arms folded.

Or maybe it was not black, just some dark color, one of those she could not see.

"No," she heard him growl, "no more room tonight," even as he removed the rope to allow a fair-haired couple to sail in.

She pushed through the line. Behind her she heard whispers, "She's here!" and "She came!"

Without pausing to look up, she tore the rope from its metal poles and motioned with her head to those waiting in line, in the rain. "Go in."

The selector slapped a big hand on her shoulder. "Hey!" he began, then he seemed to recognize her and stepped back.

Zohara stared at his eyes and turned toward the line. "Go in. But pay first."

There was a pause, then a brown-faced boy, probably a Yemenite, handed a crumpled bill to the selector, who, scowling, took it. As others still hesitated, Zohara snapped, "You want to go in or not?"

"It's her!" the first boy chortled from within. "I told you, they're afraid of her!"

As all scrambled in, Zohara dropped the rope on the sidewalk. The selector clenched his fists. "If I'm fired because of you, bitch—"

She put her hand inside her handbag. "You break my fucking heart." And as he made way for her, she marched in, throwing her ten shekels at his face.

She hated doing all this. But if she didn't, no one else would.

Why she bothered, she wasn't sure. It wasn't as if she loved her brown-skinned brethren. After all, she came here to escape them, their stupidity and coarseness, their obliviousness to any books except the insane ancient book that had killed her brother. She really went to meet Ashkenazi boys who had more than five hundred words in their vocabulary, maybe even someone with whom she could talk…

Why she helped her kind get in, she could not fathom.

The place was half-empty tonight and one of the wall bars was closed, probably because of damn Yom Kippur. Even the usual clumps of yeshiva runaways were absent, only a couple near the toilets, pale and lost and bewildered. These two were about the same age as Iddo when he fell—he used to come here when he could.

To suppress her rage, she bought a Maccabee beer, refusing the barman's offer of heroin, exceedingly cheap lately, and squiggled onto the dance floor.

The boy she had helped get in came up to her, shyly thanking her, danced alongside. She nodded then turned her back to him, and made for the toilet.

Inside was a lineup before the stalls, some men sitting at the wall, legs splayed, a few young women, eyeing the men as they waited for a stall to be free, everyone ignoring the two men at the back, one sniffing some powder off his watch's face, the other thrusting a girl's head down on his crotch. Zohara sat down. Here all were the same, Ashkenazi, Sephardi, fair, dark, white, brown.

Presently someone asked her to suck him off. She looked at his face, an Ashkenazi boy. She said no, but she'd do him by hand. And no, she didn't want any White, just twenty shekels and a name of a book.

Why she asked this she didn't know. No, she did.

Yes, she could get book names at the library, or from Batya, but she wanted something else, too, men that she could talk to about them. Unlike the ignorant *Arsim* around her, who never read anything, except the evil book that had killed her brother, or books explaining it…

The boy was staring at her with puzzlement, then nodded, and she began unbuttoning him. But when she already had him in her hand, she felt the knots of his little shawl behind the belt.

Fuck. Another yeshiva runaway. Read nothing, could hardly speak Hebrew….

Probably a total waste of time.

It was.

When she left, the crowd was already larger, but she knew it was no good. Too many of her brethren, none she could talk to. Why she fought to let them in she didn't know.

She changed her shoes outside, climbed on her scooter and drove toward Batya's flat.

As she drove she hummed a bit from the symphony by this guy Mahler, whose record Batya Feuerstein had given her the month Zohara had passed the external matriculation exams. Batya, who once was the reformatory's social worker, had been badgering her to take it ever since Zohara was released from jail.

A decent Ashkenazi bitch, imagine. And she didn't go to synagogue either. But then Batya had probably lost half her family to the ovens. Not that Zohara cared for any of these shit stories. It wasn't any of her business. It happened to the Whites, not to her people.

She tried to focus on the Mahler tune. It was complicated, not like the simple Sephardi stuff you could hear at HaTikva, or even Elvis, which wasn't bad but wasn't complicated.

Suddenly there was a whoosh behind her. She swerved instinctively and another Vespa passed her, the rider's head hidden in a bulbous helmet. For some reason she felt the hair rise at the back of her neck. But then the Vespa was gone and she was riding along the empty street, the rain in her face, the coins she just got jangling in her pocket.

It was well after midnight when she arrived at Batya's flat.

She opened the door with her key. On the living room's carpet, three bodies were sprawled, curled in blankets. Yeshiva runaways. Batya, the idiot, was providing her flat as a crash pad.

Batya herself was sitting on a high stool in the kitchen, reading. She wore the same blue pants she had worn in the reformatory, elastic band at the hip, kibbutz style, loose checked shirt, short graying red hair. She looked up as Zohara entered.

"Had a good time?"

Zohara hoisted her shoulder.

"You hungry?"

"You eating too?"

"You know I'm fasting." Batya was already rummaging in the fridge, pulling jars out, vegetables, packets.

"But you don't go to fucking synagogue."

"Don't say this word here, please."

Zohara hoisted her shoulder again, went to sit on a stool.

Batya said, "No, I am not eating. Not for me, for them." She pointed to the ubiquitous photos on the wall, of family gone into the ovens.

Presently Zohara was wolfing down a three-decker sandwich. "Your daughter called, sent a postcard, something?"

"No. And please don't talk about her."

"Why not?"

"Just because. Milk?"

Yes, Zohara wanted milk.

Batya handed her a glass. "I'm off to bed. When is your English exam?"

Batya had pushed her to do her matriculation exams. But once Zohara started, there was no need to push anymore.

"In three months."

Batya nodded, gave Zohara a half-hug—Zohara froze, as always—said good night, then went to her room and closed the door.

Zohara went to the empty room of Batya's daughter, and for the umpteenth time thought it strange that there were no photographs of the daughter anywhere in the apartment. When she asked Batya once to see a picture, Batya said no.

Only once, rummaging in drawers, did she see a photo of a beautiful young woman with golden reddish hair, small even teeth, a lightly freckled nose, just like a movie actress…

Why not show her photos then?

Strange Ashkenazi Jews. They plastered their walls with photos of the ovens' dead but did not want to show photos of the living.

Zohara undressed, emptied her mind and lay down, curled under the clean sheets, her razor under the pillow. She often had nightmares about the reformatory and the women's jail. Feeling the shiv nearby made them easier.

Just before she fell asleep, for no reason, the image of the scooter that had passed her came to her mind, and again she felt the hair rise on her neck.

Then she plunged into sleep.

-15-

**Wednesday, October 7, 1981, 11:55 p.m.,
Tel Aviv**

IN THE TEL Aviv rain, bent over the Vespa's handlebars, the killer drove around the contaminated city for an hour, looking for targets to cleanse. There was no one about. Yom Kippur and the rain had emptied the streets.

He rode east, toward his safe hideout at the Carmel Market, stopped near the public washrooms at the market's edge, parked, got off.

Down the stairs a metal shutter had been lowered, blocking the entrance to the toilets. Two bodies lay curled on the steps, sleeping, and he bent over them. No, these were girls, probably runaway *Frehot* from some Negev town. No.

He went back up, mounted his Vespa, hesitated. Maybe try one more place.

Down King George, streets still empty, bus stations empty, usually some human flotsam sleeping there, but tonight nothing. In Gan Meir Park, the public toilets at the back, yes, a form huddled. He parked but kept his helmet on, just in case.

He entered. Yes, inside the toilets one dark boy, shivering, looked up, questioning with his fingers, circle moving up and down.

He took off his helmet, nodded, helped the boy to his feet, pointed down. Yes. The boy rubbed thumb and forefinger.

It was easier this time, not even hard to find the boy's third vertebrae. He just pushed the dark head down when he finished and shot downward.

It felt good, knowing he was doing it for his father, who, he hoped, would finally be proud of his selflessness. The father he both loved and hated, the father whose honor he was avenging, like all of them did.... Yet who never once thanked him for his work....

He stuffed the body inside the toilet where it could be easily seen and inserted the note in the boy's pants pocket, half-in, half-out.

The rain was coming down in steady torrents as he put the helmet back on before he left. The streets were mercifully empty. But just in case, as he mounted his Vespa and drove back to his hideout in the Carmel Market, he again used the standard precautions, both on the stairs and at the upstairs door.

Outside the rainstorm went on, thunder and lightning coming fast, like crackling pages in the Book above as names were being written and erased. But inside him all was Cleansed and calm.

Just before he went to sleep he copied some of the Prophet's sentences for the next note.

-16-

**Thursday, October 8, 1981, 5:30 a.m.,
Tel Aviv, HaTikva Quarter**

WELL BEFORE DAWN Zohara heard the phone ringing and Batya picking it up, then speaking into it in a low voice, in what sounded like German.

Zohara came into the living room just as Batya was hanging up. Batya's face was glowing, even though she had tears in her eyes.

"Who did you speak to?" Zohara asked.

"No one."

Zohara had a flash. "Was it your daughter?"

"No, no. Go back to sleep."

"But why in German?"

Batya hugged Zohara. "Please, no questions. Go to sleep."

In the morning when Zohara awoke she wasn't sure if it had indeed happened.

17

December 1973,
Beit Sarah Reformatory

MORNING STAFF MEETINGS at the Beit Sarah Reformatory were held daily at eight o'clock and were usually short. Yet the morning after Zohara's arrival, the meeting lasted longer as there was thrilling intelligence about the strange new *Freha*, which Batya Feuerstein had obtained from Zohara's school principal.

Principal Blumenkrantz was miffed.

"We can't spend too much time on each *Freha*. We still must finish the report about the suicides."

But the staff, not eager for the tedium (for weren't these suicides all the same?), preferred to hear more about the *Freha* whose father was a police superintendent.

"Yes," said Yael Segalovitch, the houseworker and part-time Bible teacher. "What did she do, that even her policeman father couldn't get her off?"

Well, Batya said, the girl did admit to breaking a teacher's arm—

"Breaking his arm?" yelped Tova Shpigler, the cook and commissary. "You could've told me! She might have broken my arm too."

There were snickers. Tova's arms were as thick as a man's thigh.

"What else did they tell you—so I'll know what to watch out for?"

"Well, the principal said she was probably insane...."

At this, there was a general buzz. Just how, where, when did the new *Freha* display her insanity?

Principal B. put down the report draft. "So why didn't they send her to the asylum in Bat Yam?"

Bruria Shlaif, the cleaning teacher who liked to help Tova restrain girls, said this was probably because of her father.

"Or perhaps," said Tova, "she was so insane even the asylum refused to take her?"

All looked admiringly at Tova who had tied the dangerous *Freha* to the Isol's bed all by herself.

"Or maybe they were full," Principal B. said.

"But if so," said Tova, "why send her here?"

However, Batya could only repeat what she had been told: the girl was a crazed rebel, had read forbidden books, mocked authority, and encouraged other girls to do likewise.

The part about books caused alarm.

"Which?" asked Yael Segalovitch, the Bible teacher. "Not the pocket kind?"

However, Batya had gotten no details about this either.

Principal B. said they really should start writing the suicides report, "because I am not writing it all by myself again, like the one last month."

But Tova Shpigler would not hear of it. "I must know what she did, for when I put her in Isol next time. Because maybe one set of shackles is not enough?"

"So use two," snapped Principal B. "Batya will call the school to find out more."

The incident in question, Batya told them next morning, took place after art class.

Since it was Hanukkah, the girls had read the lovely story of Hanna and her seven sons—yes, the one about the devout mother who defied the Emperor's order to tell her sons to kiss the Roman idol's feet, commanding them to choose death instead.

Yael Segalovitch nodded. Yes, a beautiful story. But why in art class?

Well, all girls had learned it for an exam. But to highlight its moral beauty, the teacher also had them draw the sons' various deaths and color them. Each girl could choose the death scene of her choice: one son was eviscerated, another skinned, a third pierced with irons, a fourth strangled, a fifth burned in the oven, and so on, as the mother tenderly looked on, heroically urging her sons to accept death rather than kiss the idol's feet.

"And the *Freha*," said the Bible teacher, "got mad because she couldn't draw? And then she broke the teacher's arm?"

"No," said Batya. "She just refused to do it, and when the other girls hung their drawings on the walls, she screamed and tore them down, and stomped on them…."

"Why?" said Tova Shpigler. "Just out of envy?"

"Maybe, no one knows—she just went crazy…."

There was a puzzled silence.

Batya said, "And when other girls tried to stop her, she climbed on a table and screamed that all the teachers were insane, and that she was not going to let them make her insane too…."

Principal B. twirled his finger near his temple, meaningfully.

There was silence. It was clear all were wondering whether the crazy *Freha* would do it here too.

"And she started screaming just like that?" the Bible teacher said. "Maybe she was in a drug *kriz*?"

"No, the police doctor checked her. Then, when the *Freha* had finished destroying the class's drawings, she ran into the corridor and trashed other drawings the girls had made the week before, of Isaac's binding—"

Principal B. asked, "Why didn't the teacher tie her up?"

"Because by then she had gone into hysterics, hollering that this was how they had killed her brother and she would not let them do it to her sons too—"

Tova asked, "What brother? Was he in the same school?"

"No," said Batya, "it's a school for girls."

The confusion now was complete.

"And what sons?" asked Yael Segalovitch. "Was she knocked up before?"

"No, or the Social Services report would've said it."

Tova asked, "Maybe she was to be married soon?"

It was known that *Frehot* were forced to marry young if they were knocked up.

"No, there's no mention of this either in the report."

Yael asked slyly, "But did she have a brother at all? Or was he a part of her insanity?"

All snickered. Yes, this was possibly it.

But Batya surprised them. "Oh," she said, "she did, and he did die."

This confused everyone completely.

"He died? And who killed him?" Tova asked. "Someone in school? Was he in an *Adon's* gang?"

This finally began to make some sense. All *Arsim* were in gangs.

"No, her brother fell in the army," Batya said. "On the Golan, two months before, in a tank."

"Ah," Tova said weakly and added that this provided some extenuating circumstances, but still, one could not condone such mad behavior, dead brother or not.

"Certainly not," said Principal B., who never saw a day of army service, nor did any of his children, having found refuge in a yeshiva.

"So what happened then?" someone asked.

Batya said it was then that the *Freha* began to break chairs and windows, and the principal had to slap her lightly, as one must do with violent hysterics—

Several nodded. Of course, yes.

"And then," asked Principal B., "she broke his arm?"

"Yes. She did."

Tova said, "Broke it how? With a hammer? Or with something else?"

"No. Just with her hands, they said, she twisted it somehow—perhaps she had seen her father do this to prisoners—"

Tova leaned back and licked her lips; so did Bruria.

"And the superintendent father?" asked Principal B., who had a bitter experience with the Hadera police in a misunderstanding about some young *Frehot*, "why didn't he intervene with the judge?"

Batya said, "I don't know." For some reason she found the story disturbing. "The social worker's report says her father wasn't at the trial because he was still in hospital and had to get a special release to accompany her here—"

Hospital?!

This was totally new, and they all pounced on it: Which hospital? Why? When? How? What?

Batya referred to her notes. "It says he was in Haifa Hospital, in something called the Special Ward...."

Ay yay, yay!

At this they all clicked their tongues in unison, and Principal B. said it was well known that Haifa Hospital had a special wing where completely hopeless loonies were sent and often didn't come out.

Tova said, "So maybe her father is the insane one? And the *Freha* got it from him?"

A few nodded. Yes, things now began to clarify.

But Batya dampened it and said it was also possible the father had gone insane independently because his son fell about that time. This happened a lot too.

"So the *Freha* got it from him?" said Tova.

"Or maybe she got it from the brother," said Bruria Shlaif, adding that this was a real fine *meshiggene* family.

That was a fresh angle, so they went around and around with this, but by then it was close to nine, and by the level of noise downstairs, it was time to let the girls out of their cells to be searched.

"And I'll need help to take her out of Isol," said Tova, "and also later, if she gets to go back in, until we decide to send her to the asylum."

"Why don't we wait a few days," said Batya.

18

WHEN SHE FIRST met Zohara, Batya Feuerstein was fifty-five, wrinkled and sun-dried, a teachers' seminary graduate with two years' extra study in sociology, who, fifteen years before Zohara's arrival, had taken the job at the Beit Sarah Reformatory to help feed her baby daughter after her husband was killed during a cross-border operation.

He was Batya's second husband. The first, whose name she still carried, was bludgeoned to death by Hitler youth in 1938 in Berlin. But she managed to escape Germany, miraculously, came to Palestine, a girl of nineteen, to an aunt who housed her while she studied and married again. And the second husband, though not as good as the first, but still, a husband, gave her a daughter...

Then he, too, was taken from her. Her entire family gone into the ovens, no one left except the daughter, who had to be fed, and the reformatory paid a little better than a social worker's job. So she took it but always maintained that it wasn't just the money. The reformatory was also a mission for her because her husband had given his life for the state, and what had she done? Nothing much except keep house and light candles on the Sabbath (for him, only for him, to synagogue she gave up going. Two husbands gone and her entire family, too, enough was enough).

But in the reformatory she could help because someone had to help these poor Human Dust who had arrived at our shores. It really was not their fault that they had gotten their blood mixed with Arab blood during the two thousand years they had lived among them. That's how they became darker and dumber, one of her teachers at the seminar said with compassion, just as we became fairer and smarter after mixing up with our oppressors. (Her own daughter was blessedly almost blonde).

Why, just look at all the Nobel Prizes we got, a professor at the University said, enumerating them, and our Ashkenazi geniuses, enumerating them too. And how many Nobel Prizes did these *Schwartze* Human Dust get? Not one. Like Negroes in America, they were simply not up to it. Still, they were Jews also and they were here, because the state needed more people, even simple soldiers, which is why they had been brought in. So it was really up to all of us, but especially us teachers, to help these poor souls along, bring them closer to modern cultural standards if we can.

In this, Batya completely concurred, until she met Zohara.

It wasn't that Zohara was particularly smart (except for her skill at stealing exam answers, no one knew how), or adept at any task except getting other girls to somehow follow her lead in rebellions. Rather, it wasn't what she had or did, but what she didn't have or do that marked her as different.

Of course she also had the same deficiencies that all her dark brothers and sisters had: Disdain for authority, a penchant for violence, and horrid social manners, cursing as luridly as the worst Yemenite grocer in the Carmel Market (though, for some reason, not when she spoke to the old Yemenite washerwomen who worked in the reformatory's kitchen). Yet in her, somehow even these deficiencies were manifest in a weirdly different manner. Her disdain for authority did not seem a challenge or obstinacy. It was as if she really didn't know that authority existed, or as if she was blind to it, just as she was blind to some colors. More than one warden remarked that Zohara was probably mentally defective—which was also what her school records said.

Then by and by, it became clear she really could not understand the simplest concepts since her brain was really wired differently. Once Batya even suggested that maybe whatever made Zohara color-blind also made her blind to some simple words, but everyone else scoffed at her. Zohara was just an ornery *Freha* like the rest, only more cunning and sly.

Not that Batya liked to refer to Zohara by that ugly name, which she knew meant an Arab slattern. Nor did she like to refer to Eastern Jewish men as *Arsim*, which she knew meant pimps in Arabic. Because of course, not all of them were. At least not many.

As for Zohara's inability to understand certain things, this was only what she said, all teachers agreed, because it was clear she was only doing it to annoy and to escape her duties.

And annoy everyone on the staff she surely did, especially since what she could not understand was what all took for granted and revered. In particular, anything to do with religion, Zohara could not comprehend and flatly called insanity. She absolutely refused to participate in any religious ceremonies whatsoever, dubbed the prayer books and the Bibles that girls were encouraged to have in their cells crazy word cartoons, and more than once was found to scribble nasty words on them.

Some of this was attributed to her shock at having had both her two uncles and her brother die at wars. But other girls also had relatives die in wars—who hadn't? One of the other girls did Zohara one better—Rivka Molcho—she had three brothers and one cousin die all in one war, and yet another brother expire from an overdose—and *she* certainly did not stay away from Friday night dinners or call those who participated in them insane. She just bought herself some shit with hand jobs, which the guards allowed her instead of blow jobs, out of compassion, or instead of her daily ration of cigarettes. So if there was anyone who could claim insanity, it was she. Yet Zohara did not say she herself was insane, but rather that everyone else was.

After the first month, Zohara's claim that everyone around her was mad almost got her sent into Bat Yam asylum for observation. Twice her observation forms were signed, but each time Principal Blumenkrantz shied away from the final step at the last moment, probably because of Zohara's police superintendent father who—although she refused to see him—still came to visit her once a month.

As for her violence, unlike the other girls who could explode any time, Zohara seemed to employ it cunningly and circumspectly so that no one could ever catch her in it.

Rivka Molcho, who hated Zohara's accumulating authority, more than once ambushed her and cut her with her hidden razor blade. But Zohara said nothing, just walked away to sop up her cuts in the toilet— until one day Rivka came to breakfast with one of her fingers broken and refused to say who had done it. Later that day she cut Zohara mercilessly again, so that even guards who did some drug commerce with Rivka had to intervene, half-heartedly. But the next day Rivka came to the infirmary with one more finger broken, and from that moment no one touched Zohara anymore. And little by little, even though Zohara did not seek anyone's company, girls began to sit beside her and talk to her in low voices, though no one of the staff could learn what about. Zohara did not seem to speak much, just listen, occasionally saying a word or two, but little by little she began to be surrounded by girls who could not wait to talk to her.

Batya Feuerstein, whose job was to talk to each inmate once a week, asked them all what they talked to Zohara about, but all were evasive.

"Anything, just anything," said Margul, the small Yemenite who had claimed that Ashkenazim had stolen her baby. "She understands."

"Understands what?"

"Everything," said Margul. "Can I go now?"

Other girls did not give any better answers, and it remained a mystery. It was also a mystery how the suicides seemed to stop. The last attempt was by Rivka Molcho, who, ever since her fingers were broken, seemed also to have something broken inside her, and one morning her supplier found her in her cell with her wrists slashed half-heartedly, her face to the wall. Then, to everyone's surprise, she refused to be taken to Hadera Hospital and said she wanted to stay in the infirmary.

Then, to everyone's greatest astonishment, Zohara came to the infirmary to visit Rivka, closed the door, and stayed with her for an hour. No one knew what Zohara said to her, if anything, because it was also possible that she just listened and Rivka talked, as was the case with all other girls. But the next day, Rivka was back in her cell and from that day on she was Zohara's self-chosen slave, until the day before Zohara was to be released, right after the final and fatal rebellion, when Rivka finally cut her wrists more competently than ever before. And it was then, after Zohara's rebellion, that Batya Feuerstein also had a complete change of heart about her charges. But this came later, well after Zohara had been sent to women's jail and the reformatory closed down for two years.

19

Thursday, October 8, 1981, 9:15 a.m., Latakia, Syria

RAHMAN AL-ASSAD STARED at the French agent standing before him in the metal-clad basement in his villa. Narrow shoulders, narrow face, eyes close together, a fox serving a wolf.

Rahman said, "When will we get the decrypted message?"

"Very soon. An hour, maybe less."

"They're afraid the Americans will get wind of it if we ship more?"

"Yes, ya Zaim…"

Zaim, exalted leader. Rahman felt a little *frisson*. Usually only his brother was addressed thus.

He said, "And you believe this?"

Colonel LeLoup's man made a face. "We don't know. Our listening posts picked up some conversations… some Israeli assassins in Beirut have been grumbling…. It is they who do not want us to ship more…."

"The assassins? But why not?"

The Frenchman lifted his eyes and eyebrows, twisting his mouth down, in a Gallic gesture usually reserved for the irrational behavior of women.

"We don't know why. But the full report should be in soon—I asked them at the embassy to bring it here the moment they got it."

The *barbouz* sat down on the metal bench, and Rahman sank to his metal chair. He preferred his plush chair upstairs, but the metal chair was impossible to bug, as was the entire room. The room was a metal box under his villa, ventilated and insulated, without any phones or electronic equipment. A metal desk in the middle, a metal chair for himself, padded, two metal chairs for guests, unpadded, a glass and metal table for coffee and cigarettes, the gold lighter with the diamonds his third wife gave him as a birthday gift. Nothing on the walls except the row of electronic bafflers.

Rahman looked up. "Or, we can ask them for another meeting, offer more money—"

"No, Zaim. This would not be safe, two meetings in a row...."

Rahman hit a fist against palm, not too hard. The diamond-embedded rings hurt. He walked up to the steel door and rattled the handle to make sure it was locked, came back and began to speak about his need for more money—his brother was not paying the troops in the Biqaa on time. "On purpose! I am sure it's on purpose! He wants them to resent me, to think I am stealing their pay—this way I couldn't take them to Damascus—" He stopped, knowing he had gone too far. "A joke. A joke of course."

The Frenchman laughed almost naturally. "Of course, Zaim."

There were muffled sounds outside, then steps. A knock on the door, not timid, just respectful. He knew that knock. He marched to the door, turned the handle the correct number of turns to the left, then to the right, counted eight seconds, and pulled.

His third wife stood there, her golden reddish hair like a halo, eyes modestly downcast, freckled cheeks blushing. He could feel his erection rising. Four years, having given birth, she could still excite him.

"Yes, *habibti*, my love," he said, adding, "*meine liebchen*. What is it?"

She was German, liked to hear the sound of her mother tongue. He had met her in Berlin by chance, at his doctor's, where she was the new nurse.

She now said in halting Arabic that there was a message for his guest, an envelope, "From the embassy..."

"Give it here."

As she handed him a vellum envelope he kissed her roughly on the lips, then pinched her thigh, turning a little so the Frenchman could see.

He closed the door and gave the envelope to the *barbouz*, who wordlessly took out his notebook and a small card with gaps in it, slit the envelope open and began to scribble.

After ten minutes the scribbling slowed, then stopped. The *barbouz* stared at what he'd written, his mouth slack.

Rahman could barely contain his impatience. "What is it? What?"

The Frenchman kept staring at his notebook, then, carefully, he picked up the lighter from the table and burned the page he was working on, in the aluminum ashtray.

"Ya Zaim," he said, his voice trembling a little. "They made another offer…"

"What? What more do they want? More names for their killers? Men perhaps?"

"No…."

"Ya Allah! What? What did they offer?"

The Frenchman seemed more ill at ease than Rahman had ever seen him. "They said you can ship more, if—if you promise to help them get what they most desire…" The thin lips seemed to tremble.

Rahman stared at the man, uncomprehending.

The man went on, "And, ya Sidi… there was one more thing…. If you so promise to do this, in return they'll help you get what *you* most desire."

Rahman tried to keep his voice level. "Did they say what this meant?"

"No, ya Sidi."

"But what did they mean? What?"

The Frenchman was silent, as if his throat caught.

Rahman snarled, "What is it that they most desire? What?"

"To end the war."

"But we already help them avoid it—"

"Not the war in the Biqaa, the war with your brother."

Rahman felt cold at the back of his neck. "This is what they want? In exchange for… for helping me…."

The man's cheeks turned pale. "That's what they said…"

Rahman found his voice. "So the Israelis will help me get to power, help me finance it, and in exchange I will end the state of war with them?"

The Frenchman gave the tiniest of nods. "That's what it seems."

"This is official?"

"We don't know."

"But how can I know if I can trust this offer?"

The *barbouz* said, "We know the man who made it." He paused. "Colonel LeLoup does."

"And his word is good?"

A nod.

Rahman said, "But how can they help me in… in this?"

The Frenchman took his time. "They can do it many ways. If you sell more in Europe, you can accumulate capital for… the operation. Then, in the Biqaa, if you move your troops… east, they won't take advantage, maybe even retreat and make way…. Then, if you take charge in Damascus… they have friends in Congress, in Europe… See for early recognition…."

"Your local agent wrote they had said all this?"

"No. That's what we think."

Rahman paused. "And the Americans?"

"We… we think they won't oppose."

"Why? Why would they not oppose?"

The man spoke quickly. "Because they see your brother as Moscow's man—he learned to fly in Russia, and the Baath is a Socialist party…."

"And me?"

"You are a capitalist." The man gave a tiny smile.

Rahman pulled a cigarette and the Frenchman unconsciously lit it for him, then lit one for himself. For a moment both men looked at the curling smoke, then at each other, the moment's power imprinted on their faces.

At last Rahman said, "And what's to prevent me from saying yes, I ship more, make millions, they let me, then I don't come through?"

"No. They'll set the Americans on you."

"They said this?"

"No, but that's what you'd do too."

Rahman did not react to this. "Or, I go through with it, get to

Damascus, use their help, take charge of the country, then don't change anything? Still war?"

"No, they'll kill you."

"Not if I am head of state. There's an agreement that heads of state are immune—"

"Not if you do this deal and don't come through, they'll send someone, he'll get to you. They are good."

"They said this?"

"No. But that's how they work."

Rahman pursed his lips. He knew enough not to discount this risk. "And what do you think I should say to them?"

"We think you should ask for someone to come talk to you, verify the details, see how official it is...."

"But who will come? And where?"

"We don't know. If they're serious, they'll send someone, you see how high he is—"

Rahman said, "Because I am not going there."

"Of course not."

Rahman got up, walked about, every now and then looking around him, as if his brother lurked nearby, hearing these death-bringing words....

The Frenchman said, "Ya Sidi, they are waiting for a reply. We should send something back today."

Rahman thought of his mother. He could see himself explaining to her that Haffez was sick and in the hospital, his heart not strong, and he was now taking over....

Aloud he said, "Tell them we'll arrange a meeting here, not Paris. Not Beirut, here." He paused. "This transmission, how secure is it?"

"One part would take two years to decode, with computers. The other part, never, unless they have the one-time pad."

"Alright. Send it. No names. Meeting desired, only this."

The Frenchman touched finger to forehead, almost reverently, got up, did what he rarely had done before, extended his hand. Rahman took it. They shook.

"Yallah," Rahman said roughly. "Go."

He twirled the door handle left, right, waited, pulled. Together they climbed the stairs. Upstairs Rahman pressed the little buzzer, the outside door opened and the *barbouz* walked to his car.

Rahman came back, looking for his wife, feeling the need.

-20-

ON THURSDAY MORNING, Yom Kippur, Ehud woke up in the Unit camp near Jerusalem to the sound of a ringing phone. He cursed silently, grabbed the receiver and pressed the scrambler.

Gershonovitz's voice said, "It's a yes. They want a meeting."

"Who with?"

"It's up to us."

Ehud waited. "Who will you send?"

"You just volunteered."

"Me? I don't know what to tell him—"

"We'll talk about it."

"But I leave for Beirut Friday night…."

"Before you leave, go see the Briefer."

Ehud said nothing.

The Briefer was a man who knew all about the area an agent was going into. Often he was also the local agent on the spot, but not always.

"You heard me?"

"Yes sir."

He waited for Gershonovitz to say "End," but the line kept warbling. Then Gershonovitz said, "About that other thing—"

"What thing? You found out who screwed up?"

"No, we're still checking." There was a long pause. "Can you check also?"

"Check, how? I can ask—"

"Yes, ask, but also—pay attention to what they say."

Ehud said, "You mean, you think one of us lied to cover up what he did? One of us?"

Anons were taught never to lie when reporting. On the job, yes, as required, but never in a report.

"It's a—possibility."

"You serious?!" Then something in Shimmel's tone caught his ear. "There was something else?"

"Yes. But not over the phone—"

"Shimmel, this is scrambled—"

"Even so."

Ehud tried to think clearly. "Alright, I'll come see you before I leave—"

"No, tonight. Come to my apartment, tonight."

"No, I got to take a break, to Reverse properly—"

He really had to Reverse out of the Other or the next one in the psych ward would be him.

"Screw a break," Gershonovitz snarled. "This is more important …."

Suddenly everything seemed to crowd at Ehud. "Listen, Shimmel, you handle your *dreck*, I'll handle mine. Okay?"

"Okay, okay," Gershonovitz said. "Okay, okay, okay." The line warbled. "And do a trail, when you go back to the boat. End."

A trail? An operational checkup for being followed? Shimmel was really losing it, maybe getting the Blackness, too, like all of them.

Shutting his eyes tight, Ehud leaned back in bed, trying to Reverse. It didn't come.

How many have I killed already? he asked himself.

Oddly, he didn't even know.

-21-

Thursday, October 8, 1981, 5:20 p.m., Tel Aviv

I T TOOK THREE days before the killer's second victim was found.

Right after sunset, the end of Yom Kippur, the heavens' gates seemed to open and torrential rains thundered down onto Tel Aviv. Dark water flowed down Allenby Street, toward the sea, down King George Street, flooding stores, swamping Gan Meir Park. Trees became uprooted, shrubs floated down the river of mud. Two of the carob trees in the park toppled, one smashing through the roof of the public toilets, destroying the ceiling and cracking the water pipes. As a result, the stalls were flooded, the toilets overflowed, the walls washed away.

An hour later when the rain slackened, Gan Meir's public toilets were a large puddle of brown and blackish mud, broken tiles and fallen walls, so the body of the second victim was not discovered until three days later, Sunday. And by that time, his neck had been bloated so badly that the bullet hole was not discovered in the hasty autopsy done at Abu Kabir morgue until Sunday afternoon, when the note was already half-dissolved in water.

-22-

Thursday, October 8, 1981, Yom Kippur 6 p.m., HaTikva Quarter

AMZALEG WAS AWAKENED in the evening by a call from Jacqueline, asking if he wanted her to come fix him something to eat after the fast.

He thanked her gruffly and said he had eaten already, which both knew was a lie. But there was no point in her coming. It was over.

He made himself coffee, put on his tunic and went to talk to *Adon* Leon, HaTikva's crime lord.

The HaTikva Skewers restaurant was empty. Only the owner, reading the sports page, was seated at the central "Jerusalem" table, his white shirt stretched over his prosperous stomach.

Adon Leon Elfasi had once been a skilled car thief. Because of it, thirty years ago, after the state was born, he was invited to teach basic car-tampering at the Unit. He did a good job, so after returning to civilian life, he was picked by someone in the Interior Ministry as one of the eleven *Adonim* to oversee crime in the nascent state. He now sold drugs in HaTikva, owned two garages where stolen cars were dismantled for parts, and partnered with Jaffa's *Adon* in a teen brothel.

Amzaleg pulled a chair, flipped its back forward, sat at *Adon* Leon's own table.

Adon Leon looked at him sideways. "Not even 'With permission?'"

Amzaleg leaned over. "I need to 'have words' with you."

"Having words" was part of the Code.

The Code was never written but it was well understood: the state was organized, and so was crime, the two entangled like ficus trees and strangling vines, grown together so as to become one.

Adon Leon looked at Amzaleg from under his thick lids. "Is this from you or Chief Levitan?"

"Levitan can kiss my ass." That is, it's personal.

Adon Leon snapped his fingers. A brown-skinned teen girl appeared in the kitchen's door.

The *Adon* said, pointing to the outside door, "Close it."

"No, leave it open," Amzaleg said. "It stinks here."

The girl scuttled into the kitchen and banged away at pots to demonstrate she was not listening.

Adon Leon's eyes burned, his cheeks tightened.

Amzaleg pulled out a cigarette single-handed. "Nachum Sabag worked for you?"

He blew smoke away from *Adon* Leon's face. But just.

"Sabag who?"

Amzaleg got up, closed the door, sat down. "Nachum, Eli's son. Was a friend of Iddo. Three days ago was plugged with a two-two in the neck— you heard?"

He put the cigarette pack on the table, pushed it forward, and presently *Adon* Leon extended a manicured hand and pulled out one. "Yes. Nachum worked here, every few days—why?"

Someone knocked on the door, looked in, saw the two seated at the same table, and disappeared.

Amzaleg leaned back. "Did Nachum... stick his nose in someone's drug deal?"

Adon Leon made a face, neither confirming nor denying.

Amzaleg let it alone. "What else did Nachum do here?"

The "else" hung in the air.

Adon Leon said, "Cleaned dishes, served food, loaded soda bottles,

I took pity on him, let him make a few shekels...." He shook his heavy head in sorrow. "You think I had a hand in this?"

"I don't know what to think yet. Did you?"

"Really, Amnon, he was like a son to me—"

"But did you have anything to do..."

"No, no!"

Adon Leon began to rise, said in Moroccan Arabic, "Leave this alone, Amzaleg, listen to me."

Amzaleg stayed seated. "No, you listen to me.... Was a friend of Iddo, his sister was once Iddo's girlfriend—"

"Pirchiya? Was everyone's girlfriend—"

His voice strangled as Amzaleg caught his collar and twisted. Leon had been after Pirchiya too. He'd asked her to come to his love nest in Ramat Gan, even stay there; she kept saying no.

Amzaleg hissed, "If I find you had anything to do with this I'll call some friends from the army—"

He stopped.

Who would he call? None in the Unit returned his calls, nor his former police partner, Feldman...

But *Adon* Leon went a little pale. "I had nothing to do with it, Amnon, nothing—"

"On your children's heads?"

A muscle twitched in the *Adon's* cheek. "Yes."

Amzaleg let his hand drop and *Adon* Leon stumbled, got up and went to the door.

Amzaleg called after him. "Who would know?"

Leon had already opened the door. Outside stood a few wet men holding prayer-shawl bags, aiming to break the fast after synagogue. One by one they kissed *Adon* Leon on his cheek.

Facing away, *Adon* Leon muttered, "Sorry I can't help you, Amnon. If I hear anything, I'll tell you." He turned his head and mouthed a name, silently: *Ashmedai.*

Satan.

Amzaleg went back to his cruiser, got in and sat awhile, watching the rain whipping the skinny eucalyptus trees, just like at the morgue.

He thought of the name Leon had mouthed.

Shimon Gershonovitz, once of the Defense Ministry, later minister of the interior, was known as *Ashmedai*, Satan.

But he was retired, wasn't he?

He suddenly recalled that Munger at the morgue had said that if Amzaleg wanted to rejoin, he should call Shimmel.

Again, Gershonovitz.

Was he now with Amzaleg's old Unit?

And most odd: why was *Adon* Leon suddenly willing to help?

-23-

**Friday, October 9, 1981, 10:00 a.m.,
Kiryat Shaul Cemetery**

NEXT DAY, FRIDAY, was Nachum's funeral.

The Kiryat Shaul Cemetery was one shallow lake of water hopping with the onslaught of rain. Amzaleg stood near the dug grave. It was covered by soggy plywood, but Amzaleg could see the darkness below, like a ship's hold. His head spun, and for a second he felt as if he was about to fall in. But he held on to a tombstone and turned his eyes away.

At the entrance he saw Jacqueline's old car, saw Pirchiya holding an umbrella for her parents, both dressed in shabby black. Amzaleg looked around. Half of HaTikva was here, for a mere drug pusher. The grocer and his wife, Jacqueline and her hairdressers, Pirchiya and her parents, Zohara standing with them, far away from him. Then a crowd of former and current burglars, car thieves, small-time pimps, panhandlers, more drug dealers…

Amzaleg noticed a few waiters from *Adon* Leon's restaurant, and behind them Leon himself, and further behind, some stallholders from Central Bus Station who allowed Eli to panhandle.

A Moroccan rabbi chanted "God Full of Pity," then Eli read out the Kaddish prayer. A mutter went through the crowd and Amzaleg saw many staring at him, the man who must find the killer. He saw Pirchiya looking at him, too, her eyes softer.

He flushed and stared into the distance, at the military section. His two brothers were buried in its midst, and a bit further, Iddo. And in other sections all around, old Unit members and HaTikva friends in whose funerals he had been a participant—how many?

Too many to remember.

The rain kept falling. The rabbi had finished and the shrouded body was being dropped into the grave, mourners hitting the soggy earth mound with shovels.

Without ceremony, some began to leave. Pirchiya, Amzaleg saw, was putting a stone on Iddo's tombstone. In grade school, age ten, they had been friends. He should put a stone too... also on his brothers' graves, and on others too...

All at once the back of his neck tingled and he felt eyes on him.

Without thinking, he whipped around, arms crossed. But there was no one, only a lone mourner a short distance away, bending over a tombstone, hid by a soggy prayer shawl.

Fast and meticulously, Amzaleg scanned the sea of tombstones, widening his eyes, but there was no one else. And when he turned once more to look, the lone mourner was gone.

Jacqueline's car door was open. She seemed to be offering him a ride back. He shook his head.

Back home he drank one glass of araq after another, raising it for each of the photos, but again seeing the bullet hole.

Why was Nachum Sabag killed?

-24-

Friday, October 9, 10:05 a.m.,
Tel Aviv

THAT SAME FRIDAY morning, Gershonovitz drove himself to his office.

Since he had returned, intelligence reports had been piling on his desk faster than he could read them. They weren't what he'd come back to do. Still, he knew he'd better go over them.

He saw Moshe was already there, looking worried.

"What?" Gershonovitz grumbled. "Nothing happened to me last night, see? I'm fine—"

"No," Moshe said. "Call Ehud. He had a phone call yesterday."

"What about? Who from?"

"Didn't say. Someone named Amzaleg, from the police…"

Gershonovitz let out a sharp Polish curse, grabbed the radiotelephone and dialed.

-25-

Friday, October 9, 1981, 10:40 a.m.,
Kiryat Shaul Cemetery

S TILL THAT SAME morning, the killer bent over a grave he had picked at random. Carefully wrapped in the prayer shawl, he tried not to stare at the mourners standing around the grave of the little *Ars* he had cleansed just three days ago.

He knew he shouldn't be here, but he felt he had to come. His first selfless act.

He tugged the prayer shawl tighter to hide the scratch marks on his arms and muttered the Kaddish prayer. Then he kept silent so he could hear theirs.

There were women there, too, which confused him. He didn't like women and tried to stay away from them, although in the line of duty he occasionally had to fuck some. But that was duty.

The rain kept falling and he squinted through the opening of the prayer shawl at the mourners. So many beige and brown faces.... So much Arab blood had contaminated us....

Then, just as he turned away, he saw a face and froze: the stocky man by the graveside, in the dark blue tunic, was Amnon Amzaleg.

What was he doing here?

Then he remembered. Amzaleg was no longer an Anon, not even in Reserves. He was with the police now.

He felt relief but it quickly dissipated: were the police looking into it? Or maybe not.

Amzaleg was retired, last he'd heard. Still, one could not be too careful. He'd have to check....

He inched his way to behind an old gravestone of some soldier who had died in '48, then behind another, and he was out of the cemetery, his prayer shawl flapping as he galloped away.

The Vespa was where he had parked it, and he mounted it almost at a run. Soon he was racing away, his mind awhirl.

He hoped Amzaleg would not get in the way.

-26-

Friday, October 9, 1981, 1:45 p.m., Jaffa

THE JAFFA POLICE station had begun as an ancient Turkish prison. Its narrow corridors were barely passable, the ceiling low, the dank cubicle offices smelling of stone rot and nicotine.

An eternal corporal, as old as Amzaleg and also waiting for retirement, was at the duty desk.

There was no one else about, all in a morning meeting.

Amzaleg asked if anything special had happened. "Why is the meeting taking so long?"

"Don't know. Some orders from Chief Levitan."

From his office, Amzaleg called sergeants he knew in towns around Tel Aviv, asking for original reports on any drug dealers' deaths for the last month. "Also if anyone new gets offed, call me."

All said they would get back to him, yet somehow he doubted they would.

Something here did not compute.

He took a deep breath and called Feldman, the Security Services chief, at his home number. Once they were partners, two years in the same cruiser in Haifa, ass against ass. But Feldman played his cards right, while Amzaleg seemed to have played them all wrong.

But Feldman owed him. Too many favors to count.

Amzaleg held his breath as the line kept ringing. Then a voice barked.

"Who is it?"

"Me." Amzaleg said, "The one who lied for you in Haifa, about the whore."

A long pause.

"What the hell do you want?"

"A list of everyone in the Unit, Avigdor, anyone still in…"

The Services had lists of everyone, but they never shared.

"A list of who?"

"Don't play dumb. You owe me from Haifa."

"I owe you nothing, you fat *Ars*."

But Feldman didn't hang up.

"Yes, you do. If I had talked then…"

And now Feldman hung up.

It was worth a try, Amzaleg thought.

Or was it?

-27-

Friday, October 9, 1981, 7:20 p.m., Tel Aviv Beach

BECAUSE THE RAIN had slackened, the Friday night outing of the girls to Tel Baruch beach was back on. But only four girls came, climbing into the back of Moshiko's cab in a jumble of legs and perfume and teased hair, leaving Zohara the seat by the driver. They all brought little umbrellas, and Sigalit had brought a plastic sheet from the hair salon, which she stuffed in Moshiko's trunk. They all pretended they were just giving hand jobs, perhaps a blow job if the client was clean and sympathetic, but nothing more. And they did it not for the money but for the fun. Because what else was there to do in HaTikva on Friday night? Go to synagogue? They couldn't go to good clubs in Tel Aviv because they couldn't get in if Zohara hadn't come along, and the jazz clubs were boring: a bunch of Ashkenazim seated on low chairs, smoking and drinking coffee and listening to boring, complicated music.

The dance clubs were where they wanted to go. But even when Zohara forced the thug at the entrance to let them in, they just stood alone in a corner because the *vooz-vooz* boys did not speak to them, and the brown-skinned ones that Zohara had let in, they disdained. So after a while they often left, took a cab to the Tel Baruch beach, and, Zohara standing guard over them, did a few *vooz-vooz* clients each, charging almost double, in revenge.

Once a client, a fat old *vooz-vooz* who spoke mainly Yiddish, objected to the high price and tried to punch Sigalit, but Zohara knocked him down and he ran off, crying like a baby, brandishing his tattooed arm at them like a curse.

Next day they didn't speak about it, but afterward Zohara always came with them, her straight razor in her bag, standing guard while the girls had a good time and made some money, and also met some clean *vooz-vooz* who actually talked to them. Pirchiya used to come too but she no longer did, which was good, because with her looking half a *vooz-vooz* herself, no other girl had a chance.

Today was better, though. When they arrived at the beach, there were only a couple of old Jaffa hookers standing on the gravel trail past the Haifa Road, eyeing Zohara warily and keeping their distance. A few feet away stood a group of young men, smoking nervously and tittering, presumably students from Tel Aviv University. It was clear they did not like the bored, older hookers. The hairdressers, younger and nervous, were more to their liking. In a few minutes, the hairdressers dispersed, each with a young boy in tow. Zohara remained behind, leaning on Moshiko's cab, reading in the faint interior light. Moshiko himself had gone with one of the bored, older hookers. Every now and then Zohara raised her eyes and watched the dunes, smoking, to make sure the girls were okay.

It was fairly dark, but here and there she could glimpse flitting firefly pairs in the drizzle, as girls and clients had a smoke. Another firefly, a lone one—she looked hard and saw it was one of the students, a red-haired boy of twenty-two or three, freckle-faced and snub-nosed. When he saw her staring, he averted his gaze. She smoked on in silence, listening to the sounds of the girls having a good time. Sigalit had gone with a gawky boy into the dunes, carrying her plastic sheet, and Zohara could hear her groaning, getting into it. Zohara stubbed out the cigarette and lit another. The freckle-faced boy was still looking at her, and so she called out to him, asking him if he wanted something, else why was he staring at her? But she saw him nod.

"What?" she asked.

"Anything," he said. "How much is it?"

She had never done it before in Tel Baruch, only in the clubs and in exchange for conversation or book names, is what she used to tell herself. But now she suddenly felt she didn't care. "Twenty," she told him. "But only by hand."

He stuttered that it was okay and they went into the back of Moshiko's cab—she made sure she locked the door from the inside and turned off the light, just in case Moshiko returned early. She sat beside the boy and helped him unbuckle his pants. It didn't take long, and soon he came with a deep grunt and a sigh. Then, to her surprise and consternation, he said, "Thank you, this was lovely."

She didn't know what to say. She stared at him sideways, barely stopped herself from saying "You're welcome." Somehow it felt like rudeness. At last she mumbled something, pulled out of her pocket a sheaf of paper napkins, gave the boy one, and wiped her fingers with the others. She felt confusion, which she had never felt before doing this, perhaps because the boy had thanked her. The seat felt hard and a little wet and she longed to leave the cab but wanted to be paid first. Finally the boy pulled his pants up and she waited for him to pull out his wallet, but he kept still, looking outside the window, breathing shallowly. At last he said, "What's your name?"

She almost was rude to him then and considered giving him a false name, Hana, or Shulamit, but found herself saying her true name. She didn't know why.

"Ah," he said. "Just like the holy book?"

Surprised, she said yes, she was named after that book, what was it to him?

"Nothing," he said. "I didn't mean to—"

"Besides, my great-grandmother chose it," she said, as if she needed to justify it.

There was a short silence and she was on the verge of asking for the money straight out, when he said, "Ever read it?"

"Yes." She was again caught by surprise. "But it's fucking nonsense, just superstition mixed with primitive psychology—" She stopped, confused at her volubility, as if she were talking to Batya.

"Yes. Did you read all of it?"

She hoisted a shoulder. "Yeah, sure." She wanted to ask him to name another book, feeling greedy, but it seemed too late. Also the seat was getting colder by the minute, yet suddenly she didn't want to get up. Outside she could hear grunts and giggles, the girls were really getting into it.

He looked at her. "Where?"

She said it was in the library, at Tel Aviv University.

He laughed, a short honking sound, and after a moment she laughed too.

He asked her when she had gone to university.

"I didn't—just snuck in once, to see the books...." She couldn't be accepted to the university, not with her criminal conviction but didn't want to say it.

Someone knocked on the window. "You okay?" Sigalit's pinched face looked in, her mouth pursed, then she was sashaying away. "We're going soon."

"Yes, yes," Zohara called back. She turned to the boy. "I have to go—"

Still he didn't get up or pull out his wallet, and for a moment she thought he was going to haggle, though it didn't seem likely, but one never knew. There was an awkward silence. Then just before she gathered her legs to get up, he said, "What else do you read?" and her heart gave a thump. "Lots," she said, "lots of things."

"Like what?"

Her heart still thumping, she mentioned a few Hebrew and English books she had taken from the American library, and on a whim, said she had gotten the *Little Prince*, from her uncle who died. Then, feeling reckless, added that she sometimes read her father's books, when he wasn't looking, poems of Paltiel Rubin and Cohen Kadosh—

"Rubin? You read Paltiel Rubin?"

"Yes, my father has actually—"

More cries from outside. "Zohara! We gotta go!"

The bearded face of Moshiko appeared outside, then his hairy knuckles, knocking on the window. Zohara leaned over and unlatched the door.

"I gotta go," she said, and extended her hand. And still he made no move to pull out his wallet, just got out.

She followed him, feeling herself getting angry, him forcing her to ask for her due. All around stood the girls, disheveled. The other students were gone, the last of them departing on foot.

The boy said, "Listen, I know this is stupid, but do you want to... to go have a coffee maybe?" And before she could answer—not that she could talk, she was so astounded—he went on in a rush, "Or maybe eat something? In the old harbor, maybe Italian?" Then, blushing, he said, "Or even falafel, whatever you want."

Behind her, the girls had gotten into the cab, and Moshiko had started the engine, the seat by his side vacant. Sigalit leaned out. "You coming, Zohara?!"

"No," she said.

The boy had thought she was talking to him and turned, but she grabbed his arm. "Yes," she said to him, "thank you."

Screw her payment.

Behind her she heard the girls giggling, and then mercifully the cab was gone before they could whoop, as she was afraid they would.

She said to the boy, "You want to take the bus?"

The rain was barely a drizzle now.

"No, I have a Beetle. I left it on the Haifa road." And he turned toward the road, and she followed, stumbling a little in the sand. Once, he turned to see if she was following, though not extending his hand, but still her heart gave a lurch. Not because she liked him particularly but because he was an Ashkenazi, and he worried about her.

Just as they reached his car, Moshiko's cab passed alongside on the narrow gravel trail, the tires squishing, the girls' white faces peering at her through the window, like the faces at Beit Sarah Reformatory when she was taken to women's jail, neither she nor they knowing what was to come.

-28-

**1973, Beit Sarah Reformatory,
then Neve Tirtza Women's Jail**

THE SILENT REBELLION that got Zohara jailed began at the reformatory's library.

The library was managed by Margul Shaharabani, the mousey little Yemenite of fifteen who always wailed that Ashkenazi nurses had stolen her baby. To put an end to her whining, Principal B. put her in charge of the reformatory's library. It was a small stash of schoolbooks, educational Bible stories, and religious children's magazines.

Hardly any inmate went there except for Zohara, who went up to talk to Margul, usually after Principal B. had gone there, closed the door, and helped Margul arrange the books.

When one day Margul cut her wrists, Tova Shpigler, the commissary, prepared to take her to Hadera Hospital, just like the year before. But Zohara was already by Margul's side and would not leave. When Principal B. tried to open the door, it appeared to be closed with a chair against it. Tova was about to break the door when Zohara opened it herself, came up to Principal B. and spat full in his face.

This shocked everyone because Zohara had never attacked any of the staff before. She then raised her hand with three fingers pointed at Principal B. and spoke rapidly in a high voice in Moroccan Arabic. Principal B. slapped Zohara's face, Tova grabbed her, and when Zohara somehow removed Tova's hand, Principal B. and Tova shackled Zohara and dragged her to the storage room to be locked up.

However, on her way, with all the girls wailing, Zohara stuck her heels in, turned around and said in a clear voice, "No one talks to them, understand? Not one word to the scum." Then she allowed herself to be locked while Margul was taken to Hadera Hospital after being warned that if she kept telling fibs, she would be sent to the psych ward and be bed-strapped for a year.

Yet apparently Margul did tell some fibs because a day later, a bored policeman came by, spoke with Principal B. for an hour and then departed, after shaking hands with him and taking two cartons of cigarettes.

Zohara remained locked up two days, Batya bringing her food. And all that time the entire reformatory was silent as a cemetery, girls talked to each other in whispers but to the staff none at all. Not even when threatened with lockup or bed-strapping. For some reason this upset the staff tremendously. "After all we do for them," Tova said, "this is how they repay us," and everyone agreed. Only Batya said nothing, just kept crying and wouldn't say why.

On day three, however, with the silence ongoing, Principal B. signed a criminal complaint against Zohara and had a friendly judge in Hadera cosign it, and a two-person crew from Neve Tirtza jail arrived and carted the criminal off.

The trip to Neve Tirtza jail should not have taken long, but the traffic was horrendous. And the driver, a Druze whom Zohara knew vaguely from Shfar'am, drove the long way and stopped once to buy soda and chocolates, which he handed to her and was surprised when she asked him to give it to the policewoman instead. And when the jeep arrived at the prison's gate, the policewoman handed Zohara's file to the huge warden at the entrance and said to Zohara, "Just do as you are told and you will be okay. Your father will come to visit in a few days, after the funeral."

Zohara turned to her sharply. "Which funeral?"

The policewoman said it was the funeral of his grandmother. "Your great-grandmother. Didn't they tell you at Beit Sarah that she died yesterday?"

Zohara shook her head, and the policewoman conveyed her sympathies. She was sure it had nothing to do with Zohara's going to jail. "She must have been old and sick, no?"

By then the warden, already impatient, said she would take over and grabbed Zohara by the arm. Zohara tensed her bicep, then forced her arm to relax and followed the warden, hearing both the keys in the woman's belt and her own shackles clink, and her own breath.

All she could think about was the funeral of Great-Grandma Ruja, whose location she didn't even know—probably where her uncle Moshe was also buried.

The following week every night Zohara dreamed about Great-Grandma Ruja, who seemed to be trying to tell her something. But it was impossible to grasp what it was.

Everyone feared Zohara's Great-Grandma Ruja, but not Zohara.

Ruja lived in a Jaffa slum in a small flat bequeathed to her by a grateful supplicant whose husband agreed finally to a *Gett*, after discovering an amulet of Ruja's under his pillow.

Ruja was known to do *sh'chur*—Moroccan black magic—that even the greatest rabbis were said to fear. Besides scribing amulets, she buried hard-boiled eggs with clients' wishes scribbled on them in urine, advised lovelorn women how to lace steaks with their monthly blood, to be served to their love object. Or in the hardest cases, adjured evil spirits to return a supplicant's potency, calling curses upon the supplicant's enemies and offering the enemies' souls to Ashmedai, Lilith, and their three progeny.

Everyone in HaTikva feared Ruja, all but Zohara, who scoffed at her.

And yet, or perhaps because of this, Ruja came to see Zohara as her heir, and despite Zohara's scowls, revealed to her names of demons and the right way to curve one's fingers to summon them. She showed Zohara curse books she'd gotten from a Moroccan Berber chieftain, a long-ago admirer.

At the time, Amzaleg's parents had a flat behind the HaTikva market, and on Friday nights Ruja would sail in for the Shabbat meal, and afterward a small crowd of supplicants would shuffle in. She'd listen gravely to their tales of woe, then scribble parchments with names of spirits, wrapped garlic clove and a coin in them and, discreetly pocketing her fee, muttered incantations while the fearful supplicants trembled.

But not Zohara.

She never felt afraid of Ruja, not even when the old woman performed clumsy dances and stuck her finger down the throat of supplicants—small-time burglars who lost their nerve, cantors who could no longer hit high notes, women whose husbands no longer touched them—to pull out demons that had snuck in and made their lives hell.

The demons looked like chicken liver or gizzards but Zohara could not be sure because Great-Grandma would throw them out the window to the cats below, who fought over them.

"Do I really have a demon inside me too?" Zohara asked once, fascinated despite herself.

Ruja gravely stared into her eyes and didn't answer, but Zohara saw what the answer was.

"Can you take it out too?" she asked. She'd like to see it.

Ruja said she would be afraid to. "And you should be afraid also."

Zohara said, "I am not afraid of it, and I am not afraid of you." Then, with a flash of insight she added, "You fear me."

At this, Ruja spit three times and hissed that Zohara's was the most fearful demon of all, the one who prevented her from seeing what others saw, and so made her able to see the Other Side.

Iddo said he wanted to see the Other Side too.

"You'll get there soon enough," Ruja snapped, at which Amzaleg became enraged and said that if Ruja continued like that she would end up in the psych ward. "They'll tie you down."

"Well, you would know," Ruja snapped.

Later in Neve Tirtza jail, Zohara, tied down for punishment, often thought of Ruja, how she died when Zohara was brought here, as if Ruja's heart were broken or something, which of course could not be, because as far as Zohara could tell, Ruja did not even like her.

-29 -

A MZALEG STAYED LATE in the station, poring over reports of drug pushers' altercations. But none seemed connected to the killings. On the way home, he passed by the hair salon. It was closed, but there was a light inside and he saw a figure moving about.

At first he thought it was Zohara. Then he saw through the glass door that it was Pirchiya.

On an impulse he parked, knocked on the door and went in.

He took off his cap, offered stuttering condolences. Then, after Pirchiya had mumbled her thanks, he asked, "Zohara now staying with you?"

She nodded.

"That's good." He didn't ask where Zohara was now. Probably in Tel Baruch, guarding the other girls. He hoped that this was only why she went.

He felt himself blushing as he looked at Pirchiya; a man who'd been married, still blushing like a boy.

Pirchiya said, "You want a Nescafé maybe?"

He nodded and she turned to the storage room, while he leafed through old magazines, staring at impossibly wide-eyed blonde *vooz-vooz* women, the kind that *Frehot* turned into when they died and went to heaven, or after a few treatments at Jacqueline's.

"Here," Pirchiya said. "I made it black, with one sugar."

He stared at her and she blushed. "I saw how you take it, when you came to visit, once."

They were both silent, then, without meaning to, he asked her how she was doing now, both brothers gone, a moment later regretted it.

But to his relief Pirchiya said, "It's so-so, I always knew that one day—" She swallowed, traced a line on her knee. "Anyway, I have to work, father and mother can't—"

"Yes," Amzaleg said. "But Zohara probably pays some rent, too, now?"

"Yes." Tracing another line on her knee, Pirchiya said, "So you are investigating already?"

Amzaleg nodded.

She flushed too. "I knew you would—mother said you are just saying it, but I said—" She looked away. "You want some more Nescafé?"

He nodded, and when she came back, he said, "Can I ask you some things?"

"Yes, anything. Like what?"

"About Nachum," he said.

She hoisted a shoulder. "Yes. Ask me anything."

He watched her hair ripple and his throat felt tight and warm. "Tell me about him, Nachum. What was he like?"

It was nearly an hour later that he heard a knock on the door, both he and Pirchiya raised their eyes, saw Jacqueline at the door, in her synagogue clothes.

She entered, eyes narrow. "I saw a light, didn't know who it was—" She watched first Pirchiya, then Amzaleg.

"Oh!" Amzaleg saw the time on the clock. Nine thirty! "I was asking her about Nachum," he began—only to hear Pirchiya say, "He was asking me about Nachum—" at the same time.

Then they both laughed, embarrassed, but also a bit breathless.

Jacqueline sat on another chair, heavily. "He used to come here, too, I used to pay him to clean, sometimes."

It took another fifteen minutes before she left.

At close to ten, Amzaleg said, "Once I find something, I'll let you know—and if I have any more questions—"

"Yes," Pirchiya said. "Ask me."

And just before he left she said, "I am usually here, I don't go to Tel Baruch anymore—"

He nodded and left. The rain was falling harder now, but he hardly felt it.

- 30-

**Friday, October 9, 1981, 8:45 p.m.,
Tel Aviv Beach**

ZOHARA PUT HER hand on the Beetle's door but the boy rushed around, opened it for her, and only then went to sit behind the wheel.

She nodded, her heart thumping, not knowing if she should thank him or say something. This was new to her.

As they drove he didn't speak either, but occasionally looked at her, blinking, all the way to the old Tel Aviv port.

It seemed like a foreign country. She'd never been there because there never was any reason to go. It was Ashkenazi territory, like jazz clubs, Tel Aviv bookstores, North Tel Aviv, *vooz-vooz* land.

As they left the car, the boy took her arm, not possessively, to direct her into a pub. The pub was stuffed with people, standing two rows deep at the bar, drinking, gesticulating, many more sitting at crammed tables, eating and hallooing to passing friends, several arguments in progress all at once, loud but not screaming, just all together. The White tribe.

Zohara trailed behind the boy, half-dazed, half-hypnotized by the free clamor, the conversation, the laughter, the easy use of long words, the banter, not one curse word. It sounded almost like a foreign language, no glottides, clear and precise, like on the radio.

A waiter beckoned, not much older than the student, a folded bill changed hands, a table became free, not at the back but in the middle, under a glowing lantern enmeshed in a fisherman's net.

Was it red? One of the colors she could not see?

They sat down, leaned back simultaneously, she looked all around, drinking it in, then looked back at the boy, their eyes came together, strayed a little, came together again. He smiled, she smiled back, hesitantly, they began to speak together, laughed, tried again; she let him speak.

"You've been here before?"

She shook her head and felt her hair dance, letting it.

He said, "You like fish? They do good fish here."

Was he using bad Hebrew for her sake? Or just as a joke?

She nodded. "Okay."

"Would you like some wine, too, perhaps?"

Now he used the conditional tense, pronouncing each word properly, without making an effort. She was almost afraid to speak, with her Arabicized glottides.

"Yes," she said. "Okay, thank you."

Like a child. Yes, no, maybe. She must seem dumb to him. No you don't, she told herself. He wouldn't have spoken to you like he did, in the cab. But it was dark, he didn't see you. Yes he did, partly.

But now he had seen her. What did he think? And what was his name? She had not asked, and any moment that passed—

Another waiter appeared, he and the boy conferred. The waiter came back with a bottle of wine.

"Okay?" the boy said, showing her. French.

She read out the name, pronouncing it properly, as her uncle had taught her, when he read *The Little Prince* to her before bedtime.

The boy seemed surprised. "Yes. That's right. Where did you learn French?"

"At home," she said, feeling guilty, as if admitting a deficiency.

He poured and they drank, not clinking the glasses, not raising them, just drinking.

Again they both looked around. This was the time to ask for his name. She opened her mouth, but he had already begun to speak of the book they had talked about before. Did she really read all of it? *Madame Bovary*? He had to read parts of it in school, for the matriculation, in French. It was hard going. Such complicated sentences.

She gathered her courage. "Why in French?"

"Oh. I went to Alliance High School. We took French as a first foreign language." He made a face. "My mother says it's better than Arabic." He paused. "Where did you go to school?"

She mumbled about the Bnot Yaakov School in HaTikva, then the religious high school—

"You don't look religious," the boy said, smiling.

She flared. "I'm not."

He raised his arms, "Okay, okay," laughed.

The fish arrived, and more wine. They ate and talked about books, and what he did—studied economics, had been in the army. The "and you?" prominently missing, one-sided conversation, not forced, but pointedly not asking her anything, just books.

And just as she was telling him about the books she got from Batya, a "friend," a trio approached, two young men, even teeth and pressed jeans, checkered shirts, like advertising photos in *Maariv*. Between them skipping a wavy-haired young woman wearing colored jewelry, loose shirt, her arms around both men. In a flash she scanned Zohara, top to bottom, right to left, a raised eyebrow. Then, without pause, the woman burbled, "Hi, Yoav! Where've you been? And who's that?"

The boy blushed, turned to her.

"Zohara," she said.

The girl giggled. "Like the book?"

"Not really," Zohara said. She felt the blush start at the top of her head and spread down.

The two boys flicked a look at her, then were slapping Yoav on the shoulders, the girl reclining, and in a carrying whisper in the boy's ear, "Who's this? Your cleaning lady's daughter?"

Zohara had never seen a man flush so deep, only her father before he punched the wall once. But this boy said nothing, then gave a sickly smile, said something about they'd just met, and he would come soon, don't wait for him.

After the trio was gone, Zohara waited, but did not know for what. After a minute, the boy got up to go to the washroom and she was left alone, a swarthy island in that sea of white faces, a foreign people.

When he came back he said, "Well, yes, was so nice to meet you," his eyes already looking outside, straying. His wallet out, leaving bills on the table.

Brief hesitation, then, a bill for her, too, a bashful smile. "Thank you again…. Now I really must run—"

She felt the blood rush to her face, her temples, grabbed her handbag, rose to her feet, nearly pulled her shiv out. Then picked the first thing she saw, a half-full wine glass, threw it at him and spit, barely able to purse her lips through her tears.

Ran out past him, into the rain. Only when she was out, she saw that the bill he had left for her was in her handbag. She threw it out, into the rain, and it fluttered into a puddle, floated.

Her first thought was, go to Batya, stay there. Then, no, she couldn't, didn't want to talk about this, couldn't.

She began walking, walked all the way to HaTikva, in the rain, nearly two hours, no cabs stopped for her. When finally she saw Etzel Street, almost three in the morning, she was wetter than a rag, her mind a black swirling wetness without color or shape. She distantly wondered if this was what her father felt when he got the Blackness.

For a long while she stood in the middle of Haganah Street, rain streaming on her, from her, found her way to the boarded up Amidar hovels, the drug dens, knocked on one, where the totally gone druggies slept. At last a corner board was pushed out.

"What?!"

"I want some shit," she said.

"Forty shekels."

She only had twenty left.

Had bought cigarettes, gave Pirchiya's father some money for rent. The whore's fee she'd thrown away.

"No, forty."

She said she'd do him by hand. No suck.

"Alright, thirty, and you bring the other ten tomorrow."

She went in. Four mattresses, bundles of clothing on two, human forms. The boy handed her an aluminum foil, its edge wrapped with toilet paper, lit another piece of toilet paper underneath.

The White bubbled, and he gave it to her. It bubbled and she sniffed, then sniffed more, crying, and little by little the Blackness in her spread, warmed, dulled. She sank to her knees, then onto her back, to the edge of a mattress.

"You can sleep here," the boy said. "He went to Tel Aviv, make some money in Gan Meir, probably stayed there."

She curled up on the mattress, her handbag under her head, her hand on her shiv, limply, all her force gone.

"Hey," the boy said, "you said you'd do me."

She nodded, half-asleep, fumbled at him, but before she could start she was already asleep, plunging into a black place she had never been to before. Deep, teeth-knocking darkness.

Once in the night she awoke, hearing herself wracked by hoarse sobs, seeing it as if from afar. She had never felt such utter hopelessness, such Blackness, not even in the darkest days of the reformatory.

Beside her, the other three druggies slept, snuffling, and finally she slept, too, the rain hammering on the boards.

-31-

Saturday, October 10, 5:00 a.m., Tel Aviv

A S THE GRAY dawn broke over the drenched city, the man rode out, the helmet over his head, his tools and gear in the Vespa's trunk. After crossing the Yarkon bridge, he turned left, parked near a hut whose door was locked. Opening the door he slid the Vespa in, rolled out the motorcycle. It started easily, and he rode on.

It was not quite six o'clock when he passed the Mossad's hilltop camp, where the blinking lights probably meant those inside prepared for the Heads of Services Committee meeting. He wondered whether anyone there would mention his selfless voluntary deed, perhaps even read out the note…

As he bent lower over the handlebars, he felt himself blushing, thinking of the whispered praise for his having so well articulated what they were all thinking. Or perhaps there would even be handclaps? He hoped not. He wanted no reward for his selfless deeds. Someone had to do it, for the sake of the people's purity, and so he volunteered.

The machine between his legs purred, as he was already thinking of the next job in Beirut. Unlike others in the Beirut hideout, he liked it. He had never known why but now realized it was merely training for what he had to do here, his unique destiny.

Just before Netanya, the Unit's close-combat training facility passed on his left—not visible from the road, but he could see the telltale sign on the eucalyptus. Then the white buildings of the nearby kibbutz, and the Beit Sarah Reformatory, the young *Frehot*'s semi-prison, then the Yemenite villages beyond… like a contamination in the middle of the miraculous country that was meant to be so pure….

Gradually the road widened and presently he was riding between green wet patches on either side, of sorghum, alfalfa, orchards, of pure-stock Ashkenazi communal villages. There were few cars, just some produce trucks and a jeep or two, and then the road opened wider and he sped up, on his way to the boat to go back north.

As he rode, he chanted the Yom Kippur prayer detailing the kinds of death the HolyName had chosen for the sinning Jews whom He'd marked in His book to be Cleansed.

He had always liked that prayer. It was so apt, bringing to mind those of his family that the HolyName had cleansed away in the ovens so that their remnants, like him, could start again pure.

Only now the Jews' purity was again threatened, this time with Arab blood, and it was up to him to cleanse it.

He rode on, chanting the lines he liked best, in his mind composing his next note.

PART TWO:

THE MOLOCH

1981, Saturday, October 10, to Wednesday, October 21

-1-

Saturday, October 10, 10:05 a.m.,
HaTikva Quarter

IF FRIDAY HAD been bad for Zohara, Saturday and Sunday were worse. She had woken up Saturday noon in the Amidar hovel, cold and wet, curled on the mattress, at first not knowing where she was. Then as memories of Friday night swarmed over her, she gasped with the pain and shame of it, of being a *Freha* and unable to do anything about it.

Without thinking, she asked the Yemenite boy on the other mattress if he had some more shit. "Anything... even Brown...."

The boy fumbled in his pants. "Alright, suck."

She shook her head. This was her last defense. "No."

"You want another hit, you suck first."

She couldn't talk, just shook her head.

Sullenly the boy relented. "Fine, the first was forty... if no sucking, this is fifty."

"Alright... I'll pay you Friday."

The boy poured powder into a cigarette foil, handed it to her. She was too weak to hold it, he had to light the bunched toilet paper underneath, then hold the boiling bubbling tar to her nose. "It's good shit, White, but cheap... just came in... sniff deep... yes, like that...."

She gulped the smoke, couldn't wait for the sickly-sweet fumes to again obliterate the freckled boy who'd opened the car door for her, spoke to her about books, then threw her pay on the table and left because she was a *Freha*.

She swallowed bile, slept again, got up once to pee into the floor's hole in the other room, went back to her mattress.

The rain kept drumming on the roof, on the walls, inside her.

She awoke Sunday morning, gagging—she could smell herself, rancid sweat and burnt drugs and urine, like a Central Bus Station beggar, or a Beit Sarah inmate after two nights in Isolation....

Suddenly she had to escape. Her watch said ten-fifteen. With an immense effort she got up, her legs wobbly.

The boy called out, "Listen, you can stay. Rahamim didn't come back yet—"

"No, no. I have to go..."

She staggered to the empty room, threw up into the hole: the fish, the wine, pieces of toasted bread. Her price.

She was wracked by coughs; she had to flee.

Grabbing her handbag, she pushed at the plywood covering the opening, crept out.

In front of the half-finished building was a lake of mud. She stomped through it, in her high-heeled shoes, dragging her handbag.

There was a light in her father's flat. Turning her head away, she made her way to the hair salon, hesitated, climbed, knocked.

Jacqueline opened, went pale. "Whatever happened to you?!"

"Nothing, nothing happened...."

Jacqueline pulled her in, "Go wash and change, go, or you'll scare the clients. You want Nescafé?"

Pirchiya and Sigalit silently watching, Zohara nodded, the void inside her jagged and sharp, like a broken bone.

Jacqueline handed her the coffee and she poured sugar into it, endlessly. And as she drank, in the midst of the peroxide stink, she felt the void inside her mend a little, though crookedly, the darkness turning into a sort of rage, without form or target yet.

She spooned more sugar into the Nescafé, more, couldn't have enough of it.

Behind her, Pirchiya began to cry.

"What?" Zohara said. "What? Nothing happened."

Later customers came. She swept the floor, did two bleaches, one hair-ironing, ate a pita with halva, another coffee with more sugar. She almost felt better, but by eleven thirty she felt like doing shit again, knew it was a drug-withdrawal *kriz,* did not even try to resist, cornered Sigalit, asked if she had some left. "Just a little, I'll pay you Friday."

Sigi looked aside. "Friday is okay... You need a loan, ask *Adon* Leon, he takes only two and a half percent a week, Rabbi Bardugo wants three percent, but he'll take two if you do him."

She handed Zohara the packet.

Zohara cooked it behind the synagogue, two boys alongside, boiling theirs on can lids, all silent, not even ashamed.

Batya called her at noon. She didn't take the call.

Sunday, October 11, 5:00 a.m.,
Tel Aviv

S UNDAY, THE HEADS of Services meeting started badly and then
got worse.

Just after dawn Gershonovitz had woken abruptly, knowing where
he'd seen the words on the killer's note. He sat up in bed, the air rattling
in his mouth like a man with his throat cut.

Pnina turned around in bed. "You okay, Shimmel?"

"Yes, yes," he croaked. "I had a dream, it woke me up."

It was the same dream he'd had for years, following his six weeks in
Europe right after the war, hunting Nazis with Asa and the elder Reznik.

The dream always ended the same way: he'd cornered the Damn
HolyName in a frozen forest near Birkenau, or Aachen, the DHN
dressed in black SS uniform, begging on His knees for forgiveness, and
he, Gershonovitz, spitting in His face and slitting His throat with a
Unit knife, feeling his Blackness lift as the knife's serration bit into the
divine throat.

Only now the supplicating Hand offered him a book; and as
Gershonovitz recognized it, his blood went cold, and he awoke.

"You want me to make you tea?" Pnina said.

"No, no, go back to sleep. I have a meeting soon."

He lowered his feet to the floor as his hand sought his inhaler, and heard her getting up too. Soon he heard her fussing in the kitchen, and for the hundredth time he thought he'd love to marry her, but did not dare give the Damn HolyName one more target. Two were enough.

As he pumped his inhaler, the book rose again before his eyes and he heard himself whisper the plagiarized words of the note and what Chief Levitan had said about them:

"Like they were written in German...."

Ten minutes later, sitting in the kitchen drinking his tea, Pnina back in bed, he finally grasped the sly mockery of the latest divine move: *Cards on the table! Here is my move. What's yours?*

And fuck You, too, he thought savagely. I'll stop Your war yet, even if it kills me.

It was gray and raining outside when, fifteen minutes later, he sank into the backseat of his official Lark, Moshe at the wheel.

"What happened?" Moshe asked. "You look like shit. You okay?"

"Yes, yes, I am okay, nothing happened." He lit a Kent and coughed, waving aside Moshe's reproachful scowl. "What are you, my doctor? Just drive."

It was 7:25 when they arrived at Army HQ. Moshe parked in the mud before the gray chief of staff building with its ancient Bavarian crossbeams. It used to be a German Templars' hotel, before it was taken over by the Brits in the Palestine Mandate period, then by the victorious Jews.

Two jeeps were already parked in front, and one Volvo. Moshe shut the engine. "You want me to come in with you?" He switched into a jocular tone. "In case it goes too well, and the HolyName comes after you—"

"Don't be over-smart!" A blast of rain sprayed Gershonovitz as he opened the door. "What will you do, shoot Him? But don't worry, they won't let Him in here, He doesn't have an ID.... What?! What? It's a joke! I'm not good for the asylum yet. Go. I'll call you when we finish."

The car door slammed as he lumbered out into the rain.

Inside, there was a small crowd before the elevator that would take them down to the secure hole six floors below. He saw Mossad department heads, Foreign

Office smoothies, and a knot of Military Intel boffins in pressed khaki, all told to come and reveal their sources, to prevent double recruiting.

Gershonovitz gave them only a cursory look.

He knew where each service stood on the invasion: the Security Service for, the Mossad maybe, Foreign Office against, Military Intel for, the prime minister neutral, all evenly balanced.

Or were they?

The Damn HolyName was for the invasion too. Of this Gershonovitz had no doubt. And He would be here today also. The dream was as good as a warning.

And it was up to him to stump His tricks. But could he?

"Oh, here's Shimmel," someone chuckled. "How many did your guys send to a better world this month?" Avigdor Feldman, head of the Internal Security Service, the Shin Bet. A small and nondescript man, except for a zigzag scar that gave his mouth a sardonic twist.

"Shut up. That's not for here. Wait for inside."

More bleeps sounded from the door.

Four sunburned lieutenant colonels came in: cross-border agent recruiters.

The Security Service's 2IC growled, "This is going to be a zoo."

"Oh, yes," the Foreign Office man chortled. "Here's Kiddush."

A balding man with a yarmulke came down the stairs: Tzvi Kadishevitz, PM Begin's right-hand man, presumably back from a chat with Defense Minister Sharon, the Bulldozer himself, at his office.

Kadishevitz came down slowly, groaning about his bunions.

"So how did it go?" the Shin Bet's 2IC asked in a low voice.

The PM's CabSec twisted his mouth. "The same like always, Arik wants to go into Beirut yesterday, finish the Palestinians by hand, he already has the maps and the plans—"

"Sha," Gershonovitz said, pointing to the crowd. "You can't wait for inside?"

"What, it's such a secret? Even in Café Cassit they know it. But we didn't have much time to talk."

The debate about best killing methods lasted all the way to the secure hole, six floors down.

The steel doors' hydraulics hissed open and participants filed in and one by one sat down, congregating by their invasion stance: pro to the left, con to the right, fence-sitters at the corners.

The secure hole was an oblong box the size of a large living room carved out of the chalky gravel. Rows of metal cabinets stretched along the walls—bafflers to prevent eavesdropping and recording.

Gershonovitz remained standing, trying to gauge where the DHN would make his next move.

The Security Service's Feldman paused by his side. "Where's Chief Levitan?"

"He couldn't come, too many *Arsim* killing each other."

Feldman made a farting noise. "I told Ben-Gurion years ago, Katzenelson's book was right, it was a mistake to bring over all these *Schwartzes*…. You okay, Shimmel?"

Gershonovitz stuck his inhaler in his mouth. "Yes… yes…."

"It's probably all this ash. They never clean it."

At the room's end stood an enclosed steel barrel ending with a chimney that disappeared into the ceiling. Through a side opening an ash heap could be seen. All handouts and notes were gathered and burned before anyone was let out.

On the furnace's door an old wit had scratched the words "The Moloch." The old Canaanite god to whom babies were sacrificed.

"Here," the Security Service's chief handed Gershonovitz a glass of juice. "Drink something."

"I'm okay, I said."

The clock over the door ticked away. Finally the hydraulics hissed again, and the Mossad chief and chief of Military Intelligence walked in, their seconds-in-command behind.

Asa, the Mossad's chief, sat down, stretching his huge arms. With his white-reddish beard and bent shoulders he looked like a cross between a rabbi and an aged orangutan. His 2IC sat by his side, picked up a spoon and began to flip it like a knife.

The Mossad's chief said, "So we can start finally? Anyone has anything to hand out?"

The various seconds-in-command gave out lists of newly recruited agents and Gershonovitz handed out a page of the latest Beirut take-downs, summed up in columns.

Kadishevitz passed a sheet of attendance to sign. "That's the only thing I keep, everything else goes to the Moloch…. Oh, where's Chief Levitan?"

"Working," Gershonovitz said. "Too many *Arsim* killing each other."

Asa threw him a sharp stare. A seat at the Heads of Services meeting was not given up so easily. Gershonovitz met his stare until Asa slid his eyes sideways.

"Alright." Asa read out the new agents' names. Military Intels and the various 2ICs wrote them down, stared at their papers to commit them to their famed memories, then slid them into the center pile, to be burned.

All watched the fire flare and die.

Asa said, "Alright, let's call the first in line… no, wait. Shimmel, how're your thugs doing?"

Gershonovitz said, "Running off their feet, and we're almost out of poison-gas ampoules. They can't make them fast enough."

"So why don't you import some?"

"Nah. They're only made here and in Austria, so I said no."

There was a short pause.

Asa leaned forward. "How are the other guys in Beirut doing? Can they handle it? I mean, they're doing how many takedowns a week, each? Two? Three?"

Gershonovitz lifted his hands upward, palm up.

The Security Service's Feldman turned to Asa, "I told you before, let's stop with this foolishness, have the army go in, do the fuckers in the camps wholesale—"

"Shut up," Asa said. "I asked Shimmel a question."

"No problem with my guys," Gershonovitz said.

Asa said, "How about mine? Yaro tells me some are not doing too good, working on their own for the first time, no team—"

Yaro, Asa's son, was a Unit member, also in Beirut.

"Yeah," Kadishevitz said. "I heard this, too, from my nephew there."

The silence seemed to linger.

The Mossad's chief scratched his wide beard. "What do you think, Shimmel? They'll be okay eventually or not?"

"They'll have to."

The Shin Bet chief said, "You know my opinion—just let the army do it wholesale—"

"Fuck your opinion," Gershonovitz snarled. "You think this is not wholesale?" He stared at Feldman, hard, feeling his old chops coming back. If this was how the DHN was making his play, he could handle it. "When I came back, the PM promised me on his honor I got nine months before it'd go to cabinet for debate—we've only been at this what? Two months? So no one give me—"

Asa said, "Enough, Shimmel, don't get a hernia. What else you need, to do it faster? Should we open another shift for poison-gas ampoules?"

"Yeah, this would help."

Asa turned to his silent 2IC, raised his eyebrows.

The 2IC nodded. "Okay. I'll call them at Ness Ziona, see if they can do another shift."

"Okay?" The Military Intel chief said, "My guys can come in now, finally? It's almost nine."

"No, give me all the papers first," Kadishevitz said. "In case these talkers have good eyes." He fed the paper into the Moloch, his nose wrinkled.

"This smell," he said, "I'm asking you."

Gershonovitz got up, ready to empty his bladder. If this was all the DHN could throw at him, then fine. He could take it.

But the day was not over yet. Not by half.

-3-

**Sunday, October 11, 7:00 a.m.,
HaTikva Quarter, then a Tel Aviv Suburb**

S UNDAY MORNING ZOHARA still had not returned. Amzaleg
called Jacqueline's hair salon.

"No," Jacqueline said. "She's not here." When she began to ask how
he was doing, he mumbled he was fine and hung up.

He certainly was not fine, not with who he was about to visit.

It was a regular nursing home, but also had a wing for *shoo-shoo* residents
who went gaga and had to be kept in isolation in case they'd babble or try to
harm themselves or others.

Amzaleg showed his old Unit card to the sentinel at the entrance,
signed his name and walked in. It was four years since he'd been here last
to visit another Unit member.

Room number seventeen was at the end. There was another sentinel before it. Amzaleg again showed his card, and the guard thumbed
numbers into the lock. "Ten minutes. You understand? And if you need
anything, call."

Amzaleg pushed by him and entered.

The room was entirely beige, from the bed linen to the carpet. Even the
picture on the wall was of beige dunes somewhere in the Sinai. Only the
wrinkled old man seated on the bed was a pale white, like sand bleached

in the sun. His legs barely reached the floor as he stared at Amzaleg with dark puzzlement.

His old Unit commander, Yitzhak Shafrir: forty-two registered take-downs to his credit, now mostly a shell, with only an occasional flicker of consciousness.

Would he also be like that one day?

"Yitzhak," Amzaleg said, "it's me, Amnon."

Emotions flitted across the face in a procession of ticks, then the eyes lit up. "No shit, it's you, Amnon! Where are you now? In the Shin Bet?" The Security Service.

"No, the police. How are you, Yitzhak?"

His old commander's mouth opened, closed. "Amnon who?"

"Amzaleg..."

More emotions flitted across the face, like wind waves on dunes. "You have a smoke?"

Amzaleg pulled out a filter-less Gitanes and gave it into the huge palm. The cigarette dropped to the floor and he picked it up, put it back into the pack.

It was probably useless but he tried nevertheless. "Listen, Yitzhak, you remember the names of everyone? All the guys?"

"Nah," Shafrir said, "they are all *fakakt*, like me. You not *fakakt* yet?"

"Sometimes, but now I am okay," Amzaleg said, surprising himself.

"How's Feldman?"

"Surviving. But Yitzhak, listen, I am in the police, and I need—"

"Not the Shin Bet?"

"No. Listen—"

The old man said, "Maybe you have a cigarette?"

Amzaleg said nothing.

"Or maybe chocolate? They never give me anything."

There was a small pile of Reznik chocolates on the table, untouched. Maybe Ehud had visited.

Amzaleg looked at the bare room, some black-and-white faded photographs on the table behind the chocolate pile: a man, a woman, three girls in long skirts, on the wall more black-and-white photos, from years back, from Over There.

Shafrir saw him looking. "May the HolyName avenge their blood."

Amzaleg said, again surprising himself, "We avenged them."

"Yes," Shafrir said. Then, as if reading Amzaleg's thought, he cackled. "By killing Arabs."

He laughed hard, exposing toothless gums. Then the laughter stopped, the eyes went blank. Amzaleg waited, but it was hopeless.

As he got up to go he tried one last time. "You heard from Shimmel maybe?"

To his surprise, Shafrir's beige cheeks turned darker. "Yeah, he came to visit."

Amzaleg's heart skipped a beat. "When?"

The old killer gave a shrug. What was time here?

Desperately Amzaleg went on, "What's Shimmel doing now?"

"Running the Unit," Shafrir's eyes focused suddenly. "He said he couldn't say no…"

Amzaleg's heart beat faster. He recalled Munger saying Gershonovitz was the one to call if he, Amzaleg ever wanted to return…. And *Adon* Leon, too, hinted that Gershonovitz was involved…. But heading the Unit?

"To whom Shimmel couldn't say no?"

"Begin, probably." The old eyes began to lose focus. "Or maybe Kiddush…."

Amzaleg started. Kadishevitz, nicknamed Kiddush, was PM Begin's private secretary.

Amzaleg spoke desperately fast, "And what's Shimmel doing in the Unit?"

The old jackal-eyes lit up. "Killing Arabs wholesale," he cackled again, "… in Beirut…."

Amzaleg recalled Munger's new Mossadnik trainees. "For Beirut," Munger had said.

"Why there? For what?"

Amzaleg grabbed the man's large hand with which Shafrir could encompass a man's throat. But it stayed inert in his.

"Yitzhak, Yitzhak, try to remember…"

But it was no use. The gray eyes had turned opaque. "You have a cigarette maybe?"

"No," Amzaleg said, his heart felt squeezed. The man was gone.

Still, he stayed ten more minutes, holding the old man's hand, watching the gray eyes go into and out of focus. Once or twice he tried putting a question to the old killer, but there was no answer.

Presently there was a knock on the door and a muffled voice asked him if he was okay.

"Yes," he said. "I am okay."

Outside, the sentinel said, "You were with him in—the Service?"

Amzaleg nodded. "You?"

"No. They didn't want to take me."

"You were lucky."

Sunday, October 11, 10:15 a.m.,
Army HQ, Tel Aviv

A S THE HEADS of Services meeting resumed after coffee break, things got out of hand. But Gershonovitz almost missed it.

During the morning session he semi-snoozed, listening with half an ear to one after another agent-runner droning about old tanks in the hands of the PLO, Bulgarian surplus bazookas, Russian flame throwers—all better destroyed soon with their operators before it was too late.

He stared at the photos being handed out, then gave them to Kadishevitz to feed to the Moloch.

"Next!" Asa called.

Military Intel's Syrian desk maven droned on about Rahman's latest business deals: drugs, crime, whorehouses, dollar printeries....

Asa thumped on the desk. "Enough with this. You have a new agents list?"

The maven read out several names, then mentioned one was no longer with them.

"Why?" asked the Foreign Office man.

"Assad's mother caught him, sent him to Tadmor jail."

"Ouch!" The FO man clasped his genitals.

Kadishevitz collected the list and fed it to the flames.

"Next," Asa said.

Gershonovitz listened with his eyes half-closed, trying to gauge where the DHN would make his next move. Or perhaps the move would come only later? It was getting close to lunchtime.

Last presenter: A Mossad department head with details about Arafat's staff and household: who of his fuckboys was up, who down, who retired because he'd reached seventeen.

The FO man said, "How's Agent Judah? Still bearing up?"

Agent Judah was a twenty-two-year-old Yemenite-Israeli looking sixteen, a graduate of the Mossad's TempleWhores course, now sacrificing his ass for his country.

"Yes," said Asa, "and better than you did."

The FO man flushed. Before transferring to the Foreign Office, he'd been a Mossad gigolo with three women suicides to his credit. Afterward he spent a month in the psych ward getting electroshocks but never recovered fully. He never lived it down.

The hydraulics whined.

"What is it?" said Asa. "Lunch already?" It was only eleven forty.

The sentinel was at the door. "No, a message." He handed Asa a note. "Shimmel's driver asked him to call."

All looked at Gershonovitz.

Gershonovitz said, "Tell him I'll call after."

No way was he going to leave the field to the Damn HolyName.

Asa flicked his eyes at Gershonovitz, then away. "Any more questions before we eat? Anyone want to add something? Private operations? Secret agents you forgot to share? Last chance…"

All shook their heads. Gershonovitz too.

"Okay, then… All papers to Kiddush, before we eat."

Kadishevitz fed the sheets to the Moloch and watched them burn, his face lit red.

"Lunch," Asa called out.

Everyone rose amid the usual *shoo-shoo* chatter: where in Beirut to buy the best Armani suits, thickest Rolex watches, most real Gucci loafers, highest rate for D. Marks, best whorehouse on Rue Verdun.

The doors began to hiss open.

"Oh, wait, one more thing," the Shin Bet's Feldman said to the sentinel. The hydraulics paused. "I almost forgot. Asa, we want to recruit someone at Rahman's new coke lab—"

Asa thumped on the desk. "You thug! Only now you mention this?"

Gershonovitz pulled out his inhaler and drew on it, hard.

Well fuck You, he thought savagely. So this is how You want to play it now? Let them find out about my secret deal with Rahman via some Shin Bet agent?

Then he heard Asa say, "No need. We already have someone close by."

"Who?" Feldman said. "There's nobody on the lists."

Asa said, "Can't tell you who."

The room fell silent. Only the wall bafflers were heard.

Feldman said, "I think you said, here we tell everything, no? Didn't we say this, Kiddush?"

Kadishevitz flushed. "Yes...."

No one talked or breathed.

Feldman murmured, "You got any other private agents maybe you don't tell us about, except for Judah? Him we understand...."

It was well known that if Judah's father found out about his doings, he would kill him.

Asa said, "This is none of your business."

The silence deepened, hardened into palpable curiosity. Which agent was Asa keeping secret?

Gershonovitz watched Asa through half-lidded eyes.

Kadishevitz said mildly, "Asa, I thought we said no secrets here...."

Asa said, "You don't like it, Kiddush, you can call Begin right now, I go back to the cows."

In the silence, Gershonovitz got up, walked over to Asa, bent over to whisper in his ear. "Asa, there's also something else, we gotta talk—"

Asa snarled, "You got anything to tell me, Shimmel, you say it to everyone here."

Gershonovitz shook his head. "No, nothing." He formed zeros with thumb and forefinger of both hands.

"So fuck off," Asa said, then added improbably, "there are no secrets here."

Feldman made a farting sound, loud and long. No one laughed.

Asa said, "Maybe you want to call the PM, Feldman? Go ahead."

Slowly Feldman shook his head.

In the midst of the silence, Asa snapped, "Enough! Lunch!" and the doors hissed open.

Everyone streamed out to the elevators, tense and curious, a few exchanging looks, whispers.

Who was this agent of Asa's he was holding on to, against his own new rules?

Gershonovitz dallied then went to the washroom, a nook in the gravelly chalk marked with 0-0, European style.

Asa was already at the urinal, alone. In two quick paces Gershonovitz was at his side.

"We gotta meet and talk…."

Asa said into the wall, "Coffee upstairs, after?"

"No. Don't want Kiddush to see us talking."

"So call me at home and tell me where—"

There were steps outside. Gershonovitz scooted into a cubicle and shut the door. He could hear men come in. He waited, silently. A few minutes later when he emerged, all were gone.

Instead of joining the others for lunch he went into the sentinel's nook, picked up the phone, dialed the Lark's radiotelephone.

Moshe picked up, said his code number, and Gershonovitz said his. "What happened?"

"You secure?"

"Yes. What?"

"Chief Levitan asked me to tell you there's just been another killing."

- 5 -

**Sunday, October 11, 10:00 a.m. to 11:45 p.m.,
Tel Aviv, Jaffa**

ODDLY, THOUGH, IT was again Amzaleg who'd first heard about the second victim, not Superintendent Klinger nor Chief Superintendent Levitan.

The way it happened was this: One of the policemen dispatched Sunday morning to Gan Meir to look at the body was from the Jaffa station. Once the dead body was fished out, the policeman recognized him as Rahamim Tzan'ani, part-time waiter at Leon's restaurant and a drug pusher, who also used.

His father had OD'd in jail, and his mother was in prison. But her sister, Jacqueline Cohen, lived in HaTikva and ran a hair salon.

The policeman remembered that Amnon Amzaleg once had a thing with this Jacqueline, so he called him on his cruiser radio and asked him to tell her. "So she can come identify the body—it's in the morgue now—"

Amzaleg closed his eyes briefly, mid-drive. "How did he die?"

"Don't know—he doesn't look too good after three days in the water—probably did drugs and fell in."

"Do me a favor," Amzaleg said. "Can you put it in the OpLog only at noon?"

If he could keep Klinger from seeing it for two to three hours, in case it wasn't an accident....

"Alright."

"I owe you a coffee," Amzaleg said and pointed his cruiser toward the morgue.

"I thought you did your repentance wash only once a week," Dr. Munger said.

Munger was signing the notebook of a police sergeant who had just brought in a body. It now lay on the slab by the desk's side, staring sightlessly up.

Amzaleg knew the policeman and nodded at him before pushing ahead.

"Munger, I want to look at someone—"

"No, you wait in line. And put rubbers on your shoes. Show respect for the deceased."

Once the policeman left, Munger waddled away. "I have work, Amnon, be quick. Which one do you want?"

Amzaleg followed the pathologist. "Where is the deceased from Gan Meir?" He looked around. Every slab in the hall was taken, some with two cadavers each.

Munger spit sideways. "Nah, can't do him yet. He's full of water, you'll have to let him dry out first, at least two more days—"

"It's not for a repentance. I just want to see the body. Did you do the autopsy yet?"

Munger scoffed. "What autopsy? He fell in the ditch and drowned—"

"Munger, I want to see him." Amzaleg took out his policeman's notebook.

The pathologist scowled. "Alright, but don't tell me I didn't warn you."

Despite the warning, Amzaleg had to close his eyes when he saw the stripped body.

"See?" Dr. Munger said. "Told you."

The dead Yemenite really looked now like a *vooz-vooz*, pasty-white and inflated and flabby.

Amzaleg said, "Any water in the lungs?"

Munger shrugged. "Who knows? There's water in his gut, in his balls—three days in the water...."

"Did you look?"

But Munger was striding off. "You saw how many I got? So many shitheads going *fakakt*...."

Amzaleg bent down and removed one galosh, stuck his hand in it and used it to lift the head.

The distended head wobbled as Amzaleg bent it forward then turned it.

The puffed flesh had closed over the hole, but there was no mistaking it.

"Hey, Pesach!" he called. "Come take a look."

Munger was already by his office door. "What do you want from my life, Amnon? What?"

Amzaleg said mildly, "He got it in the third also, just like the one on Yom Kippur...."

The fat pathologist waddled over fast, grasped the head in his hand, turned it, probed with a pen.

"Yes, third vertebra," he muttered at last, "just like I taught you guys."

Amzaleg kept his eyes on the puncture. "The bullet's still in?"

"Maybe, if it didn't fall out—here—"

It took a short while.

"Two-two," Munger said at last, holding it up with rusty tweezers.

"Can I have it?"

Munger pulled his hand away. "So you'll be doing the Initial?"

For a moment Amzaleg wanted to lie, then reconsidered. "No."

He couldn't. He was a "floater" now, without access to the lab, the photographer, his old team...

"I thought so." Munger dug out of his apron's pocket a crumpled paper envelope, dropped the bullet in, licked the flap, and pressed it shut on his stomach.

"Here, you sign on it."

Scribbling, Amzaleg asked, "Where are his clothes?"

"With the rest... where you going?"

As Amzaleg strode toward Munger's office, the pathologist tried to overtake him. "Hey—"

Amzaleg got there first, elbowing aside the pathologist and going through a pile of empty formaldehyde bottles.

Inside, under an army field cot where Munger often slept, lay a heap of old shoes and rags of the dead derelicts. It was usually incinerated once a month. But to the side, under the occupied slab, was a smaller pile of rags, the top ones wet and muddy.

Amzaleg bent over them, his stomach churning.

Behind him Munger yelped. "Don't touch them! They gotta dry now before going into the evidence bag—"

But Amzaleg was already burrowing into the soggy rags, using his pen. "Where's what he had in his pockets?"

"There was nothing," Munger said. "And leave these!"

Unheeding, Amzaleg probed further. There was nothing in the pants' pockets, but the shirt pocket yielded a wet lined sheet of scribbled paper, half-dissolved.

Amzaleg pulled it out with his fingernails, lifted it to the gray light. The ink ran, but the letters were well formed, in standard "square" script, *shoo-shoo* style.

Amzaleg's neck tingled as he made out some words.

Munger tried to grab at the paper but Amzaleg twisted away.

The scribbled lines were smeared. He could only make out a single sentence fragment, but it was enough.

He felt Munger breathing over his shoulder and he held the paper up so the pathologist could see.

"Read this."

The color drained from Munger's face as he read out the lines. "...to cleanse the land from dark evil seed... Purify Jews' blood from Arab contamination..."

Munger gulped, stopped, raised wide eyes.

"A madman," he whispered. "Who writes a thing like that?"

When Amzaleg did not respond, Munger said, "You think one of *ours* did this?"

There was no need to ask who *ours* were.

Amzaleg said, "What about the new guys you are training every week—"

Munger's voice was a squeak. "I'm not responsible for what they do with what I teach them—"

The rain sound rose as the morgue's front door was opened. Amzaleg did not look up. "You have another envelope?"

Munger handed him one and Amzaleg slipped the wet paper into it, then handed the envelope to Munger, who sealed it, licking it twice.

"Now I'll sign this too," Amzaleg said. "Here, take it, put it together with the bullet."

Munger stared at the envelope as if it was about to bite him. With shaking fingers, he put it into his apron's pocket, his face doughy.

Amzaleg said, "The one I did, before Yom Kippur, he also had a note like this on him?"

Munger sat down heavily behind his desk, mechanically picked up a half-eaten bagel. Absentmindedly he muttered a blessing and began to munch, eyes vacant.

"I don't know... Ask Klinger...."

"You have a list of all those who you gave the 101 to?"

101 was short for Cold Killing 101, the basic intro course for *shoo-shoo* assassins.

"No, I don't keep records like these...."

Amzaleg persisted. "How many new guys did you train here last year?"

Munger seemed to come out of his stupor. "Who knows?.... Ask Gershonovitz, or Feldman, or ask Asa.... What d'you want from me? I only do what..." He stopped. "Amnon, please, I gotta call Klinger...."

Munger's hand hovered over the phone, eyes pleading.

Amzaleg rasped, "Did he ask you to tell him if any other stiff is brought in, done like the first?"

At first Munger didn't respond. Finally he nodded.

The rain-staccato rose again as the door opened and another muddy policeman appeared. "Munger, we have another—"

"In the back!" the pathologist hollered. "Put him in the fucking back! Any place you find!"

The door closed.

Munger said, "So many now, all from drugs, the morgue is full almost like in '73—" He stopped. "Sorry, Amnon…."

Amzaleg felt a vein throb. "You still have the bullet of the first one? The one Fishkin and I did?"

Munger shook his head.

"Why? Where is it?"

"K—Klinger has it."

Amzaleg had a flash. "He did the Initial? Him?"

Munger nodded jerkily.

Amzaleg said, "Was also a two-two?"

Munger nodded again.

"Both by the same gun, I bet."

Munger hoisted his shoulder. "Maybe."

The phone rang. Munger grabbed at it. "What? No. We are full."

Amzaleg said, "So you think one of ours did this? The note, it was written in SSS—"

The pathologist seemed to awaken. "Anyone can write like this—"

"Not anyone, just those who were taught it."

"Yeah, maybe… but I told you." His voice rose. "I am not to blame if one of you went crazy…."

Amzaleg pulled out his notebook, wrote down the date, time and the name of the dead boy, added a line about the bullet extracted by Dr. Munger and another about the half-dissolved note.

The exact words he kept out. "Barely legible" was all he wrote.

Aloud he said, "Munger, can you give me two hours before you call Klinger?"

"Why? You don't want them to catch this madman that's killing your people—" He stopped.

Amzaleg breathed in and out, giving Munger time to understand the obvious.

For wasn't it clear? A *shoo-shoo* Undertaker gone mad, killing *Schwartzes*, leaving notes like this…. Would it be in anyone's interest to catch him? Especially now?

Munger stuttered, "Maybe... maybe they'll catch him but keep it quiet...."

"Quiet how?"

Munger shrugged helplessly.

Amzaleg said, "No.... This one's mine.... Just two hours, Munger... I want to tell this boy's aunt about it, prepare her, before Klinger starts badgering her—"

The pathologist's chin went up. But to Amzaleg's surprise and relief, Munger agreed. "Okay, I'll do the autopsy, then I'll call him. Now get out—I have so many to do...."

Outside, the rain had turned thicker, soupier, but Amzaleg drove fast. He only had two hours, if Munger would keep his word.

Sunday, October 11, 11:50 p.m.,
Tel Aviv-Jaffa

B UT OF COURSE Munger didn't. Either his fear of Superintendent Klinger was stronger than his promise, or his conscience pangs at having trained the killer was. But a minute after Amzaleg had gone, the pathologist phoned Klinger.

Klinger was not in, so Munger called Chief Levitan.

Thus less than an hour after Amzaleg had left, Chief Levitan and Superintendent Klinger barged into the morgue, clamoring to see the latest victim.

A minute later Gershonovitz strode in, with Moshe right behind.

"So arrest me," Moshe snapped at him. "I am not staying in the car like a shmuck. Why can't you tell me who got killed?"

"It's just another *Schwartze*," said Munger.

"Well, I am half a *Schwartze* myself," Moshe said. "What kind of *Schwartze*?"

"Yemenite."

Turning to Gershonovitz, Moshe said, "And what about the first victim? Also *Schwartze*?"

Chief Levitan put hands on hips. "Shimmel, who the fuck is this? Did you bring a military policeman?"

"Sha, Leizer," Gershonovitz said. "He's one of those trying to keep your son from being sent into Lebanon." And turning to his driver he said, "You have a big mouth."

Levitan eyed Moshe. "That you do. You can stay, but keep it shut."

Moshe said, "You're not in my line of command."

Levitan said, "Shimmel, will you tell your snotnose to shut up, or I'll shut his mouth for him."

"I wouldn't advise it, he bites." And turning to Moshe, Gershonovitz said, "Keep quiet and put on some galoshes—and close the door, you came in last."

Moshe did, then followed the others as they trailed behind the pathologist into the mortuary hall.

-7-

**Sunday, October 11, 12:25 p.m.,
HaTikva**

AMZALEG'S STOMACH TIGHTENED when he knocked on the hair salon's door.

To his disappointment and relief, Zohara wasn't there.

"No," Sigalit said. "Don't know where she is—"

An old woman in the hair-straightening chair looked up, Pirchiya fussing behind her with a towel.

"Hi, Amnon," Pirchiya said shyly. She wore a faded black skirt, in mourning.

Amzaleg nodded at her, to his surprise just as shyly.

Jacqueline appeared, drying her hands. "Who is it—Ah, Amnon!"

He felt unease at how her face lit up.

She said, "Zohara isn't here—"

Amzaleg asked if they could talk somewhere. Something in his face alerted her.

"What is it? Something happened?"

He found himself nodding.

"Rahamim?" she said.

He followed as she led him into the back room. She asked, "He's again in the ER?"

He shook his head. "In the morgue. I'm so sorry…"

She began to cry. "OD?"

He shook his head again.

Sigalit appeared in the door. "What is it?"

"Rahamim," Jacqueline said.

Sigalit began to cry, companionably and noisily.

Amzaleg waited for her to leave, and when she didn't, said, "Jacquie, can we talk somewhere?"

"I'm leaving, I'm leaving," Sigalit said. "What, I didn't know him also?"

When she'd left, Amzaleg shut the door. "Was killed," he said. "Shot."

Jacqueline sat down on a pile of towels. "Who did this?"

"We don't know. When did you see him last?"

There was a long pause. "Two days ago—he came to ask for a loan, I said no—shot how?" She pulled a cigarette out with trembling fingers.

Amzaleg lit it for her. He noted that his fingers shook too.

"I already went to ID the... the body—if you need anything..." He stopped.

"No, thank you—I'll ask *Adon* Leon to help me with the funeral...."

Amzaleg hardened his tone. "Wait until I talk to him."

And then, because it would be strange if he didn't, he asked about Zohara. "She's okay?"

Jacqueline nodded hesitantly, then shook her head. "No, I don't know."

"She came to work?"

A nod, clamped lips.

"She stayed with Pirchiya?"

"I don't know." Her eyes strayed aside.

Amzaleg wanted to ask more but couldn't. At last he said lamely, "Let her know I was here."

Jacqueline nodded, then again began to weep, formally now, uttering little wails.

As he was leaving, she said in a low voice, "And if you want to eat something Friday—" not saying she was completely alone now, and so was he.

He nodded, noncommittal, and left, feeling his cheeks and neck heat up.

Outside, Pirchiya came up to him, her soft eyes red. She, too, was crying. "It's true? Rahamim went *fakakt*?"

He nodded. Her proximity, her faint smell of soap, made his head swim.

She said, "I told him not to use so much—"

"Wasn't OD," Amzaleg said. "Someone did him."

Her eyes grew. "You'll catch them?"

Amzaleg rattled his head, then nodded. "I will."

She held on to his arm, unexpectedly, mumbling her thanks, both for her brother and for Rahamim. He nearly pulled his arm away, but didn't.

Presently she said, "And Zohara—she—she still doesn't talk to you?"

Feeling her fingers in the crook of his elbow, like a warm drug, he shook his head. "No."

Sigalit, he saw, was eavesdropping shamelessly, her face pinched.

Pirchiya saw where he was looking. "I'll talk to you later... I should tell Zohara something?"

"Only that I was here... that I asked how she was...."

"Of course. Yes."

As he went down the stairs, the rain hitting at him, he saw the young pickpocket who was the Yom Kippur cantor, climbing up the stairs, going in.

From the street, he looked back through the rain and saw him talking to Pirchiya, and he wondered what it was about. Then he castigated himself.

She's half your age, Amzaleg, shame on you....

Yet his heart gave a strange lurch, then his groin, the kind he hadn't felt for a while.

The rain was coming down on the large puddle before the Amidar hovel, where Rahamim had been living. Ignoring the rain, Amzaleg waded through the shallow edge of the puddle, pushed aside the plywood slab at the doorless opening, and entered.

When his eyes accustomed to the gloom, he saw the floor was strewn with bunched toilet paper, half-burnt, and pieces of blackened aluminum foil. There were four mattresses on the floor, only one occupied.

From the other room wafted a strong smell of urine. It probably served as a latrine.

He kicked the nearby mattress. Its occupant, a bleary-eyed stick of a boy of perhaps twenty, jerked into half-sitting.

"W—what?" His eyes focused. "Hello, Amnon."

He was a distant cousin of the grocer.

Amzaleg said, "You know Rahamim?" He kicked at the mattress.

The place stank—a mixture of feces, burnt drugs and mold.

The boy stuck out his lower lip. "No."

Amzaleg kicked the mattress again. "Don't lie, you donkey. You want to get arrested?"

The boy fumbled under the mattress but found nothing. "You got a cigarette?"

"No."

Amzaleg waited. The boy waited, too, gave up. "Yeah, he was here Friday—" He pointed to a second mattress, whose blanket was still rumpled.

"Was here at night?"

"No, didn't come back—"

Amzaleg pondered. "Where did he hook?"

"You sure you have no cigarette?"

Amzaleg gave up, pulled out his Gitanes, gave the boy his next-to-last one and lit it for him, wincing at the boy's rancid smell.

The boy exhaled smoke. "Used to go to Gan Ha'atzmaut, Gan HaHashmal—"

"Gan Meir Park too?"

A nod.

"With anyone in particular?"

A shake, puzzled eyes. "No, anyone who came." The eyes focused. "What happened to him? OD?"

Amzaleg rasped, "Was shot."

The effect on the boy was immediate. He sprang up, tried to stand. "Who did—" Then his legs gave up and he fell on the mattress.

"You tell me."

The boy began to babble—he knew nothing, never had any business with Rahamim, who was a known user, an idiot really, three, four times a day, crazy—who in his right mind did more than two....

Amzaleg turned to go. It was useless. "Where are the others who were here?"

"Gone." Then the boy seemed to remember, the sly look came back. "Your daughter was too—"

In a flash Amzaleg grabbed him by the shoulder. It felt like holding a frail baby bird. The boy mewled out in pain and Amzaleg immediately relaxed his hold.

"She slept here?"

"Yeah… Friday, also last night…."

Amzaleg wanted to ask if she had used, too, but held himself back. "If you see her, tell her I was looking for her."

The boy nodded, whimpering.

As Amzaleg pushed at the plywood door-plank, the boy called his name, asked if he had another cigarette. "Or anything… some shekels…."

Amzaleg shook his head, went out into the rain.

Cars passed, splashing him, but he didn't notice, nor that his cruiser's radiotelephone was chirping. And when he finally heard it, he had already walked past.

He let it ring.

Sunday, October 11, 12:50 p.m.,
Tel Aviv-Jaffa

RAIN HAMMERED ON the morgue's roof. Inside, the five men stood around the stone slab.

"Three days in the water?" Levitan bellowed to overcome the rain's drumming.

"Or more." Moshe poked the dead abdomen.

Munger snapped, "Don't touch!" He lifted the balloon-like head. "Here, in the third vertebra, exactly in the middle. See?"

"Yup." Moshe leaned close. "Good job."

Levitan said, "You think the same one from before did this one, too, Shimmel?"

Gershonovitz could hardly speak, he was so enraged. He could smell the Damn HolyName's stink, His evil Hand pushing for war…. "Yes, probably."

Munger muttered, "Was also a two-two, like the first—" He pulled out an envelope and shoved it at Klinger. "Send it to the lab and ask them to compare."

"Yes, alright." Klinger stuck the envelope in his pocket.

There was banging on the outside door. "Hey, Munger! Open up, we have another OD—"

Munger shouted, "Go to Sdeh-Dov morgue! We're full!"

Moshe said, "Pfff. You need another morgue."

"We need another people. These fucking *Schwartzes*, killing themselves and each other...."

Moshe said, "Not this one." He poked at the inflated head. "When was the first one killed?"

Levitan hesitated. "Yom Kippur eve."

Gershonovitz seemed to awaken. "Hey, Munger, did he have anything in the pockets?"

Munger gave a start. "Oh yes, I forgot. There was a crazy note in his shirt—" He pulled another envelope out of his pocket and began to slit its flap.

"Wait!" Levitan grabbed at it. "Who signed on this?"

"Sergeant Amzaleg... he was here before—he found the note...."

"How? When?"

"This morning."

Levitan snarled, "This fucking *Ars*! Always sticks his dick in what doesn't concern him...."

Moshe said, "What was this Amzaleg doing here?"

Munger began to say that Amzaleg came to do a repentance-washing, then stopped. "No, he asked to see the stiff from Gan Meir, he came to look at him specifically...."

"How did he hear about it?"

Munger lifted his palms, made an "I don't know" face.

Gershonovitz seemed on the verge of an explosion.

"What?!" Klinger said. "Just before Yom Kippur, I told him to stay out of this."

Munger stuttered, "Actually he was the one also saw the bullet hole—"

Chief Levitan roared, "Klinger, go call Amnon again—right now. Tell him it's from me—if he doesn't stay out of this, I'll cut off his balls."

Without a word, Klinger turned and went toward Munger's office.

No one spoke until he came back, shaking his head. "He doesn't pick up."

Chief Levitan began to speak, but Moshe interrupted him. "Wait... wait... Shimmel, there was an Amzaleg in the Unit, no? The one called the slaughterer. Once, years ago? Any relation—"

"The same."

Moshe said, "And he's in the *police* now?"

Gershonovitz gave a terse nod, mouth clamped.

"So why's he just a sergeant?"

Levitan boomed, "Because he was demoted!"

"Twice," said Klinger.

Moshe stared at each policeman in turn, then at Gershonovitz. "Shimmel, that's the same old fart Amzaleg came back in '73 to do Reserve Service?"

"Himself. I always told Shafrir it was a mistake to take him—"

"The one did six jobs in a week? Went into the psych ward afterward, second time?"

"Third time," Gershonovitz hissed. "Pity they didn't keep him there."

"Damn right," said Chief Levitan.

There was a pause.

Moshe said, "So what's he doing here, investigating these killings?"

Gershonovitz hesitated, anger meeting caution.

Chief Levitan made a rude noise. "The first victim was a friend of his son, so Amzaleg volunteered himself...."

Moshe said, "Well why not ask him to help—"

"No way," Levitan snarled, "If he fucks up again, this all comes out...."

"How did he fuck up before?"

Klinger shouted, "He didn't obey orders."

"Oo-ah," Moshe said. "And you always do?"

"Shut up, Moshe," Gershonovitz said. "This thing comes out, all you guys are doing in Lebanon goes straight down the sewer."

There was a short silence.

Gershonovitz said, "Munger, lemme see this second note."

As he read it his face turned red, then white. "Worse than the first one...." Without raising his eyes he read out aloud the legible words, pausing where the water had made the ink run.

He stopped, wiped his forehead. Munger spit three times, fast.

Moshe said, "A final solution to the *Ars* problem, no?"

Munger yelped, "Bite your tongue."

There was a pause.

Moshe said, "Who's the madman who wrote this?"

Gershonovitz whispered, "Name of Kalman Katzenelson—Shazar's brother-in-law—" He took out his inhaler, pumped it.

Zalman Shazar was Israel's third president. Twenty years before.

"Ach!" Chief Levitan slapped his temple. "Yeah, now I remember his book—"

"Wait, you know him?" Moshe said, "A mad *vooz-vooz* racist shot this guy? The first victim too?"

"No way," Gershonovitz said. "I don't believe it. Kalman's not a shooter, just a scribbler. He used to write for a newspaper, was fired when his book came out—He couldn't be the one doing this… He's maybe seventy-four years old—"

"So what?" Moshe said, "You're seventy-seven, Shimmel, and you can sure shoot….You say this note is from his book?"

"No, no," Gershonovitz said. "There was nothing in Kalman's book about killing. Just the style is the same, also some words… Besides, Kalman's a talker, not a doer. Someone must have gotten his book, copied some pages and became gaga, then went out and shot some young *Arsim*, 'to cleanse the land'…" He stopped, breathing hard.

The rains lashed at the roof.

Moshe said, "What's the book's name?"

"Oh," Munger said, "I remember! *The Ashkenazi Revolution*, no?"

"Yes," Gershonovitz said.

Moshe said, "Who'd publish this kind of garbage?"

"Kalman himself—it was his manifesto for an Ashkenazi party. He said the Eastern Jews suffer from genetic inferiority… so if Ashkenazim mix with them, it would sunder the state—"

"An Ashkenazi *Mein Kampf*," Moshe said.

Munger yelped, "Bite your tongue!"

"You bite yours."

Chief Levitan seemed to shake himself and become a policeman again. "Anyone have a copy of Kalman's book that this madman is using as a Bible?"

Head shakes all around.

Gershonovitz said, "Moshe, get me the list of the men who came in from Beirut last week—" He breathed hard.

Levitan said, "Came for what?"

"Later," Gershonovitz said. "First things first. Moshe, Ehud is in HQ now? For the ampoules?"

Moshe nodded.

"I want to talk to him…."

Moshe cocked his head. "How d'you know it's not him?"

Chief Levitan said, "That's Reznik's son? From the chocolate factory?"

"Yes. No, it's not him, I know his father."

Moshe said, "Or me? Could be."

"Nah. I know yours, too, also you're only half a *Schwartze*."

"So what? Mad is mad."

The men looked at each other, then at the cadaver.

Klinger said, "What about Amnon? He also learned from Munger, years ago. Right?"

Munger's eyes were large and wet. Slowly he nodded.

Gershonovitz shook his head. "Couldn't be him. He's an *Ars'* son of *Ars*."

"So?" Klinger said, "Maybe he's gone crazy. Three times psych ward, you said."

"Don't be an idiot." Moshe pointed to the cadaver. "This wasn't done by some madman killing his brothers, this was done by a *vooz-vooz* …."

He paused. The unsaid words "like you" rang in the air.

No one spoke.

Moshe addressed Gershonovitz. "What else did this *vooz-vooz* Nazi write in his *Mein Kampf*?"

Munger uttered a choked cry. No one looked at him.

Gershonovitz breathed in, out. "He wanted Israel to make sure Eastern Jews couldn't vote… disallow mixed marriages…. He also wanted to make Yiddish the official language, stop teaching Hebrew…. Too close to Arabic, he said…. Yiddish was the language of culture…."

"That's all?" Moshe said drily, "No ovens for us *Arsim*? No checking of bloodline purity?"

Gershonovitz's face got redder. Munger choked. Levitan stayed silent.

Moshe hissed, "Fucking *vooz-vooz* Nazi… I'd do him for free…." He tilted his head, "Shimmel, you don't think someone ought to speak to him? Maybe he has little Nazi disciples?"

Chief Levitan said, "No one talks to him anymore, not even his wife. But sure." He looked at Klinger, who nodded, lips tight.

There was a general stirring. Gershonovitz was wheezing in spurts.

Moshe said, "Shimmel, where's your inhaler?"

Gershonovitz took it out, pumped on it.

Levitan said, "Shimmel, we got to catch this madman before he leaves more notes. If Begin hears one of your guys is killing off his *Schwartze* voters…"

Moshe turned to him, "You sure you don't want to bring Amzaleg in to help—"

"Goddamit, yes I am sure!"

"Alright, alright."

Without speaking, the four men marched to the door, Munger trailing.

"Just curious," Moshe said to Levitan. "Why didn't you fire this Amzaleg if you think he's so bad?"

Levitan said, "No."

"But why not?"

"He's a sergeant, it'd go to the Policemen's Union, half are *Schwartze* like him—" Levitan growled. "He'll open his mouth in a hearing, this crazy note comes out…. No, no. Better to keep Amzaleg where we can keep an eye on him."

Moshe shrugged. "I'd like to meet him."

"No!" said Gershonovitz.

"Why?"

"You don't need to know."

Sunday, October 11, 2:05 p.m.,
Tel Aviv

IN THE CRUISER, Chief Levitan said to Klinger without preamble, "Call Amzaleg again."

After a minute Klinger hung up. "No answer."

They drove on in silence. Presently Levitan snarled, "And I want Amzaleg's phone tapped, also the phone of this old hooker he used to fuck... runs a hair salon, in case he uses her phone."

Klinger said, "You'll sign for it?"

"No, go to the judge on call and he'll give you a warrant. Tell him it's security, he'll jump."

Klinger said, "Maybe also the phones in the grocery store, also the public phone in the HaTikva market—"

"Whatever you want, but don't do a whole production. I want it quick."

Just before they arrived at Police HQ, Klinger said to him, "Listen, Amzaleg's daughter goes to Tel Baruch beach with these HaTikva hookers. We can pick her up, explain to him what'll happen to his *Freha* if he opens his trap, doesn't obey orders—"

Levitan, his foot on the cruiser's step, paused, gave a terse nod. "I didn't hear anything."

Then he strode straight in, not even returning the desk-man's salute.

All the way back to Dizengoff station, Klinger whistled a Chassidic tune.

Monday, October 12, 9:50 a.m.,
HaTikva Quarter

NEXT MORNING, AMZALEG called Ehud Reznik again. This time the phone was picked up.

"So why d'you think it's one of us?" Ehud said, after Amzaleg had told him what he was after.

If Ehud was surprised at the call, he did not betray it.

Amzaleg said, "The MO, the weapon—" He went on, explaining, not mentioning the note.

Ehud said, "Could also be someone in the Mossad or the Shin Bet. Not just us."

Amzaleg recalled Munger's training session at the morgue and Shafrir's words. He said to Ehud, "So now these guys are doing *dreck* for you too?"

Ehud said nothing, but he didn't hang up.

Amzaleg went on. "Shafrir told me Shimmel is now the Unit's boss, and everyone is up north, in Beirut, doing it wholesale. You too?"

Ehud said, "You went to see Shafrir in his loony bin? When?"

"Yes, yesterday."

"And he talked to you?"

"Off and on," Amzaleg said. "He's got this, what do you call it? Alzheimer's?"

"Nah, he'd wish. It's Blackness, permanent. And I didn't know he talked."

"Maybe he didn't know who I was."

"Maybe."

There was a short silence.

Amzaleg said, "One day we'll be there, too, maybe."

"Not maybe."

Amzaleg clicked his pen open, discreetly. "So there are Mossad and Shin Bet guys there also? You have a list of names of—"

"No fucking way, Amnon. You're no longer in."

Amzaleg persisted, "Or if anyone has gone so crazy he could... you know, do it here too—"

Ehud snapped, "Every one of us could. Every fucking one."

And then he finally hung up.

-11-

Tuesday, October 13, 1981,
Village of Elyachin, 30 miles North of Tel Aviv

THE THIRD, "ELYACHIN" murder victim was finally discovered on Tuesday, October 13.

He was discovered by chance—and it was yet again chance that led Amzaleg to hear of it before others did, just as he'd heard of the first two.

A boy from the Yemenite village of Elyachin found the body in an almond grove, ran to the village and called the police. One of the policemen whom Amzaleg had called the day before got the call and called Amzaleg. And so Amzaleg managed to arrive early and ask a few questions.

Superintendent Klinger, on the other hand, learned of the murder only two hours later. And once he'd arrived, Amzaleg had already come and gone.

Since Amzaleg only copied the killer's note, Klinger could bring the note to Chief Levitan. However Amzaleg had also talked to another boy who had been solicited first by the killer and refused. That boy described the motorcycle helmet of the man who had spoken to him, as well as the motorcycle, and also specified the time they spoke.

Amzaleg noted it all down and tried to find a connecting thread between the times of the killings. But since he did not know the exact time of the second killing, it did not yet help.

-12-

Tuesday, October 13, 10:05 a.m., Unit HQ near Jerusalem

AFTER EHUD HAD hung up on Amzaleg, he called Gershonovitz and reported the call.

Gershonovitz was incensed. "What did that donkey Amnon want?"

"He's looking into the killing of that drug dealer and asked for the names of Anons now active." Ehud paused. "But he's not active anymore in the Unit, so I didn't tell him—"

"You did right. How long since you'd last heard from him, before today?"

Ehud began to feel irate. "What is it about, Shimmel? This drug dealer was offed last week, Amnon said it had all the marks of a Unit hit. Did you have anything—"

"Just answer the question!"

Ehud said he hadn't heard from Amzaleg for three years.

"So why'd you talk to him at all, now?"

"Fuck it, Shimmel, why not? He was in the Unit once.... And he'd just gone to see Shafrir, so he knows about Beirut...."

Gershonovitz cursed fluently, then stopped. "Listen up, Ehud. From this moment you owe him nothing. Understand? Nothing. And don't call him. If he calls you, don't answer. Leave it to me. I'll handle it." Gershonovitz breathed in, out. "Did you ask Ronen in Beirut to call me?"

"Yes, but what's all this about? This dead *Ars* drug dealer, who did he work for? What is—"

"I told you, leave this alone! End."

Ehud hung up, seething.

What had gotten into Shimmel? Had he lost it? Or maybe the old man was getting the Blackness? If so, he'd have to report it. But to whom?

Gershonovitz hung up the car phone and cursed again, methodically.

"None of your business," he said to Moshe, who, in the rearview mirror, had raised his eyebrows. Then he called Levitan's private line.

"Put the scrambler on," he said, then tersely told him about Amzaleg's call to Ehud.

Before he'd finished, Levitan interrupted, saying that Amzaleg had also gone to the second murder site, how he heard of it he didn't know. "I'll have his balls!"

Gershonovitz said, "Can you suspend him? He's a floater now—he's not supposed to stick his nose into things—"

Moshe said, "Lower your voice, Shimmel, you'll get a heart attack."

"Shut up and drive," Gershonovitz said. In his ear, Levitan was saying he really wished he could. "Any suspension, this fucking police union will stick their nose in, half of them now are *Arsim*, you can't talk to them anymore like human beings...."

"Well, do something about him because if you won't, I will, and I have enough on my head."

"Don't worry," Levitan said. "I'll handle him."

"And don't tell me not to worry. I want to, I'll worry...." He hung up, angry at himself for his behavior.

This damn Amzaleg, sticking his nose into things again.... He heard his own heavy breathing and pulled out a cigarette.

Moshe said, "Put it back, Shimmel. I'll take you home, you should grab a Valium, go rest. You have a Heads of Services meeting on Sunday, they'll eat you alive if you talk like this."

Gershonovitz glared at him but put away the cigarette.

Moshe said, "What's this with the dead *Ars*?"

"I'll tell you later, maybe."

"So you don't trust me and Ehud all of a sudden?"

"I don't trust anyone now. Just drive."

"Okay, okay," Moshe snapped. "Okay. Lie back, relax."

Discretely he disconnected the radiophone.

-13-

B Y LATE THURSDAY afternoon Amzaleg realized he wasn't making
headway. When he tried to call other old Anons he'd known, no one
was home, and those who answered some phones said the men he had asked
for were on Reserve Service.

All of them? Killing Arabs wholesale in Beirut, as Shafrir had said?

Why? For what reason?

From the station he called an Arab Druze he knew in the town of
Shfar'am, a border guard sergeant he used to have coffee with. After some
chitchat, he asked the man if he had done Reserve Service recently.

The man growled, "Sure."

"Up north too?"

Looking for smugglers, that is.

"Some."

Amzaleg waited. "If I wanted to ask about it, who should I ask?"

The Druze said, "What exactly would you ask about?"

Amzaleg switched into colloquial Arabic. "Merchandise coming from
the north, who brings it?"

"The cigarettes?"

"Yes," Amzaleg said. "But also the other thing, new."

"Ah, yes." The Druze sniffed twice, audibly.

Amzaleg blinked. Drugs. "Who brings them in?"

"I do not know who," the Druze said. "No one does. New people maybe."

Amzaleg drove back home in the rain, thinking about the new smugglers, the unknowns who brought the new shit in. Who could they be? And how could they do this so easily?

The Code was iron-strict: Only the eleven *Adonim* could do big business, of which drugs was one. Yet these new ones ignored this. Who were they?

And more intriguing still: who was giving them local cover here?

-14-

ON THE WAY back from the station, the cruiser's wipers did not work, and Amzaleg drove at a snail's pace, peering sideways, and so he nearly missed it, an altercation at the foot of the Wadi bridge. A man and a woman struggling, the man's angry voice wafting up.

Cursing with fatigue, he stepped on the brake, parked on the road's bank and stumbled out.

The rain kept falling and the road's embankment was slick with sliding mud all the way down to the Wadi bed, where the man was banging the woman over the head.

Still cursing, Amzaleg slid down the muddy slope. He nearly made it, but at the last moment slipped and landed on his left side. In a rage he got up. "Enough!" he roared. "Go home!"

The man yelped and raised a muddy fist. There was a glint. Without thinking, Amzaleg raised his arms, already crossed, grabbed the wrist from below and twisted. There was a scream, then the beam of a passing car delineated everything: the young woman, the man, the brown-black puddles, the rain.

"Don't move!" Amzaleg roared.

The girl was trying to skitter away, her black skirt flashing in the passing headlights, her heels making sucking sounds. She tried to rise, slid, finally gave up and lay whimpering, her hair in a puddle.

"Hey, you! Stop!"

The man, on all fours, was scooting away toward the concrete bridge. Amzaleg lunged at him, but the man tumbled into the splashing flowing mud, then Amzaleg heard the squish-squish of his shoes as the man stumbled up the other Wadi bank.

A passing headlight lit his face, and Amzaleg saw it was the pickpocket cantor.

"Go home!" Amzaleg shouted after him.

He bent down and picked up a cheap sailors' jackknife, then wiped it on his pants.

He felt the water streaming down his face, his shirt, his shoes.

The girl whimpered in the mud.

"Your client or your pimp?"

She said nothing, and, stumbling alongside, he helped her up the slope.

Only in the fuller light he saw she was Pirchiya, Nachum's sister.

"What you doing here?" he rasped. "I thought you don't do this anymore."

She shook her head, shivering.

"Come inside the car or you'll die of pneumonia."

"What do you care?" she said.

"Yalla, go in, go in." Roughly he pushed her into the driver's seat. Once inside, he put on the heat at full blast and got in too. She sat curled, shivering, brown mud coalescing at her feet.

He pulled out his notebook. "You want to lodge a complaint?"

Mutely she shook her head and he looked at her, his heart churning.

Last time he had seen her was at Jacqueline's. She now seemed older, with hair plastered to her neck and ears. Then he saw it was not shivering—she was crying.

"Why? What?" Amzaleg said. "What'd he want from you?"

"He keeps asking me to work for him, he needs money for the shit…. He can't get any…."

"Don't worry. He won't anymore."

She whimpered. "No, don't arrest him, he'll die in jail like my older brother, they're all dying from drugs…."

"He shouldn't use, then…."

"So what else can he do? He can't work, his hands shake...." She sniffled, then sneezed like a child. "He and Nachum used to play soccer, also worked sometimes for *Adon* Leon...."

"Enough," Amzaleg said, "enough with this. I'll take you wherever you want." Then without knowing why, he added, "You want coffee, something?"

She nodded miserably. "Yes."

"I'll take you home."

"No!" She clutched at his hand. "Please, no."

"So where?"

She shook her head. She didn't know.

"Alright, come."

He draped his tunic over her shoulders but she could not stop shivering. Only when they were climbing the steps to his tiny flat, inside the dark hallway, she stopped.

"Is Zohara home?" she asked in a small voice.

"No," he said.

She nodded fitfully, and they went in, his heart thumping.

-15-

I N THE MORNING she said into his shoulder, "I don't know, Amnon, maybe it's a sin, he died only a few days ago...."

The *Shiva* week was barely over.

Amzaleg said, "I'll take the sin on myself."

He still could not believe it, dazed with the feelings waking up inside him.

"No, on me, I don't have as many as you...."

He thought he could read it in her eyes: those sins you acquired by what you did in the army, for everyone, perhaps also what you got demoted for...

It was the first time he realized they all understood. It surprised him how big a pang it gave him.

She made him an omelet, tea instead of coffee, watched him eat; he watched her. Both feeling awkward, then not. As if it was normal all of a sudden, though he knew it wasn't.

On the way to the station, he drove her to the hair salon, even though it was only one street away.

Jacqueline could see it on them immediately. She seemed to age ten years before his eyes but said nothing. Sigalit eyed them with yellow eyes.

Zohara was nowhere to be seen.

-16-

GERSHONOVITZ WOKE ON Friday before dawn, stuck his middle finger at the ceiling and scowled.

He didn't like what he had to do, but it had to be done.

To prevent his plans from being revealed too soon to the cabinet, some of whom might leak them, he had to learn who the agent was that the Mossad had near Rahman. And for this he had to talk to the Mossad's chief, away from prying eyes and ears.

Half an hour later, he made his way out through the building's rear into the street behind. A gray Lark with a dipole antenna was already waiting, Moshe at the wheel.

Gershonovitz got in. On the back seat lay a bulging side pack.

"It's all inside?" he asked.

Moshe nodded. "Yeah, half the town of Bnei Brak I had to search for it. Don't ask."

"Alright, let's go, let's go. We gotta be there by seven o'clock."

The traffic at such an early hour was sparse, so forty-five minutes later the car climbed the Valley Gate mountain pass near Jerusalem.

"Slow down," Gershonovitz said. "It's close by."

Burnt trucks left over from the 1948 war dotted the narrow shoulders; then he saw it: a whitewashed metal skeleton of an ancient jeep near a copse of pines, a black mark on its side.

"Here, stop here."

As the Lark pulled over, Gershonovitz dug a gray Motorola clicker from the glove compartment and stuck it in his pocket. "Wait until I change."

He lifted the bulging side pack from the back and disappeared behind the pine grove.

In a few minutes he was back, dressed in a black silk caftan, long black socks and black shoes, on his head a round fur hat of the ultra-Orthodox, and on his stomach the wide cloth belt.

He threw the side pack with his clothes into the back seat.

Moshe said. "Where's your beard?"

"Quiet. I have it."

Gershonovitz pulled a black furry false beard and put it on, pressing on the sticky tape. "And if you say anything, I'll break your balls."

He felt ridiculous but he could not take a chance to be seen anywhere with Asa ben-Shlomo, the Mossad chief. Not only Kadishevitz, but cabinet members, too, had spies everywhere.

Moshe said, "Nah, come here." He adjusted the beard. "And you need to wear the hat tilted at the back. Here, let me."

Gershonovitz muttered, "How do you know? You're a *Schwartze*."

"I told you, only on my father's side. My mother's a Polack *vooz-vooz*. Now don't move."

Grumpily Gershonovitz let his fur hat be adjusted, then turned and walked up the narrow trail through the pines, taking deep breaths of the mountain air, clomping over wild oregano and sage.

This is my last time defending the Jews against the Damn HolyName, he thought. *Then I'm done.*

His watch showed a minute after seven. The sun was up over the faraway ridge. Here and there, fat pine cones lay about, glistening in the early light, their pungent smell overlaid by an odor of smoke.

As the smoke crept into his consciousness, his right hand went to the gun at his back and his left went to the clicker in his pocket. But just then the simian figure of Asa ben-Shlomo came up the trail, dressed in a black silk caftan similar to his own and wearing the wide-brimmed fur hat of an ultra-Orthodox Jew. A cigarette dangled between his lips, ash sprayed the reddish-gray beard.

Gershonovitz clicked the safety back on and nodded at the Mossad's chief, who nodded in return.

They walked awhile in silence. Finally Asa said, "So what's the big rush, Shimmel? To meet in this ridiculous disguise, away from the city? Maybe you did something you shouldn't have done?"

Gershonovitz grunted. "I just thought it's better we talk before the next Varash Heads of Services meeting, away from cabinet spies.... And just in case anyone sees us, we're here on a religious duty...."

The ultra-Orthodox often roamed the Jerusalem hills looking for nesting birds, to chase away the mother and take away the hatchlings or the eggs, to fulfill an obscure duty mentioned in the Bible.

Asa said, "So it's a good deed we're doing here? Or a sin?"

Gershonovitz did not answer, and silence fell as the two men watched the sparrows twittering and flitting between the pines. High overhead, two dots streaked north, toward Lebanon.

Gershonovitz said, "Who's got agents in Latakia now?"

"Ah." Asa stared intently at the sparrows. "Why?"

"Just asking."

Asa addressed the sparrows. "He's just asking." Then he threw his head back. "Well, fuck me in the ass! You planning to have a guy go there? To send some Syrian Flathead to a better world?"

"No, no. Not without the cabinet's permission—"

"So who's the target?"

Gershonovitz clicked his tongue. "I didn't say take down. I—I'm—sending someone to talk to—somebody over there, about—something."

Asa addressed a sparrow. "He's sending someone, to talk to somebody in Latakia. About something." He raised his voice. "Talk to who? About what?"

Gershonovitz said into the horizon, "You heard I had a—a little trouble before Yom Kippur? With my guys in Beirut?"

"Yeah? What trouble?"

"They said—they said they can't take this anymore, it's too much. Can you imagine?"

"Yeah? Well, Yaro said they work a lot of overtime now in Beirut. So what? We all do."

Gershonovitz said, "They said they want to know what's at the end of this job, they can't do it wholesale anymore."

"So you told them to fuck off and just do it?"

"Tell who? It was all of them—Yaro didn't tell you this part? They got organized."

"No, haven't seen him for weeks—" The Mossad's chief paused, gave Gershonovitz an oblique glance. "Don't tell me he organized this? I don't believe it. He's a good boy, always does what he's told—"

"No, not him, someone else organized it."

Asa slapped his own backside. "Don't tell me. Ehud Reznik."

"Yeah."

"Well fuck me in the ass...."

Gershonovitz said, "Damn peaceniks, they all want others to do the *dreck* so they can afford a conscience...." He breathed heavily, then went on, "Well, Ehud at least still does what he's told."

Asa waited. "Nu? You didn't tell them they're doing this to hold off the fucking invasion? We let the army go in, we'll be stuck there for twenty years—"

"Yeah, yeah, I told them, I told them, but... I couldn't tell them there's more."

Asa's tone turned sarcastic. "That you're sending someone to talk to somebody about something?"

Gershonovitz nodded.

Asa snapped, "But talk to whom? And why?"

Gershonovitz plugged one nostril and sniffed his knuckles, demonstrably. There was a short silence.

Asa said, "No. No, no, no. I don't believe this. He approached us? Rahman? The guy whose drugs we let through, the guy who gives us cover and information? Him? The Syrian president's brother?"

Gershonovitz shrugged. "Yeah, him."

"But why do you want to send someone—"

Asa stopped, his eyes got large. "No! Don't tell me. He wants us to help him do a putsch? Get his brother's throne? I don't believe this. No, no, no…."

Gershonovitz kept silent, just shrugged.

Asa pondered. "So it's him? It's Rahman you're sending someone to talk to?"

A nod.

Asa's brows contracted. "So Rahman contacted us, asked for help? No, no. I don't believe this. He sits in the south, has all the money he needs, all the pussy, his generals getting rich—why does he need the headache, to take on his brother—"

"I didn't say he contacted us."

"So who made the contact on his behalf? Not the Americans?"

"No, no, the French did."

There was a pause, then Asa thumped his own forehead, "No, wait. It wasn't Rahman's idea, you gave it to him. It was your idea!"

Gershonovitz shrugged, as if disclaiming a compliment.

Asa marveled, "So you got the bright idea to help make him führer of Syria, so he'd do for us what Arik wants for us in Lebanon, only better? Sign peace? And you want to see if he'd bite?" Asa stopped. "And Arik knows?"

Gershonovitz nodded.

"Kiddush?"

"Also."

"And Arik won't leak it?"

Gershonovitz said, "If he does, Begin will take his head off. On this he won't be afraid to."

Asa nodded, slowly. There was no need to say more: PM Begin, the man who had signed peace with Egypt, now wanted to also sign peace with Syria.

History would write him up in letters of fire. If.

Asa sucked air through his teeth. "How long they gave you? A year?"

"Nine months." Gershonovitz raised two hands, three fingers each. "Six months left."

Asa's eyes got a faraway look. "So that's why you wanted to know if we have an agent near Rahman? So I won't learn about this on the side and tell the cabinet?"

Gershonovitz gave a diagonal nod.

Asa gave a dry chuckle. "Also ask the agent to help convince him, maybe?"

Gershonovitz said, "Possibly."

Asa said, "Let's go over there and sit down. You can see all the way to Jerusalem."

Together they shuffled up the narrow trail that slowly widened, thorny saltwort and reddish autumn crocuses dotting its margins, until it ended in a rock that broke over a chasm overgrown with bellflowers; and there, beyond the valley, lay Jerusalem, gold and beige and luminous.

The two old spooks sat a little apart and watched the faraway city together.

At last Asa gave a sigh. "Yeah, we do have—someone—fairly close to him, in Latakia."

Another silence settled.

Still looking at the faraway city, Gershonovitz said, "So I said to myself I should talk to you, in case you have someone there, he sees my guy visiting… then who knows who in the cabinet hears about it, and it leaks, and it all goes *fakakt*...."

And all of a sudden Gershonovitz became voluble. "I thought, even if Rahman says yes, if I bring this to the cabinet the first thing they're going to ask is how sure I am he'll go through with it? And I'll have to tell them I don't know. So they'd ask, why don't you send someone, look him in the eye? So before they even ask, I am sending someone to see if we can take a chance...." He paused. "It's my idea, not his, not ours, not official, so if it doesn't work it's my fat ass."

Asa's eyes were distant. "And Rahman said yes? To the meeting?"

A nod.

Asa pursed his lips. "Who you're sending? Young Reznik?"

"Yeah."

Asa pondered. "Who else knows, among your guys?"

"Besides Ehud? Only Moshe, who watches my back. No one else."

Asa opened his mouth, closed it, then spoke through pursed lips.

"I—I got someone close to Rahman some time ago, almost by chance.

We run the agent and share his stuff with others in case the—agent—tells us something they should know."

Gershonovitz said, "So who's the agent?"

Asa shook his head. "No."

Gershonovitz flushed. "If we can't convince Rahman to do this, the entire army will go in, clean up the Palestinian camps by hand, shack to shack.... Half our troops will come back in body bags...."

Asa raised his beard's edge to his mouth, chewed on it pensively.

Gershonovitz said, "Alright, so don't tell me his name. But maybe he can help at least convince Rahman to do this...."

Asa let his wet beard drop. "Maybe."

Gershonovitz waited. "So who's the agent?"

Asa shook his head with emphasis. "No."

"So how will Reznik know who to look for when he gets there?"

Asa snapped, "He won't know, because it's none of his fucking business to look for the agent."

There was a longer pause.

Gershonovitz said, "At least what's the agent's Recog Code, so Reznik will know? Just in case?"

"No!"

Gershonovitz waited. "Asa, I beg of you... he's going there alone... I know his father...."

"No." Then Asa seemed to relent, "Alright, alright, alright." He bent over and with his fingernail scratched two faint digits on the ground: Five one.

Quickly he rubbed off the number with his foot.

Gershonovitz nodded and lit a cigarette. "And in the meantime your agent could help convince Rahman we can help make him top dog? And get him American recognition...."

"Maybe," Asa said. "With the HolyName's help."

Gershonovitz spit and Asa ignored it.

They walked on. At last Gershonovitz said, "When's the next Varash meeting?"

"Wednesday, next week. If you want, say you're sick, then no one can ask you anything."

"No, I want to be there."

They began to descend. The last few hundred feet of the trail were hard. Gershonovitz pumped his inhaler. They were almost at the bottom as a cloud of white butterflies flew past.

Asa said, "And how will he finance this coup of his?"

"Leave this to me."

Asa stood immobile.

"How much more drugs you letting him ship?" Asa said, "The Americans will kill you if they find out."

"Fuck them all. They did worse in Vietnam, and so did the French...."

Asa lifted his hand. "I don't want to know any more, Shimmel.... Bah. I wanted to drive to Jerusalem and have some hummus, but I lost my appetite."

They stood for a moment among the pines.

Asa said, "You're mad, Shimmel, you know."

Gershonovitz snapped, "The biggest madman here is Him." He pointed his cigarette upward.

Asa spat with disgust, went down the trail, and was gone.

**Friday, October 16, 1981, 7:15 p.m.,
Tel Aviv Beach, then Tel Aviv**

F RIDAY AFTERNOON, THE girls at the hair salon decided to go to
the Tel Baruch beach. Pirchiya said she would not go and no one tried
to dissuade her. Her recent stay with Amzaleg was something no one talked
about. Zohara at first was not going, following her misadventure last time.
But after some misgivings she decided to join. One fucking *vooz-vooz* boy
wasn't going to make her stay home.

Only this time, Superintendent Klinger was waiting, two of his cro-
nies hiding behind some sand dunes, and once the girls had dispersed and
were engaged in the preliminaries, the policemen pounced and arrested
them all. The clients were let go.

Zohara was reading when the policemen appeared. At first she did not
even notice them.

"Put your hands behind your back, *Freha*," Klinger chortled.

Startled, she pulled out her razor.

At this he pulled out his gun, gleefully. "Sure. I'll be happy to shoot
you. In the leg, then in the other leg. You want? You'll be in bed a year."

When she hesitated he said slyly, "Or I can let you go if you do me
first. Yes?"

The other girls were already in the van, except for Sigalit, who was
doing the two other policemen.

Zohara said, "Eat shit, maniac."

Klinger said it was fine with him, and he'd take her to the station, "Then I'll call your father…."

"No!" Zohara said. "Don't."

"Alright then…." He unzipped his fly. Zohara closed her eyes and put her hand out.

"No, no," he said. "Not with the hand."

She nearly pulled out her blade again but thought of Amzaleg and relented.

But as Klinger was finishing, groaning pleasurably, he muttered, "Oh, how he'll love to hear this…." And then she understood. She began to clench her teeth, biting hard, but he was ready and slammed his pistol over her head. It was clear he was practiced.

She woke up in the station, blood trickling down her temple. Sigalit, too, had blood on her, and apparently was tricked in the same way. Only she also had drips of goo on her chin which had not been completely wiped. She nodded at Zohara, who looked away.

Amzaleg had just left his office when he heard the radiotelephone chirping.

He didn't want to go get it, eager to get home and ask Pirchiya to come over.

Finally he gave in and picked up. It was Klinger.

Amzaleg began to slam the receiver into the receptacle when Klinger said, "You want to come pick up your *Freha?*"

And as Amzaleg's heart froze, the nasal voice said, "We arrested her an hour ago, in Tel Baruch… I'm afraid she is not too good now…."

Amzaleg nearly hit two cars on his way to the Dizengoff station. He parked on the sidewalk in front of Berman's kiosk and ran up the broken steps.

Zohara was seated on the bench with the other girls, her face dark brown, her jaw clenched so hard her mouth was all but invisible.

Klinger was filling the forms. "Ah, Sergeant Amzaleg. Since you are here, why don't you take the hookers to the back—"

Before he could finish, he was on the floor, Amzaleg holding him by the throat, thumb on the larynx, forefinger on the jugular vein.

Zohara said, her voice strangling, "Father, don't."

Amzaleg did not even lift his eyes. "Say your prayers, *vooz-vooz*. Fast."

"Off him, now!" Levitan's voice roared behind him.

Amzaleg looked up. He felt his cheeks sag as the Other took hold.

"NOW, I said!"

Amzaleg said, "You fuckers, was an ambush, eh?"

"You are suspended!" Levitan snarled. "Sunday morning, in my office! Now, out!"

Amzaleg did not get up. "Not without her."

"She stays here," Levitan said.

Amzaleg pressed harder and Klinger made rattling sounds. Levitan advanced but Amzaleg raised an open hand and Levitan stopped.

Amzaleg said, "I'll kill him slowly, I'll say he raped my daughter, talk to all the newspapers, claim battle shock, testify before Judge Fishkin, the papers will—"

"Take your bitch and go!" Levitan hollered. "And you are demoted, too, back to corporal! Out! And I want to see you in my office Sunday at eight! And shave!"

Amzaleg drove Zohara home without a word. She tried to talk once, but he shook his head. When they arrived she got out, turned toward the Sabags' flat across, stopped. Once more she tried to speak, but he again shook his head, slammed the door and parked, got out without looking back.

Only when he was climbing the stairs did she begin to cry, soundlessly.

In Nachum's old room she dug out her emergency hit, closeted herself in the Sabags' tiny washroom, and injected, sticking the needle in so deep the bruise lasted a week.

Next morning she injected again, then began doing two a day, paid for by guarding the girls and by the occasional tug, just to forget her father's silence.

She had never imagined it would hurt so much. Because, after all, she did hate him.

-18-

Saturday, October 17, 8:30 p.m.,
Tel Aviv, HaTikva, then Jerusalem

THE SATURDAY AFTER Amzaleg was demoted again and suspended, the fourth killing was discovered.

It was a double murder, the only one in the series, and one of the victims was an army colonel and an Ashkenazi, also a first.

That evening at eight thirty, a narrow complement of Heads of Services convened in the Shin Bet's interrogation center in Jerusalem.

An hour before, head of the Security Service, Avigdor Feldman, had banged on Amzaleg's door and told him to come, no questions allowed.

"You'll sit there, listen, don't talk," Feldman said. "If you can't keep quiet, you better stay here."

"Alright," Amzaleg said. "Where we going?"

It certainly was a shock. Feldman coming through.

"Shin Bet HQ in Jerusalem."

"You arresting me?" Amzaleg used a jocular tone. "For asking?"

Feldman just threw him a dirty look.

His official Volvo was parked below. Feldman drove, silent all the way. Amzaleg also said nothing, his mind awhirl, like the swirling rain outside.

Was Feldman really coming through? Or was his former cruiser partner about to use him for his own ends, in the guise of paying back a favor?

One never knew with the *shoo-shoo*.

An hour later, when they entered the Shin Bet's secure room, the discussion was in full roar about who should handle the investigation and who should be kept in the know. Police Chief Levitan snarled it was the police's purview, while the head of Military Intel insisted on Mil Intel's field security unit. Asa said mildly that maybe it was best to put together an inter-agency team to look for this serial killer.

At the explicit word, a shudder went through the room.

As Feldman sat down he said, "No team on this. One investigator, and I want all raw data once a week, in my hands."

"But why?" Asa said. "Avigdor, why not a team?"

"Just in case the perp works for one of us...." Feldman paused, letting it sink.

The air thawed a little, then began to heat.

Asa said, "But then who would you use to do the investigation?"

Levitan leaned forward. "Suissa from the Clandestine is good, also Superintendent Klinger...."

"Pff," Feldman said.

Levitan flushed and had the grace to say nothing.

"Here's an idea," Feldman said, "what about Amzaleg?"

Amzaleg kept quiet.

Levitan turned red. "He's in the Jaffa station now. Does Traffic sometimes."

The unsaid words hung in the air. A floater, an old fart.

"And he's retiring soon," Levitan went on. "Now, if you want someone with experience in—"

"He has experience," Feldman said.

"Not the kind we want." A few faces turned in polite, cold inquiry to watch the battle.

Feldman said, "He was in the Unit once, with Shafrir."

Amzaleg watched the faces. None watched him.

Did Feldman bring him just in return for a twenty-year-old favor? Or because none in the room was neutral? But then, was he neutral himself?

"When exactly you retiring, Amnon?" Feldman said.

"June second." Amzaleg kept staring at Levitan until the police chief flushed and turned away.

Asa said, "You think you can finish this by then?"

"I don't know." Amzaleg felt as if his voice came from great depth. "But—I may need a few of Asa's guys to help me check—"

"No," Feldman said. "Only police in this, no *shoo-shoo*."

Asa said. "Avigdor is right. Amnon was once *shoo-shoo*, but he's police now." He turned to Amzaleg. "Amnon, you're a what, now? A Sergeant, again?"

Amzaleg shook his head, avoiding looking at Levitan. "Corporal."

Someone snickered, he could not see who.

Feldman said, "Levitan, can you make him a superintendent again for this investigation?"

There was now a complete silence. Not a paper rustled.

"Alright," said Asa, not waiting for an answer. "Numbered copies to Defense and Interior, one personal to Kiddush at the prime minister's office—" He read out a few code names, phone numbers, number codes.

No one took notes except Feldman. His suggestion, his Op.

With his eyes still on the paperwork, Asa asked Amzaleg, "How's your French?"

"Good," Amzaleg said, and felt himself reddening, as if he'd been shamed.

"And Arabic?"

Amzaleg merely nodded. He waited for the explicit orders, but no one said anything; yet it was clear. He'd have to go to Beirut, to question the men on the quiet.

Later, in the corridor, Asa said to him, "You need me on anything, call me. You hear?"

"I won't need you," Amzaleg said.

"Don't be an *Ars*," said Asa. "I said 'if.'"

Amzaleg went out into the rain. He stood in it, smelling the wet sycamores, watching the clouds through the thin branches, and beyond, the far-off Tower of David sheathed in rain.

At the end of the row of trees, Feldman was seated in his Volvo, Levitan bending over the car window, talking fast and gesticulating.

Amzaleg went around the hood, opened the passenger door, and sat.

Levitan stopped talking.

"*Fir*," Amzaleg said to Feldman in Yiddish. Drive.

Over Feldman's head, Levitan said to Amzaleg, "Come to my office tomorrow to sign the shoulder insignia forms."

"I'll give him my old ones when he comes back," said Feldman. "Don't bother yourself."

"*Fir*," Amzaleg said again.

As Feldman drove off in a splutter of water, Amzaleg saw in the rear-view mirror Chief Superintendent Levitan standing in the downpour, hands on hips, glaring after them.

"You don't have to make enemies on purpose," Feldman said.

"Look who's talking," said Amzaleg.

Saturday, October 18, 9:10 p.m.,
Jerusalem

P M BEGIN RARELY stayed later than six p.m. in his office. That evening he stayed late and asked his Cabinet Secretary, Kadishevitz, to stay late too.

"So, Kiddush, what about this Amzaleg fellow?"

Kadishevitz hesitated.

"A bereaved father," he began. "Was with the commandoes in the war—" Meaning '48, the Independence War.

"So, nu?" Begin said. "We can rely on him to do it quiet, or no?"

Kadishevitz made a face.

"So? Yes or no?" the PM said. "He's got family? Good father?"

"Divorced...."

Begin made a face.

"Has a daughter," the CabSec went on. "His son fell on the Golan in '73." He paused, delicately. "Was with General Kahalani, the son, a tank driver... In the battle over the Valley of Tears...."

"Ah. A hero... And where was the father then? In the police?"

"No. He'd been with the Unit before the police, so he went back in '73 after... after his son fell... did several jobs in Syria... by hand..."

"At his age? How old is he now?"

"Fifty-four."

"And not retired yet?"

"In eight months. But he came back now, because—because we asked him."

"Who asked? Someone who wants this Amzaleg to find out what goes on, or who doesn't?"

Kadishevitz blushed. "I don't know."

There was a pause, a longer one.

"Okay, okay," the PM said. "Now, this Amzaleg, he is old, but still good?"

"Asa says he is, but maybe too good."

The PM seemed alarmed. "What does it mean? What's too good?"

The CabSec seemed embarrassed. "He says Amzaleg sometimes doesn't do what he's told...."

"So? And you do?"

Kadishevitz blushed more deeply.

The PM stared into the distance. "Can he come here, I can talk to him maybe, before I decide?"

The CabSec hesitated.

"Nu?" the PM said. "What?"

A phone rang. The regular black one. Both ignored it. It kept ringing.

Finally Kadishevitz nodded. "Alright, I'll bring him."

As the door closed, the red phone rang. PM Begin stared at it, then, with a sigh, picked up.

"No," he said. "I am not here." He listened a few seconds. "So bring it to the cabinet tomorrow."

He listened some more, then repeated, "To the cabinet. Not to me."

As he hung up he sighed, a sound encompassing a multitude of emotions.

-20-

**Saturday, October 18, 1981, 10:00 p.m.,
HaTikva Quarter**

LATER THAT EVENING, Feldman, the Security Service chief, called Amzaleg at home. Amzaleg was washing the dishes with Pirchiya and so he picked up the phone with a rubber-gloved hand.

"What?"

Feldman's voice barked, "Be in Geula Street tomorrow." Geula Street in Jerusalem was where the prime minister's office was located. "They want to see you first, before you go."

"Who?"

"Who do you think?" Feldman said. "Kiddush's boss, Begin."

Amzaleg blinked and stared at the rain outside, disbelieving.

"What?" Pirchiya said. "Something bad?"

"No."

"Yes," Feldman said, "And don't be late."

Amzaleg stared at the phone in stupefaction, deciding it must have been a joke, Feldman was a notorious joker.

But apparently it wasn't. A half-hour later he received a phone call from Jerusalem. This time he picked up fast.

"Superintendent Amzaleg?" The voice was bland, in Yiddish cadences.

"Yes?"

"This is the prime minister's office. Tomorrow at ten o'clock, you can be here?"

Amzaleg stuttered that he could.

"Excellent. And keep it confidential."

There were murmurs in the background, then the line went dead.

**Friday, October 17, and Saturday, October 18,
Nahariya, then West Beirut**

EHUD AND FIVE others caught the weekly gunboat back to Beirut from Nahariya beach, paddling to it in a naval commandoes' rubber dinghy.

The trip lasted four hours and it was raining hard when the boat arrived at Beirut's aShams beach. It stopped a mile off the coast. One anchor was dropped, and the assassins descended into three rubber dinghies and paddled to shore.

Three cars were waiting at the curb, residents of the regular local Mossad station at the wheels. The assassins dispersed among the cars.

Ehud got into the lead Peugeot. "Any message from Shimmel?"

The driver shook his head.

"So any local news?"

"Arafat is back from Paris."

The Palestinian leader, the chief terrorist.

One of the two Anons behind leaned forward. It was Yaro ben-Shlomo. "Probably went to see his money… My dad says he's got a billion in the bank there. But had to come back to see why so many of his men drop dead for no visible reason…." He cackled.

"Shut up, Yaro," Ehud said. "You got a big mouth."

"What? What did I say?"

"Nothing, you just talk too much." He turned to the driver. "Can you drive faster? We got some *dreck* to do tonight."

The driver spit. "We all got some, you ain't special."

The rain was so thick that the buildings to their right and left were a blur, only the occasional hanging laundry swam into view.

The Peugeot was the first to arrive at the subterranean hideout, aka "the Sub." Zerach, Kadishevitz's nephew, got out and stretched. "Butcher shop station!" he sang out.

"You shut up too," Ehud said.

One by one they went in the low door past the street junk, past a donkey's cadaver, into the old building with the bullet-pocked facade. A few feet inside the entrance door was a steel one. A camera whined as they approached and the steel door opened on hydraulics.

Inside, the light was low, the narrow corridor smelling of rot and dust. Far off a phone trilled, a scrambler sound.

Ehud said, "Oh yeah, this reminds me, I need you all to let me know where you went in Tel Aviv, and when, until you got back on the boat."

"Why?" said Tzafi. "Does Shimmel think one of us offed this drug dealer?"

"Maybe," Ehud said. "I don't know."

"Why maybe?"

But Ehud had enough. "Because the fucker who did this left a note, that's why."

Just then the inner doors opened, and they went into the main hall.

"What note?" Yaro said.

"Nothing, nothing. Forget it. Just fucking do your jobs and get me these lists."

I must really be tired, Ehud thought, *to blab like this.*

He walked in, bent under the weight of the poison ampoules' box.

-22-

Sunday, October 18, 1981, 9:00 a.m., Jerusalem

SUNDAY MORNING, STILL half-asleep, Amzaleg drove again to Jerusalem.

The prime minister's office was a large ornate building of Jerusalemite stone, built by an Arab architect and confiscated during the 1948 war. Amzaleg had never been there although he had seen it often in passing. To his surprise, he was let in without having to show any documents and was led through a narrow corridor to an anteroom.

Outside it had been cold, but the anteroom was so warm that Amzaleg, tight and uncomfortable in his police uniform, began to fan himself after ten minutes.

He felt dazed and had to stop himself from touching his shiny new rank insignia.

The sudden turn of fortune seemed almost like a joke.

"His wife has asthma," the woman at the telephone switchboard said, "so he told us to keep the heat up. But you can wait in the other room with the guards, if you want."

"No, no. I'll wait here."

Though small, it was a high-ceilinged room of the type often found in Jerusalem in houses that had belonged long ago to prominent Arab families who had fled in 1948. A silk carpet depicting a rabbi draped in a shawl had been pinned to the wall. Underneath was an oak table displaying a caravan of hand-carved camels made of olive wood, the kind of chichi Judaica one could find in any tourist shop.

"He chose it himself," the switchboard operator said, when she saw Amzaleg looking. "His wife liked it too. You like it?"

"Yah."

Amzaleg's head ached. People came and went through the anteroom. A group of American Jews shuffled in, led by a white-suited old man chattering in rapid broken English.

"He is in?" the man asked the operator.

Before she had a chance to reply, the door to the PM's office opened, and the PM's Cabinet Secretary peeked out. "In a minute!" he snapped at Amzaleg. Then he disappeared inside.

All the Americans, as one, stared at Amzaleg. Two matrons began to move in his direction, but just then the door opened again and Begin's Cabinet Secretary came out.

"Come, come." He caught Amzaleg by the hand and pulled him to his feet. "I'm Kadishevitz. Five minutes I can give you with him."

Hooking an arm around Amzaleg's hip, the man pushed him through the door.

"Inspector Amzaleg," he said, like some majordomo. "From the police."

Amzaleg mumbled, "Superintendent." He felt himself flushing.

The PM, emaciated and pale and unshaven, in a white nylon shirt, was writing in capital letters on a large foolscap page, using a fat red pen.

"He gives the speech at two," Kadishevitz said to Amzaleg, "and it's still not ready."

Begin raised his eyes. Through the bifocals, his eyes were as large as a cow's. But the narrow bloodless lips were those of a smaller animal.

"Sir," said the Cabinet Secretary, "this is the policeman who'll investigate the murders we had talked about, of the *Schwartzes*."

At once the PM stopped writing. "This one? I thought he was younger."

Amzaleg felt hot and choking. "I am fifty-four, sir—"

"You listen here, Inspector," Begin began in a stentorian voice. "This is a most delicate matter. Most delicate." He looked at his aide. "You can leave us alone to talk for a while, Kadishevitz?"

The aide said, "I'll come back soon, sir."

When the door closed after him, the PM folded his small splotched hands and stared at Amzaleg with his large cow eyes. "At fifty-four years of age, why do you need this?"

Amzaleg said, "The first victim was a classmate of my son, so I looked into his murder, then when the second happened—"

"Yes, yes." The PM waved his thin hand. "Unfortunately even more were killed, yes." The fingernails, Amzaleg saw, were bitten nearly to the quick. "Every day I hear from Asa, from Shimmel, Levitan, Feldman—I said to them, tell this policeman to find the killer, but on the quiet, we can't let this thing grow—"

"I can't promise quiet," Amzaleg said. "If I find the killer, I'll tell you.... It may not be quiet...."

"Yes, that's what Feldman said you'd say."

There was a pause.

Amzaleg blurted, "Why are you sending me? You want to find him or not?"

He was surprised at himself, talking to the PM like this.

But the PM did not seem offended, just watched him. "You are not a Polack by any chance?"

Amzaleg felt his cheeks tighten. "I was born in Morocco—"

"Because that's what a Polish officer would say. There's honor. You look for the killer. Then if you find him you can't lie and say you didn't." The dark cow eyes drilled into Amzaleg. "Sit, sit."

Amzaleg sat down. He felt the sweat trickle down his back.

"It's a problem. A big problem." Begin shook the red pen in Amzaleg's face, as if scolding him.

The Cabinet Secretary's head poked through the door, then vanished.

Begin said, "Kiddush, Shimmel, Levitan, all say no. Don't send him. Nobody wants you asking questions there. Only Feldman wants to send you. Why do you think that is?"

Amzaleg's throat hurt. "You know why, sir... they're afraid it'll bring on the invasion…. Some want it to happen, others don't…." He felt himself flush with his impudence but went on. "I don't care about all this. If I find the killer, I'll tell you, whatever the outcome, even if it's one of the Anons…."

Begin raised a hand, closed his eyes. "No, no. This is for Shimmel to arrange." His face contorted. "Listen, Inspector, you don't know what it means—" Then the face smoothed out. "Alright. You go to Beirut to find out who's doing it to the *Schwartzes*, but on one condition. When you finish, you call Kiddush and tell him first, before anybody else." The PM paused, then added improbably, "*Schwartze* or Ashkenazi, we are all Jews first, I really believe that."

Amzaleg swallowed bile. "Yes we are."

The door was pushed open and the Cabinet Secretary came in, ushering the Americans.

Amzaleg got up. His legs felt rubbery. His throat was thick with unswallowed bile. Begin rose, too, and marched forward to shake the proffered hand of the white-suited guide. Over his shoulder he said to Amzaleg, "That's the condition, remember."

Amzaleg nodded and then Begin's aide ushered him out.

"You need something, anything, talk to me," the aide whispered in Amzaleg's ear, then handed him a small card. "Not to Levitan or anyone. Hear? Call me. Direct."

Amzaleg said nothing. The PM's aide vanished.

"Here," said the telephone operator. "You look all sweaty, they all do when they come out." She gave him a motherly grin exposing gold teeth. "You want soda or grapefruit juice? Just tell them in the guard room, they'll give you free."

The guard room was empty.

Outside it was cool. It didn't help.

The phone call to Gershonovitz came from Kadishevitz, right after Amzaleg had left.

"He's going there," said the Cabinet Secretary. "Tomorrow. Oy."

Gershonovitz cursed at length, in Yiddish, then in Polish.

The CabSec asked, "Is he good, this Amzaleg?"

"You don't want to know."

There was a little silence.

The CabSec said, "So you think he'll find who's been killing the *Schwartzes*?"

"I dunno, but he'll sure find out all the rest."

"Oy yoy."

Gershonovitz said, "It's not as if Begin doesn't know who's helping us there…"

"He knows and he doesn't want to know."

"… or what we let him do in exchange…."

"This, no. This he doesn't."

There was some more silence, suffused with a crackle of the scrambler.

The CabSec said, "You can't catch him before he goes, this Amzaleg, explain to him? Keep him here, somehow?"

Gershonovitz said, "No, not him, not in this."

"Why not?"

Gershonovitz gave a click of the tongue. "His son fell in 1973, so he went into Syria, did five takedowns, became a bit crazy when he came out… had to go into the psych ward…." He breathed heavily. "Also, the first *Schwartze* killed in HaTikva was a friend of his son…."

There was another pause.

The CabSec said heavily, "You do what you can, Shimmel."

"Yes."

"But Begin must not know anything of this."

"No, no."

Gershonovitz waited, but this apparently was all. "Alright, Kiddush, I'll let you know—"

"No, I don't want to know either."

The line went dead.

Gershonovitz stared at the wall map, got up, walked about from one end of his office to the other, sat down again. He opened the safe at the corner, pulled out Amzaleg's file, and took out a newspaper page from four years before. A photo showed Amzaleg looking at a line of demonstrators. His face showed clearly.

Gershonovitz gave a deep rasping sigh and went into the corridor to the copying machine. Two giggling girl soldiers were photocopying some article from a women's magazine. He waited patiently until they finished, copied Amzaleg's photo, pulled out a blank sheet from the paper tray, then went back to his office.

He sighed again, pulled a pair of latex gloves from the drawer and put them on. Then he pulled a plain brown envelope from another drawer, stuck in the photocopy, spread the page on his desk and began to write in French in standard "square" script. It didn't take long. When he was done he inserted both sheets into the envelope, sealed it, pressing on it with his gloved fingers.

When he pressed the buzzer, Moshe came up within five seconds.

"What?" he said, peering at the fat man's face. "The inhaler not good?"

"It's good, it's good. I need something delivered." He handed Moshe the envelope.

"What is it?"

Moshe eyed the file on the desk.

"None of your business. Take the envelope to this church in Jaffa, put it in the collection box inside, in the slot where they put money in."

Moshe said nothing.

Gershonovitz said, "And keep your big mouth shut. Not one word from you."

Moshe nodded once, his jaw clenched.

"And before you go, put on some tourist clothes so you look like a pilgrim, someone not from here."

Moshe was halfway to the door. "Maybe put lye on my skin too?"

"Shut up. There are brown tourists too."

After Moshe had left, Gershonovitz put Amzaleg's file back in the safe, then looked up at the ceiling and gave a deep sigh, almost a rattle. "*M'darf,*" he said in Yiddish. Has to be done.

Putting the inhaler into his mouth, he took a deep draw, then shifted his gaze further up. "And fuck You," he whispered. "I'll stop Your war yet."

It was four-fifteen when Moshe came back. "I should kill you with my own hands," he said, "before someone else does."

"No you won't," Gershonovitz said. "Only He will."

-23-

**Monday, October 19, 1981, 8:00 a.m.,
Israel, then Lebanon's Biqaa, then West Beirut**

AMZALEG LEFT HATIKVA for Beirut next morning, taking the bus to Nahariya, the northernmost town. At the Military Intel camp, a chain-smoking lieutenant was already waiting under the sentry booth's awning, a carpet of cigarette stubs around his boots, a jeep parked nearby under a eucalyptus tree.

They drove up the coastal road, a narrow corniche running between cliffs high above the foggy beach. Rain spattered the jeep's canvas top, the little engine revving in high gear as they climbed up the northern slope. A little after ten o'clock they arrived at the tank maintenance depot of Rosh HaNikra. Tarpaulined tanks sat in the huge yard like so many carcasses in an embalming center.

"They'll send someone soon," the lieutenant said after depositing Amzaleg in the empty canteen. "You want a newspaper? Something?"

"No," Amzaleg said. "But if you have a cigarette—" He flushed. Bumming a smoke from an underpaid army guy.

"Sure," said the lieutenant, handing him a soft cigarette pack. Amzaleg saw it was Philip Morris—expensive foreign cigarettes. He took two.

"No, take more," the lieutenant said, "we get them in Haifa for half-price, from naval commandoes, they bring them from Lebanon."

Amzaleg took two more cigarettes, and the young man drove off in a spray of mud.

The canteen was empty. Posters were taped to the metal lid above the counter, showing a woman's face with pursed red lips and the slogan "The Enemy Listens!"

Someone had defaced it with a drawing of a penis and the words, "Arik Sharon, suck cock!"

Amzaleg lit his last cigarette when the door banged open and a man burst in in a flurry of raindrops. "You the policeman from Tel Aviv?"

The new arrival was a forty-five-year-old man of narrow shoulders and misshapen teeth.

Amzaleg got up. "You the nanny?"

The man showed no emotion. "Come."

Outside, the rain had settled into a steady downpour. Amzaleg felt the wind whipping the water against his legs. The chaperone said over his shoulder, "You can walk a little distance?"

Amzaleg nodded.

"Because here," the chaperone said, "they shoot at anything that drives."

"I can walk," Amzaleg said.

A flicker of lightning showed in the west, and a minute later, weak thunder rolled.

"Let's go," the man muttered.

They set out in the driving rain, the chaperone loping ahead, Amzaleg following.

As they were hopping from one slippery rock to another, the man asked, "You with the police drug force?"

Amzaleg said nothing, but the man must have taken Amzaleg's reticence as confirmation because he became voluble, expounding on the drug trade flourishing in the Biqaa below.

"Rahman, he's a protection partner with half the producers," the man concluded, "so no one can touch them. A month ago we bombed a new H lab by mistake, and the Syrian howitzers opened up for two hours. Two hours! So now we mark them on the map—half the Palestinian fuckers run to hide in the labs when they hear our Phantom jets coming."

Amzaleg recalled vaguely that Rahman al-Assad, Haffez al-Assad's younger brother, was also Syria's viceroy for Lebanon. He also had his own businesses there; the local *Adon* so to speak.

"Before you do anything here," the chaperone said, "you check with us first, or you can start something bigger than you think."

Amzaleg said nothing. He matched the chaperone hop for hop, jump for jump. He was astonished at the ease with which he negotiated these rocks, in this driving rain. At his age.

Halfway down into the valley, as they half-ran, half-slid down, Amzaleg saw the little Peugeot parked at the edge of an olive grove, and the two men leaning on it. Even from that distance he could identify the squat torso, long arms and bull neck of Yaro ben-Shlomo. The man at his side he didn't know, but the short powerful man at the wheel he did: Ehud Reznik.

The chaperone said to Yaro, "You take him from here."

"Yah," Yaro said. "You can go." But the chaperone was already striding rapidly away in the direction from which they had come.

"*Ahalan*, Amnon," Yaro said. All hail.

Both he and Ehud wore jeans and PLO-style battle dresses, the third man was dressed like a peasant—wide baggy pants and a formless cotton shirt.

Amzaleg said to Yaro, "You came specially for me? From Tel Aviv?"

Yaro said, "Nah, I'm on Reserve Service here."

Ehud shrugged and gave a squeak with his lips, to indicate he, too, was in the same boat.

"Since when?"

Yaro said, "Last month."

Ehud nodded, giving no sign he had recently talked to Amzaleg.

The man in the baggy pants untied his belt and dropped his pants. "Anyone want to take a piss before we go?"

They urinated communally, then entered the Peugeot and it drove off, this time the man with the baggy pants at the wheel.

"They're calling everybody now," Ehud said, staring out the window. "I was already doing theater, I thought I was finished with the killing."

Yaro said, "With this, you're never finished."

They drove on among gnarled olive trees, rich green fields of sorghum, until the wet gravel road turned into an asphalt ribbon.

Amzaleg said, "We're going straight to the Sub in Beirut?"

"Yes, yes," the driver said irritably.

The scattered houses had given way to more densely built streets. Urchins on motorcycles scooted by, Kalashnikovs hanging from backs and across chests.

Yaro said in French, "From here on, Deep Penetration Rules. French only."

The Peugeot slowed down. "Here they come," the driver said in French.

A trio of gun-toting teenagers were waving at the car. The driver put his head outside and shouted in Arabic, at length, waving one hand.

"Don't argue," Yaro said. "Pay him."

A teenager approached, a Chinese SKS rifle leveled in one hand, the other hand outstretched.

Money changed hands.

"They only take marks or shekels," the driver said. "Smart fuckers. Two ex-KGB run a printing house in partnership with Rahman."

"Protection partnership," Yaro said.

They drove on. The traffic noise around them was deafening.

"Just like Dizengoff," Ehud said. "Only they don't have theater."

"Sure they do," the driver said. "In Behamdun, they have a show, two girls fucking a horse, twice a day, fifty marks."

A large lorry, green-painted in the Syrian Brigades' colors, cut across in front of them, ten mustachioed men seated in the back on spring mattresses, shooting AK-47s in the air.

"Welcome to paradise," Yaro said.

At the corner of Rue Verdun, Ehud said, "I get off here."

As Ehud opened the door, Yaro said, "How many you got left to do?"

"One more."

"You need anything, something?"

Ehud shook his head and was gone. After two minutes of driving, the driver parked in an alley. Amzaleg alighted first.

"Paris of the Middle East," Yaro said. "Careful here."

The corpse of a donkey lay across the alley, dogs scouring inside the open belly.

"Two months it's here," the driver said, "no one cares." He spit.

They hopped across, descended a few steps between two wrecked buildings. Down, down they went, the stairs turning into an earthen corridor, musty and smelling of smoke.

"A shell fell here last month," Yaro said. "Almost took us all out. But the HolyName was with us. Ah, here it is."

He thumped on a dented steel door.

Amzaleg said, "Like a coke house in Lod."

The door opened smoothly. They stooped and entered.

-24-

Monday, a.m., October 19, 1981, West Beirut

INSIDE WAS A surprisingly wide corridor. It turned and twisted, and at each turn, a TV camera swiveled in their direction.

"What's this, the prime minister's office?" Amzaleg said.

No one laughed. Presently the corridor straightened and opened on a wider hall, which in turn became a semicircular command-post pit, the kind Amzaleg had seen in the General Staff HQ.

"Shit in yogurt," Amzaleg said. "What the hell is this?"

Yaro and the driver had split off and headed to a small table piled with papers, cigarette packs, smashed Styrofoam cups. Yaro offered a cigarette pack to Amzaleg. "How'd you like to be a human torpedo again?"

Amzaleg felt his head throb. "At my age? I'm finished with all this." He lit a cigarette.

Yaro said, "With this, you are never finished."

Amzaleg kept staring about. "How long has this been going on?"

A transparent Plexiglas board rose at the center of the hall, marked by a white grid, and girl soldiers, some childishly young, climbed up and down ladders making notes in wax pencils upon the Plexiglas. They wore little thin headsets and tiny throat mics, a few were smoking. Gray metal desks spread in a semicircle around them, and unshaven men, some in khaki and others in jeans, were either taking notes, talking on phones or hacking at computer screens. At the far end was a wall bank of eight Plexiglas boards with city streets mapped on them, on which girl soldiers were marking crosses with colored pens. They were calling out coordinates in the Hebrew alphabet in monotonous voices.

"Number thirteen is at Aleph-Reish nine-seven."

"Check."

"Number seven at Gimmel-Mem zero-three...."

"Check."

A TV screen to the right showed rotating fuzzy pictures of a street corner where teenagers, some the same age as the girl soldiers, seemed to be playing with elongated tubes.

"Number eleven is at Kuf-Gimmel zero-seven, executed! Repeat, executed!"

Amzaleg felt his skin crawl. He stubbed out the cigarette and pointed to the Plexiglas board. "Which one is Ehud?"

"Him? Circle number eighteen, at the bottom, near Ma'Ber," Yaro said, using the Hebrew acronym for West Beirut. "Estimated time of target acquisition fourteen minutes. You want to know who—"

"Fuck, no." Amzaleg felt feverish. "How many Undertakers you got out there?"

"Maybe twenty—"

But before Yaro could finish, a man rose from the first row and twisted around. "Shut up, Yaro." He was long and thin but with bulgingly thick forearms. He bore down on Amzaleg. "You the policeman Levitan sent?"

"Kadishevitz sent me," Amzaleg said.

"Yeah? How did you get to Kadishevitz?"

Amzaleg stared back at him. "And who are you?"

"Me? I only run this goddamn butcher shop. What's your name?"

Amzaleg looked around him. A few men at the desks had stopped their phoning and were looking up. He pointed with his chin. "These also Undertakers? All of them?"

"I asked you what's your name."

"Fuck your mother. And I asked yours."

The tall thin man raised his voice. "Yossi! Hey, Yossi! Come throw this motherfucker out."

Yaro said placidly, "Careful. He was with Shafrir."

The movement in the room seemed to slow down.

A hirsute man emerged from a cubicle, drying his hands on a towel. "Throw who?" His eyes were so black as to be all pupil.

The tall commander grew still. "When were you with him?"

Amzaleg rasped, "One last time. What's your name and rank? Or you want me to call Begin's secretary right now?"

"Fuck Begin. He knows this *dreck* is necessary." The man gave a grimace, his entire face worked. "I am Colonel Mooky Ronen. And you?"

"Superintendent Amnon Amzaleg."

Ronen pulled out a black cigarillo and lit it. "You were with Shafrir when?"

"Fifty-one to fifty-three. And you?"

"Kardom." The Mossad's assassins department.

There was silence in the entire room. The girl soldiers had stopped marking the Plexiglas; even the TV image seemed to have slowed down. No one met anyone's eye.

"So what do you want?" Ronen rasped.

Amzaleg said, "I'll need the OpLogs of the last two months, then talk to every one of your—"

Ronen threw his head back and laughed. "You what?"

A girl soldier came by and whispered something in Ronen's ear. He whipped around. "When?"

"Five minutes ago."

"Get confirmation from the local."

Yaro said sideways to Amzaleg, "We have fifteen TV cameras set up in place. Sometimes they catch the whole thing. You should see the TV pictures they send—"

"Shut up," Ronen said. "He's from the police."

Yaro shrugged, raised one finger.

Ronen got up abruptly. "This is getting out of hand. Let's go somewhere."

He marched toward the door and Amzaleg followed. As he was exiting he saw a girl soldier march to a small whiteboard in the corner and make a simple black line on it. Other lines were already there, in groups of five, each five lines crossed out

There were perhaps ten or eleven groups altogether.

Amzaleg forced his eyes away and followed Ronen out.

The canteen was almost like any army canteen he had been to, oblong and low-ceilinged, but it had been dug out of the soft white rock, and the tables and chairs were of metal and bolted to the rocky floor, like those in a Shin Bet cell.

He looked around. A black-and-white placard said "When outside speak French!" Another said "Sign up for V.D. check."

They sat down at a heavy metal table, and a girl soldier with rounded buttocks showing against her tight bleached skirt served Turkish coffee. Amzaleg followed her departing figure with his eyes.

"You want to fuck her?" Ronen said, before she had even departed. "I can tell her to. She sucks too."

Amzaleg sipped his coffee. "How many Undertakers you got here?"

Ronen leaned forward. "Listen, donkey. You don't come here to ask questions. You don't come here to interview anyone. You are not even here. Got it? We are not even here now... where you going?"

Amzaleg had gotten up and left the canteen. In the main hall he picked up a phone and said into it, "Give me a line to Jerusalem—"

A squat man grabbed at the phone. Still holding the handset, Amzaleg hit at the man's solar plexus with his other hand, in a fast knuckle-snap, then as the man doubled forward gasping for air, Amzaleg hit at the chin with his elbow. The man stumbled, holding onto the back of a chair.

Several men scrambled up, their weapons clicking as they drew back the breeches. Ronen came running from the canteen and Yaro approached, hands in pockets.

As the men converged on Amzaleg, Yaro stood to the side, arms loose.

In Amzaleg's ear, a tinny girl's voice said, "Here you are—just dial zero two." And there was the dial tone.

He lowered the receiver and dialed Kadishevitz's number with his thumb, from memory. He kept his other hand in front, moving right and left semi-leisurely, the fingers spread.

Behind, a man pulled out a silenced Beretta.

Ronen snarled to him, "Take him."

"Nah," said Yaro. "Kadishevitz will tell Begin."

"How will he learn?" said Ronen. He had stopped, hand at the small of his back.

"My dad will tell him."

A tinny man's voice spoke in Amzaleg's ear.

Amzaleg said into the receiver, "Sir? There's a donkey here called Mooky Ronen, you want to talk to him? What? How would I know if he's a Likudnik?" He removed the receiver from his ear, said to Ronen, "You a Likudnik?"

Ronen grabbed the receiver from Amzaleg's hand. It squawked, in three short bursts. "Yes," Ronen snapped. He slammed the receiver down, looked behind him. "Everyone back to work."

A girl soldier waiting in the alley between the tables came forward to whisper in his ear.

"Verify," Ronen said.

The girl made two black marks on the small board.

Ronen said, "But you don't take any notes. We'll search you when you leave."

The man who had tried to stop Amzaleg was having his chin attended to by someone with a khaki bag. Neither said a word. Amzaleg decided to say nothing either but could not stop himself. He raised his voice. "Anyone wants to search me when I leave?"

There was absolute quiet.

Then one of the girl soldiers sang out, "I will."

The room erupted. The guffaws and laughter had a hysterical tinge to them. It lasted nearly a whole minute. When it was over, Ronen said, "In the canteen, policeman. I'll send them in one by one. But no notes." He had not laughed.

There were fifty-six "Undertakers" in the Sub. Twenty-one ex-Mossad, twenty-three ex-Shin Bet, and twelve Unit Anons. Their OpLogs were on the table, in number-locked metal binders.

"So what do you want?" Ronen said.

Amzaleg kept his face immobile. "I want to talk to all of them."

Ronen said, "Listen, all this was our idea, you understand? At the last small Varash meeting."

Amzaleg said nothing and waited.

Ronen said, "Two months ago. We could see Arik pushing Begin to go in—the whole fucking army—you want them all in? In tanks? You know what it means to die in a tank?"

"Yeah," Amzaleg said. "I know."

Ronen stared at him hard. "Me too, my youngest, in '73."

Amzaleg pulled out his cigarette box, saw it was empty. Ronen took out a box of plain Dubeks, lit one and pushed the box on the table toward Amzaleg. "So we said to them, wait. Give us nine months. We'll take out the leaders. The ones who set the tone. Alright? The organizers. We'll do the *dreck*. Then you won't have to send in the whole army. You know?"

Amzaleg said, "Whose idea was it?"

"Who do you think?"

Amzaleg nodded. Only one mind could come up with this. Gershonovitz.

He said, "The first ones I want to talk to are those who went to Tel Aviv on Yom Kippur, for the refresher. You got the records on these?"

Ronen leaned forward. His face acquired the color and consistency of clay. "Someone, I am telling you, doesn't want us to do this, that's why. If we can make the Biqaa quiet, then Arik doesn't get to go in and clean up the Palestinian camps—you see?"

Amzaleg shook his head to clear it, but Ronen took it as an answer. "Listen to me, policeman. If they get to prove one of us did these killings in Tel Aviv, Begin will pull us all tomorrow. He's a Polish officer. Know what that means? He knows, and he doesn't want to know. You rub this in his face, he'll have to admit to himself he knows, then he'll tell Arik to go in and do it properly. With the whole fucking army. Now you see?"

The air in the canteen seemed to solidify into some gooey mass. Amzaleg said, "You think someone's been taking down small-time drug dealers just to pin it on one of the Undertakers here? So that Begin pulls you all out? Just for this?"

Ronen's forehead darkened. "You think I'm crazy, huh? That's what you think?"

Amzaleg said, "Why don't you just send the first one in?"

Ronen got up. "Just be careful what you do, okay? That's all I ask. I don't give a fuck if they kick me out tomorrow. But someone must do this *dreck* here or the army will be stuck here for ten years, twenty, like the Americans in Vietnam. You want this?"

Amzaleg said, "I'm a policeman. This is none of my—"

"You were with Shafrir once? Then everything is your business."

A girl stuck her head in. "Two more."

"Verify."

"Already done." She was gone.

Ronen paused at the door. "Fifty-seven jobs done up to now, this month. Thirty-three PLO, twenty-two PFLP. Not bad."

Amzaleg said, "And the two?"

"Civilian, collateral. Not a bad ratio."

He was gone. A second later his head stuck back in. "Why don't you take the first one of those you know? Yaro? Ehud? Who?"

"Ehud is back from the Op?"

"Should be."

Ronen nodded and was gone again.

Outside, a burst of cheers erupted. Some handclaps and a whistle. Probably an important target was taken down.

Presently Ehud came in. "Fifty-eight now. What else you want to know, Amnon?" His face was streaked with sweat.

Amzaleg flushed. "Sit down, Ehud, sit down."

Ehud stayed standing. "I've got a list of alibis for all the times in question."

Amzaleg's flush deepened. "Give it here." He avoided looking at Ehud's eyes and looked instead at the list Ronen gave him: fifty-two names, each name followed by a list of names in Arabic and dates. No time. Some dates had a pair of names, one had a triple.

Amzaleg raised his eyes. "No hours?"

"No." Ehud said, "It's still like in your day. Once an Undertaker goes out, he's on his own, Ronen doesn't know what he does or where, until he reports back."

"When do you report, about the—job?"

Ehud sat down. "Some report only when they are back, some right after the—job, by clickers." He stared at Amzaleg. "You still think it's one of us?"

"Don't know yet," Amzaleg said. "Which of you were out working during the Yom Kippur week?"

Ehud pulled out a pen and pointed to the list. "These were out," he made little V's with the pen. "Eight Anons, seven Mossad, ten Shin Bet."

Amzaleg said, "And you?"

"I was—not here."

"Not here, where?"

Ehud shook his head. "Can't tell you."

Amzaleg had a sudden illumination. "No shit! You were in on the Tel Aviv trip."

Ehud's face flushed. "I am not confirming."

"Who else was there with you?"

"Can't tell you."

Amzaleg sat back. "One of them with you probably did the drug dealer." He paused, choosing a question. "Who is the worst madman here?"

"Who? All of us, after two months.... Some go to sleep with the Other still inside...."

When Ehud did not continue, Amzaleg said. "So give me the names. How many?"

Ehud breathed out. "Six, seven with me." Still red-faced, he marked little dots on Amzaleg's list. Amzaleg looked at the dotted list. He knew them all, except one.

Outside rose muted cheers, perhaps another successful job.

Ehud said, "I didn't talk to you and I didn't tell you anything, understand?"

Amzaleg had enough. "Alright. I want to talk to all who were with you—no, I'll talk to everyone." Then he said, "Can you ask Ronen to come in for a second?"

When Ronen came in, Amzaleg said, "Where were you in the week before Yom Kippur?"

The man brought his head close to Amzaleg, nose to nose. "Here, with Varda, the one who wanted to search your ass. You want to talk to her?"

"Maybe later. Anyone else saw you?"

"No. This time her girlfriend was on home leave."

Amzaleg at first thought Ronen was making a bad joke. Then realized he wasn't.

A head showed in the doorway. The driver. "We threw a coin, so I'm first. You want to talk to me? I'm Zerach."

One by one they came in. It took four and a half hours, with two breaks. Amzaleg filled nine pages of notes, in small SSS script, then added a page of names, and quick questions to himself.

The last two he saw were Yaro and Tzafi. They came together.

"You want us separate?" Tzafi said.

"No, it's okay." He turned to Yaro. "Thanks for the cover, before."

"Nah," Yaro said. "Didn't want you to do Yossi. He owes me twenty shekels."

"Fifty here," said Tzafi.

When Amzaleg asked where they were during the week before Yom Kippur, both said they were in Israel, taking a refresher.

Tzafi snickered. "Maybe also for someone to look us over, see if we are cuckoo."

Yaro said, "So now we're back, it must mean we're all sane, certified." He laughed.

Amzaleg said, "Well, one of you guys isn't."

Both Anons shrugged.

"One druggie less," Tzafi said.

-25-

Monday, October 19, 1981, 5:00 p.m., West Beirut

AFTER AN EARLY dinner, one by one, Amzaleg asked the six Anons again about the first murder on Yom Kippur, in great detail. None had an alibi. And Moshe was still in Israel, with Shimmel.

"Good luck talking to him," Ehud said. "But he won't have an alibi either."

Amzaleg said, "So I'll need the OpLogs for the days of the next killings."

"Talk to Ronen."

Amzaleg had to threaten again to make a phone call to Jerusalem before Ronen gave in with bad grace. "If Kadishevitz didn't know about you, you'd never go back."

Amzaleg did not respond. He looked at the sheaf of tables. The logs went back almost two and a half months. "You started when?"

Ronen said, "August 2."

Amzaleg lit a cigarette, picked up a random OpLog. "When they go out for a job, how long they stay out?" He looked at Ronen over the smoke, focusing on the eyes.

Ronen said, "I don't know, there's no rule. Once an Undertaker goes out, you can't call him back; like a bullet." He looked Amzaleg in the eye. "You know how it is."

Amzaleg did not nod, did not let his face twitch. He was no longer part of the killing machine. "So they could be anywhere?"

"Yeah, just about."

Amzaleg read the names again. He thought of asking for the ammo logs but reconsidered. One day at a time.

"You have a place I can sleep, in case I have to stay a few days?"

"How long you figure on staying?"

"We'll see."

Ronen leaned back and called out, "Varda!"

The girl soldier who had offered to search Amzaleg came in.

"Take him to the commissary and get him what he needs."

Amzaleg said, "No need for her. I'll get the stuff myself. Just show me where."

Ronen said, "I can't let you walk around without—"

"The fuck you can't." The truce was apparently over.

Amzaleg found the commissary at the far end of the Sub, saw an empty bed in a room containing a small heap of blankets.

It took him a long while to fall asleep.

26

Tuesday, October 20, 1981, 9:00 a.m.,
West Beirut

THE NEXT DAY Amzaleg had a quick boureka from the pile on the main room's table and a cup of black coffee. No one came close, as if he was contaminated. No one spoke to him either as he walked to Ronen's small office.

Ronen did not seem surprised. "How much money you need? A thousand? Two? Five?"

"What currency do you have?" He only had a few shekel coins, which were not good here.

At last he took two hundred Egyptian pounds, a hundred D-marks and a hundred dollars.

"You want me to sign somewhere?"

The man laughed out loud, as if Amzaleg was joking. He wasn't.

Amzaleg turned to go, then turned back. "You have a spare clicker maybe? In case I go out, want to call back. Emergency or whatever."

Wordlessly Ronen opened a drawer, burrowed inside. "Here." A gray Motorola, marked with a number which he copied to a logbook, then looked up into Amzaleg's eyes. "You want to do a job when you're out, or maybe two? Five hundred per hit, no income tax. Marks, real." He laughed.

Seething, Amzaleg put the clicker in his pocket, said nothing.

Feeling put out and angry, he dashed out through the tiled corridor, the cameras buzzing as they followed him out.

Outside: Weak sunshine, air salty and wet, nearly all men with mustaches, women with tight skirts, pungent smells. Like Casablanca of his childhood.

Still seething, he went into the first café he saw, a faux French bistro resounding with local songs from a scratchy radio; bought an espresso, spoke Moroccan-French.

The bistro was like one in the new tourist section of Jaffa. Drinking his espresso standing, he calmed down, watched men beseeching the backgammon dice before casting them. No one paid him any heed when he exited via the rear door into the small alley at the back.

For a minute he stood immobile, listened, watched. No one had followed him. He looked up. No hanging laundry, just some barred windows, probably Palestinian flats by the music coming out: Umm Kulthum, Abdel Wahab. Smell of frying bread, wild oregano. Like in Jaffa.

He removed his windbreaker, turned it inside out, tied it around his waist sloppily. Untied his shoelaces, peeled his pant legs halfway up, one higher than the other. Regretfully he removed his belt, stashed it inside a pocket, unzipped his pant front half-open.

A sloven, he exited from the alley's other end, humming an Arab tune, limping a little, extending his hand for handouts. He was happy to see people giving him a wide berth.

There were a few policemen about, some Lebanese, a few grim Syrians in their green duds, looking into people's faces. He limped harder as he passed a duo, humming, and they barely gave him a look.

By the time he arrived at Rue Emile Eddé he had collected eight marks and two dollars in alms.

For an hour he roamed the streets. Rue Tabet's crooked flats turned into Rue Rachid Karami, small cafés, a garage, another café. He sat on the sidewalk's edge, hiccupping and scratching his ankles. No one minded him: just another Beiruti lowlife out to collect *sadaqa* from fellow Muslims.

He lowered his pant legs, buttoned the shirt, wrapped his belt back around his waist, turned the windbreaker right side out and put it on.

Feeling almost human again, he continued up Rue Wahash until he saw what he'd been looking for.

The barbershop was no more than a large kiosk. Two customers in chairs, two others sucking on hookahs, a third empty seat with a free hookah.

As he pondered, two Syrian policemen across the street gave him a look, and conferred.

Touching the jackknife in his pocket, he went in, sat in the free chair, bought a wooden hookah mouthpiece for half an Egyptian pound—all currencies accepted in this Levantine Casablanca—and was soon chatting with one of the smokers.

Outside, the two Syrians were gone.

Amzaleg relaxed, spoke Moroccan Arabic mixed with French, felt worlds better than earlier. This place was like the Tel Aviv Central Bus Station. His world, really.

Waiting his turn, he chatted, asked sly questions, soaked in the answers: the drug prosperity, the Syrian overlords, Maronite Christians pissed off at the newcomers, camp Palestinians still killing each other.

"Who's killing whom?"

"Why, everyone, settling scores, maybe the Israelis too...." The smoker stroked his nose. "With a local protector, probably..."

Amzaleg scoffed. The Israelis had a local protector? "Who? The Maronites?"

"No, no." The smoker sniffed his knuckles, slyly. Drug lords.

Amzaleg felt a buzz. The Syrians?

The barber called to him, "Come, ya Tunisi, you're next."

Amzaleg sat in the chair. The place reeked of a hundred odors, the floor covered with large black-and-white tiles, checkers style, like in Jaffa. The ceiling had reddish tiles, the wall displaying dozens of bottles of hair unguents, potency elixirs and faux French eau de cologne.

The barber trimmed right and left, snipped a parting in the thin middle, then quick as a snake's tongue, trimmed both eyebrows. He hummed a song, a soccer fan paean for some Beiruti team.

Feeling oddly at home, Amzaleg let his eyes roam: Magazine photos of the singer-actor Farid el-Atrash, and Fairuz, the Arab jazz singer. Photographs of local bigwigs, also a young Rahman al-Assad with three pot-bellied bodyguards, black Carl Gustafs in hand, most photos signed.

Amzaleg asked the barber if he was from here.

"No, Hama." In Syria.

"You *Ikhwan*?" Muslim Brother.

"Nah, left because of them. One day…" The man passed a hand fast across his throat.

Amzaleg nodded. The al-Assads were always fighting the fanatic Muslim Brothers. As if reading his thoughts, the man spoke of his two brothers-in-law under the spell of some preachers. "One day," the barber repeated, "the al-Assads…" He stopped, blinked.

The two Syrian policemen Amzaleg had seen before came in, looked leisurely around. Amzaleg put hand in pocket, released the jackknife's safety, took the hand out.

Don't be paranoid. No one knows you're here.

As the barber snipped, he hummed an old song by Fairuz, eyes roaming everywhere except the Syrians. Amzaleg hummed along, trilling, as the barber nodded approvingly, calmer now, the Syrians both reading an old Playboy, waiting their turn…

Policemen waiting their turn? Amzaleg put his hand in his pocket again.

"There!" The barber swung a hand mirror.

Amzaleg leaned to one side, then the other.

The two green-suited Syrians wide-stepped upright, one fat and old and with frizzy hair like a Maghreb-born, the other thinner and younger with the flat head of an Alawite.

"Up!" the older policeman said to Amzaleg.

At first Amzaleg thought they were looking for a bribe or maybe harassing him for fun. Then he saw the policeman consulting a photo, clipped from a newspaper. No, a photocopy.

Amzaleg meekly stood up. What did the *Sayeeds* require?

The younger policeman stuck his foot between Amzaleg's legs, laughed as Amzaleg stumbled and slapped his head, twice.

The older one said, "Yallah, out."

Amzaleg pulled a few bills to pay the barber, already fussing with another customer, eyes away.

The younger Syrian grabbed the bills. "Hair tax." He snickered.

The older one consulted the photo again and pulled Amzaleg out through the door. Amzaleg followed quietly. Kept his hand inside his pocket.

Why him? And where was the picture from?

Outside he limped faster, made for a gap between two buildings, lumber lying around, long nails sticking out. Serendipity.

"Hey, you!" the policemen shouted after him.

"Me?" Amzaleg stumbled, bent, picked up a long nail, stumbled into the gap.

The younger man was now consulting the photo. *"Hada huwa."* That's him.

The two converged on him, squeezing serially into the opening. Amzaleg slipped the nail into his fist, sharp end protruding, and, his innards already aflutter, closed his eyes and let the Other out.

The street went nearly black and white. Time slowed down; his heart thumped in his ears. Boom, boom, boom, just like all the other times. But now there was a strange gray halo over everything, luminous, it made his neck itch. He heard his Other say something in Moroccan Arabic.

"What?" the fat policeman said.

The man grabbed Amzaleg's shoulder, twisted him around. The younger one behind fumbled with his gun. Without pause, Amzaleg swung his hand like a scythe, elbow locked, long nail protruding between knuckles, punched it into the older man's ear, felt it slide in, rotated, pushed.

The man's knees buckled as his eyes turned in their sockets.

As the man writhed on the ground, Amzaleg stepped on his throat, not hard enough to break it, just to stop the breathing. The younger man behind was snarling curses as he pulled at his gun, the flap stupidly caught, front sight not even filed away. Gun finally free, the man let out a shot. Amzaleg felt a tug at his cheek, like a quick slap of a hot knife.

Bending fast, he pulled out the nail and, still bent, stepped over the fallen body, deflected a wild swing of the gun barrel, stuck the nail upward at the man's nose. Deep, then turn, he could hear his old killing instructor saying "It's the turn that does it. Turn and pull out."

Invisible entry wounds, will take time to see how they died.

The younger man stumbled, tried to turn, Amzaleg caught him in one stride, slammed the nail into his ear, missed, went into the side of his neck.

Damn, damn and fuck.

He pulled the nail out, watched the man topple across the other, luminous gray haze over both.

Amzaleg breathed in, out. He felt odd, as if something had taken hold of him, not the Other, but something else, made his movements quicker, more assured.

He shook his head to clear it. The gray halo was dissipating.

It had taken less than twenty seconds. No one in the street saw it, apparently, or minded the shot. He stood for a long minute, breathing hard, knowing what was coming. He could feel it.

Quickly he removed his shirt, wrapped it around his right fist, tight, then felt the bile come up and the vomit erupted in a yellow gush, he didn't know where it came from, he had barely eaten.

And then the Blackness hit and Amzaleg punched the wall to his left, once, twice, aiming for pain, mashing his wrapped fist into the bricks. He tried to lower his hand but it swung again, not him, the Other.

Just like all the times before. At last colors came back, slowly, as he pushed the Other down.

He bent over and, grabbing the dead men by the legs, pulled them one by one deeper into the alley. He picked the photocopy from the hands of the older Syrian, saw a four-year younger Amzaleg, 1977, face up and sideways, standing before some demonstration. It was the newspaper photo. Someone had copied it there and sent it here. Amzaleg was sure he knew who.

But how had Shimmel managed to send it to the Syrians so fast? How did he contact them? And why? And what secret was he trying to protect?

Presently Amzaleg unwrapped his hand, put on his shirt, his anger cold and hard.

When he returned the Motorola clicker to Ronen, the man asked why there was blood on his shirt, and what was with the bruised knuckles.

Unthinking, Amzaleg said, "Some local in a café called me an *Ars*, so I punched him."

Ronen stared at him in stupefaction, and Amzaleg was immediately ashamed of his idiocy. But then Ronen said, "Here everyone is an *Ars*," and it was Amzaleg's turn to stare, his ire rising, when Ronen went on, "Me too, and everyone, otherwise you can't do the job."

Amzaleg turned to go, feeling the insult, though unintended, his stomach stirring. The Other was not completely down yet. He knew it would take him at least two hours to Clean it.

Or probably it was hunger. He passed by the hall, bourekas still on the table. He ate three, then a fourth, then a croissant with jam, strawberries, two Dannon yogurts, drank three coffees, still felt the hole in his stomach, an erection too. Every time the same, every time.

Back at his room near the commissary, he lay down to do Clean up, breathed in, out, trying to recall the Reverse procedure, but in two minutes he sank into sleep. He slept eighteen hours.

27

**Wednesday, October 21, 7 a.m.,
West Beirut, then Israel**

WHEN HE WOKE up next morning, the chalk-stone wall dripped with water, perhaps leaks, perhaps condensation. It was barely dawn, and he felt suffocated: He wanted to leave as soon as possible but could only dress slowly—his knuckles still hurt, despite the wrapping, and it was hard to button his shirt. There was a thin film of gray before his eyes. Most likely the chalk dust, not the Blackness again, he hoped.

In the main hall a table was piled with fresh croissants, bourekas, fruits, hard-boiled eggs, tomatoes and pickled fish, like in a Tel Aviv hotel. No one was there yet.

Skipping shaving, Amzaleg ate until he felt no need for more: yes, Clean.

He smoked a Gitane then called Kadishevitz in Jerusalem at the number he'd been given.

"Yes?" The CabSec's voice was annoyed, fidgety. "Who is it?"

Amzaleg said, "The *Schwartze* superintendent here."

There was a second of silence, then a high-pitched chuckle. "Yes? You have something for us, commander?"

"Yes. You have time today?"

"For you, yes. How about three? The Varash meeting is at five o'clock. You can get here by—"

"Yes I can," Amzaleg said. "Thank you."

The line went dead.

Behind him he saw Ronen, the local commander, drinking coffee, listening, his eyes red.

"What is it?" Ronen asked. "You found something?"

Amzaleg shook his head. He was not going to give anything away here.

Ronen said, "Maybe something I should know?"

"No."

He pulled out the bills Ronen had given him the day before, whatever was left and put them all on top of the remaining ouureakas. "Count them."

"Alright, alright," Ronen said, "go fuck yourself, policeman, and don't come back."

Amzaleg lifted his middle finger and exited. The door hissed slowly shut, the camera following his move through the long corridor.

Outside, past the donkey's cadaver, a command car without license plates was parked for the weekly home leave run. Two Mossadniks and two girls sat in the car, all with eyes closed, snoozing after the night's shift, or maybe the nightly exertions. The drive passed in silence.

At the hotel's dock, a large dinghy with two taciturn rowers was waiting to take them to the boat anchored a few miles offshore—a tiny gunmetal blob in the haze.

Amzaleg said. "Can't everyone see it?"

The hotel's terrace was full of early morning bathers in bikinis and beach towels, none looking at the dinghy.

"Yeah," said a girl soldier, "but so what. That's West Beirut. Everyone's been paid."

Amzaleg sat at the other side of the dinghy, and it nearly tipped. Everyone laughed. It took half an hour to get to the boat, which immediately hoisted anchor and pointed south. The sea was calm, and less than two hours later they arrived off the shore of Nahariya. Mist lay on the road where a jeep was waiting. Once in town, Amzaleg looked behind and around him but could spot no followers. Nevertheless he spent an hour in a canteen at the Central Bus Station but still could spot no one.

As he focused on his surroundings, the entire Beirut episode was already a blur, even the killings were fading; his knuckles still throbbed a little, but the Other was gone.

On the bus to Jerusalem he still seemed Clean: no one in the bus seemed interested. From the Jerusalem bus station he walked to Geula Street, where the PM office was. It seemed as if he had been here years ago, not just days.

A fine rain fell, and he raised his face to let the drops fall into his mouth, his eyelids, like on the hike to Beirut across the mountains.

He threw glances around him. There still seemed to be no one following him. He arranged the report in his mind as he turned the corner, and then he saw them, walking toward him, not even hurrying.

-28-

THEY WERE TWO large men with thick upper bodies and hanging arms. He could see the hair braids on their wrists, the informal IDs of Samsons, retired bomb loaders fed steroids while being trained to lift quarter-ton bombs, some of them nukes.

Apparently they had been waiting for him around the PM office, no need to follow him: just eavesdrop on his call to Kadishevitz, then wait.... Or was Kadishevitz in on this—he and Shimmel? Both aiming to prevent him from coming to the meeting?

He'd been so stupid....

Amzaleg felt the flush of shame as he spun on his heel, but there was another Samson behind him, a single one but larger. Putting his hand into his pocket, Amzaleg grasped the jackknife but then took his hand out without the knife. What would he do, stick these three mid-street? They were Jews too.

The hesitation cost him a precious second. He began to twist for a knee-kick when the two behind grabbed his arms unhurriedly, their hands like steel clamps. He tried to raise the Other, but all he could feel was anger at his own stupidity. Yet almost automatically he caught one, grabbing a hand, lifted one finger hard and fast, heard it snap, but all he heard was a grunt. They were probably on prebattle painkillers, useless to break any more bones.

He lifted his legs to hang on their arms but they did not even seem to notice. Still cursing himself, he twisted, and seeing an exposed jugular, bared his teeth to bite, yet again hesitated when he saw the knitted skullcap; and then it was much too late.

The one in front stepped back and kicked him in the hip, fast and repeatedly, like a horizontal metronome. As Amzaleg dropped, he felt more kicks land on the back of his hips and he rolled into a ball, elbows defending his kidneys, but it was no use. The kicks continued, absolutely silently, now raining downward on his head, rolling him this way and that.

And still no one said a word, no sound uttered except for that first grunt. Amzaleg opened his mouth to holler, but a heel crashed into his solar plexus and he could not breathe.

And then the world slowed down as the Other uselessly came up, belatedly, and the colors melted into white and black. But the rage was for naught. All around walked men and women, averting their eyes: Chassidim in fur hats, women in long dresses, old women with grocery bags. More kicks hit him, rising higher, and as if from a distance he heard his jaw snap. For a second the pain was delayed, then it crashed into him when the bone moved, and he nearly fainted from the agony and smelled the coppery odor of his blood. And somehow this finally filled him with useful rage. A crotch swam into view and, abandoning his kidneys, he grabbed onto it and tugged hard. But there was a hard cup inside, a crotch protector. He dug under it and extracted a small grunt from the Samson, but a second later his fingers were almost wrenched as his hand was pulled away.

He felt deeper rage now, coming from the Other, at the stupidity that had blocked it.

With blood slowly filling his throat, the Other melted, role-exited on its own, and Amzaleg wondered if this was his own death finally. Without any transition, he saw the scrolls in synagogue, and Pirchiya's head on his shoulder, then Suissa smoking, and oddly enough, Zohara sitting on his lap, age ten, reading *The Little Prince*, which her uncle had given her, her eyebrows tight with concentration.

His eyes began to dim. There was a chill wind on his neck, like a faraway breath, and across the road he saw a jeep with the border guard insignia on it. Did the men look at him?

He gurgled something. One of the border guards eyed him, eyebrows knotted. It was the Druze he had met in Shfar'am when he used to visit Zohara.

"Ya Amzaleg?" The call came as if from a great distance, reverberating.

A moment passed. More kicks fell, the pain a mere throb. He was losing consciousness.

The Druze stood beside him, rifle pointing down. "What you doing—"

"*Rooh!*" the Samson snarled in colloquial Arabic. Get lost.

The rifle poked into the Samson's stomach. "I know this man."

"I told ya, *rooh min hun!*" Fuck off.

The sound of the safety being clicked off was clear. "What's he done?"

Amzaleg felt himself sliding into soft Blackness, his body a mass of pain.

The Samson was snarling, "I told ya—"

But a second Druze was near, an older one, his weapon a heavy platoon MAG, carried lightly. "He asked you what you doing to him?" Good Hebrew, that, polite.

The Samsons paused. Taking on a Druze would open a *ghom* forever. A blood feud.

One Samson aimed a final kick at Amzaleg's jaw. The second Druze caught it on the MAG's barrel, slid the barrel up between the man's legs, hoisted.

The Samson walked backward, seemed to confer wordlessly with the other two. All walked a little way off, stood waiting for the Druze to leave.

Amzaleg saw the Druze bending over him, heard him asking something in Arabic. Amzaleg whispered in Moroccan Arabic, could not recall what. His voice gurgled through the blood. He was fading into a blue abyss, being lifted into the jeep on a wave of pain.

Time passed, and more time. When he tried to open his eyes, he saw through the blood he was at the entrance to Bikur Cholim Hospital, two men carrying him through a corridor, one holding his legs, the other his shoulders. He tried to tell his rescuers something, he did not know what, but then pain swallowed him and plunged him into the blue-black nothing.

-29-

**Wednesday, October 21, 3:45 p.m.,
Jerusalem**

I T WAS FORTY-FIVE minutes after the designated meeting time.

The PM looked at his watch. "Nu?" He was sitting at his desk, piled with beige-colored files, a few blue folders, two with black borders.

Kadishevitz said, "He should've been here an hour ago."

"Maybe he got delayed," said the PM. "Let me know when he comes."

But the afternoon rolled on, and no Amzaleg.

By quarter to five, the PM said, "Check what happened. Call them in Beirut, in the what-do-you-call-it."

"The Sub," said Kadishevitz.

"Any place he might be."

But no matter how much they checked, there was no sign of Amzaleg. The Sub reported he had left that morning, the boat's captain reported he landed in Nahariya, and someone saw him arrive at Jerusalem's Central Bus Station, but after that, nothing.

Kadishevitz said, "Maybe he went to a girlfriend."

Begin seemed offended. "Just because he's a *Schwartze,* you don't have to insult him. He said he'll come here, he'll come. I believe him. Maybe there was an accident?"

Kadishevitz made an "I have no idea" face. "I'll check."

But there was no report of an accident yet, and so the meeting that afternoon went on as planned, without any report by Amzaleg. And when that evening the PM was told that Superintendent Amzaleg had been hit by a car and was now in hospital, it was no longer relevant, the decision was already made to give Shimmel three more months.

"And send him flowers," Begin said to Kadishevitz. "So he'll know we didn't forget him. And when he's awake, you go talk to him."

But Amzaleg, they were told, was in a coma, so what he had to say would have to wait.

"How long?" the PM asked.

Kadishevitz made the same face.

-30-

**Wednesday, October 21, 4:15 p.m.,
Jerusalem**

AMZALEG'S COMA CAME and went.

Only once, when the nurse was injecting something into his arm, did he open one eye.

By the peaceful warmth spreading from the needle, he guessed it was morphine, or Novocain, or some other shit, only legal.

A Druze was seated by the door, the young one. He had his rifle across his thighs, his knees spread wide. He nodded at Amzaleg peaceably.

The other Druze was by the door, smoking, despite the no smoking sign.

Amzaleg heard the nurse asking a question. He made an effort to focus on her. "Wha…"

She said, "…want to call someone?"

His head swam, he could not speak.

She repeated her question.

He nodded, tried to say a name, but his jaw could not move, it was apparently taped. He felt like he was floating as she handed him a crumpled pad and a pen. He clawed at it, and with his last strength wrote HaTikva's grocery's phone number in SSS, then a name.

The nurse read it aloud. "Call Zohara?"

He nodded. Yes.

Then the Blackness swallowed him once more and he sank in, leaving the pain behind.

PART THREE

TEL AVIV NOIR

1981, Wednesday October 21, to Wednesday June 16, 1982

**Wednesday, October 21, 1981, 4:20 p.m.,
HaTikva Quarter, then Jerusalem**

THE GROCER'S BOY had to call her name several times before she opened her eyes, mere slits.

"Wha…" She was curled on the dirty mattress at the back of the Amidar hovel, saliva dribbling from her mouth, the rubber hose still tied to her arm.

He averted his eyes, spoke into her ear. "There was an accident…. Your father…"

Zohara jerked up, her eyes coming into focus. "Wh-wh… happened?"

"He's in hospital, Bikur Cholim, in Jerusalem…. He asked to call you…."

She grabbed his hand. "Me?"

"Yes…. His jaw is broken, also some other bones… but they think he'll be okay…."

Before he had finished, she was out the broken door, shirt unbuttoned, shoes unlaced, stumbling through the puddles, her bag trailing behind.

Jacqueline, dressed in a frayed smock, her hair in curlers, was reading a cinema magazine in the towels room when Zohara barged in. "Can you come with me to Jerusalem… now?" Zohara's breath came in spurts, her eyes wild. "He's in Bikur Cholim Hospital—" She tore the magazine out of Jacqueline's hands, threw it to the floor.

"I know where it is, near Talpiot." Jacqueline went pale. "Is he—will he live?"

"I don't know.... I'll pay for the cab...."

"What? No, I'm coming. I'll drive you."

Just then the grocer came through the salon's door. "If you need money for cab..."

It would be at least three hundred shekels, all the way to Jerusalem, an hour, more.

"I said I'm driving," Jacqueline said.

Zohara turned away and swatted at her eyes. She was astonished at the sharp pang she felt suddenly. Of course he'll live. He always did, even though she hated him. She felt the anger rising, and the panic, and tamped both down. She said. "No, I'll pay you for the gas, Jacquie—"

Jacqueline's mouth twisted. "I'd slap you if you weren't his daughter."

Pirchiya ran in—"I'm coming too!" She, too, was crying.

"Me too," said Sigalit.

"There's no room," Jacqueline said.

They piled helter-skelter into Jacqueline's car, an Israeli-made Susita, fiberglass body, eaten through in places. The engine took its time turning on.

"You want me to push?" Zohara said.

"I can help," Pirchiya said.

Jacqueline said there was no need. "And you," she said to Pirchiya, "should take it easy."

Pirchiya reddened and looked at her feet, then aside, everywhere except her stomach.

Belatedly Zohara remembered she'd not had a fix since morning and put her hand on the handle to rush out. Her bag felt heavy—there was a full syringe inside wrapped in a towel.... And then the engine caught, and they were off.

The trip was slow—heavy rain, thick traffic, a mudslide after the Castel ridge, the old car barely moving in the steep rises of the pine copses, then heavy mist. At last they entered Jerusalem, the ancient car crawling between stone houses, the narrow streets, Hasidic Jews walking in the middle of the street. Zohara leaned over Jacqueline's shoulder, honked and screamed at them; they barely moved, oblivious to her honks….

At last, the hospital, a large fort-like monster surrounded by iron fences and stone walls, her father somewhere inside.

Zohara jumped out of the car before it came to a stop and ran up the stairs, slip-sliding on some wet stains, ignoring Pirchiya's calls to wait.

She pushed through a knot of clacking Orthodox Jews in gabardines, scanned the hall quickly and ran to the info desk. The place was half-dark, the walls emitting a medieval smell, a rot deep in the walls mixed with ancient medications that had seeped in. It smelled worse than the hair salon.

Suppressing nausea, she stuck her face at the info window and demanded to know about her father. "He's a policeman, Amnon Amzaleg, a… a sergeant… no, corporal… was just brought in…. I got a call—" Fear and anger filled her to bursting and she could not continue. She needed a fix….

The nurse peered at her, ready to scold, but something in Zohara's eyes made her pause. "What was he brought in for?"

"I don't know…." She could not continue.

Behind she could hear Pirchiya padding near. The walls' odor was unbearable, for a moment she felt as if she was again at the reformatory. She needed a fix soon. Her veins seemed on fire.

"We only have two policemen, one had an appendix attack last night, the other was just in a traffic accident—"

"I'm sure it was no fucking accident. Where is he?"

Two male nurses came closer, perhaps in response to a silent signal. Zohara turned on them, but Pirchiya pulled at her arm. "Shhh," she said, then addressed the men, humbly explaining Zohara was an only daughter, her brother fell in '73, her father was all she had. The two men nodded and went on walking, and the nurse relented, said the wounded policeman was on the third floor, he just came out of surgery. "But visiting hours are only—"

"What surgery?" Zohara snapped, but Pirchiya again said "Shhh," pulled at her arm, and in a moment they were walking-stumbling into the elevator, the nurse calling at them they could only stay a few minutes— then the door closed and the elevator rose, Zohara opening and closing her fists as if to accelerate her blood flow, her veins about to burst.

"Shhh, you can't bully people," Pirchiya said, "especially not Ashkenazim, with them honey is sometimes better then vinegar—"

The elevator opened and Zohara was off, Pirchiya still explaining. Zohara snarled over her shoulder, "They must have ganged up on him, or shot him, because otherwise they'd be here, not him." She ran down the corridor, wiping her cheeks furtively.

"They who?" Pirchiya panted after her.

"Anyone." She wiped the corners of her mouth, tears flowing down so fast. "All of them."

Pirchiya was now running, too, to keep up. "Wait, wait for me...." She, too, was weeping. It took an eternity to get to the door at the corridor's end. It stood slightly ajar, and Zohara nearly banged it open as she rushed in, her fists bunched.

Amzaleg was in the middle bed, the two other beds empty. There were two Druze sitting by the bedside, Galil rifles on their knees. They barred her way.

"Who are you?"

Then one recognized her. "Ahalan, ya Zohara... Your father... *Shater*..." a hero, "fought three of them..."

She drew closer to her father.

His eyes were shut, his jaw taped with gray tape, wire under it. Head wrapped in white tape, all around, like a papier-mâché Purim mask. A plaster cast on one arm, shoulder to palm, only fingers showing, the right arm bandaged to his chest, but palm free, tube going to the elbow-crook. One leg in a cast, ankle to knee, over the blanket, the other leg under the blanket, toes protruding.

A nurse came in and began adjusting an IV drip into his taped arm, looked at her.

"I'm his daughter...."

"Not too long, please... he must rest.... You Zohara?"

She nodded.

"He asked for you." Pointed to a yellow pad.

Zohara could not trust herself to speak.

-2-

**Wednesday, October 21, 1981, 5:45 p.m.,
Jerusalem**

S HE SAT BY the door of Amzaleg's room. Her head swam. She wanted
to pee and to get a drug fix; her skin itched, felt both hot and cold, but
she wouldn't leave her station.

The hospital stank, and it was noisy. She could not breathe.

She could look inside the room, see Amzaleg asleep, his jaw taped, a
tube in his arm. Her heart raced but she didn't know whether it was because
of him or because she was burning for another hit. Her hand was inside her
shoulder bag, touching both razor and the syringe. But she stayed put.

The two Druze had left a few minutes before, telling her to let them
know how Amzaleg did.

"And call us if you need us, *ya Saeeda*," said the elder one, using the
honorific she had never heard addressed to her before.

She waited for Jacqueline or Pirchiya to return, her heart and her
body on fire. But she could not leave Amzaleg alone.

Jacqueline had gone to park the car, and Pirchiya went downstairs to
get some coffee. She should come back any moment....

Finally Zohara could take it no more. With her handbag on her shoulder, her bladder full and her head throbbing with her desperate need, she
jumped up and rushed down the corridor to look for a washroom where
she could piss and inject.

Here it was.

Luckily no one was in. She dashed inside, half-sliding on the recently washed corridor floor, leaving the toilet's door open a crack so she could see into the corridor.

She pulled down her panties, sat down, then quickly bound her arm with the rubber and waited for the vein to show. In her ears came the rhythmic sound of her heartbeat, mixed with steps and voices from the corridor, as if in some one-sided dispute.

Overcoming her need, she pulled up her panties, half-rose and peeked out, her hand inside her bag, touching the razor.

She saw two big men striding down the corridor, followed by a waddling bald doctor in a flapping white coat, calling on them to stop, to get out, tugging on one man's shirttails. Her brain had not taken it in fully when, without knowing how, she found herself outside the toilet, sliding on the wet floor with one leg extended forward, the other extended back, her bag trailing behind, the straight razor in her outstretched left hand, the blade whipping from side to side. It was like watching someone else in action a long way off, her mind clear and cold, her body doing things apparently on its own volition, as if controlled by some other entity.

"Get out, both of you, your mothers' cunts!" Her voice came out a shaky croak, and, as if she was operating at a speed faster than they, she saw the leftmost man's head rotate slowly, slowly, in her direction. He had something in his hand, behind his curled palm.

In the same slow speed, under the first man's shoulder, she saw into her father's room through the half-open door. Amzaleg's eyes fixed on her, his hand twitching slowly, the wired jaw working, as if trying to tell her something.

The bald doctor was running now, in slow motion, his coattails flapping, then he was speaking to her, saying something about dropping what she held. But she pushed him aside, and, her veins burning, fixed her eyes on the leftmost big man who seemed somehow looser in his movements, more assured. He was also closer to her father's room, his hand pushing at the door. Her brain on fire, Zohara directed her sliding somehow with her right leg dragging behind, then as she tumbled-slid under the man's arms, she slashed clumsily with the razor, left up and right, not more than two feet above the floor, as if sharpening the razor, pressing down on its spine with her forefinger.

She felt the cut down in her wrist as the blade caught in the man's pants leg, and she gave it an extra push and felt it bite at the calf as it sliced in. She sensed the bite in her throat, as if she had bitten his calf with her teeth. She pressed the razor harder and felt it bite deeper still, like carving a chicken thigh, only a thicker bone.

There was a sharp grunt and a blunt swoosh as the man's beefy arm swung at her, partly stunning her as it glanced off her temple and paused to strike her again.

Half-blind with pain and her need for a fix, she flipped the razor up, twisted it and brought it back, slashing up blindly, and felt it catch at the man's forearm, bite sideways, and slice diagonally. Through the ringing in her ears she heard a muffled snarl, and then the other man came at her, both arms stretched.

Her body barely obeying her as she ducked under his arms, she tumbled-rolled, her legs entangling, and slashed upward wildly, instinctively aiming at the crook of the elbow, and as through a narrow tunnel she saw the flesh-slits spurt blood, then saw another doctor in a white coat rushing in, shouting.

Her view began to speed up, the sound acquired volume, words. She brought her left leg in and stayed crouched low, her thighs trembling, her razor flicking from side to side as the two men paused, and she hissed at them in glottal Hebrew and Moroccan Arabic, like a Yemenite washerwoman, cursing them in the name of evil spirits whose names she had heard long ago from Great-Grandma Ruja and did not even know she'd remembered.

"I call on Senoy, Sansenoy and Semangelof!" she hollered, darkness rising in her. "I adjure you..."

She had no idea how it all came back; her neck tingled as she mouthed the old names.

The two men stopped, gaped at her. The rightmost one had pushed the doctor at the wall, but now paused, arm still dripping blood, his palm raised to touch his skullcap, his eyeballs showing white-yellow. The other man had something in his hand. He, too, stopped. Just then Zohara saw Pirchiya coming up the stairs, half-stumbling, a Styrofoam cup in her hand.

More people were coming down the hall, a few nurses and another doctor. The first man threw an angry glance at the second man, who put the object back in his pocket, and in a flash both were gone down the stairs, a trail of blood drops behind, and the side door swung shut. Just then Pirchiya threw the coffee at them and the cup slammed at the door, brown liquid trickling down the dirty beige surface.

Pirchiya cried out, "Did they try to—"

"Yes."

Zohara stumbled as she rose, flipped her razor closed and stashed it in her bag, her veins aflame. The doctor came up to her. "What the hell are you doing? Give it here!"

She began to refuse, but another doctor came by, then a nurse, and she plopped the folded razor sullenly into the outstretched hand. "And don't fucking lose it." She could hardly stand. She needed a fix so bad, if she didn't have it in a minute she knew she would have a *kriz*.

Pirchiya was looking at her with fear. "What did you just say—"

"Nothing."

The doctor said, "Don't go, we called the police and they—"

"Fuck them," Zohara said. "They'll do nothing."

Her neck felt scratchy, she felt hot and cold. She wanted to run to the washroom to inject, but the bald doctor was speaking to her. No, she said to him. She had no idea who they were, but she knew they wanted to beat her father again.

He tried to ask her something, but she ignored him, called Pirchiya over and told her to go down and look for a border guard jeep.

"Which jeep?"

"Any jeep. Tell them you want to speak to Abed. Tell him Amzaleg needs his help."

"Who is Abed?"

"One of the Druze who were here before. Don't worry, any one of the border guards will know."

Indeed they did. Fifteen minutes later, after she had already injected and stopped shaking, the drug coursing through her, the two Druze returned. So when three big men came half an hour later down the corridor, one of them with a bandage on his arm, all of them looking determined and grim, the Druze sergeant was sitting by the door, his Galil with the magazine in, the safety off, finger lazily caressing the trigger.

Another doctor trailing behind the trio kept asking if they were the police. He got no answer.

When they came nearer, Abed said, "If you scummy dogs want to file a complaint with the police, I'll be happy to give a statement."

Zohara kept quiet, just looked backward at Amzaleg in his room, who looked back at her.

The doctor said to the Druze, "But you were not here, before."

"I was there before when they beat him up."

The doctor looked from one face to the other, in stupefaction. "Where?"

"On Geula Street. Ask them."

The doctor seemed lost, looked around, faced the three Samsons, who stared stonily back.

Abed said, "And my squad mates can testify too." He gave a white-toothed smile.

After a brief consultation the men spit on the floor, two made an obscene gesture and all left.

-3-

**Thursday, October 22, 3:30 a.m.,
West Beirut, then Latakia Beach, Syria**

THE DAY AFTER Amzaleg's beating, Ehud was to be infiltrated by boat into Latakia, Syria, to meet Rahman al-Assad to negotiate the deal Shimmel had cooked up.

"We got to know if he's serious," Shimmel said.

"Know how?" Ehud still couldn't believe it.

"Feel him out, look him in the eye, see what you think."

"And if I make a mistake?"

"So don't make one."

Ehud snorted.

Shimmel said, "You know a better way to stop the war?"

Ehud shook his head.

He left on the boat a few hours before dawn and the trip north took three and a half hours. This time the torpedo boat cruised much further from shore, without any lights, and sailors were at battle stations without respite. As before, the weather was like thick soup. The crew put him on shore in Syria a little after six a.m. in a small rubber dinghy, four miles southeast of Latakia on the outskirts of Ad Dabbaghah. Dawn was just breaking.

Ehud wore a laborer's garb—baggy pants belted with a rope and a well-laundered handwoven shirt. His checkered headdress had no marking and like the shirt, was old, all bought the week before in the Aleppo Market by the local agent and sent by the truck that also carried the weekly microfilm.

The two commandoes said little. But when Ehud began to wade ashore, one said, "Any message to anyone, anything?"

"Just pick me up here tomorrow, an hour after I click." He clicked one of the beads in his plastic prayer chain, and a clicker inside one of the rowers' pockets chirped.

The man nodded.

Lugging his sack, Ehud walked up the beach to the road, his feet sinking in the sand. He trundled up the narrow road, looking at the map inside the back flap of his Koran, then up. Far away, car lights moved on Abd al-Qadir al-Husseini Road, a few miles to the north. Then a yellowish light blinked three times, close to his left. He froze; then a fourth blink. A motorcycle was parked at the roadside, with a sidecar, a man in a burnoose and a hennaed beard holding the handlebars.

Ehud said, "*Sabah el hir*," two times. Good morning.

The man coughed three times, then said, "*Sabah el nur*." Morning light.

He handed Ehud rough gloves so as not to leave fingerprints. Ehud put them on, climbed into the sidecar. "*Fir*," he said. Drive, in Yiddish.

"*Uskut!*" the man hissed in Arabic. Shut up!

"*Yallah, yallah.*" Alright, alright, Ehud said, contrite.

He was the visitor, this man had to survive here.

They took a convoluted long way around, through Ad Dabbaghah, into Abd al-Qadir al-Husseini Road, snaking between early trucks, the chichi structures of Tishreen University blinking in and out of the haze to their right, around Yaman Square into the little streets of Latakia town, white buildings, small stores, no hanging laundry. Just like Tel Aviv if not for the mosques and the acrid smells, then on toward the sea and up and down Gamal Abdel Nasser Road.

"You want them all to see us?" Ehud muttered in village Arabic.

"Just losing tails, in case."

But there was no one they could see, either of them.

Ehud said, "Tell me when we get there."

He actually managed to snooze fifteen minutes when the man said, "It's over there."

It was a surprisingly modern house, but like most of the others, a mongrel of Italian and chichi design, though not without some grace. It stood at the end of a cul-de-sac; no exit.

The man said, "Leave you here?"

The light was rising, soon it would be day.

"Yes, go, go." Ehud descended, handed back the gloves, and looked for a place to change. Perhaps among the trees.

The man bent over the handlebars. "Yallah, *Mabruk*." Blessing to you.

"And to you," Ehud said.

When the motorcycle had left, he quickly made his way to the copse of trees. A trio of schoolchildren passed but none looked at him.

Among the trees he pulled some more clothes out of the sack, looked around, and quickly changed. It took him six minutes, as in the rehearsal. When he was done, he stuffed the laborer's clothes inside the sack, hid it under his abaya, and lay down to snooze.

When the muezzin at the Abdul Hadid Mosque called out the dawn prayer, he got up. It was the designated time and it was important to be on time. Such things mattered.

As he went into the street, he saw Rahman's villa was no longer clear. Two olive-green jeeps were parked in front, a brown Russian ZIL truck at the back. A man in olive garb sat at the villa's door, snoozing, a long-barreled Avtomat Podvodny APS leaning on the doorframe.

The street also had woken up. Girls in drab green were walking to school, tittering, some old men entering the mosque, prayer mats under armpits. A woman sweeping the road, oddly, in front of a house, maybe she, too, was one of Rahman's crew.

Ehud stopped, clicked three short and one long on his prayer beads, and walked on toward the villa.

**Thursday, October 22, 8:20 a.m.,
Tel Aviv, Army HQ**

GERSHONOVITZ'S OFFICE WAS quiet.

He and Moshe sat at both ends of a long aluminum desk, staring at a little gray square marked Motorola and a seven-figure serial number.

The clicker chirped.

Gershonovitz slammed his beefy palm on the desk. The clicker jumped and so did Moshe.

"Esau arrived safely, going in, on time," Gershonovitz rasped, using Ehud's operational name. He pulled out his inhaler, took a long pull, and said to Moshe, "What did I tell you?" He picked up the phone, dialed a single digit, waited. "Tell Itzik, Esau five-five." The old Haganah code for "All is well."

He listened, put down the phone grumpily. "They know already. Their man clicked." He made a face. "Doubling the risk. Idiots. They can't trust me to tell them?"

"No," Moshe said.

They were quiet and stared at the clicker, waiting. It was going to be a long morning.

-5-

**Thursday, October 22, 8:30 a.m.,
Latakia, Syria**

RAHMAN WATCHED THE street through the reinforced glass, the French *barbouz* at his side, waiting for the Israeli messenger.

There was nothing.

Only a few children, old men entering the mosque, two girls late for school, an old woman lugging bags, wobbling, another walking with a stick, yet another sweeping the street—idiot, should change her spot—the children paused before the villa, ogled the jeeps.

The soldiers scowled at the children. The girls passed by. The soldiers scowled at them too. The girls giggled.

Where was the messenger?

One of the old men came by, spoke to the soldiers, gave them cigarettes. The old woman came by, stopped and put down her sacks.

The French *barbouz* said behind him, "He doesn't come soon, I'll call." Pointed to his watch.

There was some shouting outside. Rahman put his hand on his gun. "What?"

The old woman cupped hands to mouth, "Rahman, ya donkey!" she shouted. "Where's the money for your mother?"

She was fat, rolling from side to side, the soldiers were chuckling.

"What money?" Rahman opened the window. He could smell her all the way from the curb.

"She said you didn't pay your share for the new mosque! Jamal paid already, you didn't!"

Jamal? That skinflint? Couldn't be.

The old hag shouted, "I came all the way from Qardaha, the Lady said to tell you—where's the money? Allah is watching!"

The soldiers were now openly snickering. One of them poked at her, and she slapped his hand away. "You take your hand away from what belongs to my husband, you thief." Turning to the window she shouted, "The Lady Naisa said—"

His mother?! "Come here, you old hen," Rahman said. He looked at the *barbouz*, who twisted his lips in an "I don't know" face. "What money?"

He said to the *barbouz* at his side, "Go call, he's late."

The *barbouz* nodded, disappeared inside.

The old woman waddled near, her smell unbearable. He turned his face. She climbed the stairs, grunting. She pushed by him, spat. "You donkey," she cackled. "I could've killed you five times."

He froze as she pushed by him, got inside, just as the *barbouz* was returning. "They said they tracked the boat, it already turned—"

He stopped.

Ehud had thrown off the woman's abaya and the large bra, and the dud grenades inside, grooved Mark II frags rolled down the floor.

It may have been stupid to bring them, but their effect would help ensure his safety.

He wiped his face, removed the wig, bowed.

"Dirty fucking shit!" the *barbouz* said in French.

Ehud made a little bow, said to Rahman, as proper, "With permission of the homeowner."

Still blinking, Rahman said, "Granted." He took his hand off his pistol, stopped himself from bowing just in time.

The soldiers appeared at the door. "Master," one said, "We heard a noise...."

"Yallah, out! All is fine."

He stared at the messenger, who stared back, but also touched hand to forehead.

The *barbouz* said to Rahman in French, "It's him, the director."

"Bfff," Rahman said. "I didn't believe him, he said Jamal gave money."

The newcomer shook his head. "He'll give his children first."

They both laughed, Rahman's forced a little.

Presently Rahman's manners returned. "White or black?" That is, tea or coffee, Bedouin manners.

"Black," said the newcomer, "and a place to wash my face later, with permission."

Rahman clapped his hands, shouted something in broken German.

Ehud looked at the *barbouz*, then at Rahman, and spoke Syrian Arabic. "Anything happens, I don't go back, someone else will come for you both, next time you won't know the time and place."

The *barbouz* said, "No, I am just the trustee, to ensure—"

"You are a signatory also, if we make a deal."

There was a frozen silence as Ehud wiped his face.

The *barbouz* said in French, "We don't do business like this—"

"We don't give a fuck. That's how we do it. You don't like it, I go back now...."

The Frenchman looked at Rahman, mouth pinched.

Rahman shrugged. "Yallah, let's begin." Again he clapped his hands. "*Liebchen!*" My love.

A youngish woman appeared in the door, carrying a tray, a three-year-old boy clutching at her long dress. She had clear skin, even teeth, glowing reddish-yellow hair, and freckles. A beauty. She put the tray on a small glass table, blushing as Rahman slapped her thigh.

Her blush deepened, and she made a little curtsy, a German *knix*, toe behind the ankle.

Rahman lifted his hand in a Nazi salute. "*Jawohl!*" Yes sir! he chortled and laughed. Then he said, "Pure German, the best."

The Frenchman took his cup, sipped, said, "*Enchantée, Madame.*"

When Ehud got his coffee, he said in Arabic, "Thanks, blessed be your hands," as proper. Sipped and said, "Well made."

She blushed further, thanked him in German and pushed the plate with cardamom seeds toward him, five on one side of the plate, one to the other.

His heart stopped, then resumed. Five One. The local agent's Recog Code.

This fucking Shimmel, he thought. No, more likely Asa.

He took two of the seeds, left four, two to each side. Query, standard response.

Rahman slurped his coffee, then said, "*Raus, raus.*" Out, out.

The woman left, hand spread at her side, five fingers showing. Then just before the door closed she clenched her fist, left the forefinger.

Fucking shit, Ehud thought. *Here!*

Rahman said, "Let's go down to the secure room, you can wash there, too, ya *Saeed*."

They went down, Rahman leading, to negotiate the deal.

-6-

Friday, October 23, 1981, 1:00 a.m.,
Latakia, then Beirut

THE NEXT DAY, Friday, Ehud returned to Beirut.

When they had finished dickering it was late, after midnight. The beauty brought some food: kebab halebi, lakhma meat, mahshi fingers, sweets: basbusa, baklava, strong mint tea, bitter honey. There were no more codes, nor did her young boy trail her. As she left, Ehud saw she was pregnant.

He ate sparingly, asked for a bag for some of the leftovers. "For the others," he said, "in the boat. Show them how well you feed guests."

The Frenchman laughed, thumped Ehud on the knee, as if it was a capital joke.

Rahman said they had to make haste. Ehud changed clothes, packed the leftovers in a paper bag and asked to be driven to the beach. Two bruisers in civilian clothes drove him in the ZIL truck, throwing fearful glances at him, and all around, perhaps fearing agents of Rahman's brother. They drove fast.

"Here, ya *Sidi*?" they said, when they arrived.

"Yes, thank you."

They left him on the beach near a desolate boardwalk, no one about, drove off in a shower of sand, impatient to get away, still looking around them. Ehud walked in the sand three miles to where he was left before, at the canal river's mouth, and was picked up on time.

The sailors could not believe him bringing the leftovers. "Just don't talk about it," he said, knowing they would, realizing he had been extremely stupid, giving them such a tempting reason to talk. But there was no note among the leftovers, no sign. She was not stupid, took no further chances.

Once back in the Sub, Ronen wanted to put him to work right away, but Ehud overrode him and called Gershonovitz to report.

After he had finished summarizing the deal he had reached with Rahman, Ehud asked, "When do you take it to the cabinet?"

"Not yet," Gershonovitz said. "We need more proof Rahman's following up."

"Following up how?"

"He has to move some tanks back, cut some SAMs, then we'll have to verify...."

The line chirped as Shimmel paused. Ehud knew what he was going to ask. "And you made contact there?" Meaning the agent on the spot.

"Five-five," Ehud said, using the Haganah code for perfect.

"And?"

"You are scum," Ehud said. "You and them." Whoever had sent her.

"So are you," Gershonovitz said. "But better we do shit to ourselves than the goyim do it to us."

Ehud said, "Anything else? What about Amzaleg?"

Gershonovitz said, "Oh, he had an accident."

Ehud said, "Scum is not a good enough word for us."

"Go, go to work," Gershonovitz said. "We don't have much time."

But it was easier said than done.

The news that Amzaleg had suffered an "accident" after returning from Beirut sent everyone into a tizzy, with everyone suspicious of everyone else. Finally Ronen felt compelled to address it.

"Accidented" or not, he said, maybe it was better like this because anything Amzaleg reported would've gone straight to Begin, and "all our work would've gone down the toilet."

"Then we'd all go back," he told them in the canteen on Friday eve. "Is that what you want?"

"So who accidented him?" someone asked.

"What the fuck do you care?" Ronen said. "Someone did the necessary *dreck*, like we all do."

"A true Zionist," someone said, and all laughed.

At this, someone said that maybe they should do the Bulldozer, save everyone a lot of trouble.

A few laughed. But Ronen thumped the table and said, enough. "Fuck this talk, no! We are soldiers, and we do what we are told. We are not a banana republic. We are a democracy."

"Yallah, yallah," someone else said. "I gotta go to sleep early, I have two jobs to do tomorrow."

"Me too," said Varda. "I got two jobs to do tonight."

"And do me too?" said someone, and everyone laughed.

"Anyway," said Yaro, "let's hope this madman is done with killing."

"Yah, let's hope," said Ronen.

-7-

Saturday, October 24, 1981, 5:15 p.m.,
Tel Aviv

G ERSHONOVITZ DID NOT rely on hope. Ten hours after he had gotten the report from Ehud, he called him on the scrambler. "Send me a copy of the personnel files of everyone who was here with you before Yom Kippur."

"You want mine too?" Ehud said, pissed off.

"Yes, also the OpLogs, everything."

Ehud said, "What about Amzaleg's notes? He talked to everyone, maybe he found something."

Which got him accidented, he thought but didn't say.

Gershonovitz said, "I don't have the notes, so he probably destroyed them or hid them, maybe."

"Maybe," Ehud said. "I'll talk to Ronen and see what we have."

But Amzaleg hadn't destroyed his notes.

As he'd been taught, he put them in his socks, and later, when he was sent home from the hospital in Jerusalem, they went with him. All the time he was lying in bed, recuperating, the notes were in the hall closet. He almost forgot about them.

Saturday, October 24, 7:15 p.m.,
West Beirut

THE KILLER FOUND it hard.

Ever since he'd returned to Beirut the previous week, he'd missed the post-Cleansing good feeling, because of course here he couldn't do any.

Of course, doing the jobs here was important too. But once he'd felt the pleasure of Cleansing the holy land itself, he knew he could not stop.

Yet although he read all the Israeli newspapers that came to Beirut daily on the boat, he saw nothing about his notes.

He could not understand it. Was he not concise enough? Not clear enough?

Perhaps because of this doubt, he found himself getting more tense as the week progressed. On the boat back, Ehud had given him a scare when he began to ask everyone where they had been and what they had done during Yom Kippur, and he resolved to lie low for a while, but it was hard.

As a self-reward for his patience, Saturday evening, when others drove to West Beirut for dinner and to relax, a few going to the new House on Rue Verdun, he went on his own to a Turkish-run men's house with *Atatürk's* pictures in the hall, dating from the days of the Ottoman Empire. Photos of Janissaries on the walls, and half-dressed bacha bazi boys, and painted Parisian *tantes* dancing…

He had been there once before, on a job. But today he returned as a customer, dressed in Syrian garb, wearing rimless glasses and speaking in Damascus slang.

There was much choice that night, young boys from the camps making a few pounds in their spare time. He did not detest the Arab boys. It was the brown Jewish ones who made him itch to Cleanse them and so purify the Jews, and also himself.

He lingered in the *Atatürk's* guest room downstairs, with old armchairs on a large Ferraghan carpet older than Methuselah. He smoked a hookah with Latakia tobacco and rose water, read the latest Tishreen paper, tracking the Damascus soccer league.

Later on his way out he tipped the doorman—not too much, so as not to be remembered, and also left five D-marks, voluntary charity in the UNRRA box for orphans at the Shatila Camp.

He felt good about it, and once back at the Sub, he felt less tense. Oddly enough, though, his need to go south again became even stronger.

Next week, he promised himself, right after Muharram.

He could hardly wait.

-9-

**Sunday, October 25, 11:15 a.m.,
Jerusalem, then HaTikva Quarter**

FOUR DAYS AFTER Amzaleg had been carried into the hospital, Zohara took him home. They almost did not let her take him. Finally a doctor was brought in—the one pinned to the wall by the Samson—who seemed not unhappy to rid himself of both Amzaleg and Zohara, and he signed the release with a near flourish.

A half-hour later, someone in the hospital made a phone call notifying someone in Police HQ. But it was only the next day that two policemen from Jerusalem's Poriya station came to the hospital, accompanied by a single Samson, and by that time Amzaleg was already gone.

Suissa and two of the Clandestine detectives, ben-Harosh and Zarnooga, drove in with the Abu Kabir morgue's old meat wagon, which for that day served as an ambulance. They wheeled out Amzaleg with his hospital bed, down the antique elevator, then carried him into the wagon onto a bed chained to the floor, and departed.

When they arrived in HaTikva, Munger was waiting, pacing to and fro in front of Amzaleg's flat, holding a black satchel with medical supplies and a plastic bag containing chicken livers.

"For the blood," he said.

But all Amzaleg could eat was liquid mush, and it would be weeks before the wire would be taken off his jaw, and weeks more before the cast on his wrist and ankle would be sawed off, then a month or two more before his muscles got back into shape. The ribs were just cracked and did not need a cast, but the thick bandages were as good as one. Even to the bathroom he could not go, and Pirchiya blushingly said she would put the pan under him.

All would take time. In the meantime, Amzaleg was a mass of dull pain, for which he refused to take anything Munger offered. He just shook his head, looking all the while at Zohara, who looked away—she was full of the drug, having injected the moment they got home, blowing half a day's pay on it. She could not bear to watch him, unable to do anything more than just protect him. And she still could not understand why she wanted to, after all he'd done to her, to her mother, and to her brother.

Maybe because he was one more *Ars* hurt by the *vooz-vooz*.

The metal bed monopolized half of Amzaleg's room, and his own went to the kitchen terrace. Pirchiya stayed with Amzaleg and so did Zohara.

Four boys from the Amidar hovels arrayed themselves before the hallway's entrance, armed with sticks and scowls, and two others deposited themselves at the back stairs leading to the kitchen terrace, as directed by Zohara. She needed them there because she kept trying to get off drugs and kept failing, as they all could see, but none mentioned it.

Wednesday, October 28, 8:25 a.m.,
HaTikva Quarter

THREE DAYS AFTER Amzaleg had returned home, Klinger and the police union's attorney came to see him. Neither Munger nor Pirchiya were there.

It was early morning. Klinger wore his usual crumpled uniform and a smirk, the union attorney a black yarmulke and a striped suit. He had plump jowls and carried a black briefcase.

As the two alighted, the three boys sitting on the front steps sprang to their feet and grabbed the whistles hanging from their necks.

Klinger barked, "Move aside, police business."

He tried to pass but when the boys stayed put, he shrugged, turned around and made a beeline through the yard to the back, the attorney following.

As they climbed the back steps leading to Amzaleg's kitchen terrace, they encountered the single boy there, a skinny runt from Jaffa. As Klinger began to push him aside, the boy saw it was useless to resist. But he had on his neck a soccer whistle that Zohara had made them all wear. He put it in his mouth and the shrill whistle brought out three boys sleeping at the back of the Moroccan synagogue, and it also brought Zohara out of her room, holding her razor.

Her face went white with rage. "What the fuck do you want?

Klinger's smiled, his long teeth showing. "You people kill each other, what can I do?"

Zohara hissed, "He should have killed you then…."

Klinger made a kissing sound. "Well sweetie, look who's half-dead now…."

Zohara took a step forward, felt dizzy and held the back of a chair. "You have a warrant? If not, get out, both of you."

The Amidar boys all nodded. One thumped on his palm with a stick and was shushed.

The lawyer made a soothing sound. "No need, we just want to talk to him."

"He can't talk. His jaw is broken. Get out."

The lawyer harrumphed. "Also, he has to sign something…."

In the other room, Amzaleg made *mmff* sounds. Zohara kept herself where she was. Fuck them. "He'll sign nothing. Out!"

"Or what?" Klinger said.

The boys looked at Zohara, seeking guidance.

She raised her left hand, three fingers forward. "You want me to lay a *sh'chur* on you?" Black magic. "A big one."

"Pff," said Klinger. "You think I'm afraid of your primitive *Schwartze*…."

Zohara probed the air with thumb and two fingers in front of Klinger's eyes, rasped from the bottom of her throat, "You shall not live out the year, ya accursed, and your wife will stay a widow—"

She felt dizzy, swayed, grayness before her eyes. Two boys caught her and tried to make her sit. She stayed where she was, blocking the way to Amzaleg.

Klinger clutched at his cap and said, "Move aside, sweetie."

Zohara said to the eldest boy, her voice a whisper, "Go to the grocer, ask him for his camera, say Zohara asked for it, come back…" she stopped.

The attorney said, "Yechiel, you want to arrest her? Arrest her. If not, let's get out of here. I got things to do. You too."

Zohara's eyes burned and she could hardly see through the gray fog, but she forced herself to stand straight and looked at the lawyer, "You don't leave, I'll lay a *sh'chur* on you too."

He raised his hand, gave her an uncertain smile. There was a red string on his wrist, an amulet by some miracle rabbi.

Zohara flashed her eyes, probed the air with three fingers. "I'll ask Ruja Up There to put a black *sh'chur* on your dick, every time you stick it in, you'll see my eyes, and you'll feel it shrinking, you won't be able to feel it, you won't be able to—"

The lawyer yelped, "Yechiel, let's get out of here. You don't need me for this...."

"Alright, alright," Klinger said. He made another kissing sound at her. It didn't come out well.

"Enjoy the time you have left, ya accursed," she whispered at him.

The two men left via the kitchen terrace stairs, the lawyer throwing wide-eyed glances behind him, Klinger cursing in Yiddish.

Amzaleg moaned from the other room. He could not yet speak. Zohara went over to him.

"What?" Zohara asked him. "What?"

His eyes asked her what it was about.

She said, "Two fucking idiots tried to scare you and me again. Klinger and this lawyer."

He shook his head, rolled his eyes at her, clenched his mouth.

The boys crowded in, each trying to outdo the others in telling him what took place.

"Out," she said. Her sight was better, the gray fog gone, but she felt tired; she needed a fix urgently. For the last three days she was trying to kick it, but it kept coming back, stronger still.

Just then Pirchiya came in and asked what happened.

Zohara said, "A policeman and a lawyer tried to come in, and the Amidar boys chased them off, tell everyone. Can you sit with Amzaleg for a while? I gotta go do something."

She grabbed her bag where she had a full hit in reserve, another half-day's pay. Stumbling into the tiny bathroom, she injected fast, and soon she felt it spread through her, the only good moment of the day. No, it was also good to scare them with a *sh'chur*. Not like the drug, but good nevertheless.

When she went to check on Amzaleg again, Pirchiya was mopping his forehead. Zohara tried to catch his eye but he would not look at her. He knew what she had just done in the bathroom.

She grabbed the pad, hid it from Pirchiya, wrote on it in rounded script: "Teach me what you learned in the army. I'll go look for the killer."

She surprised herself. She hadn't known she was going to write all this.

He read it. But when Pirchiya tried to read it, too, Zohara covered it with her hand.

"What is it?" Pirchiya said, alarmed. "Something bad?"

Zohara said, "No, it's okay."

Amzaleg was writing something back, in square letters. She read it.

"Get clean first."

She said, "I will." She looked at him, waiting.

"Will what?" Pirchiya said. "What?"

Zohara said, "Nothing. It's okay."

Amzaleg kept writing. "First."

She nodded. Suddenly she felt as if she was twelve again, understanding that she really didn't understand much.

"You okay?" Pirchiya said. "What did he write to you?"

She removed Zohara's hand. "Yes, you should," she said. "You should." She began to cry.

Pirchiya cried over everything, Zohara thought. *If I'm not careful I'll catch it from her.*

Pirchiya said, "Why 'first'?"

Zohara said, "Nothing, nothing."

But it was not nothing. It was suddenly a scarily big thing.

-11-

Friday, October 30, 7:40 p.m.,
First Muharram, and Saturday,

October 31, 9:45 a.m.,
Town of Shlomi, North Israel

THE NEXT KILLING took place at the end of the month, Saturday, October 31.

All week the killer had tried to stay quiet, but it was hard.

Luckily, First Muharram, the Muslim New Year, fell on Friday that weekend. The end of the Muharram feast was the best time. Their targets were either out celebrating or exhausted after their feast, their guard down.

He fulfilled his two assignments fast, then stole a Lambretta and rode it fast to aShams beach, broke into a small boat, cruised it south in the semi-dark, past the Dove Rock, and left it hidden in the rocky bay-nook, just beyond Rosh HaNikra in Israel. He walked a mile through fallow fields to the derelict hut, took out the motorcycle he'd hidden there, and rode to Shlomi, the little town of former Moroccans and Tunisians, his heart singing within him.

Luck was with him, or maybe the One Above was. With daylight just breaking, he saw a swarthy boy come out of the town's bomb shelter to pee. The boy agreed on the spot to do it for thirty shekels, behind an acacia hedge.

Later he finished the boy fast, a trio of palms rustling in the wind not far off, a calming sound. He scribbled the note from memory—he'd forgotten to write it before, silly him.

As he stuck the note in the boy's dirty shirt, he felt good. He was doing it for everyone and of course also for his father, whom he both loved and, he now realized with a pang, also hated for what he'd made him do, first in the Unit, then in the TempleWhores course, yet had never acknowledged his sacrifices.... Never hugged him and also told his mother not to do it either... to toughen him up, his father said.... Only when he missed shooting targets in the yard did his father slap his neck... so often he missed on purpose, just to feel his father's hand....

Without thinking, he slapped the dead boy's neck, for a moment he his father, the boy him.

He left half an hour after dawn on his motorcycle, and on the road back north, he could almost feel the Hand from Above caressing his neck.

He shivered with ecstasy. For a moment he could imagine it was his father.

All the way to the hidden boat, he hummed prayers and passages from the Prophet's book, composing the next note he'd leave.

-12-

**Saturday, October 31, 12:30 p.m.,
Shlomi, North Israel, and Tel Aviv**

THAT LATEST VICTIM was discovered faster than any of the previous ones, even though it was a weekend. When the other druggie who slept in the bomb shelter came out to take a pee, he discovered the dead victim and immediately called the police. Fifteen minutes later Klinger got a call.

"Don't touch anything," he said, pissing off the locals, "and if there's any note, don't read it, just put it in an evidence bag."

Which of course meant that all three policemen read the note thoroughly, smudging whatever fingerprints could have been on it. The text's incendiary language and the peculiar square script imprinted themselves so strongly on all three minds that nine hours later, all could quote it almost verbatim to a cub editor from Tel Aviv, who took the trouble to travel to the scene that night when she learned of the murder.

The newspaper published a part of the text the next morning on the back page's bottom, but it caused a stink nevertheless—bigger than anyone could remember since the Haifa riots: "…To cleanse the land from evil seed, to purify all Jewish blood from its Arab contamination…."

There was more, but the paper did not dare print it.

-13-

RIGHT AFTER KLINGER had gotten the phone call, Amzaleg's phone also rang. He, too, had asked a number of police stations' deskmen to tell him if and when such a killing took place. Only now it was Zohara who took the call.

She wrote down all details on a torn grocery bag, thanked the caller on behalf of Amzaleg, went into his room and told him.

He motioned with his fingers to the paper pad, which she pushed to his bedside. He quickly wrote, "Tell Suissa about this, then tell the heroic Amidars."

She looked at him and rolled her eyes. "Tell them what?"

He wrote, "Whatever you see fit." He rolled his eyes back at her and added. "You're in charge."

It gave her a queer sensation in her stomach to read this. But then he wrote, "And keep clean!"

Evading his eyes, she nodded and left, because, of course, she hadn't.

-14-

November, 1981,
HaTikva Quarter

EVER SINCE SHE had brought Amzaleg back from Jerusalem, she made a vow every morning to get off the drugs, tying it in her mind to a promise on Iddo's grave. But every evening, when the need for a fix gripped her, she again and again failed.

The sense of shame she felt when injecting was so overwhelming that she began to hope that it, rather than her resolution, would keep her from failing yet again. But the need was stronger.

Munger, who saw her struggling, said, "Hindelle, keep trying, I know it's hard."

"Don't call me that name!" she flew at him. "I'm Zohara. And how would you know?"

"Oh, I know, I know. I keep trying too," he said, and absurdly pointed his formaldehyde-stained finger to the ceiling, as if his drug was there.

She knew he was half-crazed. Every day it was proven anew. But he helped Amzaleg, which was what mattered. Still, she watched him, in case he did something really crazy, even when she was in a between-fixes *kriz*, she watched him.

But neither the *krizes* when she tried to prolong the times between injections nor the daily fixes (now two a day) prevented her from giving the boys their orders.

Right after she'd told Suissa about the latest killing, she called the boys in and made sure they all had their sticks and their whistles, and each knew his areas of patrol.

"And I want you to call the waiters at restaurants in Jaffa. They should go around, too, see if there's anyone new they don't know, looking for a fuck, a suck, whatever. Also in any other city where you know anyone."

The oldest boy said, "And then what?" meaning if anyone heard or saw anything.

"Then call me."

"And if you are, you know..." he said, leaving his meaning clear, that is, in a *kriz*.

"Then you're in charge," she said, saying to him what her father had said to her, seeing him inflate ridiculously. She hoped she had not reacted like this. What did she care what Amzaleg thought of her, what he said to her?

But she did. She kept resisting it, just as she kept trying to resist the drug's pull but failed.

That afternoon, however, after this latest killing, it was different. It suddenly became clear to her she couldn't kick the drugs. But she had to. If she didn't, more boys would die.

Munger had just come from the morgue to look at Amzaleg and to feed him the mush of fried liver and onions, with vitamins mashed in. Oddly, Amzaleg did not refuse and seemed even to like it, Pirchiya wiping his dripping chin.

Zohara waited for Munger to finish, then said, "Munger, I want you to tie me to the bed."

He grasped her meaning immediately. "Hindelle," he said. "No."

She had stopped objecting to the ridiculous *vooz-vooz* name he gave her. "Yes," she said. "And you don't untie me, no matter how much I beg. How long, Munger?"

Meaning how long it would take before she'd be clean.

Munger just twisted his mouth and shook his head. He didn't know.

Pirchiya began to cry, as usual. Zohara told her to stop. "Can you feed me too?"

Crying harder, Pirchiya nodded.

Munger said, "I'll make you liver also—"

"Fuck, no," Zohara said.

She went to Amzaleg's bedside and told him what she planned to do.

He wrote back, "You're sure?"

She said, "I'm not asking you, I'm telling you."

"Well then," he wrote in the square script he had adopted for the notes. "Do it."

She stared at him, her mouth clenched to hide her fear.

Two of the boys dragged Amzaleg's old metal bed from the kitchen terrace into her room and put hers on the terrace. Munger found some of Amzaleg's old plastic cuffs in the hall closet and brought them to her. But before he shut the closet door, the prone Amzaleg began to make *mmff* sounds, which meant he wanted to write something. When he did, Pirchiya read it then dug in the closet and came out with his shoes, his old socks in them. She rooted in the socks and came out with a sheaf of scribbled paper.

"These?" she said.

"*Mmff,*" Amzaleg said, and nodded his broken jaw.

Zohara put on her oldest clothes, lay down on the bed, and spread her hands. "Don't ask me again if I am sure, Munger. Just do it."

He tied her, like it was done to her in prison, tightening the plastic cuffs, first putting old towels on her skin. She saw Pirchiya, still sniveling, lifting the scribbled pages to Amzaleg so he could read them. But he only looked at her, Zohara.

That night she had her first nightmare, about Neve Tirtza jail. It was just like being in prison all over again, and again the following night, and the next.

-15-

**November, 1981,
HaTikva Quarter**

DURING THE THREE weeks Zohara was tied up, Pirchiya fed her, slid the pan under her, wiped her, emptied the pan and washed it. Even when Zohara was half-gone after her nightmares. Pirchiya also fed Amzaleg and did the same for him.

Pirchiya never flagged, never complained. She slept beside Amzaleg, even as this prevented her from sleeping properly. Because Amzaleg apparently had his own nightmares, or maybe his Blackness had come back, because often at night Zohara could hear him moan, then hear Pirchiya crooning to him, as if he was a baby and she, his mother.

Eli Sabag came every now and then, bringing some food that his wife had made; she never came in. "But she says *Mabruk*," Eli said. Blessings.

"And to her and you," Zohara whispered, her voice nearly gone.

Once, when she had just woken up, she thought she heard Amzaleg weep, but she must have been mistaken, or maybe it was she herself who was weeping. Because the nightmares kept recurring every night, sometimes several a night, or during the day, too, if she snoozed, when Pirchiya tried to feed her, weeping because Zohara, in her rage and need for the drug, called her names, called upon devils she had heard Great-Grandma Ruja call upon, to come and finish her misery. How much more can this last, she asked Munger, how much more until the cravings go?

He shook his head. He didn't know. Maybe they didn't, he said, but you learn to live with them.

Big help this was.

However, what always quieted her at the end, besides her exhaustion, was the knowledge that unless she kicked the habit, not only could she not stop the killings, but she'd never get out of this hellish country and never help others to leave. Yet the drug's pull was so great that more than once she demanded that Pirchiya untie her so she could get a fix; and then she adjured Munger in the name of the same devils, then cruelly in the name of his dead sister that he had idiotically given her, but neither complied. "Untie me, Munger!"

"You made me promise!" he shouted at her, weeping like Pirchiya, who just shook her head and did not reply, just kept feeding her the same food she had spit out.

"I release you from the promise!"

He wept some more. "It's not for you to release me, but for me to release you."

"Release me then!"

But Munger shook his head. "No. A vow is a vow."

"Wasn't a vow, was only a promise."

She raged and tugged at the cuffs until her wrists bled, like in prison, but it didn't help.

Amzaleg said nothing, not even *mmff* anymore, he just occasionally looked at her, when he was not looking at Pirchiya, his eyes now nearly fully open, most swelling gone, watching, saying nothing, his gaze inscrutable.

Zohara stayed shackled to the bed for three weeks before it was over.

-16-

Sunday, November 1, 4:30 p.m.,
Tel Aviv and West Beirut

THE AFTERNOON THE Shlomi killing was reported, Gershonovitz called Ehud and asked for the personnel files he'd asked for before.

"Where are they? It's a week now."

Ehud said, "We're collecting them, we've got no time to wipe our asses, we're running off our feet."

"What about Amzaleg's notes, you found them?"

"No, they're nowhere."

"Good," Gershonovitz said. "But keep looking. We gotta find out who of you went crazy on us."

"We are all crazy," Ehud said. He wanted to add "and you the biggest," but refrained. Aloud he said, "If you need help in this…"

Gershonovitz said in a Yiddish accent, "Neither your honey nor your sting."

It was from the Talmud. Don't do me any costly favors. Ehud said, "You religious all of a sudden?"

"No," Gershonovitz said. "He and I are enemies."

"You and Munger."

"No," Gershonovitz said. "Munger is only having a spat. With me, it's *ghom*." Blood vengeance.

"Alright, alright," Ehud said. He'd had enough of Shimmel's craziness. "We'll get you the fucking files, enjoy them with good health, and enjoy your *ghom*. End."

He went to find the files. Let Shimmel play detective if he liked.

Next morning, the personnel files of the six who had come with him on Yom Kippur, together with his own, were sent to Shimmel on the daily boat.

Amzaleg's notes, however, were nowhere to be found.

Monday, November 2, 11:10 a.m.,
Tel Aviv

E VER SINCE THE newspapers had published part of the killer's first
note, the police came under intense pressure to release the text of the
other notes.

For surely there were others?

At first the police spokesman refused to confirm or deny even that,
lamely directing all inquiries to Superintendent Klinger, who did not
want to comment either, more lamely still.

But did not the police see a common hand, since they had put in the
same superintendent to investigate all the murders, namely, him?

Superintendent Klinger, flustered, directed all inquiries to Chief
Superintendent Levitan, who first blew his top at the reporters, then at
Klinger, and finally at the police spokesman, who in a fit of pique leaked
that yes, there were other such notes, all in Chief Superintendent Levitan's
possession, but don't quote him on that.

At this, all newspapers plunged into a feast of wild speculation. But as
rumors began to reverberate about a special investigatory team, the very
next day an extraordinary Editors Committee was convened, and Judge
Fishkin handed out formal silence injunctions.

And so all mentions in the press stopped, even as the killings continued.

-18-

Sunday, November 8,
West and East Beirut

ASHURA, THE SHIITE parade mourning the prophet's grandson's killing, fell on Sunday, so the man couldn't sneak out Saturday. Instead he snoozed, reread the Ashkenazi Prophet's book, checked the poison-ampoule squirter, the various pencil knives, the backup garrotes, preparing.

Next day the Ashura festival was indeed madness.

Millions thronged the streets, pouring in from refugee camps and small towns, self-flagellating, blood streaming on their faces and their bodies. Fathers cut their toddlers' foreheads, lifted them up, the small white bandanas turning red.

It disgusted him that people would do such things to their children! What fathers would hurt their sons for the sake of an old book?

As he walked down Rue Mahmood Pasha tailing his first target, he saw others from the Sub, also disguised, crisscrossing the avenue. Nearly all the Sub's operators were out—a once-a-year opportunity. Both Anons and Mossadniks had long lists of targets. The killings would be hardly noticed amid the religious orgy of blood.

Later that night Ronen commended everyone on jobs well done. "Forty-nine in one day," he said. "Not bad, almost a record."

A small burst of clapping broke out.

"Enough," Ronen said. "Go get Clean. Well done, but we can do even better."

**November 14, 8:20 a.m.,
Elyashiv Village, near Hadera,
North of Tel Aviv, then HaTikva**

NEARLY TWO WEEKS passed and there was one more killing before Zohara was at last untied.

On Saturday, November 14, a young Yemenite was killed in Moshav Elyashiv. The next Saturday, however, there was nothing, though every policeman and reporter held his breath.

Still, the fact that all the latest killings occurred on a Saturday was a source of speculation in both the police and at Varash, where the matter acquired more and more urgency.

Of Amzaleg, and his accident, no one seemed to inquire; only Avigdor Feldman, head of the Shin Bet, sent Amzaleg a bunch of poppies.

The tied Zohara did not get any flowers. But her mother came every few days, and Batya Feuerstein came to visit and spoke to her in a low voice, got just nods, and left wiping her eyes.

The Amidar boys just kept their proud vigil, always there.

November 20, 8:20 a.m.,
HaTikva

ZOHARA WAS FINALLY untied, a little after eight in the morning.

Munger announced that his vow was now off, medically speaking. Two days before, he had drawn Zohara's blood and dipped a stick in her stool, sent both specimens to Maccabee Health lab and had just received the result.

"You are clean, Hindelle!" he chortled. "Clean like an innocent dove!"

Down below the kitchen terrace, the few boys standing guard there cheered weakly.

Munger used the rusty morgue clippers to cut her plastic cuffs, now crusted with dried blood. Zohara tried to sit up and speak, and failed.

After three weeks of lying down, she could barely speak or move, and her thinking was fuzzy, her eyesight dim.

"It'll come back," Munger said. "It will."

She flexed her legs and arms for a few minutes, then, supported by Pirchiya, went to look at herself in the bathroom mirror.

Her upper arms, thighs, neck, had become skinny and chicken-like, her breasts had flattened, her ribs showed, her hair thinned, her period stopped.

She looked like one of the stray Arab dogs in the Hirriya garbage dump.

At that same moment, to everyone's surprise, Amzaleg sat up in his bed, first time.

"*Zmmff,*" he said, and wrote something on the pad. Pirchiya rushed to see what he wrote. "*Mabruk,* Zozo!" Blessings, she called out, and as expected, burst out crying.

Zohara nodded weakly, felt anger at the wetness in her eyes and at her weakness. It was the name he used to call her when she was ten or twelve.

Munger just beamed, as if he had done it, not she, and said something in Yiddish.

Pirchiya gave Zohara a hug. "From me too."

"Yallah, get off me," Zohara whispered. "You are heavy."

Indeed, Pirchiya was. Though only in her second month, her stomach was beginning to bulge, perhaps also since she now ate more. Besides, Zohara and Amzaleg ate so little, and Jacqueline cooked so much, there was always food left.

Zohara could not stand for long. She sat down. "Tell me," she said to Munger.

Without being prompted he told her of the latest killing. "Last week, nothing this week."

Zohara turned her head to Amzaleg. "You heard?"

"*Mmff,*" he said.

"So now you'll teach me?"

He nodded, winced, blinked, then blinked again. Pirchiya wiped his eyes.

They started a day later, right after Amzaleg's jaw was unwired.

-21-

November–December, 1981,
HaTikva Quarter

IT TOOK A long while for them to recover.

When Zohara had first gotten out of bed, she could hardly walk. Amzaleg was the same. She had lost twenty pounds, he had lost forty. Both now looked like skinny dogs. The wire on Amzaleg's jaw was loosened by Munger, the cast on his ankle was taken off (again by Munger), and the hard bandages on his ribs changed to soft ones.

Amzaleg still could eat mostly mush, though he could chew it a little. But Zohara could eat, and she did—in large quantities. And every day, they sat at the kitchen table and went over Amzaleg's copybooks from that first Takedown course in the state's early days.

Zohara marveled at how legible and clear it was and, oddly, how fast she could take it all in. It all seemed so obvious to her, so natural. Most oddly, Amzaleg's pay suddenly increased and went straight into his bank account. Someone had pushed through his new rank, though he didn't know who.

Probably Feldman, he said; he was always a joker.

But now Amzaleg could pay back some of his grocery debt. They'd eaten less when bedridden but Pirchiya was eating more, even fattened a little, and her breasts grew.

"You got what I lost," Zohara told her. Her own breasts grew back a little, but not much. The rest had turned into muscle from the daily exercises, hard like a man's.

From the third week on, after Amzaleg's cast was taken off, every day she did push-ups, sit-ups, curls, lifting stones, chairs by their legs, doing splits and rolls, Amzaleg putting her through an accelerated regimen on the roof behind the hanging laundry, so no one would see. It was most important that no one knew they were getting better, he said. Not even the Amidar boys, who talked incessantly like old fishmongers.

Some of the training, then more and more of it, Amzaleg did alongside her, shaming her: "Hey, Zozo, I can do it, you can't?"

From the fourth, fifth week on, the pace increased. He timed her hits, her punches, her spins, with an old stopwatch Munger had brought. Faster, faster still. Spinning while cutting at two opponents, evading punches, slashes and stabs, kicks, feints, and again. Again. And again.

The one thing she couldn't do well was the splits. Amzaleg, by then nearly recovered, amazingly, could fall fast, one leg forward, the other back, his scrotum touching the floor. Like a ballet dancer doing *shpagatt*, Munger said. An old man like him.

She remembered doing something like this in the hospital in Jerusalem, this odd split, not even thinking, sliding on the floor toward the Samson; but she could not do it again.

"Why do I need this?"

"In case someone hits you, you fall flat like this, you disappear, much further than he expected, then you hit at his knees. You break a man's knee..."

Yes, yes, she knew this part.

"Now again," he said, and again. And again.

After a month, he brought out an old flat pistol, took her to the building's roof, showed it to her, made her take it apart, put it together. And again, and again, eyes closed: Everything again and again and again. He took a few bullets apart, poured out half the powder, put them together, loaded the magazine.

"Why did you do this?"

"Short distance, you don't need more, less noise. Now shoot at this paper, lock your elbow."

"What gun is this?"

"This? A Batya."

She laughed. "What?"

"The Israeli version of the Beretta, made here without a license. Now shoot, but lock the elbow. Breathe, stop, then squeeze."

The shot went in. And the second. The third missed.

"Again."

Then he brought regular bullets, and a potato.

"What's this for?"

He took out his jackknife, sprung it, burrowed in the potato and stuck the gun's muzzle into it.

"Silencer," he said. "Cheap."

She shot again, and again. The gun burped, barely. This time she hit all three shots. And again.

"Why do I need all this?"

"Because he's dangerous."

"He's crazy, that's all."

She wanted to say, I am dangerous, too, but by now she had learned to keep her pride in check, or the learning didn't stick. It took an effort.

Amzaleg said, "No, he's most dangerous. He's been trained to kill, no second thoughts; he learned the human body as a geography of targets, like a painter sees a landscape, doesn't see mountains, trees, road, whatever, he sees a line of lemon-yellow here, a thick patch of red ochre there, the shadow is not a shadow but Prussian blue—he breaks it apart, sees it differently. The light is a titian white, the cloud zinc white, not a cloud…."

She stared at her father, mesmerized.

He went on, "… He doesn't see a body advancing at him, he sees solar plexus, base-of-throat, kidney behind hip, kneecap indentation, mid-scrotum, earhole, soft temple… jug-u-lar."

His voice had become singsong, evidently reciting.

She looked at her father, blinked. "You did this too? Learned it?"

He nodded curtly.

"They made you paint also? Teach you to break things up, see them differently, like this?"

He seemed oddly shy all of a sudden.

"Yes, a little, draw upside down, to see things in parts, not the way they show themselves…. Learn to see the body as a target map… knife for this, pencil knife for that… we didn't have poison ampoules then, we had… other things… also had to just use what's at hand…."

His voice slowed, stopped.

She felt awed all of a sudden, shy, too, of the father whom she never knew she had. Who was he? What was he?

"Now again," he said, and again.

At night she slept soundly, her body felt new, but not fresh, just revamped, the yearnings for the drug still in there, somewhere, smoldering, but she in charge.

Munger saw it too. "Keep at it, Hindelle," he said. "I know it's hard, it'll always be with you."

"Get off it, Munger," she said. "I'm fine. Really."

She hoped.

One morning, late December, she went on the roof with Amzaleg, saw a frayed mannequin that a tailor had thrown out in the municipal dump, it now leaned against the water pipe. The boys had brought it, probably.

"What's that for?"

"Teach you how to hit, show you where."

"I know how to hit!"

"No, you don't. You still hit to hurt, to make them fall, to stun, you punch. No. You hit to break, to penetrate, to shatter, to kill, like a knife, not a sledgehammer, like an axe. Now repeat."

"To break, to penetrate, to shatter, to kill."

"Now again. See it before you while you say it."

She repeated after him, and again, seeing it, feeling the beginning of a buzz, like a joy.

The mannequin was broken in two days. He said, "I thought it would last the week."

"Well," she said, "you thought wrong."

In the evening they ate together now, which surprised her the most. She had never eaten with him, never eaten much with everyone in the family, because they used to say those crazy prayers. But now he said nothing beside regular talk, a little about what he did in the army—not operations, just the course, and about the first instructors, Gershonovitz, Munger, some others already dead. And some from HaTikva also.

"No!" she said. "Like who?"

"Oh, *Adon* Leon, and Eli Sabag, and the cantor's father, rest in peace...."

"No!" She exclaimed, "Leon too?"

Yes, he was the best car thief, and also not a bad pickpocket. And the cantor's father, talented burglar. And one Zacharia, a slaughterer, a *shoychet*, still giving knife refreshers, but also working—

"I thought the *shoychet* was you, that's what they called you."

At this he clammed up for a while. She tried to bring it up later, he clammed up again, and she learned not to speak of it.

Again and again he brought out his old copybooks, blue-lined and musty, went over them with her, line by line. How to raise an Other to take over while you do a job, then how to Reverse. You first find a Good Place you can Reverse to, by the Stanislavsky Method, both.

"You learned all this too?"

He nodded, yes.

"From theater people?"

"Yes, was called self-support skills, don't know what they call it now. If they teach it."

Line by line they went, she repeating it, again and again, reciting it almost.

Once she said, "You're teaching me like in a religious kindergarten, where they teach them the Torah when they're young. So it'll stick."

To hypnotize them, she thought, *so they'd agree to be killed;* but didn't say.

He looked at her fast, blinked, began to speak, stopped, just nodded.

Yes, he said, his father had taught him the Torah, he was teaching her this.

"*M'darf,*" she said to him, surprising herself. She had caught some Yiddish words from Munger. It's necessary. The killer was still out there and the *vooz-vooz* did not seem to want much to catch him. So it was up to them, apparently.

"Yes," he said, "*M'darf.*"

They looked at each other, blinked, one of those moments, both embarrassed, getting too close suddenly to something, even if it was necessary.

She hoped it was necessary. She felt herself changing, transforming, and didn't recognize herself anymore: Who she was becoming, as if she was turning into something she'd always been but didn't know it. She was almost afraid of it.

At times she thought that Batya, too, seemed to fear her a little, her mother, too, but not Munger. It was as if he could see the transformation and was resigned to it, had seen it before.

She caught her father, though, often looking at her not with fear, but with deep sadness, as if he was losing something, too, as she changed. Like something he had undergone before, and knew where it was leading. It made her even more afraid, yet also more determined.

But she liked him calling her Zozo again. No one else did, she wouldn't let anyone, though maybe in the future, if....

If, if, if.

She was now twenty-five years old, had tugged men's dicks for pay and for conversation, sucked a dick once because she was coerced, but had never yet fucked a man, let alone made love to one.

Or must she, too, kill before she had managed to love? Just like her brother?

-22-

January, 1982,
Beirut, Israel, Jerusalem and HaTikva

MEANWHILE THE KILLINGS in Beirut went on, and so did those in Israel.

Nearly every week or two another swarthy boy was taken down, in some low neighborhood, all shot behind the neck.

The mode of killing was never published, but Amzaleg and Zohara learned of it from police stations' deskmen, contacts of the Clandestine, or Amzaleg's friends in Crimi ID lab.

Not all killings were reported in the press. Some were hushed, others made into something else. Weekly Varash meetings were now reporting directly to Kadishevitz, who gave the PM the expurgated version: Drug-crazed pushers killing each other, the police and Shin Bet doing their best. He did not dare to blame the Anons directly, because who knows, Amzaleg might recover and it would all come out—Shimmel's part and his own. One had to be careful.

Indeed, once or twice the PM even inquired: "And this *Schwartze* policeman? He is better now? I'd like to talk to him."

"No, he's still recovering, jaw wired, poor man, can't even talk. I'll let you know when."

"Alright, Kiddush.... Oy, what would I do without you?"

The boys patrolled HaTikva, others patrolled Jaffa, Bat Yam, and neighboring slums; older local volunteers did too.

The police didn't like it. "But we have to help ourselves," Zohara said.

"Like we should've done Over There," Munger said once.

"But you are helping now," Zohara said.

"Well, no one helped us."

"You should've helped yourselves."

In a rage, Amzaleg told her to get off this. "He doesn't sleep afterward. Why do you say these things to him? He loves you."

It astonished her. "No, he loves his dead sister, from the ovens."

"No, Zozo, it's you. You throw it in his face, now he finally can love again?"

She felt as if she'd been slapped.

Amzaleg went on, "You'd be doing him a kindness, let him, even if you don't like him."

She whispered, "I… No, I like him, I… I'm sorry."

The realization was like a hot stab. Did Amzaleg talk about himself too?

Surprising herself, she touched his cheek then quickly lowered her eyes, unable to look at him. But he covered her fingers with his, and with his other hand raised her chin so she had to look.

She felt her eyes grow hot, then wet.

"Be kind, Zozo," he said, "if you can."

She shook off his hand and dashed out, unable to stand the sudden knowledge. How far did her blindness go?

And during all that time, the killings in Beirut and the Biqaa and environs continued, as Ehud's negotiations with Rahman continued, and as Gershonovitz went on with his quiet investigation.

By the beginning of February, however, all these things changed.

-23-

Sunday, January 31, 10:35 a.m., West Beirut

ON SUNDAY, EHUD received a rare phone call from Rahman's French *barbouz*.

He listened in disbelief when told that the coup would have to be postponed, since Rahman now had an urgent job to do for his brother, the president.

The scrambled line chirped and warbled as the call was rerouted many ways to hide its origin.

Ehud's heart flipped when he grasped what the *barbouz* was telling him.

"Like what, urgent, where? What?"

"Something in Hama," the *barbouz* said circumspectly, his voice crackling. "I can't tell you more. The Muslim Brothers are getting uppity, making trouble. If they start a rebellion there, it can spread…. All the family's business would be at risk. I shouldn't be telling you this. But he's not canceling, just postponing."

Ehud said, "I don't know if we can hold back much longer."

"You should keep trying," the *barbouz* said. "It's only a month, maybe two. Rahman still wants to."

"If we can," Ehud said.

Fuck, he thought, Shimmel will plotz, and so will the guys in the Sub.

How much longer? How many more? Haifa Hospital's psych ward will have to build another wing, buy a dozen more electroshock machines, hire more psychiatrists.

He said, "And your side?"

He could almost see the shrug. "I hope," said the Frenchman.

"You don't know? You have to consult them, before you continue?"

The *barbouz* said in French, *"Je ne consulte point pour suivre mon devoir."* I don't consult to follow my duty.

Fuck, Ehud thought. Pompous ass, quoting plays.

"Yallah," he said, "I'll let you know. End."

Shit, shit, he thought. What will Shimmel say?

But to his surprise, Gershonovitz did not plotz, did not blow his top, unbelievably he almost barely paid attention to the delay.

Most probably because, as Ehud learned much later, Gershonovitz finally found who the rogue killer was. He'd learned who it was that same morning, two hours before Ehud called.

All through December and January, Gershonovitz had been meticulously collecting data about the probable movements of each of the seven who had come to Tel Aviv for the refresher during the week preceding Yom Kippur.

He then kludged together their probable whereabouts during each weekend since, via their Beirut jobs OpLogs, skimpy as they were. He called Ronen almost weekly, driving him crazy, checking and cross-checking. Then he browsed through the personnel files, made phone calls to the psychiatrists who patched up Mossadniks and Anons.

Then by the end of January, Gershonovitz knew.

You are an idiot, he told himself. You should have known from the beginning. The question was, what should he do now?

It was then that he got the phone call from Ehud telling him of the hitch.

"We got a postponement," Ehud said straight off. "His *barbouz* called."

Gershonovitz said, "It's the Hama thing?"

Ehud tried not to show his surprise. "What do we tell him?"

Gershonovitz said, "Later, I'll call you soon. Listen, I gotta do something right now. Can you hold the guys for a while?"

Ehud was more astonished at this than when the *barbouz* had called, and also more enraged. "What do you mean, hold them?"

"Just a day or two, I'll come back to you. Just two days. Please. End." Gershonovitz hung up.

Ehud stared at the scrambler, flummoxed. Shimmel had said please. What was going on?

Someone knocked on the door. It was Ronen.

He said, "What's with Shimmel?"

"No idea."

Ronen said circumspectly, "It's still on?"

"Yes," Ehud said. "Still on."

But was it?

Zohara was finally making headway too. It began with her performing the last task she needed in her training, to test her Other on a real job—as real as she could make it.

She didn't tell Amzaleg she was going to do it, and he didn't ask.

When she came back from the Jaffa garbage dump, having done it, she went straight to the bathroom and washed the blood off her hands, put iodine on the scratches. She tried to throw up as Amzaleg said might happen, but nothing came.

She just washed her hands, again and again.

Amzaleg looked at her from the doorway. "A dog?" he asked.

She nodded, still seeing the slit throat, the wild eyes losing luster as life ebbed. "Yes."

He nodded diagonally and left, saying nothing.

But it took her a full day to Reverse. What she couldn't get over was the feeling during the kill, the sheer joy of it, as if she had found what she was meant to do.

Was it like this for him also? She wanted yet didn't want to know.

Only once Amzaleg mentioned it, later. She hadn't asked him anything but he said, "Because you must be sure, if the time comes and you face him, it's either him or you, that you can do it."

She said nothing. She understood that with the Samsons, he had hesitated. Because they were Jews, probably; but it wouldn't matter to her.

He said, "There's no other way to be sure."

"Yallah," she said. "Enough."

That evening Amzaleg went over his Beirut notes one more time, then said, "It must be one of the seven who came here before Yom Kippur. You should speak to them all." He gave her the list of names. "Go see them. They're probably in Beirut, but some may be on monthly leave. Maybe you'll learn something."

"What about those without addresses?"

"Find them yourself."

She didn't ask how, felt it was some sort of test. "Then ask them what?"

"Whatever you think, see what you can find out."

She waited for him to tell her to watch her step, take care, because of the obvious danger; but he said nothing.

It gave her a hot pang. Didn't he care about her? She knew he did. He had almost killed Klinger for what he had done to her. Just the memory of Amzaleg straddling Klinger, hand-on-throat, made her all warm inside. Yet Amzaleg said nothing to her about being careful, as if he was sending her to war, where one did not need to be reminded of it.

Just like when he had sent Iddo to the army?

She wrenched her mind away from this. She was not Iddo, and Amzaleg had not forced her to go and fight. She had asked him to teach her so she could catch the killer.

She didn't have to ask why Amzaleg didn't go out himself. He was still not completely well, and the Samsons lurked out there. Or, maybe he just wanted to train her. It was possible.

He gave her money, of this there was no lack now, courtesy of the Shin Bet's Feldman, who had pushed for Amzaleg's new rank. It was more than what he had made before. She didn't even have to work anymore at the hair salon. She almost missed it, but not quite.

It took her half a day to fill in the rest of the addresses, then she set out. The first man she went to meet was Ehud Reznik, the one Amzaleg said was the top guy in Beirut, after Ronen.

-24-

Sunday, January 31, and Monday, February 1
HaTikva, then Jerusalem, then Kibbutz in Upper Galilee

S HE DID NOT phone in advance, just took the bus to Jerusalem, scanning her surroundings all the way like Amzaleg had taught her, but saw no followers.

Ehud was not at home. The Jerusalem trip was wasted.

The next two men on her list were not home either, one in Kibbutz Sha'ananim, near Hadera, the other in Acco, north of Haifa. To both places she traveled hours more by bus. Both men, she was told, were on Reserve Service. These trips were wasted also.

But she found she didn't mind. She had never traveled so far on buses before. It was as if she was seeing the country for the first time. She had rarely ventured out of HaTikva, except for her time in Shfar'am, the Arab town in the lower Galilee, and of course, the reformatory. She realized that all her life she seemed to have lived in Black Israel, where she and her kind lived, not the place the newspapers and magazines wrote about. She was really seeing White Israel for the first time now, it was a new country for her but she did not dislike it. Some of it was pretty. She returned home late to HaTikva, then set out once more the next day.

The fourth man on her list lived on a kibbutz also but was only renting there. His address she had found on her own. After futilely checking in several places, she contacted the subscription manager of *Davar*, the

Labor Party's newspaper, and learned the man's whereabouts—a kibbutz on the Western coast of Lake Tiberias, in the north.

"He got some inheritance," Zohara said, in response to the question, using her Ashkenazi voice. "From an aunt in Poland, and we are looking for him. I am with the lawyers…. What? Oh, Rubinstein, Klinger and Levitan. Thank you so much."

She scribbled the address, rolling her eyes at her father, who had rolled his first.

Again she took the bus. It took her three and a half hours to get there. Even though the previous trips were all duds, she felt oddly exhilarated as the bus meandered between mountains. This Anon, too, would probably be away on Reserve Service, but it almost didn't matter. She had never done such a thing before, gone on a mission; and for her father, too, also for all those killed, and for those who would be killed if she and Amzaleg did not stop the madman.

She told herself to tamp down what she felt, but it kept coming up.

"Gidi?" said the kibbutz secretary when Zohara had pushed his office door open. If he was astonished to see a beige woman with a casque of frizzy hair, he did not show it. "One of the renters?"

"Yes," said Zohara.

"What's he done?"

Apparently he had taken her for a police detective because of the accent she now used.

"Nothing. I just want to talk to him."

The secretary, a large man with the rolling walk of a paratrooper, shrugged, got up and pointed to a house in a row of decrepit houses, not far from a wire fence at the edge of a fallow field stubbled with thistles. "Over there," then he added in a tone of gruff apology, "the first houses we built, before '48, we now rent them out—but not to Arabs."

"Of course not," Zohara said, but the man had already gone in.

She tramped down the muddy trail toward the first of the crumbling structures, some barely standing. Rags had been laid on a wooden horse, perhaps to dry, but were now soggy with water. It gave the place the air of a refugee camp or a Moroccan immigrants transit station. Even the scent of the faraway lake seemed overlaid with rot.

The rotting smell was stronger as she trampled up the trail. The house that the secretary had pointed out was just as derelict, but someone had given it a coat of crude green paint and the paint had bubbled up in the rain.

From within came the honey sound of violins, two of them, playing what she'd heard at Batya's. After a few seconds she realized she knew the piece. She waited for the second violin to come in, for the final scherzo, then knocked.

After a moment the door opened. Inside it was dark, but she discerned a tiny kitchenette and a metal-spring bed. On the floor was an Arab raffia mat on which a record turntable was turning.

The man in the door was neither tall nor short. He stood in complete attention, as if focusing all his faculties on the visitor. The quality of his immobility was so complete that he reminded her of her father, she could not tell exactly why.

She stood just as immobile. "You Gideon Sukenik?"

Without speaking, the man opened the door and moved aside in one smooth motion, his other hand held sideways, the fingers spread.

She slid into the room and waited, one hand inside her handbag.

The sound ended and the needle kept bumping against the turntable's middle. The man did not move to stop it, and after a while Zohara bent over and lifted the needle, keeping her eyes up. As she straightened, she looked around her, carefully.

The room was small but clean. Bare walls, a military metal bed with a seaweed mattress, spread with a fluffy down blanket in a white cotton coverlet embroidered by hand. A plywood table, two wooden chairs, one black armchair overflowing with old newspapers, and a heap of softcover books.

On the floor stood a tiny porcelain coffee cup, with dregs of black in it. On the kitchenette counter was a Bedouin coffeepot and a lopsided paper bag.

Without being invited she walked to the armchair, pushed the newspapers to the floor, and sat down.

"You were with the Unit when?" she said without preamble.

Sukenik extended a hand, curling the fingers rapidly. The fingers were long and tapered, like a violinist's, and seemed foreign to his wrist, which was as thick as a stevedore's and just as scarred.

She leaned forward, pulled her father's wallet out of her shoulder bag and put it into the waiting fingers. The man flipped through the documents one by one. Then handed the wallet back to her and she stuffed it in the bag.

He raised his eyebrows at her.

"I'm his daughter," she said.

"Your father is the *shoychet*?" The "slaughterer."

She nodded, "That's how you still call him?"

"Not me. I'm from sixty-nine. Course number seven. He was first course, from what? Fifty-two?"

"Fifty-one, he said."

The man stared at her. "How come he told you this stuff?"

She said carefully, "I'm helping him in something."

"You? In what?"

His eyes were so pale as to be nearly transparent. His hair, too, was pale yellow, and his eyelashes, though long, were barely visible. Some sort of smell, disconcertingly faint, emanated from him. She could feel her crotch moistening and clenched her stomach angrily.

She said, "There were some killings…"

The man said, "Yeah, he came up north, your father, asked questions. I talked to him. I heard he went back, had an accident, went to hospital."

Zohara said dryly, "Wasn't an accident."

The man kept looking at her. He seemed to be looking right into her, she didn't know how he did that. Could her father do it too?

She said, "You—working up there too? Or you're done with it?"

She didn't say Beirut, somehow it seemed to be too explicit.

"No, I gotta go back tomorrow."

She raised her eyebrows, meaning, what are you doing here now?

He paused and blinked, as if surprised.

She felt surprise, too, didn't know how come they were talking like that, how he had accepted her so readily, she him. Just in case, she kept her hand close to her handbag, near the shiv, but it didn't seem as if there was danger.

Still she kept her hand there.

He said, "I had to go into hospital for a few days."

"Black?" she said.

He started. Then he said, "Ah, the *shoychet*... your father still got it?"

She said, "The Blackness? It used to come and go, then it almost went away, then after—Jerusalem—he got it back...."

The man looked at her, eyebrows raised.

She said, "He's okay now." She waited. "Recovering." She paused again. "Also they broke his jaw, and his ankle, and one hand... it takes time...."

He nodded slowly. "Why you here?"

"I have some questions.... He sent me to ask.... He can't leave the flat.... They are watching it...."

She didn't know if she did right, to confide so fast in this man. But her father had told her to trust her instinct, both in action, and before and after. Well then.

He waited, and she said, "What are you doing in a kibbutz?"

"Living."

She searched for something to ask, but her mind didn't seem to work. There was a faint smell coming from him, like a cake freshly baked. It made her mouth water, and she felt it also between her legs.

Was she as bad as that? It hadn't happened before, not like that.

There was a short silence as they stared at each other, like two feral animals who'd found themselves indoors, trying to gauge whether this had made them into enemies or temporary allies, or maybe something else.

Outside a distant tractor rattled to life. Presently Zohara said, "Since when you're here?"

"Seventy-four." He stared back at her through his pale eyes. "Seven years now."

"Doing what?"

Sukenik shook his head.

She persisted. "Where do you get money to pay the rent? And food?" She indicated the coffee- bag with her head.

"None of your business."

"You working? Or grandmother gives you money?"

A touch of color rose in Sukenik's transparent cheeks. "I work in the cow-shed for the rent, and in the kitchen." He paused, hesitated.

She said, "Reserve Service? They pay?"

He nodded, then said, "But I don't take it."

When it became clear she could not understand, Sukenik shook his head. "Don't want to."

She still did not understand.

Sukenik added, "Every year they come, I tell them to fuck off. What about the—your father? They asked him too?"

"I don't know." He never said anything. "Besides, he is in the police. And he's too old."

"You're never too old."

She breathed in, out; the smell in her nose was turning her head. She wanted to stretch out her hand and touch him, and she didn't know why.

She said, "But now you said you'd do it?"

Sukenik's cheeks flushed more. "Three months ago they came again, asked me to be an instructor in a knife course, maybe do a demo. I threw them out. I said, go talk to Munger."

She waited, nodded, to show she knew who Munger was.

Sukenik said, "Last month Reznik came, he told me why they need everyone."

She shook her head, to show she didn't know the man, hadn't met him.

There was a brief silence.

Sukenik bent down, picked up the coffee cup, and drained the dregs into his mouth. He picked up the record, put it back in its sleeve. "You like this?"

Zohara said, "Bach is okay. But I can't listen to him and talk at the same time."

They stared at each other. Zohara knew she should be asking more questions: her father's copybooks had shortlists, said what to ask when,

when to wait, or say nothing. Now she said nothing, but not because of the lists, she just found she wanted to hear him talk.

She blinked, felt the flush rise up her neck all the way from between her breasts.

Sukenik said abruptly, "My grandfather helped found this kibbutz, walked all the way from Kishinev, on foot. Took him two years. For years he had dreamed of Zion, and organized the first self-defense group against Cossacks, after the pogroms. You heard about the Kishinev pogroms?"

"I don't know, maybe," she said. "I studied in Bnot Yaakov."

Sukenik nodded absently. "Don't know it. I went to the Reali school in Haifa, after my parents divorced, left here. Lived with my father, he was high up in the army... so I went to the army too...." He fell silent. "My grandfather dreamed of his grandchildren being soldiers. Jewish soldiers."

She said, "My grandfather, he didn't want a policeman son."

There was a short silence. Finally Sukenik said, "What do you want to ask me?"

Her heart beat faster. It was a simple question. What did she want to ask?

Instead she said lamely, "You read about these killings?"

Without taking his eyes off her face, Sukenik nodded. "The drug dealers who also sold their ass?"

She felt herself going rigid, forced herself to relax.

She said, "You were where, those days?"

A spark of expression came into Sukenik's eyes. "The first time, here, with Reznik and the rest, then at the time of the other killings, in Beirut. First time I came back is now, after two months." He paused. "I don't know why I came." He paused for a long moment. "Had to, I guess, for the Reverse."

She nodded.

He suddenly seemed eagerly keen to talk to her, as if he saw her in a new light. "You... he taught you? To get into... an Other?"

She nodded again, curt, reserved. Your Other is nobody's business, her father had said, but your own.

But the man now persisted. "And you can get in, out, no problem?"

She said, "I don't want to talk about it."

He nodded slowly, with seeming approval, not at all put out.

She said, "You been here how long now?"

"Since Sunday."

"Anybody seen you here?"

The man shrugged. "I eat at the dining room." His lack of interest now returned. Or perhaps it was a show. "You think I did any of this?" It seemed to amuse him.

"Or someone like you."

Sukenik stared at her for a long while. Two conflicting emotions seemed to battle in his face. At last he said, "You want a coffee? Something?"

"Yes. Bedouin, if you can make it."

She didn't say, like my father does, but Sukenik already turned to the kitchenette. "Can do."

She said, "You have something to eat too?"

Saying this seemed to have cost her a lot—she felt her heart beat, and the image of the ginger-haired student blinked before her, the boy who had thrown her hooker's fee in her face because she was not *vooz-vooz*. This one did not seem to care.

She struggled to rise from the deep armchair, and without looking, he extended his hand backward and helped her to her feet. His touch sent a buzz all through her.

She said, "You never… never did any Reserve Service? Before now?"

He did not look at her. "No. When I left I went to hospital for a month, then… then I went to another service, for two years… didn't like it…. Then I came here."

He watched the water boil, then withdrew the Bedouin coffeepot from the little gas burner.

She said, "What other service?"

"I'll tell you later."

As he served her the coffee, he asked with amusement, "You are not afraid I would, you know, attack you, if I were the guy you are looking for?"

She said, "What could you do to me?"

Without putting down the coffeepot, he struck at her neck with the other hand, not sideways, but straight in, fingers stiff.

Before the finger blade came near, she caught his wrist, twisted it up, her thumb between the thin bones at the palm's root. She was not even aware of it until she had done it but now waited for what he would do. There were only two ways to get out of a wrist lock, Amzaleg had said.

But Sukenik just smiled, put the coffeepot down, and with his still-warm hand he patted her cheek, then the back of her neck, and she trembled and felt herself letting go.

"What did you do?" she said. Amzaleg had never taught her this.

Sukenik shook his head. "They don't teach it. At the Unit they only have men as targets."

She didn't understand, but before she could ask him what he'd meant, they were kissing, not hard at first, just insistent, then she made it harder, didn't care anymore, despite a blink of surprise inside her—how long since she had met him? Thirty minutes? Less? She didn't know when they had taken their clothes off, nor how they got into bed. She became conscious of her actions only when she heard the bed squeak, then heard herself cry out as she came, marveling that there was hardly any pain—apparently she was no longer a virgin, after what Betty did to her in Neve Tirtza. But it was sweet, so sweet, she felt she would melt with it, knew it couldn't get any better.

But she was wrong. As she lay on her side, looking at him with wonder, smelling him, he inserted his fingers inside her, began to stroke upward, under her navel, looking into her eyes, his eyes not even blinking, as if he was looking into her, all the time his hand inside her stroking up.

She felt a buzz start through her, then a violent trembling, and when she came again, it was almost painful, so strong it was, she jackknifed and cried out full throat, felt a big spurt coming out of her, like peeing, but not that, something else. Then she came again, and again; and as she heard her own shouts she glimpsed at the edge of her vision what must have been colors—at least she thought they were, bright and luminous. Like the heat halos around the dancers at the Velvet, only richer, but when her shudders quieted down, they melted and vanished.

Her heart was hammering so hard she felt dizzy, her body still shuddering every few seconds, but less and less hard, also the spurting stopped. At last he got up, brought her a towel.

"What did you do?" she whispered, her voice hoarse. "Where did you learn this?" He shook his head but she insisted. "Tell me! You a doctor?"

Again he shook his head. "Later, I'll tell you later."

"No, tell me now," she said.

He did, and then she almost regretted he had.

After he'd Blacked out of the Unit, he still wanted to do something for the country his grandfather helped found and his father served. So he entered a TempleWhores course, *Kdeshim veKdeshot*. It took place in Jaffa above a café, one of the first such courses, both men and women.

They were taught it as a science and an art, by both doctors and psychologists, and yes, some high level prostitutes also, and one old graduate of the Russian school, now married with children. She came to teach them as a favor to her new country.

Zohara listened, transfixed. It did not seem real. More than once she said, "I don't believe you."

No, it was true, he said. It sounds like fun but he hated it, worse than takedowns, what it did to you. And there was no Other to protect you. "They didn't even think you needed it, the idiots."

Finally he had to leave. He had fallen in love with a woman in the course who was trained to marry a foreign target, so he didn't sleep with her, to preserve her virginity. All others, of course, fucked each other, both during the lessons and after, it was encouraged, for training, and to teach them not to see it as something special. Not as special as the country, that is.

"So you didn't?" She didn't know why he was telling her all this.

No. Whatever he and she felt was stronger than they, but their sense of duty was stronger. So they didn't, though they did practically everything else, spending whole nights with each other, against strict orders. Of course they were found out, a sentinel heard her singing in his room, her voice like an alto-flute, he playing his violin. Saw them kissing, too, which was another no-no. There was a quick trial. She could stay, since her father had fallen in a border operation, so she had credit with them, but he had to leave. He was given one chance to redeem himself; however, he failed in that one also.

"Failed how?"

He was set on a *Dossit*, a religious wife with two children, in Mea Shearim, in Jerusalem. The task was to fuck her, then get her to withdraw 100 shekels from her husband's bank account, just as an exercise.

Zohara shook her head. She could not believe such a thing.

No, he said, they do similar in the Mossad to test you, even worse things, to find what comes first for you: your honor or your country, your conscience or your country.

"You are making it up," she said.

Oh no, he said. He wasn't, it was all true. But he couldn't do it, so he was let go. "I only came back now, when they asked me, both Ehud and Shimmel, and told me why they needed me."

Shimmel was who?

He looked at her, eyebrows raised. "You don't want to meet him. He's Satan, the devil personified. He'll do anything. Luckily he works for us."

What she didn't say: You didn't, and that's why you failed. Also Amzaleg didn't, which is why he's at home now, half-broken.

He traced lines on her breasts, avoiding her nipples, then on her neck, finally on her lips. She trembled, closed her eyes, said, "This woman, where's she now?"

"The *Dossit*? Don't know. Probably still in Mea Shearim, with more children—"

"No," she said, "not her, the one from the course, with the voice like a flute."

He shook his head, hard. "Don't know, don't want to know. She's gone, will never come back... as good as dead, somewhere far, probably."

"But what if she comes back?"

"She won't."

She grabbed his hand, stopping it. "You still love her?"

Again, he shook his head. "She's gone."

Presently they fucked again, she trembled again all over, saw colors again. It scared her now because if she suddenly saw this, what else would she see?

It was dark outside when he said, "Stay until tomorrow."

She said she had to call her father. "He'll worry about me." To her surprise she felt warm inside when she said this.

"So call him."

She looked around. "You don't have a phone."

He rummaged inside a backpack, pulled out an oblong gray box, unfurled a flat antenna. "Here." He handed it to her. "Dial."

She did, the line crackled, and presently Amzaleg answered. When she said she would stay the night at the kibbutz he said nothing for a while, then said, "Call me when you leave. End."

"I will. End."

They ate later at the communal kitchen hall. No one paid her any attention. Later at night when they fucked again she tried to keep a portion of her apart. She didn't know if she had succeeded, but this time she didn't see colors or squirt.

Just before they fell asleep, he told her all Anons had it easy with women—it's the aura of blood on them, having killed with their own hands, women can sense it.

Her father too? She couldn't even think about it. She only knew about Jacqueline. She asked, "What about Anons that fuck men?"

He stiffened. "None of us does that," he said. "But yes, the course the year before mine, a guy, Bentzy something, was kicked out, he was peddling his ass for money on the side…. Another guy, perhaps his boyfriend, left on his own, or maybe his father found out what course the army had sent his son to…" Sukenik laughed suddenly. "Give your life for your country, okay, give your soul to the Unit, also okay, give your son's life, sure, but would you give your son's ass?"

She said, "I wouldn't give anything."

He said, "You'd give it all for something, for sure, but for what?"

She realized he was giving her a compliment but didn't like it said like this. "My children," she said. "For them I would kill. But they won't be born here, that's for sure."

"Who else?" he asked. "Your father?"

She had to stop and think, then nodded. Yes. "Also Pirchiya." She didn't explain who Pirchiya was, and he seemed to understand.

"And who else?"

She felt stumped. Who else? Her brown brethren? The idiots who let themselves be killed and oppressed? No she wouldn't, she decided. Once she was done helping her father catch the madman who was killing them, let them take care of themselves.

"No one," she said.

He nodded slowly, his mouth twisted. Then he kissed her. "I got to catch some sleep, I have to catch the boat tomorrow and I can't be late."

But then he asked her about herself, and it all came out. Her dead brother, breaking the teacher's arm, the reformatory, the drugs (though she didn't tell him why), then how she got rid of it. "Because Amzaleg said he wouldn't let me help otherwise."

"Wow," he said. "Three weeks! It's worse than jail-check!"

Jail-check, he explained, was the mock-prison course Anons had to take, to prepare them for being captured. "Though, of course it won't help you if they are Syrians and send you to Tadmor."

When they fell asleep she wrapped herself around him and he hid his head in her neck, breathing into her, falling asleep fast. He smelled wonderful, like a fresh cake, not like blood at all.

She woke up when he did, and watched him wash his upper body in the sink, soldier-style, rubbing water on his chest and under his armpits, then toweling himself with the same towel she had used last night. His chest was crisscrossed with fine scars whose origin was unclear, but his back and left shoulder had three small round scars likely made by bullets.

She watched his economical movements and felt a hot stirring between her legs which slowly spread up to her belly and down to her thighs. He spun around as if feeling her eyes, his hand lifted and crossed, in the way her father had taught her, and for a moment he stared at her as a stranger. Then a glint of recognition swept his eyes sideways, like vertical pupils in a cat's eyes, and he opened his arms wide and without saying a word went to her.

She was already on her feet and they met midway, their teeth knocking. He swept her up on the table and spread her legs and entered her in one motion, and she cried out with the extreme sweetness of it and the pleasure but also the pain, which was not in her legs now but higher, between her navel and her heart, so intense she could hardly breathe, and with a surprising anger over her need.

Then in a minute it was over. They broke apart without words, then both stood at the sink, washing side by side, drying themselves with the same towel, each using an opposite corner.

He said, "Like Arabs do before prayer. Ablutions."

She laughed and said something in Moroccan Arabic.

"What?" he said, then smiled. "Yes." He repeated it in High Arabic. Hastiness is from the devil.

She grabbed his head and pulled it between her breasts. "My little devil," she said in Moroccan Arabic. Then she grabbed between his legs. "And my big one." She rose on the table, spread again.

"No, I have to go...."

"So quickly."

She did not tremble this time, nor did he. But when she looked into his eyes as he battered into her, he said, "Don't look at me like that."

"Like what?"

He shook his head, and then he finished and washed himself yet again.

Later she accompanied him to the dining room again, and they sat side by side over breakfast. The server came and slopped some coffee into their mugs. She overturned half a sugar bowl into hers.

He looked into her eyes, raised an eyebrow.

"None of your business," she said. "But yes, I'm clean now."

It was then she asked him who of the others he thought could have been the killer.

"I don't know," he said. "I guess all of us, who knows? It does things to you, to learn this as a profession. Like an art, almost."

She found to her surprise it did not scare her, not even when she thought that her father was one of them, too, or rather had been, that like Gidi he had flunked out, but again like Gidi, was now back because he had been asked.

Then it was time for Gidi to go.

Outside, he climbed on his ancient motorbike. It took a while for the bike engine to start. She watched Gidi kick at it, her arms hugging herself. She said, "How long you go for?"

He shook his head.

"I don't want to know what. Just how long."

Again he shook his head.

She rattled her head, feeling that big pile of kinked wool swing from side to side. "So go, go."

He got off the motorbike, came to her, hesitated.

"Don't touch me," she said. She couldn't understand why she was so angry.

He patted her cheek and she grabbed his wrist, as she had done the day before, then let it go.

"Okay, go." She said. "Go."

She stood watching the motorbike as it roared feebly away. Then she went back into the room and searched it thoroughly. She was ashamed of this but did it anyway.

She found nothing.

-25-

Tuesday, February 2, 11:25 a.m.,
HaTikva Quarter, then the Clandestine's Hut

WHEN SHE CAME back, Amzaleg did not ask her why she had stayed over. He only asked, "What do you think?"

She shook her head. "I don't know yet."

That evening Amzaleg snuck out for the first time with her, to the Clandestine's hut behind the Army HQ. The entire team was waiting for them in the canteen. All piled into the old half-truck's back—just in case the rooms were bugged.

Amzaleg introduced Zohara, and one by one they nodded. Without further ado, they went over the list of the killings—there were seventeen by then—one by one, as if reporting to a just-returned chief.

Some made suggestions, others shot them down. It was not going well. No one said to Amzaleg, "We need you," but it was in the air. Suissa felt it, sat with his head bent, face flushed.

Amzaleg rose to go. "Gotta go back now, next time only she'll come."

On the way back Amzaleg saw all the lights in the top floors of Army HQ were lit—all the floor's windows, hallways too.

Zohara saw him looking. "That's where they sit? The chief of staff and everyone?"

"Yah," Amzaleg said. "Also Shimmel."

She said, "The Satan?"

Amzaleg stared at her. "Where did you hear his nickname?"

She said lamely, "The Anon in the kibbutz, Gidi, he told me."

Amzaleg nodded slowly, perhaps understanding more than she had meant. She reddened.

"Just be careful," he said.

Back at the flat Amzaleg sat down, laced his hands and said, "How we gonna find him?"

The day before, they had gone over the Beirut schedules and the times of the killings. It could have been any of the six who had come with Ehud, and of course Ehud himself. There was no way of telling.

Zohara said, "I don't know, but we gotta be ready, in case he makes a mistake."

"He won't," Amzaleg said grimly. "He's smart."

But it was Zohara who had made a mistake, though she didn't yet know it.

And oddly enough, four days later, Saturday, February 6, the killer made one too.

-26-

**Friday, February 5, 10:10 a.m.,
West Beirut**

FOR A FEW days, Gershonovitz had been trying to contact the man, clicking him directly with nine-nine "Call Me ASAP," followed by his own code number. But the man refused to acknowledge—he suspected that clever Shimmel was on to him and was calling to congratulate him on his private initiative. But he hadn't been doing the Cleansing for praise. It was just one more job that had to be done. He felt modest about it so was reluctant to respond.

He wished his father would call him, though, to congratulate him, but there was nothing.

On Friday, however, while out on a job following a newly promoted PLO sergeant through the Sabra's refugee camp's back roads, he incautiously answered his clicker's buzz with a three-three: Who? What? He'd thought it was Ronen, with some new details about the target.

But in response he got the nine-nine.

Damn. But there was nothing to be done: he'd acknowledged already.

He immediately exited the camp, found a pharmacy and called the number that connected to HQ via two scramblers.

"What's up?" he asked, speaking French.

Gershonovitz said straight out, "You gotta stop doing this."

The man felt a mixture of fear and pride. "Doing what?" he said, willing Shimmel to say it.

"Killing those little *Arsim*," Shimmel said. "It ain't worth the risk."

He liked how Shimmel had put it. "It's just a little extra," he said modestly, "for all of you."

He knew he should have said "all of us" but wanted Shimmel to understand his selflessness.

Gershonovitz said, "You can screw it all up, everything you guys been working for!"

In a flash the man understood that Shimmel was not against what he was doing. "No, I am being careful," he said, then added, "also, I'm leaving notes so they'll know why I'm doing it."

There was a pause, then Gershonovitz said, "Listen, when can we meet?"

He felt a prick of caution, the kind they had been taught to pay attention to. "Why?"

"Just to talk—" Gershonovitz stopped, realizing he was being obvious.

"No, I am busy," he said. "Lots to do here, lots of jobs."

He loved Shimmel, but something told him he shouldn't trust him now, just in case.

Shimmel raised his voice, "I am telling you, you should stop it! It's an order!"

At this the man didn't know what to say. An order was an order. "So when can I continue?"

Shimmel was silent for a few seconds more. "Just stop for now."

"But when could I continue?" he persisted.

Shimmel said, "I'll tell you when. For now, you stop, it's an order. End."

"End," he said, too, and hung up.

Alright, he told himself, he'd lay off Cleansing—starting next week. But this weekend he could still do one, just to take care of his immediate need. He owed it to the book's Prophet, also to himself.

He left the pharmacy, then reentered the camp to do the job. It didn't take long. The man was young and inexperienced, didn't even resist much.

Afterward he lolled about until sunset, then strolled to the aShams beach where he'd hidden the small boat, took it out to sea, and was round-ing the Dove Rock just as the moon rose. It was lovely, the light through the mist. He felt at peace.

He was at Rosh Pina before midnight and, on his bike, on the outskirts of Tel Aviv well before dawn. As he came nearer, he realized he hadn't brought the book: He'd have to compose a note from memory yet again, damn. But then, oddly, it cheered him a little. He'd have to say it in his own words now. He felt as if he had graduated into a higher level, as if a Hand was guiding him.

It was six thirty in the morning when he came to the outskirts of Jaffa.

-27-

GERSHONOVITZ SLAMMED THE phone into the receptacle and clicked the scrambler off.

"Shit," he said, then cursed in Polish.

What now?

Should he call Ronen, tell him? Or Ehud? Tell them to get the guy out of circulation?

He paused his finger on the scrambler's toggle, then shook his head and put his hand in his lap. He ground his teeth and pulled out his inhaler.

No, no. It was bound to get out. If it did, the stink would reach Begin's ears, maybe even the newspapers. A day after, all the Undertakers would be recalled and the entire army would roll in....

No. Best was to wait, hope the madman would obey orders, take it easy for a while. Until then, he better keep it to himself, say nothing to Moshe, nothing to Ehud, nothing to anyone. And try to get this madman to come back, maybe take care of him himself....

He pulled out his old Beretta from under the scrambler's drawer, looked at it, put it back.

Damn, damn... So much at stake, and now, this.

So many in-betweens, so many intermediaries. It was a miracle it hadn't leaked yet. They had to do it soon. It was such a big thing, both to prevent the war and to make peace.... It was worth any price, every price.

He looked up balefully, raised his middle finger at the ceiling, muttered a Yiddish curse, then put the scrambler on and put in a call to the Sub, to talk to Ehud.

-28-

Friday, February 5, 8:45 p.m.,
Jaffa

I T WAS RAINING lightly as the man parked his stolen Vespa behind the Ariadne Café in Jaffa, then, dressed in scruffy rags he had stolen long ago from a Carmel Market stall, the scooter helmet still on his head, hand in pocket touching his gun, he meandered down Jaffa's Jerusalem Boulevard, looking for a victim to Cleanse.

Not many people in the streets, but some in cafés, a few cars driving by: Friday eve. He kept his head lowered but scouted around for a target. He'd have to make sure it was a Jew, not an Arab—there were both, in Jaffa, somehow living together without fighting. He could not understand it.

Despite the presence of Arabs, the smell in the air was local, not like Beirut's. He could feel the tang of it in his throat, the smell of the land of his childhood. Rain kept falling and he stuck his tongue out, feeling the drops on its tip, as he had felt several times before in his other Cleansings—most were done in the rain—as if to remind himself of his youth; and for a brief moment he had a sense of disorientation, when all past Cleansings suddenly merged into each other in a single action, seeking—what? Cleanliness? Purity? Love?....

Certainly not love! His ability to love anything but this country and his people had been surgically removed by his father, then whatever shreds remained were cleansed away during his training—first in the Unit, then in the TempleWhores course, where he idiotically tried once to recapture it, and lost. It was too late now to get it back....

And without any reason, he again thought of his father, who had never loved him. Because if he had, he wouldn't have sent him to the Unit to do these deeds, nor would his mother have acquiesced....

Rain must have gotten into his eyes so he wiped them. He had no feelings for either parent now, yet he recalled he had loved both a little, once, when he was still a child, before he knew what they'd demand from him in the future.

That early little love was of course long gone, after what he had to do on his parents' behalf, and after what was done to him. Yet with love or without it, he still sought their approval, his father's especially. Because if one could no longer feel love, what else could one put in its place except that?

Perhaps once his father read his notes in the paper, he would show his appreciation, maybe even love him a little? Then perhaps he, too, could love his father a little back?

No, no, certainly not that.

He felt himself flushing at the mere thought. It was now too late for this. He would do the jobs demanded of him in Lebanon, and even do others here on his own initiative. But love? Not that, not ever. Especially not for his father....

At the mere thought of his father, his fingers twitched on the gun in his pocket, and a strange kind of heat rose in him, all the way from his groin. Just then his roaming eyes glimpsed the little *Ars* at the back of a café, staring at him with a knowing smile.... The images of his father and the little *Ars* imperceptibly merged, and he knew this one would do.

Almost without thinking, he headed toward the little brown boy, pulling out his wallet.

-29-

Friday, February 5, 9:05 p.m.,
HaTikva Quarter, then Jaffa

ZOHARA WAS IN her room, rereading an English novel Batya had loaned her, when the phone rang.

Jerked out of the hypnotic dream, Zohara stared around. But Amzaleg and Pirchiya were gone—they were at the Sabags for Friday eve dinner.

She grabbed the phone. "What?"

The book still sang in her, its imaginary people so alive she could almost see them, hear their voices. "Say it again, slowly."

It was one of the boys, babbling away.

"Someone... someone tried to—give money to a, boy in Jaffa, for, you know—" the young man stuttered, "then afterward, after—you know, he tried to—shoot him—"

Her skin crawled as her Other awoke with a snarl. "What? Who tried to shoot?"

"The client! So the boy beat him back and ran... and he used the soccer whistle... so two of us came, and... we whistled too... and he—the man—ran away.... More of us came, and ran after him... I went to call you..."

"Stop, stop! Wait. Where did it happen?"

She stuck her feet into her shoes, frantic, feeling the Other storming into her.

The boy yammered, "...Behind Café Machfooz—it's near—"

"I know where it is!" She grabbed her Vespa keys. "Tell the others to spread around and look for him but not to get near. He's dangerous. Wait for me, I'm coming…"

"Should we… call the police?"

"Fuck the police. They'll do nothing. Wait for me."

She slammed down the phone, looked wildly around her: What to take? Amzaleg had his gun on him all times. Should she go to the Sabags, get him?

No, fuck it, every minute counted, it's on you now, Zozo, on you.

She grabbed the folded jackknife, stuck it in her back pocket—fat lot of good it could do, but what else…. Enough, go, go, go!

Luckily the Vespa started fast. Damn, she was almost out of fuel, but it was only a few miles….

It took her eight minutes to get there, almost slipped twice on the rain-slicked road.

As she came near she could hear the whistles; the Other made her go faster still.

-30-

HE RAN.
Just before he had felt the shudder coming, as he put the gun's muzzle to the skinny nape, the boy looked up, saw it, and hit at his crotch.

The shot missed, and before he could aim again, the boy was running. And as he pulled up his drawers while trying to aim, the boy had put something to his mouth and gave a sharp whistle.

Incredibly, other whistles answered, then more...

And so he ran.

He zigzagged as if under fire, bent low, scooting between the dripping palms of the Avenue, among low stone fences, hovels, toward the yard where he'd hid his stolen Vespa.

He could not believe it. He'd been ambushed.

How?

The whistles were converging on all sides, and so as he'd been taught, he went to the ground. Dove behind a pile of broken stones, dismantled beds, a rotting mattress, burrowed in, waited.

Rain hammered on his scooter helmet but he kept it on. Little by little the whistles stopped. Yet he waited.

His Other was screaming at him, its need and his own unsatisfied, but he stayed quiet, enraged but quiet.

He waited. Then he heard steps, several of them.

-31-

ZOHARA JUMPED OFF her scooter.

"Where did you last see him?"

The boy pointed, finger shaking.

She said, "What did he look like? Short? Tall?"

The boy shook his head, said, "Round head, maybe a helmet."

This was something. "Anything else?"

More boys came, more head shakes. There were six of them. They encircled her, waiting for instructions, the dolts. Like in the Velvet, like everywhere. Helpless. Like in Munger's stories.

She said crisply, "Spread all around, all of you, stay low, watch for movement, anyone running, anything—whistle. But not otherwise." She paused. "Or if you are attacked."

Somehow this brought spark to their eyes. Some thumped their sticks on the pavement.

She said, "Yallah, go."

She herself joined the boy who had seen the fleeing gunman, both searching alleys forking off Jerusalem Boulevard in the direction where he had run, both getting drenched by the rain. Inside her the Other was yammering. Amzaleg never said it could do this. Maybe she should be afraid of it, but she wasn't.

She was beginning to suspect the search might come to nothing when suddenly came a whistle, from behind a hovel at the edge of Adjemi, and a figure dashed away, round-headed and fast and zigzagging, bent low. She nearly ran after it, then realized the idiocy. "You go after him, but don't get too close!" she shouted at them, and she herself ran back to her Vespa.

It started immediately, but after forty feet died. No gas.

The Other in her was hollering as she jumped off, ran after the entire flock of boys, all whistling like mad after the round-headed figure hopping between bricks of a toppled house, through the rain.

She was getting closer, too, and as the running man stopped briefly, a palm frond hid his face as he raised his arm and she felt a puff of air close to her ear, then saw him turn and jump on a dark scooter and ride away, the large head bobbing, bent over the handlebars.

The boys arrived soon after—too late, too late.... She nearly screamed with the futility of it, the Other yammering in her worse than the boys, she felt its rage in her throat, her mouth, the meat taste of the missed kill....

She folded the jackknife and put it back in her pocket. She didn't even remember when she had pulled it out and sprung it.

The boys milled around, muttering, passersby watching them curiously.

One boy said, "Maybe we should tell the police?"

She began to upbraid him, and stopped: wasn't a bad idea.

"Yes, okay."

In the rain, they walked the four miles south to the police station, she pushing the inert Vespa, the boys trailing, two dragging their sticks on the sidewalks.

"Lift them up," she said, not looking back, knowing they'd put them on their shoulders.

At the front desk, the sergeant raised his eyebrows, slow-grinned, tongue in the corner of his mouth.

"Again you..."

She ignored it, told him succinctly what had taken place.

He shrugged. "You should've called a policeman, that's what we are for." He added slyly, "Why didn't you call your father? He could've finished him with one hand…."

She gritted her teeth, turned sly in turn. "He's still in bed, after what you did to him."

The sergeant smirked. "We? We didn't do anything, he probably stuck his dick in something that doesn't concern him—"

"I'll tell him you said this." She leaned on the counter. "I'd like to file a report, please. Give me a form."

The sergeant erased most of his smirk. "You tell me what happened, I'll write it down."

"No. Give me a form, I'll fill it."

As he began to object she turned back, motioned to the boys. Three edged in, then the last three, all panting a little from running and fear.

She turned to the sergeant. "They are all witnesses, they'll all sign." Then she added, "We also have a picture…"

She must be stupid, lying like that, but her instinct told her perhaps she wasn't.

The sergeant's smirk was gone. "What picture?"

"Of him, the gunman. By a camera…"

The boys were at the desk now. They looked at each other. The quickest one said, "Yes."

"Give it here," the sergeant snarled.

She pushed the boys back, shook her head. "Only to the newspaper—"

"You wait here, I gotta make a phone call."

The boys looked at her, fearful and admiring, waiting.

She said, "You make a call, I'll make one too. Or you give me the form, I'll fill it and leave."

"Who will you call?"

She stared at him, unmoved, made her eyes flash a little.

After a brief minute he gave in with bad grace.

"Here." He peeled a form, gave it to her, added a pencil, blunt. She thought of pulling out her jackknife to sharpen the pencil, then told herself not to be stupid.

She said, "And put in the carbon paper, I'll keep one copy."

She left half an hour later, the boys trailing.

She said, "Someone help me push the Vespa to the gas station."

From the station she called Amzaleg. He listened without talking, beginning to end. "Come back and we'll talk about it," then he added in a low voice, "you okay?"

"I'm okay. You just warn everyone, and call Suissa. I'll see you later." Then she recalled they were a team now, and added lamely. "I'll be at Batya's, you need me, call me there."

He didn't ask why.

She filled the Vespa with gas, then rode out of Jaffa, cutting in through Shabazi and Pinsker Street to get to Ben Yehuda Street faster, everything around her nearly black and white. Even the few colors she could see were nearly washed away. She kept trying to tamp down its bloodlust but it wasn't leaving her; no matter how she tried, it stayed, grew, rumbled.

For the first time she could not shake off the Other. She tried to conjure a calm scene: A visit to her grandfather; talking to Pirchiya, playing with Iddo; helping Margul; nothing worked. Perhaps she ought to conjure her time with Gidi?

She didn't want to think of him, afraid of what it would raise in her, maybe worse.

For the first time, she began to feel a twinge of fear. What if the Other did not leave? Would she, too, have to go to the psych ward, like her father? If an Other did not leave, one had to go to an actual calm place as soon as possible.

Well then.

She half-drove, half-skittered, her Vespa snaking between cars, toward Batya's flat.

32

Friday, February 5, 9:40 p.m.,
Jaffa, then Tel Aviv

FROM THE STATION'S front desk, the sergeant called Superintendent Klinger at home and told him what had just transpired. "And she also said she had a photo of him…."

Klinger interrupted his babble. "Where's she now?"

"She just went off, don't know where." The sergeant said, "But listen, maybe it's nothing, just one drug pusher who tried to shoot another, then lied about it…."

"And what's this about a photo? Did she show it to you?"

"No, she said only to the newspapers—"

Klinger cursed in Galician Yiddish, got hold of himself. "Don't worry about it, I'll handle it."

Which is exactly what Levitan said to him when Klinger called and reported what the sergeant had said, and right after, Levitan called Gershonovitz in turn and filled him in.

"This *shoychet*'s fucking *Freha* is worse than he was, almost," he concluded.

"Not almost," Gershonovitz said. Then he too said what both Klinger and Levitan had said before.

"Handle how?" said Levitan.

"Better you don't know, Leizer," Gershonovitz said, "is better for you."

He knew what Levitan was going to ask next. And indeed Levitan said, "Shimmel, if she has a photo, don't you think we should get it, to see—"

"Don't be an idiot, Leizer," Gershonovitz said. "She doesn't. Where would she get a camera?"

"But what if she does?"

"I don't need a photo. I know who it is."

He cursed himself right away for having said it, but this damn Amzaleg and his *Freha* were driving him nuts. It was as if the Damn HolyName Himself was dangling them before his eyes on purpose, teasing him, using them against him just when this peace plan was so close to fruition....

"So who is he?" Levitan said.

"Doesn't matter. I told you I'll deal with it."

He hung up, glared up at the ceiling, mouthed a Polish curse at his Tormentor, then another one at himself, picked his Motorola clicker, took a long pull on his inhaler, and clicked.

33

Friday, February 5, 9:50 p.m.,
Tel Aviv

OF COURSE THE man did not respond.

He was on his way back to Beirut by now, his mind a mixture of seething and numbness.

Only when he was back in the Sub could he begin to think of it rationally. And then sanity returned: he saw plainly the hand of the One Above in this—it was clearly a hint for him not to get conceited, that the Cleansings were not meant for his good feeling, but for the good of all.

Feeling sheepish, he promised himself to be more careful in future.

Shimmel kept clicking him every few hours for the next day, and the next, but he didn't respond.

-34-

Friday, February 5, 9:55 p.m., Tel Aviv

ZOHARA OPENED THE door to Batya's flat with her key. The yeshiva runaways were asleep in their room, Batya not yet in.

She made straight to the fridge and wolfed down half a sausage and a chunk of cheese, but the hole inside her was growing bigger, the Other growling ever louder, madder.

It began to frighten her but she tamped down the fear and tried again to Reverse, sat on the sofa, stared at the living room wall, the photos of Batya's dead relatives, the small lit candle....

The Other began to rumble and she looked away to the flowers on the table, half-wilted, a small picture on the wall, a copy of a Dutch painting—pregnant woman in a kitchen with a small dog—then a photo of Batya with five girls at Beit Sarah, Zohara at the front, all smiling.... She breathed in, out. Imagined herself back in Beit Sarah, girls in her room telling her their secrets, one combing her hair in gratitude....

Without noticing it she fell into profound sleep, as if hitting a wall.

She woke up with a snarl when Batya came in.

"Where've you been?" Zohara asked. Batya rarely went out evenings.

She breathed in, out, tested herself, the Other was half-gone, half-there still.

"To my husband's grave," Batya said. "It's his year-day. Then I stopped at the Bugrashov Street synagogue, to light a candle.... Have you eaten?"

"Oh." Death again, and fucking synagogue. "Yes."

Just looking at Batya made her better: One more who, like Munger, loved her, though she could not tell why. Not like her mother, who had to love her, or her father. Yes, he too.

The Other was recoiling now, shrinking.

"But you'll have coffee?" Batya looked pale, eyes red. She set out the coffee service. "Where've you been?"

Zohara's teeth buzzed as the day's happenings roared back.

She could again see the gray form hopping on the stone fence and the dead palm fronds hiding the man's face as he raised his arm, and she felt again the puff of air close to her ear.

Was it Gidi?

"Nowhere," she said. "Here and there."

Oddly, she had not felt fear while she chased him, not even fear that it was the man who had opened her up to colors; just hot bloodlust so overpowering it was almost like hunger. She could taste it in her throat, deep and meaty.

Batya was saying something, having sat down and poured her coffee.

"What?" Zohara said, still tasting it, and now, just as strong, the fear it was him, Gidi.

Batya repeated softly what she had said.

No, Zohara snapped. She never went to one, they had gone over this before.

As cars rumbled in the street below, she thought of the fleeing killer, could imagine the razor sliding on his throat, biting in. Probably was the man who had killed Nachum, Rahamim, others too.... Surely it was not Gidi.

The car sounds faded. Batya had closed the windows and put on a record and it now played scratchily, something by Bach or Boccherini, Zohara could not separate them at the start.

"Never?" Batya asked.

"Never what?"

"Synagogue," Batya said again.

But Zohara had had enough. "Fuck no," she snapped, the Other waking. "What is it with you? You only go on Yom Kippur, why do you care? You take in yeshiva runaways with nowhere to go. You must hate the religious nuts, too, like me."

She spooned sugar into the coffee, drank up, making sure not to slurp. It tasted like meat.

"No, I don't hate them," Batya said. "And don't say this word here please."

"Sorry," Zohara said, mechanically. The melody was jumping from top note to top note. So it must be Bach, like the one Gidi had playing; the Boccherini was just one big mush. She waved her hand lightly, following what Batya had called the fugal line, pushing the Other to subside, then the image of the fleeing man. Both resisted. "I am sorry about your dead husband, but this synagogue shit…"

She waved her arm, perhaps also to chase away the image of the fleeing killer.

Batya said, "Just because you can't understand—"

Zohara dropped her hand, bent forward, hard. "No, you listen." She felt vaguely this was not the time to be voluble but could not hold back, it just came out. "You ever see a hypnotist?"

Batya shook her head, her eyebrows knotting.

"Once," Zohara's words rushed. "I saw one in Jaffa in the Ariadne Café four years ago, I was twenty maybe, I went with two who left Beit Sarah—Margul, remember her? The Yemenite, she tried twice to cut her—" She felt herself babbling.

"I remember." Batya poured her more coffee. "What about a hypnotist?"

The Bach went on, top note jumping top note, like the fleeing killer had. Now the bottom notes took over; clever, that trick. Zohara forced her mind back. "He asked everyone to clasp their hands and told them their hands were locked—some couldn't open them and he brought them on stage." She stopped, seeing it again. "I thought he'd make them shout, sing, something, but he just talked to them in a deep *vooz-vooz* voice, like the announcer on Kol Yisrael radio, what's-his-name…."

"So what?" Batya said. "Some huckster magician is not synagogue, I can't see—"

"No, no, no," Zohara said. "No. They really all fell asleep so deeply that no matter how everyone shouted and clapped, they didn't wake up. Then he told them they were on the beach in Eilat, it was hot, there were girls in bikinis, and when he woke them up you should've seen them—"

"You sure it wasn't staged?" Batya said. "Prearranged."

In the other room one boy snored, then stopped, probably having woken himself up. There was a low whimper. Many cried the first few days. Zohara said impatiently, "Yes, completely sure, I know two who went on stage. These people really thought they were on the beach...."

She poured more sugar into her coffee. Ever since she had kicked the drugs she couldn't get enough of it. Munger said it didn't matter, she could have it. It made her head buzz. Also music gave her itchy skin, especially Bach, or Mozart, their quick stuff.

She jumped. A shadow appeared in the bedroom door. One of the runaways. He looked at them both and went into the bathroom; soon whimpers were heard.

Batya got up, went to the bathroom, spoke softly. A voice answered. Apparently there was no need for her; she sat down again, took her coffee cup.

Zohara went on, "No, no, the people on stage were sure they were on the beach in Eilat, although none of them had ever been there, and all felt hot—one was sweating, even—we all saw it...."

Batya's eyebrows knotted. "And how is this—"

Zohara snapped, "I didn't see what they saw. I wasn't hypnotized. These idiots were, and they saw stuff that wasn't there, just because of some fucking words. Do you see what I mean?"

The runaway yeshiva boy came out of the bathroom, clutching himself as if he was cold, went into the bedroom. Soon soft snores were heard.

Batya just sipped her coffee and looked at Zohara over the cup's rim, her eyes dark, face taut.

Zohara said, "It was only the man's voice that made 'em see what wasn't fucking there, see? Just his voice! But it made them sore when some Yemenite in the crowd laughed at them." She twisted her mouth. "If they had guns, maybe they would have used them—" She paused. "What, what?"

Batya was deathly still, her eyes were now nearly shut, tears coming down.

Zohara went on, oblivious, "D'you think it's possible to be hypnotized by a book also? Not just a voice? Not like the *Little Prince*, or this *Bovary* book you gave me, when you know it's just a story, but words that make you believe in fucking nonsense that really isn't there?" Her voice rose, she found herself getting angry. "And fight for the nonsense? And send your children to be killed for it—" Her voice rose further, then she choked.

It all came back to Iddo, every time; then she felt the need for drugs so badly. And now she realized for the first time that she was also afraid for Gidi. That something would happen to him in Beirut. Or worse, that it was him, and she would have to kill him.

She swatted at her eyes, drained her coffee cup, put more in, poured sugar in, more, more.

The room was quiet. Batya got up shakily, wrenched the fridge open, looked inside for a long while, closed it, and came back without bringing anything, stumbling a little.

"No," she said in a low trembling voice. "I don't."

Zohara said, remorselessly, "Well, you read this fucking Bible and you get hypnotized by it, but I read it and I don't. And the fucking teacher in Bnot Yaakov School, who made us read about this insane mother who got hypnotized into killing her seven sons—he wanted all of us to become hypnotized also—only I didn't." She heard her voice rise. "So they kicked me out... not because I broke his arm, but because I didn't see the fucking bikinis they saw...."

"Lower your voice," Batya said, "and please don't say this word in my house. Please, please."

Zohara said, "Sorry."

They were quiet for a long moment.

Batya said, "I think I'd like another Bach."

Zohara said, "I can't think straight with all these violins.... Maybe I should go." She got up, looked down at Batya, who was sitting with her hands in her lap, tears down her cheeks. "Batya, please, I'm sorry about him, your husband, but can't it be that you are all hypnotized? And I am not? Because I am immune?"

"Hypnotized by whom? Or by what?"

"By the fuc... by the words in this, this book, someone wrote tall tales a few thousand years ago, he knew how to use words like this *vooz-vooz* hypnotist in the Ariadne."

"Who? Who wrote it?"

"Someone, long time ago." She was shouting again. "I don't know who! What does it matter?"

Batya seemed to be trembling all over. "I think I'd like a Wagner." Her face was flushed.

"But I thought he was a Nazi."

"Yes. But his music wasn't."

Zohara snapped, "I really don't understand you. You lost everyone over there, to the ovens, you don't go to fucking synagogue because of it—today you did—"

"Please!" Batya wiped her eyes. "Not this word, when you say synagogue."

"Why? You are not religious."

"This has nothing to do with it."

Zohara picked up her empty cup, put the spoon in it, got up and put them both in the sink. She said over her shoulder, "Maybe I am immune? So I can't be hypnotized into seeing what doesn't exist? But all of you aren't?"

She shook her head. It was hopeless. Batya seemed unable to get what she was saying.

They were quiet for a moment. Finally Batya said, "Maybe, just like you can't see red, you can't see what we see."

"Yes, exactly!"

"But there is red, it exists."

"How do you know?"

Batya smiled a crooked little smile. "Oh it does. I've seen lots of it. You did too."

Zohara flushed, remembering the colors she saw with Gidi, pushed it away. It scared her still.

She got up. "I should be going."

"No, stay, please. I—I love to have you around."

Zohara reddened. "When is your daughter coming?"

"Don't know." Batya grew quiet.

"Where's she now?"

Batya shook her head. "Somewhere, I don't know. She's doing something abroad I'm not supposed to know about."

"For the *shoo-shoo*?"

"Quiet. Don't speak about it."

"Why don't you have any pictures of her around?"

"It's—it's for her safety. Please don't talk about it."

Again they were quiet. The music rose, clashes of horns and atonal singing.

Zohara said, "I don't like this music."

"But you can hear what it's saying?"

"I just don't like it."

Batya was silent, and so was Zohara, both listening to the odd cruel music. Zohara's mind wandered. This was when she missed the drug worst, to calm the madness... as improbably high voices sang with mad emotion, images floated before her: her mother, Iddo, her stay in Shfar'am, Rabbi Shechter, whose wrist she broke and for which she was sent to Beit Sarah....

"But I'm glad they sent me," she blurted, "or I'd never—"

She stopped, flushing.

"Yes." Batya put her large red hand over Zohara's.

Zohara pulled her hand away, not quickly.

When she was leaving, Batya accompanied her to the door. The rain had stopped. "Be careful with the scooter," Batya said. "And look around you. This madman who's been, you know—"

"Yes," Zohara said. "I will."

She couldn't tell Batya she had seen him, nearly gotten him. Why worry her.

"And drive carefully," Batya said again, and as usual, tried to hug her; as usual, Zohara escaped.

As she was riding away, she realized that the Other was gone.

-35-

**Friday, February 5, 11:50 p.m.,
Tel Aviv**

AMZALEG WAS WAITING for her, sitting at the kitchen table, read-ing a book of Paltiel Rubin poems, a glass of araq before him. Pirchiya was sleeping.

"You're Clean?" he asked her first thing as she came in.

His voice was different. His jaw had mended a bit crookedly.

She nodded.

"Sure?"

"Yes, sure."

"Sit then, tell me."

When she told him about it all over again, he said little, but when she came to the part of telling the sergeant she had a photo of the shooter, Amzaleg turned white—she at first thought he'd rage at her, but he just became silent and immobile, then told her she had been exceed-ingly stupid.

"You just put a target on your back, Zozo, why?"

"Well, fuck them," she said. "Let them come after me, I'll do to them what they did to you—" She heard the foolishness in her voice and stopped.

To her own surprise she said, "I—I wasn't thinking. I'm sorry."

He nodded, grudgingly approving her contrition. "Just be extra careful now. Someone sure doesn't want this madman caught—I don't yet know why."

But he did, she sensed, only didn't want to burden her with it, maybe increase her risk.

He looked at her long. "Go eat something. Then we'll talk more."

"I ate."

"Alright, let's do it."

He sat down. "You have the names of the seven who were here on Yom Kippur?"

"Yes." She read them aloud, one by one, said, "Do you know any of them?"

"Not all, only some."

"Any you can rule out, that you can call and ask to help you?" Like this Ehud Reznik, who owes you. Or Gidi, yes.

But Amzaleg shook his head. "No. Can't rule out anyone now…" He paused. "But I know someone who maybe does know, at least most of them…. He was in the Unit, once…"

She said, "I can go talk to him, you want."

He shook his head. "You can't. He's in Canada."

This stopped her, then she understood. "And you can't call him from here."

He made a face, not having to say it.

She said she could call from Jacqueline's, but he shook his head again: He knew the *shoo-shoo*. Here or any place around—Jacquie, the grocery store—was probably tapped. Maybe even public phones in the market….

She said, "Wait, wait. Batya has a phone."

Amzaleg said, "I can't go there, someone may see me…." He left it hanging, his meaning clear. Let them think he was out of it, while she did the legwork.

It made her feel warm again. She said, "But I can go to her, call from her place, you'll tell me what to ask…."

Finally he nodded. "Alright."

"What's his name? The one in Canada?"

"David," he gave a twisted smile. "David Starkman."

"And how do you know him?"

Amzaleg hesitated. "He came back four years ago for his father's funeral, then he stayed a month and staged a theater play with Ehud—" Again he paused.

She had an illumination, "The show you got demoted for, for letting it run during the elections?"

"*Hada huwah.*" That's him.

"So he has to talk to you, no?" Owes you.

He gave another odd smile. "Maybe, maybe not."

She let it go. So much she didn't know.

Just before she turned in, well past midnight, she said, "Oh, and what if they are listening to his phone too? In Canada?"

"Why would they do that? He's out of it now, gone."

She nodded, unconvinced: she wouldn't put anything beneath them.

Amzaleg said, "It's a chance we have to take."

-36-

Friday, February 5, 11:55 p.m.,
Tel Aviv and Beirut

GERSHONOVITZ COULDN'T TAKE the chance that the madman would kill again. But no matter how much he clicked him, the man stayed silent.

He was now certain he must do something soon, but how?

What also rankled was not just that the guy went gaga and began to kill *Schwartzes*, but also that he became a *feigele*. A fag. That's what comes from having dealings with Arabs, Gershonovitz thought bitterly. We sacrifice ourselves for the sake of our people, and our best boys get corrupted. As Golda had said, we'll never forgive the Arabs for forcing us to teach our sons to kill. And now also this, this Arab sickness, like what Arafat has....

Still, what's done is done, and what must be done must be done. If only he could get to him!

He gritted his teeth. So much to do!

Maybe first he'd better do something about Amzaleg's daughter. That damn *Freha* was causing most of the trouble now. At least Amzaleg was out of it finally, the damn troublemaker. For at least one, maybe two more months, he'd be flat on his ass, Asa had told him. These Samsons could time it to the day. Someone you could rely on, finally.

What he still couldn't grasp was how this druggie *Freha* could have cut two of the Samsons. How was it possible? He took a big pull of Swiss cortisone. The more he thought of it, the more he realized that maybe he'd better take care of her first—not that it would be easy. Klinger had said that now she always had these young *Arsim* in tow, with their fucking soccer whistles, maybe she also did have a camera, like she said....

He ground his teeth.

If this *Freha* discovered that the serial killer was one of the Anons doing the work in Beirut, and if it became public, it could force Begin to pull them all out, let Arik have his invasion.... It'd sink the country in the shit for years, and now also screw up the best chance for peace with the Flatheads.... Just what the Damn HolyName probably wanted....

He shook with rage. No, Amzaleg's *Freha* had to be stopped. But how?

If he were younger, he'd have taken care of her himself, no problem. But at his age...

Could he ask Moshe to do it, maybe?

But after a moment he shook his head. Nah, that impertinent half-*Schwartze* probably wouldn't obey. Like the other Anons, he, too, was now obeying only orders he liked. It was dreadful, what the country was coming to, nobody following orders anymore.

Gershonovitz mouthed an Arab curse into the ceiling, at his Enemy, then an idea popped up, unbidden: perhaps, if the madman could be convinced to do one more, but a *Freha* this time....

Now this was an idea! If only the man would respond....

He clicked again and again but still got no response.

A few minutes later Gershonovitz suddenly remembered to call Ehud to get an update. So much to do, so much could go wrong, so many against him....

At least Ehud answered right away, five minutes after he'd clicked him.

"What is it?" Ehud said.

Gershonovitz, too, spoke without preamble. "Anything from the Flatheads?"

"Yes, the *barbouz* called. Rahman is still in Hama, helping in the killing. He thinks it'll take them one or two weeks more before they can bring in the bulldozers, then maybe it'll take another week."

"Why bulldozers?"

Ehud said, "Oh, they have ten thousand dead Muslim Brothers already, maybe twelve. It'll be twenty thousand dead before it's over."

Gershonovitz had a moment of disorientation, the images crowding in. "You just ask him for a firm date. Once I have it, I can take it to the cabinet, have them vote on it."

There was a pause. The line warbled. Each could hear the other's breathing.

Finally Ehud said, "How are you bearing up, Shimmel?"

He had never asked this of him before.

Gershonovitz said, "Like always, sleeping with one eye open."

Ehud said, "Wish I could help you."

He had never said this before either.

Gershonovitz said in a rough voice, "Same here. End."

"End."

They both hung up together.

Gershonovitz took a long pull on his inhaler, sat back, staring at the phone. For some reason he felt the need to wipe his eyes. All these Muslim Brothers in Hama, first burned then bulldozed, going into mass graves.... But it wasn't his job to worry about them all, he couldn't save everyone. Trying to prevent one war was enough, maybe getting a cold peace with Syria as a bonus. He only did what was necessary. *M'darf.*

If only he could stop this mad Undertaker in Beirut from doing more damage, risking exposure of everything... or better still, get him to do Amzaleg's *Freha*....

So much to do!

He clicked once more the madman's call sign but again got no response.

-37-

L EVITAN, TOO, SAT a long time staring at the phone.
　　He, too, thought of a mass of bodies. Not of the Muslim Brothers,
but of Golani soldiers and Israeli tank crews, if Arik, God forbid, ever
took all the army into Lebanon.

But now, this.

Levitan shivered. Shimmel's admission that he knew who the killer
was shook him more than he could have foreseen. If Shimmel knew this,
why then wasn't he doing something about it? Why wasn't he pulling the
madman out?

Without even pausing to think, he already knew why. The risk of the
thing getting to Begin, the news that one of the Undertakers in Beirut
was sneaking into Israel to kill *Schwartzes*, would immediately tip the balance in Arik's favor: an Ashkenazi fanatic Cleansing the land of *Schwartze*
Jews—most of them Begin's voters, yes, but Jews also....

Levitan stared wide-eyed at the wall, where Dudi's photo smiled at
him, white teeth under a brown beret of a tank driver—a sergeant already.
Dudi had his eyes, his mother's mouth, his grandfather's nose. The one
who went in Birkenau.

Dudi, the last of the Levitans.

Levitan rubbed his eyes as he looked at his boy. Only now he also saw behind Dudi the dead *Schwartzes*, those on the slabs at Munger's morgue, killed by the madman whose identity Shimmel knew, the one who'll now kill more, unless stopped....

Levitan kept staring at Dudi's photographs: from age zero to today, every year new photos, a shrine almost, birthdays, bar mitzvah, graduation from Herzliya High School, boot camp.

He shamelessly wiped his eyes, looked around him, the flat where Dudi grew up, the last remnant of the Levitans.

"Leizer, you coming?" His wife called him from the bedroom, hoarse. "I need a new refill.... It's in the bottom drawer."

She, like Shimmel, now used an inhaler, her asthma getting worse. It went on like this, Levitan thought, he'd need one, too, soon.

"I'm coming," he said. "I'll bring you one."

Only at four in the morning did he fall asleep, had bad dreams, woke up at dawn, went to the kitchen, couldn't stop himself, called Gershonovitz.

"Shimmel? It's me."

Gershonovitz's voice was hard. He apparently hadn't slept either. "What do you want?"

"Can't you... can't you send someone after this madman-killer?"

"Send who? Klinger, maybe?"

"No, listen." Levitan's voice was hoarser than his wife's. "Maybe you can borrow a Samson, do to this madman what they did to Amzaleg... you know..."

"Oh yeah? Amzaleg is old. If he was young, these Samsons would be dead. These Undertakers, anyone of them would eat three Samsons without salt. Even Amzaleg's fucking druggie daughter cut two of them."

Levitan said, desperate, "Or maybe one of your other guys, you tell him to do it—"

"No one would do another if I don't tell him why, but then it'll come out—you want this?"

Levitan passed a sweaty big hand over his face. "No, no."

The line chirped, or maybe the birds outside; the day was breaking.

Gershonovitz said, "You go back to sleep, Leizer, I told you I'll handle it."

But Levitan couldn't sleep, nor the next night either, nor the next.

Saturday, February 6, 8:50 a.m.

NEXT MORNING, ZOHARA drove her Vespa back to Batya's. The rain had stopped, a weak sun came out, the clouds now in patches, some gray-blue sky visible. Batya seemed surprised to see her, but happy. "Everything okay now?"

Yes, Zohara said, everything was okay. Could she make a phone call from here? No, her phone was working, she just wanted to make sure no one was eavesdropping....

Batya became quiet. "You're sure everything is alright?"

"Yes, yes, don't worry." She recalled Batya's German-speaking daughter, the one Batya didn't want to talk about. "But if you don't like me to call from here—"

"No, no, it's okay. Come in.... Who do you want to call?" A little twinkle in Batya's eye, clearly thinking of a boyfriend, someone Zohara did not want her father to know about.

"Oh, someone in Canada... I'll pay you for the call...."

"Don't be ridiculous." Batya pointed to the phone, went into her bedroom, closed the door.

Zohara sat before the little table, pulled a pen toward her, dialed.

A long delay, two rings, then a voice in English. "Starkman or Sowa? Whom do you want?"

She said in Hebrew she wanted to speak to David.

A long pause. "Who is it?"

"Amzaleg's daughter, my name is Zohara…."

There was a pause. "Where you calling from?"

"Why?"

"Just let me know the place, and I'll call you back."

"When?"

"Right now."

She began to read the number, but he stopped her. "No, the name of the person, and the address. I'll look up the number, I have the Tel Aviv phone book."

She said Batya's full name and the line went dead. In a few seconds the phone rang.

Flustered, she picked it up. The man said, "Why are you calling?"

"My father told me you can help, in something…"

"How do I know it's really from him?"

"He told me, in case you ask, to tell you that you owe him an araq at least."

The man gave a short bark, maybe laughter. "Alright, what kind of help?"

She said, "There were some killings—" She paused. "We don't know who did it, and we can't talk to the suspects, so he wanted to ask who of them you think could've done it."

It sounded ridiculous to her, but the man took it in stride. "How many you have, on the list?"

"Seven."

"Why didn't he call himself, why did he send you?"

"Because… because he can't…. They broke his jaw, some bones too… he can speak, but he… he can't leave the house, I can't say why…."

"What happened to the other guy who broke his jaw?"

Zohara said, "I cut him, with a razor, also the other one."

The man laughed again, a quick bark. "What's your name, you said?"

"Zohara," she said, uncertain how to go on, how to convince him.

But the man apparently had made up his mind. "Read me the list."

She did, pronouncing the names slowly. "Who of them do you think could have done this? I mean, pay money for some boys to suck him, then kill them? Then write these notes?"

"What notes?"

She explained, quoting one or two lines from memory.

"Shit," he said. "It sounds like something a German would write about Jews."

She didn't speak, just waited.

At last the man said, "Could be any one, if he didn't come out of his Blackness.... You know what it is?"

"Yes."

"So. Was anyone of them in the hospital recently?"

She said she didn't know. "All are now in Beirut, doing... something, so they are not in the hospital. But," she added, "all were here on Yom Kippur, which is when the first killing took place."

The man made a teeth-sucking sound. "Did you talk to any of them? Did Amnon?"

"He met them all in Beirut. I only talked to Gidi, here, I met him in the kibbutz...."

"Ah, yes, Gidi. And what did you think of him?"

She felt herself blushing. "I don't know. I don't think he—but maybe." She hesitated. "I don't know."

"I don't either," he said. "He plays the violin, good with his hands. Went Black once, transferred out to... something else...."

"Yes," she said and blushed some more.

He paused, as if giving her time. "I don't know, maybe. But Ehud, I don't believe he could do this—"

"That's the one does theater?"

"Yes. Gidi maybe, and Ami also, they both could. Who else you said? Moshe Mizrahi? He could, but I don't believe it. He's the opposite of crazy, teaches philosophy in Tel Aviv U, Yaro is a complete Yoram, and Tzafi Margolin has only one arm, but he's as good with it as someone with two—"

She interrupted him. "A Yoram is what?"

She was taking notes, writing fast, in SSS.

He laughed again. "A goody-goody boy. It's a Tel Aviv expression."

"Oh." It was as if the *vooz-vooz* had a language of their own and she was now learning it.

He said, "You said seven. Who else was there?"

She read out from the list, "Zerach Kadishevitz, and Ami Fogel."

"Ami is like Gidi, from a kibbutz, he is also a Yoram. And Zerach I don't know."

She said Zerach was with the Mossad. "They work there, too, now."

"Well, you know more than me now."

She asked again whom he thought was likeliest, and again he said he couldn't tell. "Really, I don't know, they are all good men—"

She lost patience. "Obviously one of them isn't."

There was a pause as the line chirped. Then he asked, surprisingly, "What're you doing besides helping your father catch killers?"

Flustered, she said she worked at Jacqueline's. A hairdresser.

"And that's it? You speak English?"

"Yes, also French, from home. And Arabic."

"Wow, quadrilingual." He said, "And where did you go to school?"

And before she knew it she was talking to him, almost like she'd talked to Gidi, telling him where she'd been, even told him about the reformatory. "And I did my matriculation exams," she added.

He said, "And what do you do besides work?"

Even more flustered, she said she liked to read, took books from the HaTikva library, the American library, too, to practice English. "And Batya lends me some, also records, I like Bach…." She didn't say anything about Mahler, how she liked his complications; it would sound like a boast.

How it all came out, she didn't know. Was she as hungry as all that for someone to listen to her?

The man said, "You should talk to Jenny, she likes books, too, she teaches at U of T…."

She asked shyly, "You married?"

"As good as," he said, then added, surprising her again, "why don't you come to visit?"

She didn't want to say she had to wait for her record to be expunged. "Maybe one day."

"Sure," he said, "come stay with us, it's nice here, only a little cold."

"A little?"

He laughed. "Come and you'll see."

She said, "One day, maybe, but I now have to help my father find this killer. The police don't want to catch him, maybe because he is a *vooz-vooz* and the dead were... you know..." She stopped. "I am sorry."

"No need." The man's voice changed. "We are first what we are born into, then it's up to us to decide what we want to be. Call me again if you want. I'm sorry I can't tell you more—" He paused. "How's your father?"

She faltered. "He... he's recovering."

There was another pause, then the man said. "Listen, I gotta run, tell your father he can call, too, for the same price." He laughed. One more *vooz-vooz* joke, probably. "And tell him not to beat up too many Samsons, leave some for you to cut."

She laughed, delighted. She liked this man.

"I will tell him."

He said, "Yallah, bye," and hung up.

She looked at what she had written, all in SSS, but could not read a thing, could not think.

Canada.

One day maybe, after she did what she had to do here, had caught this killer, gotten her record bleached.

Batya came out of her room straight away, asked her if all was okay.

"Yes, yes," she said.

"What was that about Canada?" Batya asked, not even ashamed for having eavesdropped. "You going on a trip?"

"No, no."

There was silence as Batya looked at her. "I heard the rest, too, I know you're helping your father, but please be careful, please. And if you need help, let me know, I know people—"

Just then one of the boys came out, asked Batya something in Yiddish, haltingly, and she replied in the same language. He made a little bow to Zohara, looking aside—many yeshiva boys thought it a sin to look at a woman who was not a relative—and shuffled back into his room.

Batya asked her if she wanted to eat something. She always fed her.

"No," Zohara said, "maybe later. I want to take a walk before I go back."

She felt enervated as she walked up Keren Kayemet Boulevard to the beach, past Ben-Gurion's old house, the Yemenite sentinel in front, the sun shining on her, the wind cooling her neck, tingling it strangely. She could hardly see where she was going.

Both David and Gidi were *vooz-vooz*, like that red-haired student, but they seemed to her like a different species, like aliens almost. No, like they were normal, and everyone else here alien. Or maybe everyone else was just hypnotized, and they immune, like her, maybe this David also, who said you are first what you are born, then it's up to you to choose....

It shook her, this. Her spine felt tingly and soft with the words.

There should be some way to wake up others here, too, from their evil hypnosis—but not she. She would leave this damn place as soon as she could, then bring her brothers and sisters out, extract those who, like Iddo, wanted to leave but couldn't, like Munger wished he could have extracted his family.

But first she had to catch this killer, make sure her people were safe.

Yes, her people.

At home she told Amzaleg about her talk. She waited for him to criticize her, why she hadn't pressed David about each suspect, or for any other ideas he might have about the killer. Instead, Amzaleg gave her a lopsided grin. "Canada, Zozo?"

"Maybe," she said lamely. "Yes, one day. But first we have to catch him, then I'll see." She couldn't leave her brown brethren here to be killed.

"Oh yes," she said, recalling. "I had an idea, after."

He waited.

She said, "You can ask Dr. Anton who it could be, he might know some of them."

Her heart beat hard just saying it. Dr. Anton was a topic neither of them talked about. He was the one who had treated Amzaleg for his Blackness, then married his wife.

Amzaleg did not look up. "It's an idea, but I don't know if he'll talk. They are patients, too, if they were in the ward."

"Yes, they probably all were, though maybe not all his."

"Maybe." Amzaleg looked up at her. "Good thinking, Zozo, I'll ask him the next time he visits."

-39-

Sunday, February 7, All Day

N EXT DAY, SUNDAY, Gershonovitz spent the morning browsing through the latest reports of Agent 51, as well as the raw recording of Rahman's talks with the French *barbouz*, picked up by the recorder inside Rahman's cigarette lighter.

Everything seemed on track. So why did he feel fidgety?

A little after lunch he popped into Asa's office.

"Anything more recent from her? She says he's serious, or not?"

"Oh he's serious, makes preparations, every night she tells him he'll be a fine president...."

Gershonovitz blew out air in relief, turned to leave, looked at Asa. "Anything else?"

"Yes. She wants out."

"Fuck, no!" Gershonovitz slammed both fists on Asa's desk. "She can't. Not now!"

"That's what I clicked her."

Gershonovitz said, "Every one of us has a job."

"Yes," Asa said heavily, thinking of his cows, one of them expecting. "Yes."

Back home Gershonovitz immediately called Ehud at the Sub on the scrambler.

"Tell the *barbouz* it's all five-five here," he said. "We only need a date from Rahman."

Ehud said they'd just gotten it. "It's June third."

"Good," Gershonovitz said. "So you guys can take a rest."

"Yeah, whoever is not in the psych ward then…"

There was a short silence. Finally Ehud said, "So the cabinet is okay with all this?"

Gershonovitz said, "Yes, in principle, if everyone gets his pound of flesh later. But I don't know what the Damn HolyName will say."

"Ask him," Ehud said.

"Don't be a putz," Gershonovitz said. "You know we're not on speaking terms."

"Yallah, yallah," Ehud said. "Enough with your blood vengeance. I got a job early morning."

Gershonovitz said, "Anything I should tell your father?"

"No need, he knows."

For the first time, Gershonovitz could not find words. Finally he said, "About the other thing, with the dead *Arsim*, do you have any idea who it could be, doing this?"

He held his breath as the line hummed.

"No," Ehud said. "Could be anyone."

"Yes," Gershonovitz said, relieved.

"If I hear anything I'll tell you. Go to sleep, Shimmel. End."

"Alright. End."

Gershonovitz waited, clicked the madman's call sign once more, but again got no response and felt a twinge of anxiety.

How close was Amzaleg's *Freha* to finding who the madman was?

His anxiety turned to rage. The last thing he wanted was Amzaleg's *Freha* serving as an unwitting tool in the hands of the DHN, screwing up this magnificent chance to stop the invasion, maybe a peace deal with the Flatheads on top of it….

This madman would be the perfect tool to take her down—if only he'd answer!

Gershonovitz kept clicking until midnight, every few minutes, but there was still nothing.

It was getting tight. He simply had to take her out before she found out something.

But how?

-40-

Monday, February 8, 1981, 11:30 a.m.

ZOHARA DID NOT think she was getting close.

Amzaleg did not press her, just let her go on, going over the material with her again and again.

But finally he said to her, "So who of them do you think it is?"

She said, "David said it could be anyone."

"But what do *you* think?

She shook her head, said she didn't know.

Did Gidi miss her too? She didn't know that either. He didn't call, she knew he couldn't. Still she hoped he would, if he could.

She said into Amzaleg's back, "If at least we could talk to them—"

"How? They're all in Beirut, maybe won't come home for months."

She knew that. Still. She hoped.

It was a new thing for her, hope. Not just with Gidi, but in other things too.

It might have been the mention of Canada in her talk with David, or maybe the slow expansion of her horizons due to the books, or the music Batya made her listen to, or yes, the colors she saw briefly with Gidi. But also, perhaps mainly, it was a dawning knowledge that it was possible that everyone around her was indeed mad, hypnotized like those on stage in the Ariadne Café.

It was this, and yes, the memory of what she'd felt with Gidi, that gave her hope. She held on to it every day as she burrowed yet again through the list of the seven suspects.

Once she asked Amzaleg how he would have done it, if he had to leave Beirut, sneak into Israel, come back. He said straight out he'd not cross on land, he'd take a small boat from Beirut at night, go around the Dove Rock, land somewhere past the border, in Rosh HaNikra, or Rosh Pina, maybe as far South as Nahariya, take a motorbike or a scooter from there.

"Where from, a motorbike?"

"Steal one, easy. Leon taught us."

She looked at him slantwise. "Can you show me?"

"No."

She laughed, then said, "Who of these seven can ride a motorcycle?"

Amzaleg didn't know. "Ask Gidi,"

"If he comes back on a break, I will." She reddened, went on. "He rides a motorbike...."

Amzaleg waited for her blush to subside, said they all probably could ride one.

"Also operate a boat?"

Amzaleg shook his head, didn't know. "But you are in the right direction, Zozo, thinking in the right way, putting it together."

She shrugged, though it made her feel warm, his approval.

"You'll catch him," Amzaleg said. You.

"I know we will," she said, not to let him off the hook.

More and more he left it in her hands. She liked it, and yet she didn't.

-41-

**Wednesday, February 2 to February 22, 2016,
Hama, Syria**

ON FEBRUARY 2, Rahman joined his brother Rifaat's expedition to cleanse Hama of Muslim Brothers.

Brothers. When it was all over, Rahman drove back to Latakia in triumph, having been decorated by his brother Haffez, the president.

There was no point in remaining. The fun was over and from now on it was mainly grunge work, pouring napalm on the bodies and burning them, bulldozing the remains into the mass graves. He had told Haffez they should've kept some alive, to help them dig. Haffez said he was right, next time they'd remember. Maybe even write it into procedures.

He liked that, making an impact already. It was good training.

He arrived at Latakia early morning, cars honking. He brought back pictures from the operation to show his wife Nur, to prove how brave he was.

The following week he began to move his wives and children from Latakia to the Lebanese Biqaa, to make his move on Damascus from there. He was not willing to leave hostages in Syria. He told all wives to enroll the children in Lebanese schools, the young ones in kindergarten, to show they were staying and not give any hint to Haffez's spies.

The details were important. Nur agreed too. She was the only one he could talk to who was as excited as he was.

-42-

March 1982,
Tel Aviv, HaTikva, Haifa

THROUGHOUT MARCH, SINCE there had been no further murders, several boys left HaTikva and returned to Jaffa. Others, sent by Zohara as emissaries to nearby neighborhoods, left also. And so half the street patrols disbanded, handing back their whistles to the local soccer team managers.

This worried Zohara no end.

"Do you think he's done killing?" she asked Amzaleg as they were finishing one more session of training. He never let up, despite his fatigue.

He shook his head. "Doesn't matter. We still have to catch him."

"But how? We can't go talk to the suspects—" She gave him a slanted look. "Maybe I should sneak into Beirut, like you did, talk to them there..."

He looked at her hard. "Don't even think of it."

"Or if Gidi calls, I could ask him—" She reddened, stopped.

It was more than four weeks. She knew he was working up there, doing those hard jobs, trying to prevent the war—Amzaleg finally explained this to her—but still, Gidi could have sent a message, something.

And then the dark thought she kept suppressing: If it was indeed Gidi who'd killed her brethren, and she found this out... would she kill him? Could she?

Sometimes she thought she could, other times that she couldn't. But beyond that, and stronger still, she hoped he would call or send a message.

But there was nothing.

No, there was something, a small thing she could not pin down.

At the back of her mind, something she'd heard or seen when she was with Gidi kept nagging at her. She tried to remember but it evaded her; all she remembered was him. Day by day she kept trying to fit the seven's schedules in Beirut to the killings' times, but she got nowhere.

And the thing at the back of her mind stayed hidden, no matter how she tried to recall it.

-43-

April, 1982,
Beirut, Jerusalem, Nes Tziona, Beirut

MID-APRIL, EHUD HAD to return briefly to Israel to pick up more poison ampoules. On the way back from the Unit's camp, he called Shimmel on the scrambler. "You want to meet before I go back on the boat?"

He could pop up to Tel Aviv, maybe see his father too.

"No. I got it under control. You go back and make sure the guys don't do another putsch."

Shimmel was still angry at their pushing back at him about the volume of killing.

Well, fuck him. They were not obeying orders blindly. They had a say, too, before they did it anyway.

Later, on the boat, he idly wondered what happened to Amzaleg, how he was doing after his "accident." He should visit Amzaleg, too, next time he was in town, see how he was.

Amzaleg was, after all, an Anon once, before he went off the rails.

-44-

**April, 1982,
Tel Aviv**

THE NEXT DAY, Zohara rode her Vespa to Batya's to call David in
Canada, again. Maybe he had some more ideas.

"No," he said when she'd finished, "I told you, I don't know who's
likeliest. Any one of them could be—"

She interrupted, "No, I mean, who of them prefers men?"

There was a silence. "I don't know... none of them that I know of... and
if one of them does, he'd probably keep it quiet...."

A fat lot of help this was. "But how to find out who?"

She had never even met them, except for Gidi.

David said, "Just keep your eyes and ears open for anything, no matter
how trivial."

What did he mean by that?

"Just trust your instinct," he said, sounding like her father.

Then without any transition he said, "Jenny asked when you're coming
to visit."

She was taken aback. "I told you, I... I have to catch him first, the killer,
like I said."

"So right after, come, it's nice, no army or wars and shit, you'll like it."

"I... I'll have to get a passport, and a visitor's visa.... I don't know." It
was going too fast.

But he wouldn't let her off. "No, listen, forget immigration visas and just come as a student."

A buzz went through her. Student?

She stammered, "Maybe, I... I don't know—"

She'd just assumed that when her criminal record was bleached, she'd leave and work wherever she went as a hairdresser.

She tried to ask more questions about the suspects, but he really had not much to tell her, and they soon hung up.

It took her a while to calm down. But the idea of Canada—and going there soon—now stuck to her like a burr.

She could hardly imagine it: Canada, everyone around her sane, no one teaching children about mad mothers ordering them to die; no wars, no army for one's brother or uncles to die in.

Did such a paradise really exist?

She reminded herself she had a job to do first, so she tried to forget about Canada while she interrogated teachers, neighbors and friends of the seven.

"I'm helping my father," she said when asked. "Superintendent Amnon Amzaleg, of the Jaffa station," showing his wallet with all his credentials. "Yes," she said once, "maybe one day I, too, will join the police." She gave her most winning smile to the old kindergarten teacher of Yaro ben-Shlomo in the kibbutz. "It's a family tradition, the police. What? Yes, my grandfather, too, was in the police. Where? Oh, here, in the British police, during the Mandate," she lied smoothly, happily. "He came here from France in 1900, a personal friend of Baron Rothschild...."

In Acco, where she talked to the bank manager where Tzafi Margolin, the one-armed Anon, worked as an assistant manager, she transformed her grandfather into an officer in the British Police who'd helped the Haganah on the side.

After two weeks she had three copybooks filled with notes, all in SSS. Amzaleg did not even ask to see them. Perhaps because there had been no new murders, or maybe he had begun to trust her.

Once or twice he did ask, "You making progress, Zozo?"

"What do you think?"

He smiled at her in a way he had never smiled before, soft, and she reddened.

Or was it simply that he was getting old?

Yet evenings, no matter how tired they were, he went over the knife routines with her again and again, the twirls and the attack-fending basics, the falls and the slashes, the feints.

"But I know these already!" she protested. "Once a week is also good, no? Not every day!"

"Yes every day. You have to know them in your sleep, in case he comes after you."

"Why after me? He only goes after men…."

"In case he learns about you, you have to be prepared."

She didn't think she needed the daily training anymore, but he insisted, and it was easier to comply than to refuse.

She saw that it was now more difficult for him, that the Samsons' beatings must have left real damage. His twisted jaw must have hurt, and he had slowed, occasionally faltered, and after every session with her, Pirchiya would sit at his feet and rub his legs with cream. She was now in her sixth month, so big she could hardly move. Later, with Pirchiya in the washroom, Zohara said to Amzaleg, "So make it a real family. Marry her."

At this he said nothing.

"But why not?"

"I don't want to leave her a widow, if."

Same answer as always.

"If what? If the fucker comes after you?"

He shrugged, looked away.

She said, "Don't worry, I'll defend you. I cut up the Samsons, I'll cut him too." She laughed.

He didn't, just stared away. "You just take care of yourself, Zozo."

She could not understand him, but she had no time for this now.

Mid-April, after reading the killer's note that *Yediot Aharonot* published, Zohara went to the public library and asked for the book from which, her father said, the words were taken.

As she read the book, she had to restrain herself from tearing out the pages and stomping on them. How could anyone think like that? Did Batya? Did she herself, now? She refused to pursue the thought.

And nearly as badly as she wanted to catch the killer and leave, she feverishly hoped it wasn't Gidi.

Yet other times, when both her heart and her body were aflame with her need for him, she hoped just as hotly that he was indeed the killer, so she could finish him once and for all and no longer miss him. So that she could then leave for Canada without anything holding her back.

But she did miss him, terribly, and from time to time tried to do to herself what he had done, probe herself where he had, the way he did. But something was always missing. Perhaps his touch, his smell, or his pale eyes that looked right into her, or maybe his voice.

Was this what the books she had read called love? Or was it only hypnosis by a professional seducer? A man who perhaps could no longer feel love himself but could hypnotize others into feeling it? A man who could kill women's hearts for the state, but who first had to kill something in himself?

It was then that she fleetingly glimpsed a shade of the killer's mind, and why he was doing what he did: Was it his twisted attempt to find love again? Not merely hate of his father?

At such a time she almost felt pity for him, and for all the Anons who, like Hanna's seven sons, had been handed to the state by their fathers—though with their mothers' consent, yes—and taught that both killing and fucking—and loving too, yes—were not private matters but tools to be used for their people. Just as they all were tools in their fathers' hands to keep the fathers' book alive.

Was she, too, a tool in her father's hands? Was Gidi in his?

No. She had volunteered, for the sake of Iddo and for the dead *Arsim*.

But hadn't Gidi volunteered also?

At such times she often thought that her investigation was perhaps an attempt to learn who she was, who her own father really was, what he was to her, she to him.

Because more and more, it was becoming clear she was performing the investigation, not he.

If at the beginning Amzaleg said that he had to stay home so the authorities would not be on their guard, now it was clear he was pushing her to do it all, or nearly all.

She fought with him about it.

"Why don't you call, too, Amzaleg, go, too? Why should I do it all?"

"Because they are listening to the phone, they'd follow me...."

"But you can come with me in disguise, you know how to do it." She knew he could, if he wanted to.

"No, Zozo, you do it."

She kept fighting him about it, but he persisted. It was as if he was training her to do what he had done, so she could protect herself when he would no longer be here.

She did not want to think about that part, how she'd have to change if he were gone. Maybe even more than she had changed already.

Several people remarked about the changes, none to do with her developing muscles or growing assuredness. She herself noticed some—her hair, which had been like steel wool, now became softer, lighter in color, her skin smoother—perhaps because of her sweating in the daily physical training. And, following Amzaleg's insistence on doing the theater exercises, her accent became malleable, she could now talk as a *vooz-vooz*, change her voice at will, and let herself be subsumed by a role, as a step to creating an Other via that odd theater method prescribed by the seventy-year-old Russian book, translated into Hebrew. Every month she had to do the book's exercises again and again, to make sure her Other would be there when she needed it.

And there were other exercises, too, odder ones, that Amzaleg prescribed for her, like drawing an upside down chair, trying to forget its "chairness," just following the lines, their angles, length, looking for the breaking spots, the fragilities, like searching an attacker's body for weaknesses, vulnerabilities, kill spots.

She herself, too, often felt she was breaking her essence into parts, recomposing them into something new under her father's guidance; or perhaps recomposing into something she had almost been but was stopped from becoming by the school, the reformatory, the mass insanity.

She fought against it but it didn't seem to help.

And she fought Amzaleg about Pirchiya, again and again. "Why don't you marry her?"

He just shook his head.

"Why not? Give your son your name. You don't want?"

"Or daughter," he said.

She ignored it. "So marry her!"

He said, "She's half my age. If I die, she'll be a widow—"

"But then she'll get a police pension. So why not?"

He got serious all of a sudden. "No, one more target for them."

She said he was being ridiculous. "They don't do this…."

"They do worse."

No matter how much she argued with him, he would not budge. And Pirchiya, whom Zohara thought would want it the most, did not say much about it.

"Only if he wants to," she said. "He'll stay with me anyway."

Pirchiya was now staying with Amzaleg in his room, infrequently going to stay with her parents so her mother could help her. Jacqueline, too, helped, kept paying Pirchiya even though she only worked part-time. And Zohara now wasn't working at all, maybe once every two weeks, just so that she could speak to the hairdressers, have some inane, meaningless girl talk, after her daily training.

And through it all she missed Gidi badly.

But she was making headway. At times she thought she could almost glimpse the figure of the killer through the myriad of facts, shimmering. All it took, she knew, was one clear hint sticking out of the twine ball of facts that she could pull on, then it would all unravel, exposing him.

She felt she had the detail somewhere among all those she had gathered, that it was staring her in the face, but she was not yet smart enough to see it.

Luckily the killer did not kill again.

Yet.

-45-

April, 1982,
Beirut and Tel Aviv

NOT THAT HE didn't try: One Friday eve, residents of the Sub put on a mock play of a takedown gone wrong, which Ehud Reznik helped direct. It was a roaring success. Afterward everyone got drunk and slept late. Early the next morning the man tried to sneak out and sail his boat south for one more Cleansing. But the night before, Ronen had ordered all outside doors locked, so the attempt failed.

He was enraged. Shimmel's hand was clearly in it, but there was nothing to be done. So next day, after a double job in the Sabra camp, when he couldn't take the urge anymore, he visited the *Atatürk* House secretly and had a new boy, then another. But it didn't help much. His urge for a Cleansing only grew hotter.

Meanwhile Shimmel kept clicking him, but he stubbornly refused to answer.

-46-

April, 1982,
Beirut, Latakia and Tel Aviv

GERSHONOVITZ'S PLAN, HOWEVER, was moving forward like a tank in first gear. All during the first week of April, terse messages went back and forth, with suggestions for agreed-upon troop movement coming up to June 3.

"But why only then?" Asa complained to Gershonovitz. "Why not sooner? He wants to sell more shit? Once he's president he can rob all the money he wants, no?"

Gershonovitz shrugged. "Who knows how a goy thinks?"

It was early morning. They were sitting in the Mossad cafeteria in Glilot, in the atrium upstairs, the sun shining through the glass ceiling. "I hope he's not just tricking us...."

They were both silent until the server departed. Gershonovitz said, "What does *she* say?"

Asa gave a deep sigh. "She says the Flathead is serious."

Silence descended as they watched the indoor pool, secretaries on their lunch hour dipping in and out of the water, bosoms bare. Arcadia.

Gershonovitz said, "And? She's going with him?"

"Yeah, yeah. But she still wants out, can't take it anymore...."

"No, no! She's gotta stay! Once he's in Damascus..."

They stared at each other, same thoughts, no need to say them: A direct line to Syria's president via his bedmate who is ours, doing her duty. A *shoo-shoo* wet dream.

Asa muttered, "How much is he shipping a week now? Two loads?"

Gershonovitz raised his palm in the air.

Asa said, "Three?"

Gershonovitz raised his palm again.

"More? No, don't tell me, I don't want to know."

Asa stared at the pool below. Gershonovitz raised his eyes to the ribbed glass dome, through which puffy clouds could be seen, floating in the gray sky. With an effort he restrained himself from sticking his middle finger upward.

Six weeks more. Will it still go five-five?

Gershonovitz was already counting the days to the planned putsch, when on April 27 he got a really big fright. And, as before, it had to do with Zohara.

-47-

**Tuesday, April 27, 1982,
Tel Aviv**

THE DAY KLINGER learned of Zohara's investigations, he called Chief Superintendent Levitan and, in a rage, asked what to do. "This fucking *Freha*…Why don't we arrest her?"

"On what?" Levitan said. He had not been sleeping well lately.

"On interfering in a police investigation…."

"What investigation? You want the newspapers to hear we have an investigation about suspect Undertakers? You crazy? Shimmel will have your ass, and mine."

"So what do I do?"

"Let me handle it," Levitan said.

Which was also what Gershonovitz said to him, when Levitan called to tell him that Zohara was digging up stuff about Undertakers now sacrificing their souls for their people in Beirut.

"But how, Shimmel, how?" Levitan said. "And you also said this last time."

"I told you I'll handle it!" Gershonovitz raged. "These things take time! Also I have other things on my plate…"

"Well you'd better do something about her or the other things won't work either…."

"Sha, Leizer," Gershonovitz said, "not on an open phone line."

He hung up, seething.

If she went on like that, she was bound to find something, maybe discover who the madman was. And this, when the plans were so close to fruition....

If only the madman called him back, he could unleash him on her.

But how to make him?

Gershonovitz stopped pumping, thumped on his forehead, winced.

You are an idiot, Shimmel, he hissed. You're really getting senile. Why didn't you think of it sooner?

Grabbing his clicker he keyed in the madman's call sign, his own, a double nine-nine for emergency, then bared his teeth and began to click slowly, spelling it out, not using contractions. "Call me or I'll tell your father. End."

He didn't have to wait long.

-48-

May, 1982,
Beirut

THE MAN WAS on his way to the *Atatürk* House when he got the message.

He heard his clicker chirp and looked down. A long message, probably this new dumb secretary of Ronen's at the Sub, still not knowing acronyms....

Then as the message sank in, his heart froze and he nearly dropped the clicker.

Cursing in French for safety, he looked for a café with a public telephone and called the local number via the scrambler.

"Yes," he said in French when Shimmel came on, "you dirty fucking shit, Shimmel, what?"

Gershonovitz said, "You want me to call him, your father, tell him what you've been doing?"

"No," the man said. "What do you want?"

Gershonovitz said, "I have another job for you."

Was this all?

His heart beat more sedately as he listened to Shimmel.

"We don't take down women at the Unit," he said at last when Shimmel had finished.

"*M'darf,*" said Gershonovitz in Yiddish. It's necessary.

"Alright, Shimmel," he said. "Maybe. But why now?"

"Because Amzaleg's *Freha*, the one who almost caught you last time, she's investigating where all you guys were on Yom Kippur and I am told she's getting close."

The man nearly said no, then realized he could get in, do her, then do a Cleansing at the same time. An opportunity to be seized….

But Shimmel, as if reading his mind, said, "Listen, putz, you come in, you do only her, no one else on the side, you understand? It's an order."

Shit, order. "Yes," the man said, crestfallen. "Maybe next month, we're working so hard, we have to sign in and out, I'm not sure I could sneak…"

"Don't worry about this part, I'll see to it you can get out easily. And next time I click, you thug, you answer. Understand? End."

"End," the man said sheepishly.

He stared about him, barely seeing the booth's walls.

Shit, shit. She was getting close, Shimmel had just said. But how close?

Zohara herself didn't know if she was getting close.

She had a copybook nearly filled with notes about the suspects, but no suspect had yet become alive for her, not even Gidi. Rather, all seemed to merge into one: All were Ashkenazim (except for Moshe, whose father was from Iraq, his mother from Poland), all smart loners, all either played an instrument, or painted, or did theater, or wrote poetry—at the Unit they probably looked for this artistic streak, her father said, when they recruited for lone killers. And all had served in a combat role before: paratroopers, Golani, naval commandoes. Not all made it past training, Amzaleg said. Killing alone face-to-face was worlds different from killing in groups from afar. Not in the same category even.

"Yes, yes," she said. "It's special, I got it."

He shook his head at her. "It's no laughing matter," he said. "Just make sure you know how to put it on, when you need to."

"It" was the Other, the thing rarely spoken of.

"Yes, yes, I know."

Luckily there were no more exercises with it, just that one time, with the dog, and the time she chased the fleeing killer.

It had never risen up in her even once, since. There was no need.

-49-

May, 1982,
Tel Aviv

SEVERAL WEEKS LATER, there was a surprise: A large parcel arrived for Zohara, from Canada. Inside was a huge orange and white sweater of rough wool, with a poster of Toronto and a letter from Jenny tucked into the sleeve, together with application forms for the University of Toronto.

Amzaleg and Pirchiya stared at the thing. "What is it?" Pirchiya said. "A housecoat?"

"A woolen prayer shawl," Amzaleg said. "For the winter."

"Yallah, yallah," Zohara said, miffed at both of them. "It's a sweater, you dummies."

"You never wear any," Pirchiya said.

"It's for Canada," Zohara said. "I'll be a student there."

There was a short silence.

"What about the killer?" Pirchiya said at last.

"I'll catch him, don't worry."

Zohara put on the sweater, buttoning it. It was large, warm, with a label of the Hudson Bay Company. Established in 1658, it said. More than 320 years. Shit, older than Israel by far.

On the front was woven a picture of a mule-like animal in brownish wool. A moose, it said on the sticker. "Looks a little like you, Amzaleg," Zohara said.

"But the nose is like yours," Pirchiya said, and giggled.

Amzaleg said nothing, just scowled.

"Don't worry," she said. "I'll catch him before I leave."

Pirchiya said, "But you leave only after." Meaning after the birth.

"No way I'll miss it."

I T WAS A huge thing, the baby. Everyone was happy for Amzaleg, even Jacquie, sometimes.

Amzaleg's only son fell, his two brothers, too, childless both. Amzaleg was already resigned to the idea he'd be the last of the Amzalegs; his father thought so too: Almost like a *vooz-vooz* family, his father said, everyone dead. The only one left for the family was Zohara, a daughter, and unmarried too. But even if she married, so what? She'd take on her husband's name. But now here was hope, it could be a boy.

"I don't care, a boy, girl," Amzaleg said generously. "At worse, it'll be another Zohara."

She scowled at him, not accepting it as a compliment.

"What? What did I say?" Amzaleg protested, knowing exactly what.

But yes, the baby would be special, even she admitted it. No way she would miss its birth.

Many came to ask Pirchiya how she was doing. She walked about with her arms cradling her stomach, as if it would fall and shatter if not supported. Amzaleg, too, often came to pet it, as if making sure, and Dr. Munger came once a week to check on her.

But despite her condition, Pirchiya often sneaked out mornings, waddling softly down the backstairs, loaded with pots of food leftovers, which she left at the Moroccan synagogue's backdoor.

One morning, though, Zohara got up early and saw Pirchiya sneaking out of the Moroccan synagogue, furtive, without any pots.

"What you been doing inside there?" Zohara asked her.

"Nothing, nothing…."

But on Pirchiya's wrist, Zohara saw, were two red threads, knotted and tied; and when she dug into Pirchiya's pocket, she found folded papers scribbled by red ink, in Talmudic script.

"What's that?!" she snapped. "Amulets?"

Pirchiya blushed, tried to pull her hand back, turned her head away, finally nodded.

"What for?"

Zohara felt mad at Pirchiya's foolishness.

Pirchiya stuttered, "For… for the baby…."

"And the other?" There were two threads.

Pirchiya lowered her head. "So you wouldn't go to Canada, so you'd stay here…."

Zohara slapped her lightly on her chin. "Don't waste your money."

For a while Zohara was annoyed, then relented. If it made the little fool feel better, reduce her fear of giving birth, why not.

She felt surprised at herself. She'd never used to think like that.

Amzaleg, she saw, noticed the threads also, his face going dark, but he, too, said nothing.

And all the while, despite her continuing investigations, there was nothing new, no break.

-51-

May 21, 1982,
Tel Aviv, HaTikva

FINALLY, A DAY after Zohara had sent in her U of T application and five days before the English proficiency exam, there was a break in the case, and it came because Zohara suddenly remembered what was nagging her. It was in the middle of a face-to-face combat session with Amzaleg, on the building's roof, when it happened. Both she and he had wooden knives, freshly painted, and they were trying to slash at each other, timing it, a three-minute round. Despite Amzaleg's limp, he just kept moving, not fast, just always moving smoothly, somehow knowing where to be.

"There's movement and there's motion," he said, when she grudgingly commended him on being able to evade most slashes. "Movement is sudden, motion is continuous, like that…" Even with his bad leg, he seemed to move like a fish, slithering maddeningly where she could not reach, always avoiding her grasp as if reading her mind.

"You simply don't stay still, ever," he said. "You stop, you die."

But today they seemed evenly matched somehow, and she nearly got him, when the thing suddenly popped into her head. "I remember!" she shouted, and as she stopped, he slashed at her. She parried unthinkingly and slashed back, then retreated, always moving.

"That was good, Zozo!" he said, massaging his forearm.

"No, listen… something Gidi said… I'm sorry, I should have told you…."

Amzaleg saw it in her eyes. "What is it?"

She said, "Shit, shit, I had completely forgotten… Something Gidi told me… About the course he took, the second one… I forgot to tell you…"

Amzaleg did not move.

"I… I asked him if any men in the TempleWhores course, you know, instead of being taught to go after women, were taught to go after men… Gidi said no, today they do, but not then…."

Amzaleg waited, immobile.

She plunged on, "But then he… he said in the course just before him, there was a man who 'had matters' with another man in the course, Bentzy someone, who screwed up—this Bentzy did, made money on the side with what they taught him, so they threw him out and the other guy left too…. I… forgot to tell you… I am sorry…." Her voice stuck.

She felt the shame of failure, and the hot guilt.

Amzaleg did not speak and she didn't either. For what could she say? That all she remembered was Gidi probing inside her and the colors he'd made her see? That because of this, a boy was almost killed?

David had warned her to pay attention to all details, no matter how trivial.

She should've listened.

"I am sorry," she repeated but he waved her to silence.

"So you think this Bentzy is the one?"

She forced herself to think. "I… I think it's not him… probably the other one, the one who left." She felt the gears inside her head catch and click. "Could you get the list, maybe, of the course participants? Gidi said he was in the '77 course, it was a few years before him—" Her mind was working again now. "So '74 and '75, get '76, too, to be safe."

Amzaleg nodded. "I'll see if I can, but I don't know."

She said, "What about Feldman? The Shin Bet guy who was your partner in Haifa once? Couldn't he get you the names?"

She stopped. Her eyes felt hot and wet and she swiped at them. They could've been so much closer!

Amzaleg nudged her hand. "Forget this, Zozo. It happens, we are not machines."

She nodded, still feeling low.

Amzaleg said, "Come on, at least we got something maybe."

"Yes. Not maybe." She swatted at her eyes again, ashamed he saw her tears. "Just give me his number and something to tell this Feldman, so he'll know it's from you. I'll call, you stay here."

But Amzaleg shook his head. "Not you, Zozo, I'll call him."

"Why you?"

"Because he owes me, not you," then he added, "but I'm not sure he can do it."

"Sure he can! He's the chief of the Shin Bet, no?"

Amzaleg said nothing, left in Moshiko's cab, came back two hours later.

"He can't," he said.

She felt hot anger, began to speak, then suddenly there was a little flash inside her.

"Listen, Amzaleg," she said, "this Bentzy guy, the one who was kicked out, would he still be doing this, do you think, on the side?"

"Like what, on the side?"

"You know, like a gigolo, selling his ass, or maybe a pimp, selling others' asses for a fee, so you could see his record in the police files, in case if he'd ever got arrested...."

Before she had finished, Amzaleg grabbed her head between his large hands and tried to kiss the top of her head. She was so surprised she almost did not squirm away, but she finally did, pushing at him, hard, still feeling his lips on her forehead.

When she finally got her breath back, she said, "So maybe we can look for him, this Bentzy, in the police files? Even if it wasn't his real name, because maybe he used it later." She searched for words, "for sentiment's sake...."

Amzaleg looked at her narrow-eyed. "Zozo, they should fire Suissa and put you in his place, I ought to tell them. You want?"

"Yallah, yallah," she said, sheepish but warm inside. "It's only an idea."

But to her surprise there indeed was a Bentzy in the police files, when she asked Suissa to look. A "Nehemia (street name 'Bentzy') Etzioni," arrested several times for male pimping and male prostitution.

Zohara said, "Ask your sources where we can find him."

"Maybe you want to come work here?" Suissa said, miffed. "Teach me my profession?"

"I only work for my father," Zohara said. "And he asked this, not me."

"Alright, alright," Suissa huffed. "I'll ask around."

But three days later, there was still nothing.

"Maybe he doesn't want to be found," Amzaleg said.

"So what?" Zohara said, "The killer doesn't want to be found either."

After a pause Amzaleg said, "I'll have to see *Adon* Leon again."

"You sure?" she said, because this might mean asking for a favor from an *Adon*, which Amzaleg had never done.

"Yes. I'll be doing him a favor, maybe."

-52-

Friday, May 28, 1982,
Tel Aviv

THAT EVENING, AMZALEG took Moshiko's cab to *Adon* Leon's weekend love nest at Ramat Gan.

Leon opened the door in a striped blue housecoat and felt slippers, his hair in a hairnet.

"What? What?"

Amzaleg said, "There's a guy who knows the man who killed Nachum, but I can't find him."

Leon's mouth twitched. "So? Tell Levitan."

Amzaleg saw he had caught the *Adon* at dinner. A fifteen-year-old shamelessly walked about in a flimsy pink shift. The girl was one Amzaleg had never seen. *Adon* Leon never brought his *vooz-vooz* girls to HaTikva; he had a special flat for them outside.

Whether he was ashamed of his neighbors or the girls, Amzaleg was never sure.

Amzaleg rasped, "The fucker also knows who's flooding the market with new shit that's taking business away from you."

The *Adon* fixed Amzaleg with his hooded black eyes, waiting.

Amzaleg said, "You want, I'll go now and let you eat. Or maybe you want it to stop?"

The *Adon* chewed his lips, tugged at his hairnet. "Who's the guy knows all this?"

"Name of Etziony, Nehemia, calls himself Bentzy."

Adon Leon did not ask how Amzaleg knew. He turned back, sat down, dipped his spoon, tasted, and without looking at Amzaleg, said, "You see him, tell him from me, to give you whatever you want, or he won't work in this town again."

Amzaleg didn't move, didn't breathe. At last he said, "But where's the guy? I can't find him."

The teenage girl said, "I know him."

Adon Leon said without turning, "Shut up, nobody asked you."

Then he got up, nodded at Amzaleg. "I will get back to you."

Amzaleg walked downstairs, breathing shallowly, his heart hot and cold. Who did a favor to whom?

Moshiko's cab was waiting and he took it back to HaTikva. On the way, they passed two loaded tank carriers going north, soldiers hitchhiking, all with Galils, Uzis, FNs, a few jeeps.

As they were finishing the meal that evening, the young *vooz-vooz* girl knocked on Amzaleg's door. "Leon said to tell you, tonight this guy will be in one of the clubs."

Zohara came from behind and eyed her. "Which club?"

"Didn't say, but in Tel Aviv." She turned and left.

Outside the window it began to rain, hard.

"Rain in May," Zohara said. "What is this? Lebanon?"

Wind coming through the window blew on her neck and she shivered.

Amzaleg got up to close the window. Far away, from the Ayalon road, came rumbles of more trucks driving north. Some jets high up could be heard.

"We finish eating, we go look for him tonight," Zohara said. "Which club do you want to start?"

"You choose," Amzaleg said.

"The closest to where Nachum was found."

-53-

**Friday, May 28, 1982, 10:50 p.m.,
Tel Aviv**

THE CLOSEST WAS the Black Satan club.

It was raining harder when Zohara and Amzaleg—she leading, he following—arrived in Moshiko's cab. It was not easy to find the club's entrance—Zohara had never been there; finally two boys with spikes in their hair directed them.

The Black Satan sat in a defunct shoe factory behind Central Bus Station. The building sprouted makeshift ventilation shafts, like old tumors patched by metallic tape, the stairwell going down at the back. But as Zohara pushed open the thick metal door, she was assailed by a staccato blast of yellow and darkish strobe lights and an ear-piercing cacophony of whistles and instrumental wails.

"Fucking shit!" she shouted at Amzaleg. "Better than the Velvet ten times."

It was as if a silent black-and-white film had suddenly been splashed with color by a child who also threw in a hundred-decibel soundtrack for good measure. In the flashing lights, the huge basement seemed to crawl with subterranean life: wild heads, both long-haired and shaven, popped up from among a sea of waving hands on the dance floor before sinking into an undulation of waving palms. All heads pointed in one direction, eyes bright and glazed.

The noise was head-splitting.

From behind, Amzaleg shouted in Zohara's ear, "Beirut is here; worse."

She shouted back, "But we gotta find him, if he's here."

"Find how?"

The dancers' faces were white smears blinking in and out of the strobes. The noise kept escalating, crashing at them.

She hollered at Amzaleg, "Wow. Look over there."

He turned his head, then grabbed her hand. "This is not for you! Let's get out!"

In the middle of the huge hall, on a shallow stage, a young man was slowly peeling off his silvery pants with one hand, with the other directing a military flashlight at his crotch, turned to full brilliance.

"Show it!" screamed high male voices. "Show it all, Avi!"

Zohara swallowed her saliva, transfixed.

The stripper wiggled his pelvis, and as the pants came off, red spandex underwear was revealed. The crowd hissed like snakes. The stripper twirled the flashlight, sweeping his crotch up and down. He bent forward—his upper body was bare, the nipples pierced with metal studs—and stuck a long tongue at the crowd. It was forked, having been split down its middle.

He wiggled his tongue then screeched at the crowd, "*Ashmedai chai! Ashmedai chai!*"

Satan lives! Satan lives!

Zohara's heart bumped. For a moment the man looked like Gidi. But no, it wasn't him.

All around, the crowd erupted in an animal roar. "Show it! Show it!"

Amzaleg tugged at her hand, pulling her back to the door. Without looking at him she wrenched it free. "No! We gotta stay, Amzaleg! He can be here. Look around!"

She pulled out the two police album photos, gave him one.

Avoiding looking at the dancer, Amzaleg scanned the faces winking in and out of the strobe light. "Nothing." Then said sideways to her, "You, anything?"

"No."

A throng pushed by, passing through the pulsating beams, smelling strongly of beer and puke.

"Nothing happens before three in the morning anyway!" a man shouted into her face. The man wore paratrooper camouflage pants and an undershirt of scintillating pink. He was drinking from a bottle of Maccabee beer. "Then maybe, and only if Bentzy comes."

Before she could hold on to him, a skinny girl dressed in a tight black sheath passed between them, tears seeping from her closed eyes, as the man babbled away.

Zohara pushed past her. "Where is he, Bentzy?" But the man was gone, the door banged shut.

Zohara heard Amzaleg booming in her ear, "We gotta go see other places before they close. Can't see anything here."

"Wait, wait."

She rose on her toes and cupped her hands to her mouth. "Be-e-entzy!" she hollered.

No one paid any attention.

On stage, the young man had peeled off his spandex underwear and exposed a huge erection, a bright ring hanging from a piercing at its end, and a golden Star of David.

The screams turned horrifically penetrating, as if a troupe of devils were all shrieking at once, in a pulsating rhythm.

The crowd shrieked, "Satan lives! Satan lives!"

The dancer wiggled, his erection going up and down. Zohara shook herself. "Look at his face," she shouted at Amzaleg. "You think that's him?" She stared at the police photo, in the pulsating strobe.

"No, and they called him Avi." Amzaleg's face was rigid, he didn't look at her.

She punched him in the shoulder. "Yallah, it's for the job, you didn't bring me, I brought you."

Amzaleg nodded, looked away. "Yes."

The noise rose and escalated, escalated and boomed: *Ashmedai, Ashmedai, Ashmedai chai!*

Satan, Satan, Satan lives!

"Maybe ask them!" Zohara hollered, pointing.

A quartet of soldiers were sitting at the edge of the dance floor, with their legs extended, drinking Nesher beer. The dancers seemed to avoid the out-stretched legs by some instinct, like bats' radar. The soldiers' red paratrooper boots were unlaced, their khaki shirts unbuttoned, showing undershirts and metal dog tags—they were either on furlough or going back to camp.

At their side, a girl soldier was lying curled in a fetal position, wear-ing paratrooper camouflage pants and a bleached khaki shirt open to her navel, without a bra. Her nubby breasts were as small as a prepubescent girl's. The leftmost soldier had wrapped an arm around her shoulder and was stroking her fair hair. With his other hand he was wiping her eyes.

The soldier raised eyes red with lack of sleep and drugs. "He died, Amiram. Her boyfriend, yesterday," he muttered at Zohara. "Too much shit."

Amzaleg hissed at the soldier, "Get her out of here, go someplace quiet."

"Nah," the soldier said. "Then she cries all the time. Here she can stop thinking. We all gotta be back by ten anyway, in case we're moving."

The girl gave a twitch and a whimper, curled tighter. The soldier bent over her and tenderly extended a palm. On it was a pinch of White powder. "No, no," she mumbled. "You need it more."

"No, take, take," he urged her.

Dutifully she bent her head into his palm and breathed in. When she raised her head, her chin, her nose, her lips, were covered with specks of White. "Ami, Ami, Ami…" she whimpered.

Zohara said, "You seen Bentzy?"

The soldier shook his head dully. "No."

Just then the screams turned frantic as the naked Satyr began to stroke his huge member.

"Let's get out of here!" Zohara shouted at Amzaleg.

Amzaleg turned to her, his face dark ochre, shouted something, his voice lost in the cacophony.

"No, wait," she shouted back. "Wait here!"

Before he could stop her, she grabbed the gun from the small of his back, pushed past him and the soldiers and barged into the dance floor.

She almost gagged—the smell was a mix of sweat, urine, and hashish.

Grabbing heads and necks she kept repeating the question about Bentzy's whereabouts, shouting into glazed eyes. None answered. Amzaleg, after first starting after her, had taken the other end of the dance floor and was doing the same. None seemed to respond.

Zohara unholstered the Beretta, ratcheted the breech back and shot twice at the ceiling. The sound of the shot rolled faintly. There was the briefest of lulls.

She cupped hands to mouth.

"Bentzy!" she hollered into the lull. "Bentzy Etzioni! Are you he-e-e-re?"

A few disinterested heads turned toward her, dull stony eyes. Someone shouted, "Hey, Bentzy! Your mom's looking for you!"

A brief wave of nasty laughter roiled the sea of waving hands. She felt Amzaleg grabbing the gun from her hand, shouting something at her; then the music restarted, but a second before it did, a man behind Amzaleg said to him in a normal voice, "Try in the Sahara club."

She saw Amzaleg whirl and did, too, but the man had already melted into the crowd.

She motioned to Amzaleg and they left, pushing through the sweaty, dazed throng, back through the metal doorway.

Outside, the dark hit them like a soft shock, and the sudden silence, before she heard the rushing water, billowing and surging, flowing and gushing down Fein Street. Rotting tomatoes floated away in the black rushing turbulence, like small clots of blood.

"Shit," she said. "A rainstorm in May, what a country." She galloped down the street, Amzaleg following close behind.

"Where we going?" He seemed to have relinquished control to her.

"Over there, let's take one."

At the curb a half a dozen cabs were parked, waiting for clubbers. They got into one and sailed down the river of black sludge, the water parting before it.

"The Sahara, on Allenby," she told the driver.

In the rearview mirror she saw a portion of his cheek was gone. Probably a shrapnel wound.

She said, "Can you go faster?" It was getting late.

"Take a helicopter," the driver said.

The Sahara sat at the back of a narrow apartment building on Yonah Street, with a Judaica store and a goldsmith nook in front. Water swirled around the goldsmith's window front, like a mini deluge around a small ark, past the low stone fence, past the entrance.

The bouncer inside was seated on a high chair, all bald head and tattoos. The place was one dark cavern, empty and blue and velvety. The man sat by the bar, eyes fixed on his beer bottle. His T-shirt, painted with a blue Magen David crossed with a red penis, was entirely wet.

"The dream of the prophets hath come true," the man sang sleepily, in the intonation of a Kol Yisrael announcer. "Before our astonished eyes—"

"Shut up." Amzaleg leaned over and poked at his chest. "Where's Bentzy?"

The man sing-songed, sleepily, "The Maiden of Zion would rejoice to witness the return of—"

"Shut your mouth." Amzaleg poked the man, who seemed to wake up. "Come back later," he muttered, twitching. "Nuthin' ever starts before two—"

Amzaleg slapped the doughy face. "Where's Etzioni?"

The man gave a whizzing sound, barely awake. Amzaleg punched at his stomach.

"Bentzy! Where's he?" More slaps; but the man put his head down and snored away.

Amzaleg let his hand drop. "Alright, fuck it." He wiped his hand on his pants. "What now?"

"Maybe he knows," Zohara said and pointed.

A man entered from an unseen opening at the back and began to sweep the floor with a near-brushless broomstick. Amzaleg pounced on him. "Etzioni here?"

The man shook his head, bewildered, recoiling.

Zohara grabbed Amzaleg by the hand. "He ain't here. Let's go across the street and ask."

But the pub across the street was also empty, as was the one beside it. However the bar in the basement of house No. 57 on the Prophet Habakkuk Street was hopping. All tables were occupied. Men aged between twenty and thirty, dressed mostly in black, several with military dog tags, sat silently, eyes glazed, swaying at their seats while on the darkened shallow stage, a Yemenite singer of indeterminate age was ululating of palm trees and a shepherd, in Jazz rhythm.

"It's completely dead," said a waiter of indeterminate sex who led them to a table at the back. "Nothing starts before three o'clock."

Zohara ordered a Maccabee beer for form's sake and Amzaleg ordered another. She opened her bottle with a spoon, jail style, and asked about the man called Etzioni.

"Tall? Homo?" said the waiter. "Redhead?"

She sat up. "Maybe."

"Was here before, I think he went to the Club Argaman."

She left her beer half-drunk and dashed out, Amzaleg stumbling after her. The rain, if anything, had intensified, but she was by now so wet that water no longer mattered.

But in Club Argaman no one had seen Etzioni either, nor in Café Cassit, where Amzaleg, now half-dead on his feet, suggested they go on the off chance. But some actors, seated by the kitchen at the charity table, said Etzioni had gone to listen to jazz in Bar Minan, near Central Bus Station.

"Let's go," Zohara said. "Yallah."

As they left, the clouds burst. The water streaming down was more like a heavy gray sauce. Zohara ran among the sweeping molten sheets of water, Amzaleg half-hopping behind, down Allenby Street, along the row of vendors' stalls, now shuttered and locked with large iron locks.

Rivers of blackness swept along the gutters. As they dashed from under one awning to another, Zohara glanced at her watch: 3:35 a.m. The rain, if anything, intensified into an avalanche of water. It cascaded and roared.

"Get in anywhere!" she shouted at Amzaleg, "before we dissolve like dog shit. In here! Here!"

They scuttled into the Big Mama, a pizza kiosk in front of a cab stand that was, miraculously, open. She felt ravenous. "Two medium pizzas," she snarled at the man behind the counter who also had only a white undershirt on, and dog tags. Everyone had dog tags, apparently prepared to be called up.

Zohara wiped her face uselessly. Amzaleg, huffing and spitting water, slid in after her in a slosh of water; his leg almost buckled.

She steadied him and he sat on a stool, huffing, but he did not complain.

"Take a beer also," the man behind the counter said. "What rain, eh?"

They drank up.

Amzaleg said, "You want to be in the police, Zozo? This shit is what you'd...."

Just then Bentzy Etzioni walked in. Amzaleg's eyes opened wide, bulging a little.

Zohara turned, looked, said to Etzioni, "Where've you been, you donkey?"

Etzioni was a tall and muscular redhead, his biceps inflated, his chest bulging under a wet white undershirt. Over his head he held a black umbrella, two of its spokes broken. "Who you?" he snarled. "You want something maybe?"

Amzaleg said, "You want to speak nicely to her?"

"Oo hoo!" said Etzioni, and lifted his shoulders, flexing. "Nicely, he says."

Zohara laid a restraining palm on Amzaleg's wrist, pulled the wallet out of his pocket. "We want to talk to you about someone from the TempleWhores course—"

In a blink the red-haired man was sprinting down the water-swollen street, running like a jackal, the umbrella tossed away.

She threw down her beer bottle and followed, her legs pumping. She could hear Amzaleg stumbling behind her as the red-haired sprinter winked in and out of the downpour, hopping and slipping between parked motorcycles under tarps, tarped stalls, a handcart loaded with bricks.

For a frantic moment she thought she had lost their quarry. Then she caught up with him halfway up Sheinkin Street, fell to jogging alongside him. "You'll go to jail. You want?" she huffed. "They'll fuck you with nightsticks first, then who knows? Or maybe you want to sit somewhere?"

The man stood bent, hands on knees, huffing and wheezing as rainwater streamed from his head.

Amzaleg came presently from behind, his sparse hair plastered to his forehead. He was still holding a pizza slice in each hand, gave one to Zohara. "You forgot this."

He gave the redhead his own slice. The man took it. "Fucking rain," he wheezed at Amzaleg, ignoring Zohara. "In a heat wave you'd never have caught me."

Amzaleg said generously, "Where did you learn to run like this?"

"Chasing your mother."

"Speak nicely," Zohara said, "or I'll lay a *sh'chur* on you."

"Huh," the man said, eyeing her warily.

They stood for a moment, holding the pizza slices, under the primordial gush. "Over there," Zohara said. "You want to walk or swim?"

They stumbled into the Café Piccolino, behind the Bugaiski porcelain and tea service store.

Zohara said, "And if you try to run, we'll catch you and off to jail you go. Got it?"

Amzaleg gave her a side glance, approvingly, but said nothing.

The café was dry, though water seeped in from the street. A few thin men in faded identical undershirts sat by the light of yellow bulbs, smoking, the radio playing a Yemenite medley.

Zohara ordered a coffee. "You want one too?" she asked Etzioni. "Or maybe a beer?"

"Fuck you," said the redhead.

"Speak nicely, you," Amzaleg said, "or to Abu Kabir you go."

The man looked at him, shrugged. "What can they do to me?"

"Nothing happens before four o'clock," the waiter said, depositing their coffees. "Twenty shekels."

Zohara paid. Amzaleg said to Etzioni, "You knew him? The guy left when you were kicked out?"

"Fuck you too," said Etzioni, but he seemed to be more amenable. Half his pizza slice was gone.

Amzaleg said, "Were you in the '71 TempleWhores course?"

The man said, his mouth full, "I ain't talking to you either."

"Who's the man was your boyfriend then?" Zohara said. "What's his name?"

A strange expression flitted across the freckled face. "That's classified, not for the police."

Zohara sat back, to let Amzaleg take over.

Amzaleg waited for the man to swallow. "I was with Shafrir in '51, in the Unit." He took his wallet from Zohara and out tumbled the IDs.

The man flicked his eye on them. "So what?"

Amzaleg said patiently, "Your boyfriend, he was with the Unit, too, before the course?"

Etzioni said nothing.

"Why did they kick you out?" Amzaleg said.

The man shook his head, eyes still on the ID cards. The number on Amzaleg's Unit ID was 7, one of the founders. The man watched the mythological number, transfixed, fingered the two old grenade pin rings attached to the wallet's chain.

Zohara added, "This man was your boyfriend, he's been killing people—"

"Maybe not." Amzaleg flicked his eyes at Zohara, cool it, give the man an out, in case. "We don't know yet. We just want to talk to him."

"Yes," she said, sheepish.

"Killing people?" The man's mouth twisted as he laughed. "You don't say."

Amzaleg said, "Not for the Unit, not in the army, he's been doing it private."

"Yah? So what? Me, too, what they taught me, what's the difference?"

Zohara said, "He's been sneaking in, we think, killing young boys here, none of them *vooz-vooz*, after first letting them suck him. Why do you think he's doing it?"

Amzaleg flicked her another glance but she ignored it. Obey your instinct he'd said. Well then.

The man blinked. "How do you know all this?"

Amzaleg said, "I've seen some of the bodies, did the last wash on one, in Abu Kabir."

He presumably followed his own instinct too.

Amzaleg went on, near-normal voice, "The first he did, was a friend of my son, died in '73, on the Golan."

They waited.

"My condolences," Etzioni muttered. "May you not know more grief."

"Thank you," Zohara said. Amzaleg nodded, affirming.

They drank their coffees, Etzioni too. Zohara said, "Were you in the Unit, too, before TempleWhores?"

"Yah, a week."

She wanted to ask why he was kicked out from there, stopped herself. "So you sold your ass on the side, outside the TempleWhores course?"

She expected the man to get mad; he just shrugged. "Ass, dick, what's the difference? They pay."

Amzaleg said nothing, presumably letting her run with it now. Alright, then.

She said, "And this boyfriend from the course, he was also in the Unit, before?"

No answer at first, then a brief nod. Yes.

She said, "And did you do him for money, too, on the side?"

The man sat straighter. "No, no. He and I...we just got together before they kicked me out... then he, too, left.... I don't know why, maybe because I made money with it too.... Fuck it, I didn't know it mattered to him...." A shake of the head. "But I ain't talking to you about it."

The man seemed torn about something.

Zohara said, "Because if we don't find him, he'll kill again—you want this on your conscience?" She remembered she had to leave the man an out, and said, "If it's him."

"Yes," Amzaleg said. "We only want to talk to him."

He looked at Zohara askance, eyebrow up. Talking to a pimp about conscience.

But the man looked lost. "I told you! I ain't talking...."

"Why not?" Zohara said. "We only want his name."

"To talk to him," Amzaleg said.

The man looked at them as if talking to children. "But I don't know his real name. No one in the course told it to others, so when you go back to civilian life…" He gave a high-pitched laugh, "So you can have a regular life… with family and shit… we only used the code names…."

Amzaleg said, "So your name now, you changed it to Bentzy?"

"No, no, it's Nehemia, I use Bentzy only on the street."

Zohara threw Amzaleg a look and he nodded slightly, she was right again. She felt better.

She said to the man, "Then you're now using the name they gave you?"

He actually spit the words out. "They didn't give it to me, I picked it."

"And what name did he pick?" Amzaleg said quickly, before she could.

The man opened his mouth, closed it. "I ain't telling you."

Another pause.

Zohara said, "Can you at least describe him?" Her heart hammered. Here it was.

But the man shook his head. "You can beat me up, take me to Abu, I don't care…."

Zohara got up, faking it. "Alright, fuck it, let's go then—"

But Amzaleg caught her hand, good cop now. "Wait." He said to the redhead, "Can you call him maybe? Tell him we want to talk to him?"

Zohara blinked. She had never thought of it.

To her surprise, the man nodded. "Yeah, but not call, just click him, if I want to."

"Click?" she said. "What's that?"

Amzaleg said to her, "Everyone in the Unit gets a Motorola clicker, with his code."

"Yeah," the man said, "in the TempleWhores also. But I won't."

All around them men got up and left; the place began to empty.

Amzaleg waited, said, "Listen, Bentzy, you know *Adon* Leon? He said if you don't talk to us, you'll never work in Tel Aviv again."

A long silence. "Nah. What's he got to do with the police?"

Amzaleg said, "You want me to call him, have him tell you in person? Interrupt his Friday night fuck maybe? Get him even madder at you?"

The redhead licked his lips. "No. Alright, so I'll go to New York, so what."

"Sure. You want, I make the call now, New York it is. You know anyone there?"

The man was silent, wiped his nose, his chin. Zohara gave him a napkin.

Amzaleg said, "You like hummus? Falafel? All this?" He swept his hand at the deluge, the street, the decrepit houses, the ancient shops, the flowing sludge, rain.

Zohara couldn't see how this could help, what sort of enticement it was. But to her surprise, the man said, "Alright, alright, fuck it, I can click him so at least he'll talk to you."

Zohara said, "Don't tell him we want to talk to him. Just ask him to come, to see you."

Amzaleg opened his mouth, closed it, gave a tiny nod of approval at her instinct.

The man got a strange look in his eyes. "Alright, I will, but I betcha he won't answer. It's three years now, since we met last."

"You met? After the course?" Amzaleg sat down. "Where?"

"Here, sometimes other places...."

"And how did you tell him where to come?" The *shoo-shoo* listened to phones, to clickers.

The man said, "Dead letter, you know."

"Ah," Amzaleg said.

"What's that?" Zohara asked.

Fuck all this *shoo-shoo* business, she'd never learn it all. Like a foreign country it was, like another *vooz-vooz* language.

Amzaleg explained, and Bentzy filled the rest in, all of a sudden seemed eager to talk. Maybe it was the relief of not being banished by the *Adonim*, or not going to jail, or maybe seeing his old boyfriend again, who knew; she didn't care.

"Where would you send the dead letter?" she asked.

"The post office," he said. "On Lilienblum."

"I know where it is."

It took half an hour to arrange.

-54-

DEAD LETTERS WERE simple. As in any Mossad course, during the TempleWhores course all phone calls were tracked. So to set up assignations, then and later, they resorted to the old *shoo-shoo* method of dead letter drop in enemy territory—not under a rock in the park, but via a letter to a PO box number of a person who rarely checked it, or better still, was dead.

Tel Aviv criminals sometimes used the method for drug deliveries. You sent something to a post box in some small town with no security, then burgled it to pick it up.

Anons often used to send small items to themselves in PO boxes in enemy territory. No need to carry it with them. Then burgle the post office when the item was needed. Easy.

Dropping the letter into a postal box was a matter of seconds, tailers would miss it, then the sender would send a "hi" click to let the other know a letter would be waiting.

The other would then burglarize the post office at night to pick up his letter and learn of the meeting place.

"So I can click him. He'll come pick up the letter at Lilienblum, you can then find him, ask him questions. But I'm sure he won't come. It's been three years."

Amzaleg said, "He'd better come, or *Adon* Leon will kick you out. No one will talk to you."

Bentzy said, brave again, "So I'll go to Haifa, Jerusalem, somewhere."

"The *Adonim* over there will issue the same edict."

There was a long pause. A strange expression came over his face, a longing almost.

Amzaleg said, "What's his click code? I'll click him for you."

"Fuck, no."

Amzaleg said, "So just do it. You still have a clicker?"

"No. But I can call a number then dial his code, he'll get it."

There was another moment of silence.

Bentzy said, "But you won't do anything to him?"

"No, no," Zohara said.

"No," Amzaleg said. "Just to talk."

"Yes," Zohara said.

Her heart had begun to hammer. She didn't want to think about who the recipient was.

The man got up. He seemed to have shrunk. "You got a shekel?"

Amzaleg gave him one and the man went to the counter to make the call.

Zohara and Amzaleg exchanged glances, saying nothing, waiting.

"When will he come?" Amzaleg asked when Bentzy was back.

"I dunno if he comes, I told you."

"But if, then when?" Zohara rasped.

"Next week, something, can I go now?"

Zohara said, "But don't tell him we're waiting for him."

Bentzy shook his head. "I won't."

"Go," Amzaleg said.

Bentzy left, sticking his middle finger at them, backward.

After a moment, Zohara began to speak. Amzaleg, too, at the same time.

"What?" he said. "You first."

She said, "You think he'll warn him?"

"No," Amzaleg said. "I believe him."

He was wrong, of course, not that it mattered; it may have even helped.

-55-

Saturday, May 29, 1982, 7:15 a.m.,
Beirut's Sub

B ENTZY'S MESSAGE LEFT the man stricken. After all this time
Bentzy remembered and wanted to see him.... All night the man wres-
tled with himself: Should he go? At dawn he'd decided not to, then he got
the second click: Abort; it was risky/dangerous.

His eyes watered. Bentzy still cared enough to want to see him, but
overcame it because he worried about him…. How could he not go now?

Only much later it became evident that an improbable chain of coincidences contributed to the final outcome.

The first took place two days before, Thursday, May 27.

Gershonovitz was in his office, going over the latest intel, when
he got a call from Asa telling him Amzaleg had wanted the list of the
TempleWhores courses.

"Did he call you?" Gershonovitz asked, incredulous. "Direct?"

This would be the height of cheekiness, a low-level policeman calling
the Mossad's head.

"No, no. He asked Feldman, who asked me. I told him no way, we
don't give out this information, it can ruin families…."

"Yeah, yeah, alright. And you think that'll put him off?"

"Him, maybe, but not this *Freha* daughter of his. She's worse…."

After he hung up, Gershonovitz had to walk around the flat for an hour before he calmed down.

Something had to be done about this *Freha*, and soon.

Then came the second coincidence.

Two days later, Saturday morning, Klinger called and told him Zohara had gone to the Canadian embassy and stayed there for almost two hours.

What could she be cooking there?

Gershonovitz thumped on the wall, kicked at his desk, almost toppled it, and clicked the madman in the Sub. Didn't much hope he'd answer: The day before, when he had clicked the man to tell him he had to do her before she found out who he was, the man took three hours to call back. Then when he called, he'd dug in his heels.

"Maybe, I'll think of it. Will let you know. End." The man had hung up the scrambler before Gershonovitz could again threaten him with his father.

Fucking dirty shit. Go defend a state with such people.

But now, after Klinger's call, he had to try again. This time the response was different. Because by odd coincidence, fifteen minutes before, the man had gotten the second message from Bentzy via the Mossad phone, telling him not to come.

He was just about to call Shimmel to tell him he'd changed his mind, he'd do her, when Shimmel called him. He picked up, and before Shimmel even opened his mouth, the man said, "Okay, I changed my mind, I'll do her."

"You will?" Shimmel said, his voice a mix of suspicion and surprise—he was evidently ready to lay into him, to convince him. "What made you change all of a sudden?"

"Duty," the man said, "I thought about it all night."

Oddly Shimmel accepted it. "Alright, good, I'll send you her coordinates." Shimmel was evidently elated. "Where she lives in HaTikva, her room location, everything."

"Alright, commander," the man said, all professional now.

He tried to tell himself he shouldn't mind doing her. After all, this

Freha almost got him caught. But still, a woman, not some chick to fuck in the course, for training, or now and again in the Sub, to keep up his female seduction skills and prove he was one of the guys, but actually to take her down—and a woman he knew, too, the *shoychet*'s daughter....

Yes, Amzaleg was an *Ars*, but still, one of us, Anon Number 7, no joke.

Aloud he said, "But you have to fix it with Ronen so I can leave."

"Okay, okay, I said I will. You guys will have seventy-two hours off," Shimmel said, then added, "but that's it, you hear? You do her, and get back to the Sub, and that's the end of it. No doing little drug dealers on the side, you hear?"

"Okay, alright," the man said, adding casually, "but I may stay for a day or so, just to—look around." He almost said "to see friends," but didn't.

"I don't care, just make sure no one sees you, and be back for roll call in the Sub. Ronen shouldn't know from this. Understand?"

The last word Shimmel said in Yiddish, to make it personal.

"*Jawohl*," the man said in German, and Shimmel got mad, as he knew he would.

"Don't be a putz," Shimmel snapped. "Just execute. End."

"End," the man said.

He realized he'd been hoping for a kind word for his dedication, something, from Shimmel, the kind he never got from his father. Maybe after he'd executed, if he didn't screw up....

Of course he wouldn't.

As he hung up the phone, Gershonovitz stared at the wall for a long while, then looked up at the ceiling and grimaced. "What?! What?!" Finally he lowered his gaze. You are becoming a Munger, he growled at himself; then to compensate, stuck his middle finger at the ceiling and spit. But his mouth was dry and no spit came out. His breath caught and he pulled on his inhaler, went to the kitchen and drank some water, returned, and called Ronen on the scrambler to tell him he should give everyone three days off. They were working too hard.

"Three days? You sure?"

"Just do it," Gershonovitz said. "They're falling off their feet, the boys, is what I hear."

There was a pause. "Okay," Ronen said, and later in bed told Varda that Shimmel was getting soft in his old age.

"Nah," she said. "He'll be hard forever. Not like you."

That night Ronen didn't sleep at all.

The following day he announced a seventy-two-hour break, and the man immediately began to plan. Luckily he had the note practically finished, it only took a half-hour to edit.

He split away the first moment he could. His little boat was where he'd left it.

It was smooth sailing all the way.

-56-

Saturday, May 29, 1982, 7:45 p.m.

S ATURDAY EVENING, EVERYONE met at the Clandestine to plan the ambush.

Across the backyard, at the chief of staff's floor, all lights were on. They, too, apparently were planning something. The Clandestines ignored it.

Amzaleg, by now revived, spread the post office plan on the canteen's table, pointed where the letter boxes were, where the doors were.

"But how do we know what night he'll come?" Suissa complained.

"We don't. We'll have to go there every night, keep an eye on the place."

"At night? All of us?"

Suissa's girl was sick and it was his turn to stay home. His wife worked late evenings.

Amzaleg snapped, "Yes, fuck it, at night. All of us."

"We can take turns," Zohara said. "Anyone sees him coming, will call the others."

"We won't," Amzaleg said. "We see him, it'll be too late. All of us in this, every night."

Suissa nodded weakly, giving up, like Bentzy had, Zohara thought.

They went over the ambush plan again, the click codes among themselves, not too many.

Zohara said at last, "But I may have to stay with Pirchiya, she's due any week now."

Didn't look at Suissa, fuck him, wasn't the same thing.

Amzaleg said pitilessly that Jacquie could stay with her.

"No way," Zohara said. "I don't want to miss it."

"Which would you rather miss?" Amzaleg said, still ruthless.

If Suissa could give up things, so could she.

Zohara glared at him. "I'll stay with her, and if you see or hear anything, I'll jump on the Vespa, be there in five minutes."

"Five is too late."

"Three, then."

"If we need you," Suissa said, taking a chance to pay her back.

She just glanced at him disdainfully, not bothering.

"Alright," Amzaleg said. "Click codes again."

Ben-Harosh read them out, everyone repeated them, knocking on the table, to simulate.

"Batteries?" Amzaleg said.

For the clickers, and the night goggles.

Nitza, the Hut's secretary, said, "I got fresh ones, from the chief of staff dispensary." When all stared at her she said, blushingly, "I have a friend there."

Suissa asked when they'd start the shifts.

"Tonight," Amzaleg said. "If the bugger set out right after he got the click from Nehemia last night, he'd be here in the morning."

"If," Suissa said.

"Yes, if," Amzaleg snapped.

-57-

Sunday, May 30, 1982,
Tel Aviv

SUNDAY MORNING, MAY 30, Zohara received a letter from Toronto, Canada. She was accepted to the University of Toronto, Liberal Arts program, starting September 1982.

She began to call Batya to tell her. Mid-dial, Amzaleg came in, saw the U of T letter. "*Mabruk*," he said to Zohara. "Canada, Zozo?"

She stuck her chin out. "Yes."

"But first we have to catch him," he said. "Remember?"

She said, "We will. Bentzy says he'll come."

There was a moment of silence. Then Amzaleg said, "Who do you think it is?"

"I don't know."

Her happiness over the U of T letter was nearly gone. She didn't want to think of the killer, who he was, who he wasn't. Tomorrow, or the day after, she would know. If he came.

She almost wished he wouldn't so that it would be easier.

Of course he did come, and of course it wasn't.

-58-

Four Months Later, **September, 1982,
Tel Aviv**

B ECAUSE THE UNDERTAKER murders had no formal recognition, their linked history had no official name or scribe. So after it ended, with the killer caught and taken down, Asa ben-Shlomo, just before he returned briefly to his cows, asked Tzvi Kadishevitz to memorialize all that was known at that point, and hand out a summary in the last expanded Varash meeting, which Arik Sharon attended, too, as well as Levitan, just before he, too, retired, the copies being fed right afterward to the Moloch.

Kiddush's memo had more blank spaces than was really justified, because it was already agreed by then that the first stage of the catch was when Amzaleg learned "through one of his informers" that the rogue killer had been in a TempleWhores course—which the informer had "briefly" attended also. The killer's intentions and motives were left blank also, merely alluded to as "the result of stress due to overzealous work in the service of his country."

Amzaleg, too, was present at that Varash meeting, at the insistence of Begin himself, who said they owed him at least that, considering the fourth death in his immediate family, "none of it his fault," and him a *Schwartze* to boot; it was as if he had suffered a private holocaust of his own.

However, Kadishevitz did list all the killings although he excluded the last one, because the Unit prided itself for not going after women. "This," the Shin Bet's Feldman said, looking at Asa, "the state leaves to your people, when doing such *dreck* becomes necessary." To which Asa said nothing. For what was there to say?

There was of course no mention of Zohara in the memo, nor was any note taken of her investigations, all of which were credited to Amzaleg and served to justify his additional promotion just before his retirement.

The full story of the ambush, what had led to it and what came before and after, including the improbable chain of events that almost seemed to cause each other, was noted only in a terse oral sequel. As Kiddush collected the forms to be fed to the flames, Avigdor Feldman, to everyone's surprise (he had taken Amzaleg's loss hardest) snarled, "I can only say that there were too many coincidences here," and he looked hard at Arik and Asa in turn, "but I don't want to make any accusations or suppositions."

Both looked right back at him, silently, but as the papers burned, Kiddush intoned, "Coincidences in this place are how He manages things," and he pointed his thumb up.

"Don't go all Shimmel on us," Feldman said.

At this everyone snorted faintly, and as if by an order, got up and left. Only Asa and Amzaleg (still growing a beard after the *Shiva*) stayed behind, had a few quiet words, then left also. It was six months before Varash met yet again, and by then everything was forgotten, erased, gone, like the papers in the Moloch's maw.

Perhaps because he'd been scolded in public, on his way back from the Varash meeting, Arik famously lost it. On the way back to Army HQ with two of Asa's department heads, one of them told a disparaging story about a new Mossad recruit, whom he called an ignorant Yemenite who, like all Arsim, should be made a booth sentinel or cook assistant, tops, and that Ben-Gurion had made a mistake bringing them over. Arik stopped the jeep mid-road and roared at the man that in '73, Colonel Avigdor Kahalani, a Yemenite son of Yemenites, saved the Jewish state when, with five tanks, he stopped a hundred Syrian tanks in the Valley of Tears. "Without him," Arik hollered at the man, "al-Assad would be fucking your wife, and Hama would be here." And when the poor man stuttered that he didn't mean all Arsim, only the Yemenites and maybe the Moroccans, Arik hollered it was not just Kahalani, but one of his tank drivers, a little Moroccan Ars from HaTikva who, when all other drivers, afraid to move, froze, was the first who drove into the incoming fire, shaming all the others into moving. A minute later this Ars's tank was hit and all inside it were burned, him also, but the other tanks went on. Without this little Ars, and Kahalani, the Jewish state would have been lost. "A Yemenite and a Moroccan, you son-of-a-whore, you, sitting here with your Gucci shoes...." Arik went on in a rant and ended asking the man for his name and personal ID, so he could tell Asa what sort of people he had. Later everyone agreed that Arik had really lost it. Dealing with Arabs made him again what he really was, a wild cultureless peasant.

Almost none of this would have mattered, as Amzaleg and Zohara were silently preparing for the ambush. But Amzaleg later understood that had he known what was to come, he would have said something more before leaving, rather than less.

-59-

Sunday, May 30, 1982, 10 a.m., Jerusalem,

S UNDAY, MAY 30, the government met in the underground secure bunker regarding Rahman's planned putsch, drafting orders for Israeli generals in the north to retreat once the time came, and diplomatic cables to be sent to the secret partners.

In the face of all this, Arik was greatly upset, still wanting to invade and deal with the PLO himself. Gershonovitz raised his hand and said: "Arik, lay off, no need to dirty your hands. Rahman will deal with them better, I promise."

Arik said his hands were plenty dirty, he didn't mind some more *dreck* on them.

No one laughed at that dig. *Dreck* was Shimmel's word, Arik throwing it back in his face.

But Gershonovitz stayed calm. "No, leave it to him for later, like he's just dealt with the Muslim Brothers in Hama."

There was a silence. Clearly it was a winning argument.

But Arik, pig-headed, persisted. "No, we can finish them off too...."

"No, no," Kadishevitz suddenly said, and everyone opened their eyes wide. Kiddush never spoke in the cabinet; he was just a note-taker, a nebbish with a pen. "No, we won't."

"Me, too, no," Begin said. "We go with Shimmel, it's already decided, Arik, enough. Vote."

There was a show of hands; it was carried. Right after the vote, Gershonovitz clicked to the madman from the basement's anteroom, to repeat the order and insist on no delay. But he got no answer, the man was apparently already on the road, obeying orders at last, on a roll to do her.

Well, fuck her. Gershonovitz stuck his middle finger at the ceiling. "And you too," he growled.

-60-

Monday, May 31 to Wednesday, June 2, 1982,
Tel Aviv

MONDAY, MAY 31, at seven p.m., Amzaleg, Suissa, everyone, was in place in the Lilienblum post office, lying in wait behind sacks full of letters, the place semi-dark. Only the low stained glass windows, set just below the ceiling, let in thin shafts of moonlight.

No one moved, no one spoke. But at the end nothing happened. The man didn't come.

Or maybe he did come by to scope the place—ben-Harosh later spoke of a motorcycle making two rounds, first from the direction of Rothschild Boulevard, at two a.m., then once more, from Aliya Square, at three thirty a.m., but no one approached.

"Just reconnoitering," Nitza said. "Maybe."

She sat in the Cortina outside, a Hasselblad camera ready, gun too, just in case. She also saw the motorbike pass and gave the sign to Suissa and Amzaleg inside, who called Zohara, who arrived in less than four minutes.

"Maybe that's what scared him off," said Suissa, digging at her.

"No," Amzaleg said. "She parked near the bourse, came by on foot."

"A bike was going by me in the other direction, when I came in," Zohara said. "Was already leaving. Big black BMW?"

Like the one Gidi had.

"Yes," Nitza said. "That's the one."

"See?'"

"Or maybe it's nothing," Amzaleg said.

Nevertheless, he suggested to her later that she stay with them, and that Jacquie would call her in case Pirchiya's water broke. "Nine o'clock you are here too."

"Alright."

"I know he'll come tomorrow," Amzaleg said. "If he did the recce, he won't postpone."

But he didn't come. Tuesday, June 1, there was nothing.

"He won't come," Suissa said.

His wife had complained, him not being home nights. She had done so for a month, when she was working late.

"How much longer?" Suissa asked Amzaleg.

"Until he comes," Zohara said. If she came at nine, so could he.

Suissa nodded, meekly.

Wednesday, June 2, still nothing. They stayed until seven a.m., just before the post office workers came in.

"Probably tomorrow," Zohara said.

It was killing her, not knowing who it was.

-61-

**Wednesday, June 2, and Thursday, June 3, 1982,
Jerusalem, then HaTikva, then Tel Aviv**

O N WEDNESDAY AFTERNOON the cabinet met, ready for
Rahman. But there was no message and so the ministers dispersed
until the next day, to wait for word from Shimmel. But before Shimmel had
given any word, matters came to a head elsewhere, everything all at once,
but not the way anyone thought.

The evening was cool. June already but still not yet warm, Zohara at home
with Pirchiya, waiting for nine o'clock. All day Zohara had felt something
but didn't know exactly what, as if someone was watching her, even when
she was in the toilet. It was an odd feeling, her neck hair actually rising.

Was the fucker already here? But he only attacked men and was supposed to go to the post office.

She went out, walked around the block, letting her instinct roam, but
there was nothing. Still, her neck's hair rose, vibrated almost.

On the way back she bought some more spicy olives for Pirchiya from
the grocery. Pirchiya went through them like Amzaleg used to go through
sunflower seeds.

At seven thirty Amzaleg called. "You be here by nine o'clock. Jacquie
will spell you."

Zohara said, not arguing, "Yes, alright."

Her neck twitching, again she went around the block, up and down Etzel Street. She didn't know what it was but there was something, someone, like a thin wire of heat pointing at her.

"It's nerves," Munger said when he came in briefly to check on Pirchiya. He was told they were about to ambush someone, though not where nor when. "Like I was before my bar mitzvah...."

She told him to stop. "It's not nerves, I am telling you."

After he left, Pirchiya went to lie down and Zohara tried to read, smoke, anything to take her mind off this strange feeling. Trust your instinct, Amzaleg had said.

But trust how? What was it saying?

Wrapped in Jenny's sweater, she sat at the kitchen table, her jackknife before her, trying to read, when she thought she saw, or felt, or rather heard something. It was getting close, whatever it was. She jumped to her feet, and then it came.

It was invisible, but she felt it, like a vast and luminous grayness filling the room, neither good nor evil but something beyond, perhaps both. Her heart thumped unbearably and her skin buzzed, as if an electric charge went through it. Then she felt her nipples stand up and her groin begin to throb, her nose tingled and a huge yearning went through her, as if there were something above her, fragrant and warm, smelling like Gidi only a hundred times more so, its blind eye staring down at her, neither malevolent nor benevolent yet both. And all at once, the overpowering yearnings engulfed her and she felt the need to merge with it, whatever it was, to satisfy it, to do what it wanted, to bathe in its acceptance; but just as the yearnings rose, a bud of black anger also burst inside her, and it grew and blossomed, larger and blacker and just as strong, raging at the power it thought it had over her.

In her ears was noise like much rushing water, gushing like the rain sewers ten days before.

And as she felt the yearning for whatever it was, the shivers came upon her, one after another, and she felt herself shaking all over, even as the anger in her ballooned also. Then without any conscious decision, she let the Other rise—a darkness like Great-Grandma Ruja's anger, only bigger and deeper, with huge red eyes and a large open mouth, black and wide. And as the convulsions gripped her, again and again, her yearnings became almost unbearable, like missing Iddo only ten times stronger, a hundred times more, but she also felt the rage rising alongside at what was being done to her, what it was doing, like what Gidi had done; only Gidi hadn't done it to manipulate her, playing on her like this, for his own ends.

Or had he?

As her groin convulsed, she, or maybe her Other, let out a bellow at the unseen thing in the gray air around her, and she, or perhaps the Other, slashed at the air with the sharpened jackknife quick-quick, in the way Amzaleg had taught her: down, up-up, a figure-S and a down slash then across an imaginary throat.

And as she slashed with her right, she raised her left hand above her head, three fingers pointing forward and up, and let her rage build until it was huge and black-blue and luminous. And even as she felt the wetness on her thighs, she hollered in Moroccan Arabic, "Three times I curse ye, ya *mal'oon*," ho accursed one, then she shrieked at the top of her voice, "*Mal'oon, mal'oon, mal'oon!*" Accursed! Accursed! Accursed!

All around her, and inside her and above her, there was a huge sigh, perhaps of rage, perhaps some other nameless emotion, as she stabbed forward with three fingers, again and again.

"Senoy, Sansenoy, and Semangelof!" she hollered. "I adjure you, and all hurters and damagers and dark spirits, in the name of all the dead…."

Her voice stuck, she could not continue, but she kept hollering incoherently, even as she convulsed. She could not stop; the Other that was in her, the one with the big red eyes and the open mouth, had taken over. She found herself twirling, turning, slashing at the air, at the gray luminosity, feeling its rage at her resistance, her innards throbbing, her nipples stiff, like what Gidi had done to her, but much stronger, different, better, worse.

Screeching from the bottom of her throat, she gave one more slash, felt it catch in the air, improbably, like the cut on the Samson's thigh, pressed it harder, in the air, then in a blink the grayness faded, like ink dissolving in water, and the air around her cooled.

There was a huge bang.

She fell to a flat *shpaggat*, her crotch on the floor, the Batya gun in her hand. But it was only the window, the wind had banged it open and rain was pouring in.

"Zohara?" Pirchiya appeared in the bedroom door. She had been sleeping through all Zohara's screaming, but the bang had woken her. "What are you doing on the floor?"

She looked like a sleeping child carrying a pillow before her, her stomach big and round.

Zohara swiftly stuffed the gun behind her and rose. The pain between her legs may have been from the *shpagatt*, or from whatever she had just underwent, whatever it was.

"Nothing, I fell. It's nothing…."

She still felt the rage in her throat. Her thighs were still shuddering every now and then, but she felt awake, alert, enraged at whatever had played with her, had thought it could overpower her.

She rose and sat in a chair, breathed in, out, began to Reverse. Slowly the Other's large red eyes began to fade, though not completely, as if unwilling to leave. She felt her three fingers twitch, lowered her hand.

"Oooh," Pirchiya was holding her stomach, but not hard.

"What?" Zohara said. "Do you feel anything?"

Pirchiya was not due for another week, maybe a bit more.

"No, he's just kicking, as usual." Pirchiya looked at her. "What's with your hand?"

Zohara looked down. "Oh, nothing." She still kept the three fingers pointing forward, half-curved, now halfway down. "I banged my hand when I fell. It's okay now."

She waved her hand as if she was cooling it, then made Pirchiya sit at the table, and sat down with her.

When she saw Pirchiya shivering, Zohara took off her Canadian sweater, wrapped it around Pirchiya's shoulders, got up and closed the window. The curtain flapped until she banged the window closed. The latch was broken, but the window stayed shut.

She sat down again, shivering in reaction. She had almost completely Reversed now.

"When do you go to your meeting?" Pirchiya asked.

Zohara had not told her of the planned ambush—maybe it won't happen, maybe he won't come; she only said it was a meeting she was going to with Amzaleg.

"Quarter to nine, we have time, almost an hour."

Zohara made tea, brought out some baklava and olives. Pirchiya felt the need for salty things.

"For the baby," she said, abashed, when Zohara asked. "He's still asking for it."

Together they waited for Amzaleg to come back.

"He's okay?" Pirchiya asked once.

"Don't worry," Zohara said. "Everything is fine."

But of course it wasn't.

-64-

H E WAS WATCHING the window from across the yard, lying in wait behind some bushes, between the Moroccan synagogue and Amzaleg's flat.

The *Freha* daughter was inside, with the whore Amzaleg was shacking up with. The *shoychet*'s daughter was the one making all the trouble, trying to nix all the work they were doing, Shimmel said. She had to go, for the good of all.

He had never taken down a woman before. The mere thought gave him an odd thrill, as if he was a boy again, peeking at his mother in the bathroom. He watched the *Freha*'s back through the window, prancing about in her gaudy sweater, and held his gun steady. The distance was a little far, but it was close enough. Just to make sure, he'd better try to climb higher—there was a water pipe running up the side, with flanges; he could climb that.

It was dark. He didn't mind that. He had on his night goggles, and the Nomex suit's fabric was light-absorbent. No one could see him.

He stuck the gun in his back belt holster, then, clutching at the first flange, he pulled himself up, waited, then pulled himself higher, silently and softly.

It was not hard. In a few minutes he'd do her, then go pick up Bentzy's message. He already felt the thrill of seeing him again, knowing now he cared.

Slowly, softly, he climbed, letting the Other rise in him, getting ready for the job.

Zohara said, "You okay?"

Pirchiya nodded, tugged Zohara's sweater tighter around her. "I was cold, now I'm okay."

Zohara said, "Wait, I'll bring you another sweater."

She went into the bedroom, rummaged in the pile of clothes on the chair.

There: the window.

From the hip pocket of his Nomex suit, he brought out the glass cutter. But as he pressed it gently on the pane, he felt the window move—apparently it wasn't latched. He pushed it softly, and it opened, noiselessly. He brought out his gun, raised it, minding the bulbous end, and sighted along the barrel at the woman's back, her shoulders wrapped with the garish sweater, a *Freha*'s attire.

Remembering to stop breathing, he squeezed the trigger slowly. The gun gave a burp and the woman cried out, twitched, her head fell on the table.

At that moment another woman came out of the bedroom, gave him a green-eyed stare, and he froze. Hadn't he just done her? His eye skittered between her and the slumped figure.

He moved the gun barrel, but she was no longer there.

ZOHARA HEARD THE pop, came out of the bedroom, saw Pirchiya slumped at the table.

"What—" she began, then saw the blood, and the face at the window. She screamed, and the face in the window started—it was a black mask with two eyeholes, below it a hand with a gun, a round bulb on its snout—a potato—

The bulb sprouted as the gun barked, she heard *whhhoosh*, and without thinking threw herself at the table, grabbed the jackknife, still open, and in one move hurled it overhead at the masked face.

The knife skittered on the gun barrel, slitting the black sleeve, and fell to the windowsill.

The potato barked again, louder; but the bullet went wide, Iddo's photograph cracked. She hollered with rage; the window emptied as the figure disappeared, and she heard clinking as the shooter slid down the pipe, clattering on the flanges.

By then she was at the window and saw the figure zigzagging between the Moroccan synagogue and the grocery, fading away, and then it was gone.

For a second she stood, the Other rising in her, hot. Behind her she heard a soft sound, turned, saw Pirchiya's head beginning to slip off the table; the table's edge was red.

Zohara screamed yet again—the rage she felt was unlike anything she had ever felt before—threw her head back and screeched at the ceiling.

"*Mal'oon, mal'oon, mal'oon!*" Both her throat and her shoulder were on fire.

Then, bending over Pirchiya, she felt for the pulse in her throat. It was weak and fluttering. The bullet, she saw, had hit under her shoulder blade but did not exit, half-charge probably; or maybe the potato silencer.

She phoned Jacqueline. "We need your car—take Pirchiya to hospital—"

Jacqueline yelped. "Her water broke?"

"No, been shot."

Jacqueline said nothing, was there in a minute, her housecoat untied, wet with rain. Zohara pressed a towel over Pirchiya's back; it was turning dark.

Jacqueline was firing questions at her. Zohara just shook her head. "Get your car."

Someone knocked on the door—Eli Sabag. "Who screamed?" Then he saw Pirchiya, went white, held on to the doorposts, both sides.

He whispered, "You called an ambulance?"

Zohara shook her head. To HaTikva? She said, "Help me carry her."

Together they carried Pirchiya down the backstairs, legs trailing, put her in the Susita's backseat. "Drive to Yaffo Hospital," Zohara said. "I'll call Amzaleg. Don't wait. I'll take the Vespa."

She ran upstairs, called the Clandestine's phone, got Suissa. "Tell Amzaleg I'll come later. Pirchiya was shot, we're taking her to Yaffo Hospital."

Suissa, stuttering, said Amzaleg should be back soon.

"Just tell him." She hung up, gathered her bag, razor inside, jackknife too. She raised her eyes to the ceiling, stuck three fingers at it, muttered old curses she had heard from Ruja.

She ran downstairs, searching for her Vespa. But the Susita was still there, the engine sputtering, Jacqueline crying and hitting the dashboard. Eli was in the backseat cradling Pirchiya's head with both hands, his lips moving.

"I'll get Moshiko," Zohara shouted, "his cab—"

Just then the engine caught and the Susita jerked forward. Zohara jumped on her Vespa and they were off, she following.

-66-

AMZALEG WAS ALREADY at the hospital's gate when they arrived. Under his pants and shirt he was wearing his Nomex coveralls, she saw, the hood peeled back over his collar. He must have been putting it on when Suissa told him. His cheeks went taut when he saw them carrying Pirchiya in, her legs in the air, probably remembering how he was carried into Bikur Cholim in Jerusalem five months before. Eli Sabag was holding his handkerchief to Pirchiya's back, his arthritic fingers clumped into fists. He was oddly composed, but his eyes were on fire.

"Amnon, Amnon," he said. "What did they do to her?"

Amzaleg looked at Zohara. "Was him."

"Yes," she said. "Fuck it, was him."

But she knew now that it probably wasn't. The killer was just a pawn in the hands of whatever she had seen and battled in the gray luminous smoke, the thrice-accursed that had done it all.

She could still feel in her belly the unbearable yearnings for it, and the hate.

On Iddo's grave she vowed to remember both—and keep the hate alive.

-67-

**June 3, 1981, 6:30 p.m.,
Jaffa**

THEY WHEELED PIRCHIYA'S gurney into the corridor, Amzaleg holding on to her limp palm, Zohara helping to push the gurney with one hand, the other hand absurdly dangling the jackknife. As they passed the triage station, the nurse said something to them, but Amzaleg could not grasp her meaning. There was a roar in his head. Zohara let go of the gurney and tapped him on his forearm. "There, we should take her into the operating room there."

The words still did not penetrate but he nodded and allowed himself to be directed. In all his life he had not felt a grief such as this, such rage, such guilt, not even when Iddo fell; perhaps because deep in his heart he had already known Iddo's fate when he'd forced him off that boat and brought him home.

But Pirchiya? This unexpected flower that just came to him, that gift? Why?

Like a monstrous echo of his thoughts, he heard the word repeated and stared wildly about him. The corridor, he saw, was crammed with beds edge to edge—the rooms had evidently overflowed and there were people lying in beds, some staring up, others staring wildly about, just as he was, mostly silent, but some were moaning, the entire length of the corridor, up to the end nearly invisible in the dim murk.

"Why, why?" a wizened old Jew sitting on a bed was swaying, as if praying at Yom Kippur, wailing. "Why did the Blessed Name have to give me this disease, why? Why?"

A plastic bag full of dark liquid dangled from a hooked pole beside him, a tube leading into his hip under his hospital robe. "Why me and not to Arafat, may his name be blotted out forever? Why not give the cancer to Assad? Why not to Hitler—"

"Sha, rebbe, sha," a plump nurse said softly as she bustled by, carrying corked jars with sloshing dark liquids in them. "Don't ask such things." As Amzaleg pushed the gurney past her, Zohara and the deathly pale Jacqueline assisting, the nurse grabbed the attached cardboard note, stretching the rubber band as she scanned it quickly. "Over there, there." She pointed. "Operating room Gimmel—we are so busy tonight—"

Amzaleg sensed the gurney change direction and felt more than heard Pirchiya give a little moan, as if echoing the wailing rabbi.

Just then the doors banged open in front of them as the gurney was pushed forward; two male nurses appeared and pulled at it.

Amzaleg nearly stumbled and Zohara grabbed at him, whispered at him, but he could not comprehend her words. The light had darkened and the entire scene acquired a hellish glow, like in the Black Satan club, eons ago.

"Will she survive?" he said to the nurse, astonished at how normal his voice sounded in his ears, then he noticed he was repeating his words again and again.

One of the male nurses smiled at him softly, meaninglessly, then tried to remove Amzaleg's hand from the gurney's handle. "We have to take her in now," the man said, and as Amzaleg maintained his grasp, he twisted and looked into Amzaleg's eyes. "Let it go, please."

Amzaleg could not move; he felt Zohara putting her hand on his. "Dad," she said, "Dad, let her go." He felt his fingers lose their grip, then tightened them again. No, no!

"Oh why, oh why," the rebbe wailed behind, trailing the black catheter. A voice shushed him, telling him everything had a reason, it was not for us to ask why.

"But why me? Why, oh why?"

Amzaleg's fingers had frozen, he could not remove them. He felt Zohara bend over his hand and kiss the fingers. Her lips felt dry and hot. "...Dad, Dad... they need to operate...."

He kept hold of Pirchiya's hand. He could see her eyes flutter, and for a second, thought he saw her rounded belly quiver.

"Dad, please..."

"Wait," he rasped, "wait, wait!"

He stomped with his right foot on the gurney's back wheel and stopped it from moving, then let go of Pirchiya's hand, and with fingers turned into wood, pulled out his keychain.

"...Dad, Dad, please..." Zohara was saying, her voice rising.

Ignoring her, he removed the two grenade pin rings he carried on the chain, the ones from the Castel battle. He turned around, "Rebbe," he called to the man trailing the catheter, "come here," his voice now hoarse as if he had swallowed gravel. "Rebbe, can you perform a wedding—" His voice failed.

Zohara's voice rose, "Dad, there's no time—"

"Why?" the rebbe kept wailing. "Why, oh why..."

Amzaleg let go of the gurney and pulled the rebbe's catheter stand closer. The two male nurses converged on him, a third one coming down the corridor.

Amzaleg pulled at the rebbe's thin hand, gently. "You do it," he said.

Through hot mist, he put one grenade ring on Pirchiya's finger and said the words he should have said before if he had only dared, that she was hereby sanctified to him, to him alone—his voice broke again but he swallowed hard and repeated the words.

"What is this?" the rebbe squeaked. "A joke? Shame on you—"

Amzaleg said, "Not a joke. You do it. Say it."

"But she has to agree—"

"Wait, she will." Amzaleg bent into the pale lovely face on the gurney, its lips turning blue around the edges. "You agree? Yes?"

The pale lips fluttered; there was the shadow of a whisper, the shadow of a nod.

The rebbe bent over too. "Yes?" he repeated.

The whisper was barely audible. Yes.

Zohara thumped on the gurney's edge. "If you don't let her go now, I'll break your head again, Amzaleg—"

The rabbi shrugged pathetically, "Alright, you say the words now."

Amzaleg said them, he could barely hear himself.

The rebbe said, "Who is she?"

Amzaleg said nothing, though he wanted to.

Zohara said, "Her name is Pirchiya, daughter of Eliyahu Sabag."

"And him?"

"Amnon, son of Simon Amzaleg."

The rebbe muttered, then slowed down, "By the law of Moses and Israel, alright." Then he shuffled away, keening, as if he'd forgotten everything except his own undeserved tragedy.

Amzaleg said to the male nurse, "You can take her now." And as the gurney was swallowed by the swing doors, he turned to Zohara. "We have to go." Though his heart was a live coal encrusted with ice, his voice was nearly normal, back in operational mode, the Other singing in his veins, holding the reins. "They're there already, everyone, I should be there too. We gotta catch this fucker before he does more of—of this—" and now his voice caught, red curtain rising before his eyes, the Other gaining for a moment.

Zohara said, "We'll catch him, don't worry." Then, as if to make sure he understood this was not personal anymore, she punched his shoulder, hard, as she had seen him and Suissa do to each other, and snarled, "Go, go," as if she was the commander sending him to battle, not he sending her.

Amzaleg turned to go. As he passed, the rebbe caught his sleeve, asking something, but Amzaleg removed the grasping hand and ran out, the keychain still in hand, the grenade ring on his finger.

And then he was racing in the Clandestine's old Cortina down Salameh Road in the pale moonlight, Zohara following close behind.

-68-

June 3 to June 4, 1982,
Tel Aviv

A S AMZALEG DROVE, Zohara, on her scooter a few paces behind, tried to push the Other down but could not. It yammered in her, the meaty taste in her mouth almost overpowering.

Still seeing Pirchiya's head slumped on the table, she tried to suppress the thought of what she'd do if the killer was indeed Gidi; but the image kept coming up, the deep eyes behind the eyeholes.

And all the while the gray luminosity hovered at the edge of her vision, steely and expectant, and she kept her left hand loose on the handlebar, the three fingers hooked.

When they arrived, the post office seemed deserted; in its backyard, the trees rustled and some sleepy bird tweeted, just as they did yesterday.

Her neck felt cold when she and Amzaleg entered through the back. She saw none of the Clandestines' cars, none of the scooters, but knew Nitza was somewhere nearby in the Cortina with her clicker and a gun, watching for intruders.

In front of her, Amzaleg entered the post office via the back door and she went in after him.

Inside it was dark and he put on his goggles; she didn't need to, she saw almost as well without them. He peeled off his clothes, put them in the Nomex bag and remained in his Nomex coveralls, and she followed suit.

Her coveralls felt tight at the chest, her breasts tingled, or maybe it was her breathing, so for a few seconds she closed her eyes.

He saw it. "You okay?"

She nodded, terse. All around her the air was faintly glowing, and her neck bristled. She brought her left hand up, in the dark, probed three fingers in the air, mouthed silent imprecations.

She looked around; at first she couldn't see the hidden crew, then one by one saw the tips of their heads behind sacks of letters, boxes; different spots than yesterday, proper procedure.

"You go there," Amzaleg mouthed at her, "near that exit, I go near the other."

She didn't argue, took her place. The Clandestine's crew didn't speak as she passed, just squeaked with their mouths at her, and she squeaked back.

The air glowed, perhaps the crescent moon high in the window, perhaps not.

She stretched behind a lumpy sack, careful not to rustle it, watched the half-open back door through which they'd come. Her watch said ten-twenty. Pirchiya had been operated on already, the bullet dug out, maybe even the dead baby. Zohara tried to wipe her mind clean, could not, felt the glow all around her, probed the air again, three fingers.

The Other kept trying to take over. Finally, no longer resisting, she let it rise and fill her, feeling her face stretch taut, like Amzaleg's when he saw Pirchiya being wheeled in. Then it filled her entirely and she thought of nothing else but the taste of meat inside her throat, the gun at the small of her back, and the jackknife in her hip tuck.

Amzaleg had insisted on her carrying the little gun, and so she put it in a back holster. She didn't intend to use it.

Time passed. No one said anything. She needed to pee but held it in, then let it flow into the diaper inside the Nomex.

More time passed. No one uttered a sound. Once or twice Amzaleg clicked his tongue, and after an interval there were answering clicks from those behind him: Suissa, ben-Harosh, Zarnooga. She herself answered last.

An hour passed, then two. She peed again, could smell her urine, other smells too, stronger, men's. And another, sweat maybe, sharper, possibly fear.

Perhaps she dozed, or maybe the Other did; then she didn't; there was a thin whisper of sound, the door moved. Or did it?

Yes it did. Amzaleg clicked his tongue twice, so soft the sound was not even there.

Get ready.

The door opened a shade. No one was in there. Then she saw a gray mass at the bottom of the crack. He was pushing it while crouching, waiting. Her heart stopped, restarted.

There was nothing for a while, then a blur of movement: the man rolled in fast, head tucked under his shoulder, a judo roll, behind some sack of letters, and waited.

No one moved; nothing budged.

Was it him? Zohara's heart was ice and fire, molten lead, both.

Two minutes; five; then the man unfolded, stood up slowly, walked toward the row of post office boxes, their back-openings stuffed with letters and parcels; he stood before them, counted with his finger, left to right, top to bottom.

He paused, pulled something out of a box, an envelope.

Suissa sneezed.

There was a click, and a glare of light. One of the Clandestine had clicked the overhead bulb on. She squeezed her eyes into slits, looked at the man.

The man snap-turned—all inhaled with shock—he looked like Asa ben-Shlomo, then didn't; it was really his son, Yaro, looking like a haggard version of his father.

Her heart gave a huge lurch, went into her throat, ballooned, heated.

It was not him. It was not. Not Gidi. Not.

"Don't move!" Amzaleg called out.

But Yaro was looking at ben-Harosh, whose beard was flecked with moonlight. "What have you done with Bentzy?" he lowed, in voice hoarse with tears. "Where is he?"

"Me?" ben-Harosh said.

"What did you do with him? He was here, and you took him... like you took everything else from me... everything.... I did it all for you... for you... and you did this now...."

"What did I do?" Ben-Harosh whispered sideways to Amzaleg.

Amzaleg muttered back, "He thinks you're his father—it's the beard..."

Yaro was pointing to ben-Harosh with one hand, the other, with the gun, down by his side. He was weeping openly now. "I killed for you... I fucked for you... I cleansed the land for you.... Only for you.... You never said anything...."

Zohara rose, her eyes fixed on the man. It wasn't Gidi. Her heart burned, ballooned.

"Yaro, Yaro," Amzaleg said, "please..."

But Yaro was babbling, "I wanted to make the place clean.... Like I cleaned the cowshed for you... but you never said thanks, nothing..." He waved his arms, hair flying, eyes wild. "Never..."

Amzaleg said, "Yaro, put down the gun. Listen to me...."

Zohara launched herself forward, her Other roaring, tasting meat in her throat.

Yaro hollered, "Go fuck yourself, Dad, and all of you can kiss my—" Quick as a snake he fell into a *shpagatt*, rolled to the side, and in one smooth movement snapped two shots, one at ben-Harosh, the other at the bulb.

It burst, and the man vanished.

The hall fell into semi-darkness. Zohara could hear the rustle as everyone hastened to put on the night-vision goggles, but she didn't need to. The moment he raised his gun she had already fallen flat in a *shpagatt*, rolled toward him, already slashing up, up, and a curved S.

He parried and slashed at her in return and she could feel it sliding on her wrist, biting. She parried in return just like with Amzaleg on the roof, and on the upswing stabbed at his side, up-fisted, deep, and again.

He fell sideways, tried to grab at her but she slashed at his palm, and again, then as in an afterthought, grabbed the wrist and broke it. The taste in her throat turned saltier.

He kicked at her and she evaded it, kicked sideways at his knee, heard it snap. It was as if someone else was acting, she watching. All without sound, just heavy breathing, both of them.

"Move aside!" Amzaleg hollered behind her. "Give us a clear shot!"

"Yes! Move!" Suissa's voice.

She ignored both, rushed at the man, elbowed his neck, kneed his groin, fell on him, pressed his neck down with her wrist. He began to rant confusedly, against his father, Shimmel, Bentzy who had betrayed him, tried to get up but could not, her weight on him, pinning him.

Amzaleg called to her again to move, let them have a shot.

Yes, Suissa called, move.

Fuck them both. She rose to her knees, pressed one knee on the man's neck, dropped the jackknife and pulled out the razor. He was moving feebly now, then stopped struggling, looked up at her with calf eyes, maybe beyond her, his throat extended like that picture in school which got her sent to the reformatory. A narrow moonbeam lit his face, from nose to chin.

"Ya *mal'oon!*" she hissed.

She raised the razor and flipped it open, then let the Other go. It didn't want to, but she forced it. She felt the gray luminosity intensify all around, getting closer. She pushed at it, too, hard, harder, and finally it retreated too. She looked down into the calf eyes beseeching her to do what she must, and all at once felt her heart squeeze with pity and revulsion, but as the killer's eyes fluttered at her, she recalled Pirchiya's head slipping on the table, looked down at him and slashed down and back, fast.

The blood sprayed on her feet, some on her wrist.

The gray melted, again like ink dissolving; her Other was partly gone too. She tried to breathe, and after a while, she could.

It wasn't Gidi. It wasn't.

She felt dazed, elated, then felt her stomach turn, heave. She held it down, couldn't.

Everyone averted their eyes as she vomited sideways, green bile, yellow, some half-digested food. Amzaleg was at her side first, with his flashlight sweeping the fallen figure. Suissa right after.

"Shit," Suissa said. "First I thought it was Asa."

Amzaleg said. "No. His son."

He handed Zohara a handkerchief from his back tuck. She refused it, then took it.

More flashlights were being lit: Ben-Harosh's, Zarnooga's, then Nitza rushed in, her gun held in two stiff hands, pointing forward. "I heard shots...." Then she saw the body.

"Who is it?" she asked.

Suissa told her.

She said, "You think his father knew?"

Amzaleg gave a terse shrug.

"Who knows," Suissa said.

Zohara kept breathing, in and out, and crumpled the handkerchief.

There was a pause, everyone regrouping.

Nitza was saying, "I didn't see him enter, but there was another guy, big redhead, tried to sneak in, I caught him, left him tied in the Cortina. You didn't say there were two."

"Probably Nehemia," Zohara said. She was a bit better now, but not much. "Probably wanted to come in to warn him."

There was another short silence.

Ben-Harosh said, "Should I call Munger?"

"Yes," Amzaleg said. "Tell him to come take him, leave off the autopsy, I'll do the washing."

"And keep it quiet," Suissa said.

All looked at him. No shit, sneezer.

Zohara said, "I gotta go." She left, holding her stomach, felt it coming up again.

No one said anything.

Amzaleg said, "I'm going too. All of you stay."

Ben-Harosh, like always, was quickest. "Want me to come with you?"

Amzaleg shook his head, turned. But after he'd gone a few paces, he turned back, nodded at everyone. They nodded back.

Outside, on the way to the cruiser, he saw Bentzy slumped on the Cortina's steering wheel, weeping. "I heard shots," the redhead said. "How is he?"

Amzaleg stared at him, shook his head once.

The weeping intensified. "Can I go in, see him?"

"Maybe in two, three days. Munger will call you."

He entered the cruiser, called the hospital on the radio. His fingers shook, one with a ring on it.

He saw Zohara on her Vespa, driving toward Jaffa. She, too, had things to do.

-69-

**June 3 to June 4, 1982,
Tel Aviv**

S HE WAS NEARLY back to normal when she got to the hospital, but not quite. She remained three minutes outside, Reversing, then went in.

There was no news, the operation was still ongoing, so she rode back to HaTikva to pick some things for Pirchiya.

While collecting underthings, socks, another sweater, the phone rang, from the hospital: Pirchiya just passed away, the baby survived. "A boy," the nurse said. "Almost four kilo."

Zohara screamed.

She hollered full throat and threw the jackknife at the ceiling, where it stuck, quivering. "Ya *mal'oon!*" she screamed. Ho accursed!

The room, however, was silent, no gray mass anywhere. She felt drained, beaten. She called the Other up, but as it rose she felt it was gray and used up.

She drank some water, then looked up at the jackknife, realized it could fall on someone, the *mal'oon* would kill another one, who knew whom.

She stuck her left hand her up, first three fingers, then just one. "Fuck your mother," she rasped, "ya *mal'oon.*"

She pulled a chair, climbed on it, grabbed the knife and folded it on her thigh, slid it into her pocket, went down the backstairs to her Vespa, rode fast, back to Jaffa.

But as the hospital loomed before her, she stopped her Vespa, turned it back, rode back to HaTikva, turned, drove through Tel Aviv, north.

-70-

I T TOOK A while for Amzaleg's call to the hospital to go through. It was shunted twice before he finally got the nurse of the OR.

"A boy," he repeated dully after the nurse. "She's dead."

"Yes... we did our best, but..."

He hung up, went back in, saw the Clandestines milling around Yaro's body in the post office's sorting room, waiting for instructions from someone. Suissa was lost as before.

"She's dead," Amzaleg said. "The baby is alive."

A short silence. Suissa said, "Blessed be the True Judge."

The others mumbled alongside. What was there to say?

Amzaleg turned to go. "You in charge," he told Suissa.

All nodded. Alright, if they must.

Amzaleg shook his head at Suissa and everyone, then nodded diagonally, the commander thanking them. They nodded back, turned to the body, Suissa began the Initial, he saw, checking items, taking notes, giving some orders. He'd do for now.

It took Amzaleg less than ten minutes to get to Army HQ complex. He entered the Clandestines' hut using his key, then from its backyard, squiggling through the gap in the fence, into the Chief of Staff building.

Shimmel's office was on the third floor. The sentinel, seeing his Unit card, let Amzaleg pass.

The fat man was in his office, pumping his inhaler into his mouth, when Amzaleg walked in, the gun already in his hand. Amzaleg held the Beretta steady, one arm outstretched and locked, the other supporting its elbow. The barrel didn't waver.

Gershonovitz put the inhaler down on the aluminum desk, said, "I knew the Damn HolyName would catch me, but I didn't believe He'd send an *Ars*."

Amzaleg didn't say anything.

"You think I'm crazy? Go ahead, laugh at me." Shimmel said, "We invented Him, our national Other, to make us special and to have someone to blame for what we have to do, like we taught you guys to invent an Other, to help you do the necessary *dreck* face-to-face, have someone else to blame it on…. We thought it would keep us from going crazy but it didn't work, did it?…. Then Munger said, let's take one *Schwartze*, yeah, a Jew also, but also an *Ars*, this Amzaleg, maybe like Arabs he doesn't have an extra soul like we do…. But it didn't work, did it? You got the Blackness also…."

Gershonovitz gave an asthmatic rattle, perhaps a cackle. "You got it like every other Anon, made you Blackness-mad, too, like it made all of us, like the Damn HolyName we invented is now taking over all of us, giving us a collective Blackness—" Some spittle flew out of Gershonovitz's mouth. "And we still complain about Him. Why? I say, if we don't like Him, we can kill Him, to stop it all, be like the Arabs, or leave. Like it says in the Talmud, it's all up to us…. Well I don't have an Other I can blame my *dreck*-doing on…. I do what I have to do by myself, so the rest of the Jews can stay pure, but I don't complain about it…. You guys can call your Other, I got no one to call, and even if I had, I probably wouldn't—"

As he spoke, Gershonovitz moved his arm slowly from his stomach toward the desk. Amzaleg's gun coughed a little and a puff of smoke appeared in the map behind Gershonovitz's back, somewhere in Bir Gafgafa, in the middle of the Sinai.

Amzaleg said, "Shimmel, you're mad, a hundred percent. They should have put you in the same loony bin with Shafrir, long ago, saved me the trouble now of killing you."

Gershonovitz withdrew his hand from the desk. "Amnon, Amnon," he rasped, "you don't know what you're doing! The Damn HolyName is using you! Rahman al-Assad is waiting in the Biqaa, with fifteen of his generals ready to move, I only need to call Mickey in Northern Command and tell him to withdraw ten miles, Rahman sees it, he moves to Damascus and in two days he takes over—please, Amnon…." Gershonovitz's voice turned urgent, pleading, "Amnon, Amnon, you don't know what you're screwing up—if I call Mickey now, we'll maybe have quiet with the Flatheads for a few years, maybe they'll even kick Arafat out of Lebanon for us, knock a few heads in Shatila, and Sabra, then we'd maybe make peace with the Syrians, too, like with Egypt, no more boys have to die in the war—so what if a few *Schwartze* druggies got lopped off by a mad Undertaker? Who cares?"

"I care," Amzaleg said, "was a friend of my son, the first one."

"One druggie!" Gershonovitz hissed. "One! You know how many will go kack, if Arik has his invasion? Both *Schwartze* and *vooz-vooz*? Yes, everyone? Jews! Jews can die! Enough we died! Enough!"

Amzaleg said, "I don't give a damn about all these calculations anymore. Half my neighbors are eaten with drugs, the others are in jail, whoever is left goes to the army and gets shot so you and Begin can play Jewish empire for your Damn HolyName—"

He was surprised to hear himself speaking like that.

"What empire, Amnon? What empire? They try to kill us—"

"So you killed my people in return, letting all the shit go through Haifa."

"What's this about your people? Jews are your people, not just *Schwartzes*!"

"No. Fuck this, Shimmel. No more. I now look for mine only. Only them."

Gershonovitz's eyes acquired a soft sheen. "Amnon, Amnon, I am begging you, on my knees, what does it matter, a few druggies—"

"Yeah, a few *Schwartzes*, like me—"

"What, like you? Not like you! You are one of us, always were, I don't even care where your family came from—we took you in, to the Unit, Munger took you in personally—"

"Well fuck him and fuck you," Amzaleg said. "You killed my people, sent someone to kill me, sent Yaro to kill my daughter…. Only he killed my wife…." His voice shook, but his hand didn't.

Gershonovitz sat up in his chair, his eyes losing their luster. "I didn't know you married her but yes, I did send him, and you'd have done the same if you were in my place, I'm sorry about her, but your daughter was going to screw everything up, screw the only chance—"

He lunged at the clicker but the Beretta coughed again, this time Beer Sheva sprouted some dust. Gershonovitz kept his hand half-extended but immobile.

Amzaleg said, "You think you can scream, maybe? Someone outside will hear you?"

Gershonovitz said nothing.

"Go ahead, scream," Amzaleg said, and Gershonovitz, after a brief hesitation, opened his mouth and took in a half-lungful of air, and Amzaleg, like a Russian *kozachok* dancer, dropped into a squat, one buttock settling on one heel, the other leg extended forward, toes up, both hands straight, and shot Gershonovitz meticulously through the open mouth, the bullet passing just over the desk's edge and rising a little, passing between the fat man's hands.

The flat face was thrown back for a second then fell forward, the back of the head intact, the bullet not powerful enough to exit. Amzaleg rose to his feet, rubbed the Beretta carefully with the corner of his shirt to remove the fingerprints, taking care to rub both outside and inside the trigger guard, then leaned over and put the gun into the beefy hand below the large head whose eyes were turning glassy.

He said softly into the pallid face, "Maybe we should have a twenty-year war, to learn what we can't do, but I don't give a shit anymore, I'm out of this—"

He bent the inert forefinger into the trigger guard and made sure the gun was on the fat stomach, then peeked into the still-quivering mouth. The bullet had entered the palette and gone inside, upward, just as if the fat man had shot himself in the mouth.

Amzaleg turned around and surveyed the room, looked up at the map, took out his jackknife and, springing it, dug out the two bullets, put them in his pocket, gave the room a last look, and left.

The corridor was empty, but he could hear footsteps coming from the direction of the front entrance as he quickened his pace, limping.

Outside the day was just breaking, sleepy birds chirping in the sycamore tree. He bent and squiggled through the gap in the wire mesh and soon was in the hut's backyard.

It was 6:32 in the morning when he made himself Bedouin coffee in the hut's canteen. His hand, he noticed, was shaking a little. He waited for the vomiting feeling to start, but nothing came, nor the urge to punch the wall. Nothing.

An hour later it still hadn't. He felt light-headed with grief and disbelief as he drove back to the hospital to see his son.

-71-

June 4, 1982, Army HQ, Tel Aviv

GERSHONOVITZ FELT THE bullet like a hot lump of coal in his brain, surrounded by a scintillating fog. But the fog kept expanding, as if stretched by an invisible entity whose hands were spread to receive him, without rancor, without pity, yet with limitless understanding and without judgment; and all at once he felt enormous yearnings to be received by it, as his black anger was being melted slowly by the hot coal, and the grayness, and it was turning to something else, gray and luminous also, which slowly merged into the luminousness waiting to receive him. It was not pulling him, just waiting with infinite patience; only he himself began to feel impatience, to get it over with, to merge with what was waiting for him, to see what it was, what He was.

As from a great distance he now saw and heard Amzaleg talking to him, and then Amzaleg grew smaller and smaller, and the gray fog became more and more luminous, and suddenly he saw Moshe bending over him, his angular cheeks glistening and wet. Moshe spoke, and he answered, could not tell what. The luminescence grew in intensity until it nearly blinded him, or perhaps it was his eyes that were filling with wetness. He felt the back of his neck stiffening then grow soft as a buzz started in it, or maybe in his throat, like Munger's singing, only with different words. He yearned to listen to the song, to the words, but his ears were growing numb and he was pierced with regret that no one would be left now to protect the Jews against their Damn HolyName and keep the hate of Him alive; and then all at once he died, rushing upward and melting into the luminous gray splendor.

June 4, 1982, Army HQ,
Tel Aviv

J UST AFTER AMZALEG left, Moshe came in, missing him by a few
  seconds.

Seeing Gershonovitz slumped, Moshe rushed to his side. His first thought was that it was the asthma, then he saw the gun in his hand and the hole in the upper palate.

"Why, Shimmel, why?" he hissed.

Gershonovitz tried to speak, whispered, "Call Mickey BenTov at Northern Command... tell... tell him... Operation Lion's Pity is on...."

Moshe said, "But why, Shimmel?"

Gershonovitz shook his head slightly, impatiently, whispered, "Password 1977...."

Then he slumped.

Moshe's voice was barely audible, like Gershonovitz's. "Okay... Shimmel, okay.... But why this?"

Gershonovitz, fading fast, said, "A... A..." He could not finish, just looked at the desk.

Moshe looked, saw nothing.

Gershonovitz gave a rattle and looked at the phone, breathed hard.

Moshe, holding back tears, called NC from the list. "Gimme Mickey BenTov.... Yes, Shimmel says go, password 1977—"

He'd obeyed Shimmel's order but could not yet think.

BenTov's basso said in his ear, "Moish? Tell Shimmel he's too late, didn't you guys hear? The Israeli consul was shot in London an hour ago, so the government decided to invade."

Gershonovitz's rattle became deeper.

Moshe said, "Goddamn, he was right."

BenTov said, "About what? Be quick, Moish, we going in in an hour… Golani, tanks, paras, everything."

"Nothing, nothing. I gotta go too. *Mabruk.*"

But BenTov had already hung up.

Moshe felt Shimmel's neck. The fat man was not breathing, his neck felt cold.

He closed Gershonovitz's eyes, shut his own tight for a few seconds, then called Kadishevitz.

As he waited for Kiddush to come to the phone, he looked again at the desk. There was a mark at its outer edge, nothing much, as if a hard pencil was rubbed there, indenting it. He looked closer: A gray scrape of some sort, recent…. Then Kiddush came on and Moshe informed him. "Tell the PM," he said, "Shimmel is gone, by his own hand…."

When he hung up he said out loud, "Blessed be the True Judge," automatically covering his head with his palm. The back of his neck felt cold, as if the door was open. He twirled to see, but there was nothing. Then he raised his eyes at the ceiling. "And fuck you too," he snarled, "from him and from me," and stuck his middle finger upward, as he saw Shimmel often do.

"You were right," he said, spoke to the fat man lying dead in the chair. "I'm sorry I didn't believe you. Shimmel, you were right—"

Then he felt sheepish, ashamed of his stupidity. "I'm getting as crazy as you were," he muttered, and made the other necessary calls, one by one.

The Burial Society men arrived first. "Take him to Abu Kabir," he told them, "and tell Munger I'll be doing the wash, and don't file any paperwork yet."

He gave his name and Unit number, as authorization to keep it quiet, then sat and stared at the wall map, then again at the desk.

Once again he asked why, first aloud, then silently inside.

Keeping his Other down—it strained at him hard, wanting to rise—he went over the room inch by inch, but aside from the scrape on the desk's edge, and some holes in the map where pins had presumably been removed recently, he found nothing.

Tomorrow, he promised himself, he'd look into this.

-73-

Friday, June 4, 1982,
Jaffa

A MZALEG FOUND ZOHARA in the hospital's maternity ward,
holding the baby.

"I'm not going to Canada," she said to him. "I'll raise him now for
you, but in three years I'm going and taking him with me, you hear?"

He swallowed, looked at them both, nodded diagonally, neither confirming nor denying just to show he'd heard her.

She said, "I don't want Jacquie to raise him, be another *Ars* in HaTikva."

He said, "Ilana can also help to—"

"No. Raise him in Shfar'am like an Arab?" Only thing worse than an *Ars*.

Amzaleg squeezed his eyes shut. It was all too much, his Other
receding now in the face of all this. The baby yawned, and the Other
blinked away.

"Three years," Zohara repeated.

Amzaleg opened his eyes, nodded. She looked at him, eyebrows
raised, waved her head to the outside, pointing with her thumb in the
Army HQ's direction.

"Finished," Amzaleg said. "I should've done this before, saved everyone trouble."

Outside, the rebbe was still crying out his question, a nurse muttering
at him.

Zohara raised the baby, her half-brother. "You want to hold him?"

"Alright," Amzaleg said, "for a minute, I have to talk to Munger, also call Asa and tell him."

Console the bereaved father. Asa, whose son had done it all....

Why?

There was no why; or if there was, like the rebbe outside, it was not for us to know.

He looked into the baby's eyes, his son, a new Amzaleg, new beginning. But not for here, no more. Zohara and Iddo were right all along. He was wrong.

"Alright," he told Zohara finally, and she nodded.

A nurse came in and Zohara handed her the baby.

Amzaleg impulsively hugged Zohara, and, for the first time he could remember since age twelve, she hugged him back in full, hard, her head on his neck, kissed him too. "Yallah, go," she said finally. "I'm here, Amzaleg. Go."

He saw she was crying fitfully, heartbroken and enraged, so not to embarrass her, he left.

-74-

Friday, June 4, 1982,
Jerusalem, Beirut, Atlit

AN HOUR AFTER the consul's shooting in London, the full cabinet sat for fifteen minutes and voted: It was a go, no dissenters now. Only one abstainer, pro forma.

Ronen was given twenty-four hours by the Ministry of Defense to evacuate the Sub, although it was later universally agreed that it should have been three times that.

It was five in the morning when the order came over the Sub's scrambler.

"But I have two guys still out!" Ronen shouted, pushing Varda away.

"Tough titties," said the defense minister's aide. "By tomorrow morning you're all out. You'll have six torpedo boats waiting at aShams beach…."

"It won't be enough!" Ronen shouted, not making clear whether he meant the short time, or the number of boats, or both.

"Execute, execute," said the aide, which Ronen saw as the ultimate insult, this being the traditional order for tanks to move into battle, not to retreat from it.

"Received," Ronen said through gritted teeth. "End."

It was bedlam. They made a bonfire in the back of the building, three empty oil barrels, everyone kept throwing papers into them, dowsing them with gasoline, a line of Mossadniks passing to and fro, carrying takedown records in steel suitcases to the waiting cars. Arab children standing at the far curb clapped, their mothers on the balconies, also clapping, some ululating.

"I'd like to shoot them," said Yossi, who carried two steel cases in each hand. "Just one, to make an example."

"They should be grateful to us, cleansing their country of garbage," someone said.

"Shut up, all of you, no one shoots anyone," Ronen said. "We ain't got time. Move, move."

"Not even in self-defense?" said Varda, teasing.

He said nothing, he was so furious. Nine months, so much good professional work, all down the drain.

Ehud came by carrying a steel case, the box of ampoules on his back, and said that Yaro and Zerach had not returned yet.

"I know," Ronen said through gritted teeth. "I clicked both, personally. Only Zerach answered. You got anything from Shimmel?"

"Not yet," Ehud said, went on to the waiting cars, executing the orders. He was thinking about his father, for whom he had killed so many, making himself into an Other, all for naught.

Zerach came a minute before they all left, sheepish, just as Ronen was locking the steel doors, setting the timer's detonator's delay.

He said to Ronen he still had his stuff inside. "Everything, clothes, shoes, even my Bible from boot camp." He was in flip-flops, probably went to the beach after his takedown.

"Tough titties," Ronen said, and felt ashamed, he was becoming more of an *Ars* daily. "We'll get you a new one." He waved to the drivers. "Move, move," and the caravan departed.

The boats were moored close to shore, all the aShams hotel's guests watching as the Sub's denizens climbed into their dinghies. Zerach and Ami and Yossi first, with the girls and the support personnel and their bags, the Anons and Mossadniks carrying mini-Galils openly, to discourage interference; then one by one all followed to the other dinghies, which departed in a diagonal row to the moored gray boats.

Ehud and Ronen were last to leave, saying nothing to each other, clambering on the last boat, for a moment deferring to each other, then Ronen climbed first, Ehud after him.

On the boat's deck Ehud was surprised to see the pregnant beauty, Rahman's wife, in loose jeans and a Red Company Syrian battle dress, her child in tow. The back of the boy's head, he saw, was oddly flat, like his father's. The boy kept fingering a Star of David on a gold chain around his neck—it was evidently new to him.

Ehud nodded to the beauty but she did not nod back, or speak.

After a while he said, "You're being evacuated too?"

She gave her head a hard shake. "No. AWOL."

Her voice was low and vibrant, like a Bedouin flute.

At the sound of the unfamiliar language, the child clung to her and she cupped his odd head protectively, the other hand on her belly.

When Ehud raised his eyebrows she said in a low voice, "I don't want him to grow up a murdering *Ars* like his father...."

Ehud said nothing. She turned away and together they watched the shore departing.

Presently Ronen came to stand beside them and watched alongside, throwing glances at his watch.

"Now," he said. There was a brief delay, then a dull thump, and a gray-pink flower blossomed over the city.

"Gone," he said. "Fuck it." He spit into the water and wiped his eyes.

Varda, who had come right after, burst into tears.

"Yallah, yallah," Ronen said and thumped her on her rump to console her, but she slapped his hand away and ran downstairs. It was her youth she was leaving behind, someone said, and no one laughed; theirs too.

Now more and more came up on deck to watch the conflagration, both Anons and Mossadniks, and sailors. The captain came up too.

"Thus shall perish all your enemies, O Lord," the captain intoned.

It was the biblical sentence said after Pharaoh's troops drowned in the Red Sea.

Tzafi looked at him and spit, then he said, "Ehud, where's Yaro?"

"Probably got stuck somewhere, in Shatila."

"Maybe he'll do Arafat on the way out, so something good comes out of it."

"You wish," Ehud said.

They were both silent.

"And who is this?" Tzafi said, pointing to the beauty.

She said, "Doesn't matter. I'm just catching a ride."

They arrived at Atlit, the naval commandoes base, at eleven o'clock, the boats so overloaded they had to cruise creepingly slowly. No one was waiting for them, not Asa, nor Gershonovitz, only a row of vehicles.

One by one the arrivals got into jeeps, waiting command cars, a few cabs sent by Mossad HQ, and departed in the order they'd come, silently. The Anons and Mossadniks left first, Ehud and Tzafi and the beauty got off last, after all had left. She went into a cab with her son and departed, and Ehud and Tzafi stayed behind, lingering.

Tzafi grumbled, "You'd think Shimmel at least would come."

Just then Moshe arrived, driving Shimmel's Lark alone, parked and told them. "But he'll be buried inside the cemetery. The military rabbi gave an exemption, I told him I'd do him with my bare hands if not."

Jewish suicides were buried outside the cemetery fence.

"But why?" Ehud said. "Was he depressed, something?"

"What do you think?"

Obviously, after the failure of his plan... "Wait," Moshe said suddenly, "wait, he didn't know yet it had failed.... I called Mickey at Northern Command, he said tell Shimmel...."

He paused, his nostrils pinched. "No, he didn't know yet."

Tzafi said, "You sure he did it himself?"

"I'm still looking into it," Moshe said.

They got into the Lark and Moshe drove off, speeding through the gates, telling them about it as he drove, not even trying to wipe his eyes.

Ehud and Tzafi wiped theirs. When Ehud asked where the funeral would be, Moshe said, "He didn't want one, he wanted his body cremated."

When Tzafi cackled and said Shimmel probably wanted to join his family, Ehud punched his shoulder so hard that Tzafi shrieked. "You want to take off my other arm?"

"I'll take off your dick, you're not quiet." And to Moshe he said, "You going to listen to Shimmel in this fucking thing?"

"Fuck no," Moshe said. "Kiryat Shaul, Friday, eleven o'clock, Aleph uniforms all, anyone doesn't come will have business with me."

"Fucking yes," Ehud said. "And me." He, too, wiped his eyes, shamelessly.

-75-

Saturday, June 12, 1982,
HaTikva and Tel Aviv

NINE DAYS AFTER Pirchiya's killing, Zohara was feeding the baby the day following his circumcision (she had objected fiercely, Amzaleg overruled her) when Gidi phoned.

She felt a shock when she heard his voice on the phone, but also a strange calm, as if she knew all along he would call—although of course she didn't, or she wouldn't have suffered so much.

His voice did not take away the pain of Pirchiya's death, yet it was something, perhaps even everything of something else.

Yes, she said, she was staying at home, Amzaleg too.

She could hardly breathe.

"Good," he said.

That evening he came on his motorcycle. Amzaleg opened the door and as Gidi came in he said the proper words, "May you not know more grief."

Like Amzaleg, Gidi had a scruffy beard and his eyes, unlike Amzaleg's, were hollow. But when he saw Zohara, he spread his arms wide and she, after putting down the baby in its crib, ran into them like in one of the movies in Cinema Merkaz and almost broke her teeth kissing him. He rubbed the small of her back and she pressed his head to hers, her hands behind his neck, eyes closed. She couldn't speak and he didn't either.

Amzaleg looked away, then said, "Yallah, yallah," and began to make coffee in the Bedouin coffeepot.

Later Gidi and Amzaleg sat down under Pirchiya's photo with the black diagonal patch, and after the coffee they had araq and talked in low voices while Zohara fed the baby. Gidi's face was gaunt but otherwise he seemed fine, like she remembered him from that one time they'd met, except for his eyes.

By nine o'clock she handed her half-brother to the temporary care of Jacquie and left with Gidi on his motorcycle, hugging him hard, head on his back, sideways. Amzaleg waved after them once.

Gidi's grandmother had a flat on Balfour Street, he said. She was in a convalescence home so he and Zohara could stay there a few days if she wanted, until he went back to the kibbutz, if he went, he didn't know yet. Yes, she said. Yes.

The flat was just across from the Strauss Health Center, near the primary school, on the third floor. The moment they came in, Gidi made a beeline to the sofa, extracted an elongated case from under it, pulled out a violin swaddled in velvet, tuned it, then played something fast, trill chasing trill, his fingers dancing on it, eyes closed.

Zohara stood in the hallway, her little satchel at her feet, listening with wonder.

"What is it?" she asked. She had never heard such a thing. Like Bach on heroin.

Paganini, Gidi said, and played another, slower, sweeter, the bow bouncing gently. "Kreisler," he said. "I used to play it before the army." His eyes seemed to fill, so did his cheeks. "You like?"

She said she liked it, went inside, looked around. The flat was filled with old books, records, carpets, ficus trees seen from the terrace, ancient furniture, dark and shiny, but with a clean smell. There was a large radio on legs with a record player at the corner, Blaupunkt. Gidi said you could hear best when lying underneath. "Come," he said, pulling her hand.

She let him and they lay down side by side under the big box after he'd put on some records.

He laid his head on her shoulder as he listened, then looked at her like

Yaro had, just before she had cut his throat; disoriented, she felt now the same odd pity, but also love, yes.

Later they fucked on the large heavy bed, different than their first time, slower, longer, but she saw colors all over again, cried out, he did, too, but into her shoulder.

She didn't know if she was happy or not, Pirchiya gone only nine days, her only two wishes fulfilled, the baby okay, Zohara giving up Canada, for now. She felt incomplete, glowing hot around a core of darkness. Every hour she remembered Pirchiya being shot, then how she felt as she slit the throat of the killer who at the end put himself in her hands at her mercy, which she exercised, doing as he wished.

Gidi later played again because she wanted to hear more of it, learn this side of him, the side before the killings. She wanted to live a long life with him playing if she could, if he would. She then told him she had planned to go to Canada but wouldn't now, because of her baby half-brother. "But in three years I am going, and I'll take him with me."

"I'll come with you," he said, not even asking if she wanted him to, but when she looked at him intently, he said there was nothing for him here now, nothing to make him stay.

Later he cooked eggs, chopped a salad, she washed the dishes, and at night she woke once or twice, the blackbirds tweeting in the ficus, she again and again remembering how she slit the killer's throat, how he looked at her pathetically, as if she was his mother.

It was strange how she didn't hate the man, both then and afterward, almost felt as if she had lost something with him gone, a sort of purpose.

In the morning Gidi and she made love again then talked, she walking up and down the bookshelves, asking him about this or that book—he seemed to have read them all.

"So why did you stay in the kibbutz?" she asked him once. Him having all this treasure here.

He just shook his head, and she didn't pursue it.

"And your father? You talked to him, since you came back?"

"Yes, I called him, once."

She didn't want to ask if he had told his father about her, like she had told hers about him. She just nodded. Fathers were complicated here, she understood by now.

Later she asked Gidi to play again the first thing he'd played, the Paganini, like fast butterflies flitting around top notes, blinking and winking. He did and she watched his fingering from up close, then how he bounced the bow, the tendons on his thick, scarred wrist popping even as his long fingers danced.

As she listened she felt her insides opening up, from belly to throat to nose, as when she'd read books, like buds of Rose of Jericho in water, showing their colors and, when pulled out, scents too.

After three days he drove her back to HaTikva. He had to go to the Unit base near Jerusalem for some formal discharge papers and would come see her in two days. He left his bag with her, gave her some records to listen to, and a few books. He kissed her, at length. Two days, he said.

She couldn't wait to see him again. It was a deep hunger within her, a new need, not just for the fucking, the love, for everything.

76

YARO'S AND GERSHONOVITZ'S were not the last deaths of the Undertaker case—Lebanon's battle casualties, of course, excepted.

A day after the rogue Undertaker's death, Klinger's body was found on the Tel Baruch beach, genitals in mouth. Probably an Arab mutilation, it was concluded, maybe the same barbarous hands who had slashed more than twenty Torah scrolls in a dozen Tel Aviv-Jaffa synagogues that same night. Three days later Klinger was buried with full honors in Bnei Brak, near his parents, even Levitan attended, although he was just back from his son's funeral. (Dudi died in a traffic accident on the way to Lebanon, trying to avoid running over a dog. Dogs and birds were escaping *en masse* from the Biqaa, like animals from a forest fire, or from an earthquake.)

Amzaleg performed the last wash for Yaro's body at the Sdeh-Dov morgue, so he couldn't attend.

Pirchiya's funeral took place three days after her murder, June 6, in Kiryat Shaul Cemetery. A huge number of people attended, both HaTikva people, mostly old criminals, pimps, hairdressers, grocers and all others who knew her, but also policemen of all ranks, to honor Amzaleg's fallen young wife, who "died in the midst of her days by evil hands," as the funeral notice said, may the HolyName avenge her blood.

Some boys who had come to HaTikva from Jaffa came, too, but not all—a few had already departed for Reserve Service. The army was preparing to cross the Litani River, to invade Lebanon. A number of them would not return.

The *Shiva* was held in Amzaleg's flat but as the numbers swelled, it was transferred to the Moroccan synagogue, and from there spilled into the Yemenite and Iraqi ones.

Adon Leon wanted to pay for everything, the food and the drink and yeshiva boys hired to say Kaddish for a month, but Amzaleg would not let him.

There was a thick crowd around the grave, nearly a hundred people. Batya had come, too, at the last moment, leaving her recently-returned pregnant daughter at home with her young son. Zohara came with little Menachem in her arms (this was the name given him, meaning The Consoler) who slept all through the interment, peacefully. Amzaleg said Kaddish over the grave and Eli Sabag, the bereaved father, said one too. Zohara did not shed one tear until the body was lowered, and then she melted. Batya tried to help carry little Menachem, but Zohara would not let her or anyone else touch him. And all through this he slept.

Two days later, Tuesday, June 8, a day after Israel's bombing of the Iraqi nuclear reactor, Amzaleg drove to Jerusalem to meet PM Begin.

Despite the heavy work schedule after the bombing, Begin insisted to Kadishevitz that he bring the *Schwartze* who'd suffered so much on everyone's behalf—he wanted to speak to him directly. "We owe this to him, and much more, so much he gave."

It was a most uncomfortable meeting. PM Begin did not get the full story from Amzaleg since Kiddush had asked Amzaleg not to tell it: No need to shock him too much, he said. Begin was already showing signs of his depression, perhaps dementia, and it was a delicate matter, he had to be protected.

A year later, Begin would resign.

77

Wednesday, June 16, 1982,
HaTikva and Tel Aviv

THIRTEEN DAYS AFTER Pirchiya's killing, on Wednesday morning, June 16, Eli Sabag came to see Menachem, his first grandson, to perform the ancient "Son's Ransom" blessing. Both he and his wife Bracha wore black. Bracha tried to tie a red thread furtively on the baby's right arm, but Zohara wouldn't let her.

"No, he's out of this shit."

Someone came by from the grocery store and brought araq for Amzaleg, and pickled fish and spicy olives for Zohara, which lately she had begun to crave, she couldn't get enough of them. She had also begun to put on weight, and her breasts grew.

Neighbors dropped in. Jacquie had prepared small cakes, bought baklavas, hummus spread, pita breads, all put before the lit soul candle under Pirchiya's photo.

Amzaleg came and went, couldn't sit in one place too long, his right leg had mended poorly and hurt, also his jaw hurt, it, too, had mended crookedly. He couldn't eat much, couldn't chew well, and became skinnier; or maybe he smoked more now, when looking at Pirchiya's photo.

Zohara often caught him looking at Iddo's photo too. She could almost read the guilt etched in Amzaleg's eyes: The son he'd practically slaughtered with his own hands, when he brought him back, and for what? What difference did Iddo's death in the Valley of Tears make? Or Nachum's, later? Not even catching Nachum's murderer seemed to alleviate Amzaleg's guilt.

At such times, Zohara would hand Menachem to him—she thought it might help, but it only seemed to bring up memories of Pirchiya. Her death was for Amzaleg a huge shock, perhaps even bigger than Iddo's, maybe because it was so unexpected. Every day he went to the Moroccan synagogue to say Kaddish for her. Eli joined him, sometime others did too.

Zohara just kept the soul candle going. It was a small thing, nothing to do with the shit.

Her mother and Dr. Anton came, both held the baby a few minutes, while Zohara fretted. She didn't like to let him out of her hands, so Amzaleg answered the phone calls—there were many, mostly for him: retired policemen, old farts from his 1948 days, calling to give him condolences.

Later Gidi called from the Unit's base and said he would come that afternoon. Zohara couldn't wait to see him.

Later on as she was talking to some young boys, Gidi's radiophone rang. He'd left it with his backpack and Zohara picked it up.

A woman spoke, her voice low and vibrant, like a musical instrument, asked for Gideon Sukenik, and when told he wasn't there yet, asked to give him a message about a meeting at the "office" that afternoon, in a certain room. The woman gave her the room number and Zohara wrote it down in SSS, by habit.

Several Amidar boys came, also a duo of yeshiva runaways. Batya was now sending them to her. Zohara taught them English, proper Hebrew— like savages they were, for years they were kept in ignorance of anything except the evil book that told them to let their fathers kill them.

To them, too, she spoke of Canada. It was paradise, she said, though she'd never been there.

On the wall hung the Toronto poster that Jenny had sent her, with the approved university application forms inserted under it. At its side hung Nachum's Los Angeles poster with the Haifa train tickets inserted, the ones she had helped him and Iddo buy. Zohara pointed at the Toronto poster, the magnificent towers, told them all about hockey, baseball, lakes and forests, from Jenny's letters, also what she had read. They nodded dumbly, not all listening, just happy to hear her voice, knowing she'd defend them if needed.

Iddo and Nachum hadn't managed to leave, and she was temporarily prevented, for now. But she'd surely leave soon and so would Menachem. Until then she'd tell him how his mother died and what killed her, would teach him to hate It, and keep this hate alive.

Of one thing she was sure: her children would not be born here.

When Gidi came two hours later, once she'd finished hugging him, she remembered the phone call about the meeting and told him.

Gidi said, "Did she say which room?"

"Yes, she said the meeting will be in room fifty-one."

He became deadly still, then asked, "You sure that's the number?"

"Yes," she said, looked at her note. "Five one. That's what the woman said."

She had turned to pick up Menachem who had begun to wail, so she missed the haunted look in Gidi's eyes. He remained still for a long while, then shook himself, picked up his backpack, kissed her gently on the forehead, and left on his motorbike, not looking back.

As Zohara fed the baby, she thought of Gidi's fingers dancing over the violin strings, then on her and in her, on her hair, her lips. She couldn't wait to hear him playing again, to hear his voice, feel his touch, talk about books with him, and music, introduce him to Batya.

Nibbling on olives, she adjusted her tight bra and whistled the closing bars of the soft tune he had played last, and as Menachem looked at her with dark, tear-filled eyes, she combed his silky hair and looked out the window, waiting for Gidi to return.

Toronto, 2023

ABOUT THE AUTHOR

 Avner Mandelman was born in Israel and served in the Israeli Air Force, including the 1967 war. He has a BSc in Aeronautical Engineering from the Israeli Technion, an MBA from the Stanford Graduate School of Business, and an MA in English / Creative Writing / Theatre from San Francisco State University. Alongside his stock market ventures he has published extensively: professional books, much anthologized stories, and an award-winning literary thriller, *The Debba*, the first in the Undertaker trilogy. *The Undertaker's Daughter* is the second in the trilogy, and a third, *Death of an Undertaker*, is in the works. Avner lives in Toronto, Canada, reading, writing, investing, and mentoring young people.